# CRUDE JUSTICE

## EAMON BRANDON

authorHOUSE®

*AuthorHouse™ UK Ltd.*
*500 Avebury Boulevard*
*Central Milton Keynes, MK9 2BE*
*www.authorhouse.co.uk*
*Phone: 08001974150*

*First published by AuthorHouse 9/28/2007*

*ISBN: 978-1-4343-2758-1 (sc)*

*Printed in the United States of America*
*Bloomington, Indiana*

*This book is printed on acid-free paper.*

### A Note from the Author

*Most will accept that corporations do not exist for any altruistic purpose; in fact it could be argued that the opposite is the case. The directors of corporations are there to make money for the shareholders and, despite lipservice to the contrary, incentives and pressures within a corporation are generally designed to achieve that single objective. Consequently, on occasions, in pursuit of this singular corporate measure of achievement, a cultural momentum is created that breaches the boundaries of morality. Crude Justice is a work of fiction that has used reports of actual events to construct a plausible behind the scenes scenario of this corporate life-force. The characters and corporate strategies are purely imaginary and any resemblance to real people or companies is purely coincidental.*

# *Acknowledgements*

I would like to thank some of the  people that made Crude Justice possible.

First of all my wife and family. They resisted the temptation to have me certified, and eventually, having got over the shock, became my greatest  fans and support. For this I will be eternally grateful.

Secondly I want to acknowledge my colleagues down through the years with whom I shared many experiences, and for whom I have the greatest respect.

Finally I want to thank my good  friends – Patricia Kavanagh, without whom Crude Justice would never have been started, Pat Corcoran, without whom it would never have been finished, and my daughter, Dara, without whose indomitable editing flair, it would never have been publishable.

# PROLOGUE
## DUBLIN AIRPORT, DECEMBER 1972

She watched in a daze. It was so cruel. She closed her eyes, but it didn't help; she couldn't avoid listening. She knew what was happening; she had seen it all before. She had been so brave. Tears had been close, very close, but she hadn't let them come; she didn't break down. She knew if they started they wouldn't stop. She had to be strong. For her daughter's sake she pretended to be happy, but her heart was breaking. It was her own decision. He had pleaded with her to stay, but why would she? They had no future together. She looked at the little child beside her, soundly sleeping, dreaming. She had to think of her—of her future. She had family in America, and nothing but heartache in Ireland. She didn't expect him to come to the airport, but she still hoped he would be there. She waited, and waited, before going through to the boarding area. She searched the sea of faces. She held back the tears, as those joining the line were being embraced, and hugged, and kissed, by their loved ones remaining behind. She and little Patricia had no one to hug, except one another. But how could he be there? She hadn't even told him she was going. She held Patricia's hand more tightly than was necessary. They went through to the boarding gate. The two of them. "Passengers with small children first," the announcement said. They reached their seats. It would be better when they took off; she would watch the movie and Patricia would sleep. But that's when it really hit her. How could they show that? They must know how emotional it is to leave Ireland, especially when you know you'll never see it, or the man you love, ever again. How could they? The tears that streamed down her face were not for Bogart, or Bergman, on the Casablanca set, but for her own real-life situation.

It was a wet and windy morning in December of 1972 when Maureen Harvey and her daughter Patricia left the island of their birth to make a new life in America–the "Land of Opportunity."

# PENTAGON, WASHINGTON D.C.,

## THIRTY YEARS LATER, DECEMBER 2002.

*Goddamn it, man, just stick to the script.*

Dino Papandreou, Senior Vice-President, Petroleum Operations, Global Oil Incorporated, was not a man who showed his emotions— not that his impassive posture gave any hint of anxiety as he listened to his protégé, Tim Savage, deliver the most important address of both their lives. Anyone looking at his massive presence would have thought that his interest in the proceedings was, just as it was for the other fourteen, to be briefed on the critical energy shortage facing the United States, and the reducing number of options that were available, from which they would formulate their collective recommendation to the President.

His positioning, at the end of the long oak table, gave him the opportunity to discreetly watch the reactions of the others, and secretly indicate to Tim Savage when he thought a point needed additional emphasis or explanation. The tiny beads of sweat that glistened on his forehead and heavily jowled features were not in any way due to surprise at the startling revelations of the briefing; he himself had carefully crafted every word, every syllable, and rehearsed every measured cadence, every pause, every inflection that the speaker was now, expertly, delivering. No, it was the world-changing significance of the occasion that caused this bout of anxiety. This was the pinnnacle of his career. He had devoted every ounce of spirit, every breath of almost thirty years, for this moment. It would bring him immense wealth. But that didn't matter too much. He already had more than he could ever spend. No, his reward would be the number-one job. The job that should have been his and not that goddam non-excutive Chairman's. The wimp, who took the credits for what Papandreou had really being doing all these years, without due recognition or the power and prestige that was his due. That would change now; it had to. If the recommendations that were now being carefully articulated were accepted—and he knew they would be; he had already spoken to those to whom the President listened—then Global Oil would take on a hugely important role in the energy strategy of the United States and would need a trusted, full-time executive Chairman. That job would be his. There was no one more qualified.

*But first Savage has got to convince this bunch of hard-nosed technocrats sitting around this table. Or, at least two of them.*

He studied their faces. Generally, he'd know whom he had and who needed more persuasion. He was confident of the business group. They would understand that tough decisions have to be taken. Five were already certain. Most owed him. He needed two of the others for a majority. Seven, plus his own vote, would be enough. The President wouldn't need a lot of convincing; he was already accusing the Saudis of being soft on terrorism.

He could smell, as well as feel, the tension in the room. *Goddamn, if only I had taken more time to secure a majority before the meeting. It would have been possible. Everyone has his price, or a skeleton that he wants to keep in the cupboard.* He studied them again. Their expressions were mixed; he couldn't tell. *Goddamn. And there'll only be one shot at this.*

"Never again will the United States and the Saudis enjoy the cosy relationship that has existed in the past. We've always been able to count on them for our oil. Not anymore. They still need billions of dollars to pay for their extravagant welfare system, and to support the luxurious lifestyle of the many thousands within the extended royal family, but their internal pressures are such, that they may be inclined to look elsewhere for those dollars."

Papandreou again scanned the faces on either side of the table extending down to Savage. They must understand that in the aftermath of 9/11 everything has changed. *For Chrissake, surely the fact that fifteen of the nineteen hijackers were Saudi nationals and the fact that that goddamn terrorist, Osama bin Laden, is also a Saudi, should be enough.*

There was no obvious reaction. The faces remained impassive.

"Two-thirds of the al-Qaeda prisoners taken in Afghanistan and being held at the Guantanamo Naval base in Cuba are Saudis, but despite the involvement of their nationals, they refused to allow the United States operate from their territory when we needed to take out the Taliban in Afghanistan. In fact, they asked the U.S. to withdraw its forces from the Prince Sultan Airbase. Our intelligence reports indicate that developing rapport between the Saudis and the Russians, and growing cooperation and trade with the Chinese, are matching this deterioration in U.S.-Saudi relations. The United States needs the oil, but we cannot live with the constant threat of it being used as a political weapon, to force us into shaping a foreign policy that that powerful Jewish lobby -- the American Israili Public Affairs Committee -- won't accept."

Papandreou could feel the heightened tension, and was conscious of Savage's furtive glances in his direction. *Dammit, man. I'm supposed to be just another committee member. If the others see this as a set-up, and realise that Global Oil has a vested interest in the result, it could ruin everything. Just do it as I told you, man, and stop looking down here.*

"The Chinese desperately need the oil, just as we do, but the Saudis cannot supply both them and us indefinitely. The problem is that they'll try, regardless of the fact that their crude oil reserves are being depleted at an alarming rate. We know this from intelligence reports, despite Saudi denials. This presents the United States with an unacceptable threat to its fundamental and vital energy needs—a threat, gentlemen, which no self-respecting superpower could live with. At this time, the United States is the only superpower, but that situation will not last forever. It behooves us to act now, while we can. It is our clear national responsibility to use our strength to underpin our energy supplies into the next century."

Savage's voice had risen to a crescendo, and when he stopped, the silence—broken only by the sound of Papandreou's breathing—was eerie.

"And, are you saying that the Pentagon Planners are advocating military action in Saudi Arabia to counter this threat?" It was one of the skeptics, and the tone was derisive.

Again, Savage caught Papandreou's eyes. He was met with a penetrating glare, like a blowtorch on ice. The challenge was his and his alone.

"No! On the contrary. Direct action to bolster our energy supplies would be politically unacceptable. World opinion would be scathing and would damage us economically. Our global corporations are very dependent on world markets."

Papandreou cringed at the use of his company's name as an adjective. It was too close to the bone. But he resisted the urge to intervene. Savage had been coached on all possible objections, and he was an expert. The suggestion of an economic consequence would consolidate the business support. *But what about the wimps?*

*Those spineless academics that never had to risk a dollar of their own money, or battle for survival, as I have done.*

"A far more acceptable, and infinitely better, option is Iraq. Its proven oil reserves are not as large as Saudi Arabia's, but we do know that it has vast development potential. It is largely unexplored, and due to the sanctions imposed on the Saddam Hussein regime, none of the more modern extraction techniques have been applied to the wells that are in production. From the viewpoint of world opinion, it's a far easier target. Saddam Hussein is reviled internationally as an evil despot, who unhesitatingly, used weapons of mass destruction on the Kurdish people. He is seen as part of the Sunni Islamic sect, so the majority Shiite Muslims would see his elimination, and the consequential regime change, as their liberation from half a century of oppression. The United States would be seen, both by the Shiite Iraqis and the international community, as liberators, not aggressors, and its oil could be secured for the benefit of the U.S. and its allies."

Papandreou waited for the reaction. There was none. The silence was deafening. Everyone seemed stunned at the suggestion that the U.S. would use its military might to commandeer the oil resources of another state. Isn't the U.S. the good guy? We don't do that. We prevent others from doing that. Isn't that why we drove Saddam out of Kuwait? He could read their thoughts. Shock and turmoil were evident from their ashen expressions.

"Come on, you guys. Why let some third-rate despot squeeze the life blood out of this great nation for no other reason but that the Good Lord happened to place the oil under his ass rather than ours?" It was the skeptic that had spoken previously.

*By God, I have them!*

The group was composed of another thirteen men, and one woman, who were at the very top of their professions in business or academia. They were not accustomed to being told the answer; they were decision makers. It was clear from their muted reaction that the possibility of an energy shortage in the United States, or a situation where the only superpower in the world would be beholden to a third-world regime, was not a position they were prepared to contemplate. Certainly not when the problem could be solved in such an easy and politically acceptable way. A vote was unnecessary. Their view and recommendation to the President, he knew, would be unanimous.

It was this gathering, deep inside the edifice of the Pentagon in Washington D.C., on that cold December day of 2002, that developed the strategy and the thinking behind the invasion of Iraq. As Papandreou had predicted, the recommendation was eagerly accepted by the Bush administration, which understood all issues relating to oil.

These events would have a profound affect on the lives of the Brant family, who at that time, were sleeping soundly almost three thousand miles away, in Dublin, Ireland.

# CHAPTER 1

## DUBLIN, IRELAND, DECEMBER 2002

Who would have thought that a "Mediterranean garden" five stories up made any sense? When Patricia suggested landscaping the roof, Ed Brant had assumed she meant a few potted plants. Never in his wildest dreams did he envisage tons of soil, mature trees, and hundreds of shrubs illuminated at night, creating islands out of the paved patios. Yet, he had to admit, this could be a very special place. Not right now, but later, when he had the time to spend here and enjoy it; when he had reached his goal and could slow down.

From where he stood, through the gaps in the thick foliage of the coniferous trees, especially imported from Italy, deliberately positioned to frame the views, he could see the dark green of the harbour, speckled with the white and yellow of the marina-moored yachts, far below.

*Yes, the money that she spent on creating this roof-top "Garden of Eden," as she called it, was worth every penny.*

He walked across to the perimeter wall to a spot between the trees, and looked out over the bay. The morning was cold. The

December sun was still low in the sky. He turned up the collar of his overcoat, as he felt the chill of the gentle sea-breeze. The sound of the birds signalling the start of another day distracted him, as they chirpily commenced their daily chores, and competed with the rustling of the canes and the gentle lapping of the water feature, for his attention. His desperate lonliness being momentarily suppressed, he found a pleasure in the setting that surprised even himself. This was Patricia's scene, never his, yet here he was, as she used to be, taking it all in.

As usually happened, when he had these rare moments for personal reflection, his thoughts turned to Patricia. He checked the time. She would not yet have woken. Those beautiful auburn tresses would still be strewn across her pillow. He recalled the many times he had watched her sleeping, listened to her breathing, and marvelled that such a beautiful creature could actually want him. The rasping sound of his own breathing jarred him back to reality. He sat on the granite steps to the upper level and rested. His breathing gradually eased, as did the tightness around his chest.

It was all of six months now, he recalled, when the problem first started. That's what caused the row. She had noticed his heavy breathing and, as always, she thought that he could just drop everything and attend the doctor. He would, he told her, as soon as he could fit it in. And he would, as soon as he got time. Thinking back now, he supposed he was unreasonable. She was only concerned about him. But, as was happening more and more often, she got him on a bad day. One word led to another. They had a blazing row and she left. He had tried to convince himself that it was for the best. But really he knew it wasn't. He'd have to get her back, but how? It was his fault. But as his Executive Assistant she should have understood the demands on his time.

"But that isn't the problem," she kept telling him. "You're married to Global Oil. You're obsessed with the oil business.

You've no private life outside of the office. It's not healthy. I won't just hang around and watch you do this to yourself."

For all her talents, she just couldn't understand the pressure he was under to prove himself. His father was now gone, but that didn't remove the criticism that haunted him every day of his life. He was determined that, despite what his Dad had thought of him, he would make it to the top. Maybe he wasn't the man's man that his brother Ben was, or the unconquerable athlete that his younger brother John was, but he also wasn't the failure that his father seemed to have thought. He could be something and he would be something. He would succeed in the toughest arena—one in which his father had failed. He would get on top of the corporate monster that had plagued his father. He wouldn't be there to see it, but he knew in his heart that his dad would know. He had tried to explain this demon to Patricia. He knew she didn't really understand. How could she? He couldn't make sense of it himself. But she should have known that the corporate ladder required commitment. Otherwise, he'd be just one in the bunch of mediocrities that are swallowed up by the system. *But, by God, I do miss her.* It was difficult seeing her every day and keeping his personal and professional lives apart. He again looked over her rooftop haven. *I just hope that, behind her present frostiness, she still cares.* He knew he did, more than ever. As soon as he got where he had to go, and could relax and do the things that she wanted, he would win her back. In the meantime, being too close would cause further grief, and right now he couldn't afford that distraction.

He caught the reflection of his slim, executive appearance in the bay window and knew that, despite what Patricia thought, his gym work was paying dividends. Was that a slight greying around his temples? Maybe so, but it just added to his presence. To exercise authority, it was necessary to look the part as well as be the part.

It was here on the balcony, he recalled, that it happened. He hadn't noticed her pruning the roses when he came out following his gym work. Maybe it was climbing the stairs from the basement gymnasium that caused his breathing to be heavier than normal that morning. He didn't know. Whatever it was, it just gave her another opportunity to attack him.

"Ed, please visit with the doctor; it's probably nothing that some medication can't fix, but it's something that you must see about."

"I've told you, I will," he had responded. "And I will, but not just now."

He walked away from her towards the edge of the balcony and watched a gull gliding effortlessly on the early morning breeze.

"Ed, I won't be a witness to whatever you're doing to yourself."

"Leave it...will you?...I know what I'm doing."

"Do you Ed? Do you really know what you're doing to yourself... to us...doing with your life?"

He said nothing...staring in a fixed gaze out across the bay to the blueness of Howth, feeling the now familiar tightness in his chest.

"You drive yourself so hard... you have no time...to live...for us ...please..." she said, as she moved slowly towards him.

"Please listen to me. Is this what you really want? Is this what he really wanted? Is this what your father would have wanted for you?"

As soon as she mentioned his father he swiveled to face her. He felt deadly cold. The muscles in his throat and shoulders tightened; a surge of rage engulfed him. He looked at her beautiful, anxious, pleading face and he wanted to hurt her. He had lost control.

"Shut the fuck up! Just shut the fuck up!" he roared close to her face. "Don't you tell me what I should do. What the fuck would you know? You—you never had a father."

He was immediately shocked at his own aggression. He felt physically sick. He knew he had been completely irrational. He tried to apologise but the words wouldn't come. He just stared at her tear-stained face and tried to block out her sobs.

She didn't say anything, but when he returned that evening she had already packed and left. How could he explain to her that he couldn't abandon his early morning routine? She could never understand. It isn't an option. To be a winner—indeed, to survive in the competitive world of high achievers—he had to be forever alert, to be fit in mind and body. Although she was his Executive Assistant, he had always shielded her from the pressures of his office. In his world of big business, it's survival of the fittest; kill or be killed. She just wouldn't have understood. He would compete at the highest level and reap the rewards. Despite what his father had thought, he was a winner, and would keep raising the bar until he achieved his ultimate goal. Until then, he wanted no distractions; nothing else mattered.

Of the three Brant sons, Ed knew that he was the one who had to respond to their Dad's challenge. He knew it only applied to him. The other two could do no wrong. In his dad's opinion they were already "something." Those cutting words were directed at him. It was most unfair, but that was the way it was. Ben, seven years older, was struggling with a mortgage and school bills while, as a union official, trying to extract more and more for his union members who more often than not were probably paid a lot more than he himself. John, his younger brother, was also getting nowhere. He had quit university in his first year, and went directly into the small family firm. Ed suspected that, despite the appearance of marital bliss, his brothers could not be happy or fulfilled. After all, compared to him, what had they achieved? And he hadn't finished yet.

He had taken the percolator out onto the balcony and he poured another cup. Strong and black was how he liked it. As his father used say, "It has eatin' an' drinkin' in it."

But, he wondered, what is success? Was it this multi-shaded green, pink, and lilac-speckled oasis that would be his private haven? He looked down over the lush, green, manicured grass and landscaped gardens five stories below. Was it this luxury penthouse in Dalkey, the most sought-after area of south County Dublin, with sea-views from the wrap-around balcony to rival any in Europe? Or maybe the gleaming, black S600, 36 valve, 5.5 litre, V12-engined, chauffeured Mercedes that he watched, as it sped up the tree-lined driveway, to take him to his oak-panelled executive office only two miles away on Dun Laoghaire's sea-front? Or, was it the lifestyle that allowed him be pampered to his heart's content by overpaid minions desperate to register their devotion ahead of the annual appraisal and bonus allocation time? He really didn't know. What he did know, however, was that if this was the success that his father had drummed into him as being the key to happiness, well, it was unlocking the wrong door. He had all the trappings of success, but felt empty inside; there was something missing. But maybe he wasn't there yet—wherever "there" was supposed to be. He had made spectacular progress in his career so far, and was still rising. Maybe when he established himself on the international scene the new challenges would bring a sense of fulfilment. Yes, he reckoned, that was it. He just wasn't stretched—even though, at thirty-five, he was the youngest Chief Executive within the international operations of Global Oil. Just stick with it, he concluded; more of the same, and he would achieve the position that his father, he knew, secretly aspired to but never reached. Yes, he had to think "positive," as his father used to say, and "get on with it."

Reluctantly, he left the balcony, which had now become his private refuge, and took the elevator to the ground floor, where his reflections were sharply interrupted by his uniformed driver.

"Mornin' Boss. Nice so far, but the forecast is for stormy weather. There's heavy rain and wind coming in from the west. By the way, ya better read the papers. But I'm afraid dat you're not goin' ta like that either."

Ed sank into the leather-upholstered, rear seating of the Merc and glanced through the morning headlines as he was driven along the familiar coast road to Global House, the head-office of Global's Irish operations. He was jarred back to reality:

# 'Oil Company Executive to Give Evidence to the Planning Tribunal' screamed the news headline in the Irish Times.

*'Geoffrey Fagan, Chief Executive of Independent Petroleum has been summoned to appear before the Planning Tribunal today, to give evidence against allegations that he bribed government Ministers to prevent the huge British multi-national hypermarket chain, Costless U.K., from establishing a pilot unit in Ireland.'*

The tribunals were the source of daily revelations in Ireland. They had been set up by the government in response to opposition pressure to react to allegations of corruption at the highest levels of the administration. The significance of the report was emphasised by the relegation of bellicose statements by the American President on Iraq, to the secondary headline.

"Jesus! I hope he doesn't dump the rest of us in it," he muttered.

Brant's driver, who was about to comment, caught sight of his expression in the rear-view mirror and wisely decided that silence was more appropriate.

"How the bloody hell did he get himself into that position?"

Costless U.K. was the biggest hypermarket chain in Britain. It used a cut-price petrol offer as a lost leader to attract grocery shoppers to their huge out-of-town shopping centres. It was the single biggest threat to the profitability of the oil industry in Europe.

"Jesus. Surely if he wanted to bribe someone he would have distanced himself from the payments," he muttered.

*Now the industry could be exposed to scrutiny because of one idiot's ineptitude.*

He arrived at his office to start another day in his climb to the top, to his father's vision of success.

————————◆◆◆◆————————

An old man was sitting unobtrusively in the mahogany-panelled, marble-floored reception area as Ed Brant entered on his way through to his executive suite on the third floor of Global House. He greeted the receptionist, seated at her counter against the back-drop of a wall entirely covered with a wooden engraving of the world, which represented the corporate reach of Global Oil. Normally, a perfunctory "good morning" to any waiting visitor would have been the extent of his acknowledgement, but there was something vaguely familiar about this particular visitor who made eye contact as Brant entered.

"Are you being looked after?" he asked, as he passed.

"Yes, thanks. I'm just waiting for my son, Peter. He knows I'm here."

Brant stopped as he thought he recognised the legendary Tom Stone, the founder of this company that he now managed. It was obviously a younger Stone that featured in the portrait hanging in the board-room, but nonetheless, it was, unmistakably, the same man.

Stone's submissive demeanour, as he sat on the black, leather-cushioned sofa, was what had confused Brant. It was not what he would have expected. Tom Stone was a multi-millionaire, probably the most successful entrepreneur that Ireland has ever produced. He always imagined him as a man of supreme confidence, if not arrogance.

He introduced himself. "Ed Brant, I'm the Chief Executive."

They shook hands.

"I'm just waiting for my son. He's upstairs paying my heating oil bill. Never thought you'd be sending me one of those."

Stone had sold his interest in the company, so Brant kept the conversation general. He ignored Stone's comment.

"I'm glad to be out of it," he went on. "Business today is not what it was when I started in the fifties. It's all driven by bloody computers, churning out bloody strategic plans and the like."

"Yes." Brant agreed. "But, don't you think it's great? Ireland is now thriving. The Celtic Tiger is still alive and well."

"I don't know anymore," said Stone, pointing to the gold-framed proclamation hanging prominently on the wall of the reception area. "I see nothing but those bloody Mission Statements, or whatever it is you call them. They're all the bloody same—'Our people are our greatest resource,' they say, while at the same time the management spends most of its time trying to get rid of them so that they can get cash bonuses and stock options."

"Ah, I don't know," said Brant, struggling for words.

"You know bloody well, if you're your dad's son. Great man, Paddy Brant. Knew him well. In our time we built our companies with staff loyalty and hard graft. Now, as far as I can see, its just graft. Did you read the headlines this morning?"

Brant noticed the amused interest of the receptionist, who immediately pretended to busy herself shuffling papers on her already tidy desk. But he was shocked. Here was the man who not only founded the company he presently managed, but also Stoneways plc, the largest public company in Ireland. He was more than relieved to be able to finish the conversation, when

Peter Stone, Tom's son, came out of the lift, greeting them both with a cheery grin.

"Hi, Dad! From what I've overheard, it seems that you're still enjoying your retirement. Come on and I'll get you home." They left together.

When he got to the third floor, instead of going straight to his own office, as would be his normal routine, Ed couldn't resist the temptation of visiting the boardroom—just to confirm that the portrait, dominating the end wall, was in fact that of Stone. He sat back into his Chairman's chair at the other end of the room and studied the image. Yes, no mistake, it certainly was Tom Stone; a much younger version, but those granite-like features were unmistakable. The name 'Stone' was, he thought, very appropriate. He looked closer. Stone was actually seated in the same chair, in the same position, in which Ed now sat. Funny, he thought; although he had been conscious of the portrait, he had never before really looked at it with any interest and never really noticed the detail. It had obviously been hanging there for years. He could see the darker shade of the cream wall paint where it shadowed the wall. He studied Stone's expression. *What would he have been thinking as he posed? He was obviously a very busy man, so why would he have taken the time? I couldn't see Dad doing it.* He smiled to himself at the thought. A comparison with the Mona Lisa came to mind. *I wonder did ol' man Stone fancy himself as an artist's model? Was this boardroom his private Louvre? You could not be accused of having that enigmatic smile. No, certainly not. More of an enigmatic frown or grimace. Certainly an enigmatic stare.* The eyes seemed to follow him as he stood and walked to the door. *Maybe you saw yourself presiding over boardroom proceedings, in perpetuity?* He paused with that thought for several seconds. *Well, Stoneyface Tom, you ol' goat, if you did, better forget it. Ed Brant is here now and your era is over.*

Brant walked through the lobby, into his own executive suite, to prepare for the upcoming management review meeting. As he passed the windows, he noticed that his driver had been right about the weather. The sky had darkened and the sailboats were bobbing about at their moorings. It hadn't yet started to rain, but that was not far away. He gazed, unseeingly, out of the window for several minutes. Despite the meeting preparation pressures, he couldn't get Tom Stone out of his mind. Here was a true entrepreneur. A man with just a basic education, like his father, like many of his contemporaries in Ireland, but with a real flair for business. He had built up a multi-million-pound construction empire, which when floated on the stock market had made him one of the richest men in Ireland. Not content with that, he then set up an oil company that he had recently sold to Global Oil Inc., the biggest oil company in the world. He was the epitome of business success, yet was totally cynical and disillusioned. But it was the looseness of his comments that really concerned Brant. Despite his retired status, Tom Stone was a man of considerable profile within the community, and was regularly asked by the media to comment on business trends. Ed could just imagine him putting on a performance of informed cynicism on the Pat Kenny or some other radio talk show. His prior connection with Global Oil could draw attention to the company.

He put that thought out of his mind. He was confident that they had nothing to worry about in Global. Everybody knew that payments were made to politicians. How else could business ensure that the ground rules were made to suit and not impede? But to draw cheques, for lodgement to an Irish bank account, was so asanine as to be beyond belief. If that was what Independent Petroleum had done—well, they and their sponsor deserved to be caught. The dogs in the street knew that, since the advice famously given by Deep Throat to the Watergate investigators—"Follow the Money"—no-one ever left a money trail. The same dogs also knew that there was now a well-established structure to facilitate such inducements. Payments lodged to a personal account with the Ansbacher Bank in the Cayman Islands could be withdrawn, on a back-to-back basis as personal loans, from an associated bank in Ireland. There was no way the Irish authorities could connect the two, but loose talk could be embarrassing.

The sky had now turned a nasty shade of dark grey, and his pondering was terminated abruptly by a flash of lightning that seemed to enter the sea. This was the prelude to the darkening clouds emitting a clap of thunder that heralded the arrival of the expected downpour.

As he strolled onto the bottle-green carpet of his executive office, experiencing the deep pile under his feet and absorbing the familiarity of its opulent surroundings, Ed felt a strange sense of comfort—or was it security? This was his patch. He had personally selected the carpet colour and the oak-panelled walls. Unlike the boardroom, ol' Stoneyface had never dominated these surroundings. Ed couldn't understand these feelings, or why he was so intimidated by a chance meeting at reception, and an old man's picture on a wall. Maybe he just reminded him of his own father. They seemed to think alike. They were contemporaries he knew, although that was so long ago. There was a connection at one stage but then, for some reason that Ed was not aware of, they had then gone their separate ways. Each had been successful in business although his father's company was nothing like the scale of Stoneways. It was an oil distribution business in south County Dublin. It provided a good living but required long hours. Ed's younger brother, John, now ran it.

He could clearly remember those early days, when, as children, both Ben and himself, and later young John, used be the reluctant audience at dinner table discussions when his father would brief his mother on the day's events. No, they weren't really discussions in the sense that anyone else participated. They were more like lectures on the immorality of big business. Brant senior had his difficulties with his supplier, Anglo Oil plc, and was inclined to generalise.

"Big business is intrinsically immoral, and those involved in it become corrupted before being devoured by it."

He talked of "ordinary Irish people," whom, after centuries of political oppression, were now being exploited by foreign industrialists. He derided the educational system, which, he claimed, did nothing to train people to manage their lives. Children are encouraged to "do well" at school, "to get good grades," "to graduate and then get a good, secure, pensionable job." This they generally do. They get good salaries and start to enjoy a reasonable standard of living. They are then targeted by the financial institutions. After all, they are the wealthy of the future. The problem is that only a small proportion of them ever become wealthy; the rest struggle with debt and mortgages, with pension contributions and college fees and tax—which the rich, in the main, manage to avoid. Their cost of living races ahead of their salary progression until, when they least expect it, their world falls apart because their employer has decided that downsizing is necessary, and their jobs can better be done by a machine or by young, cheap, graduate labour on the far side of the world.

"If you're in business," he said, "you've got to be either the owner or the investor—never the employee."

"When you start climbing that ladder, make sure you own it."

"How can you own it?" Ed remembered asking.

It was then that he first realised that he was an outsider; his father's advice was not for him.

"It's not for everyone." He was told.

"Don't worry. We're not all born to lead – you'll find something you're good at. You can help me out in the family business."

He never asked again, nor joined these family sessions, but his father's words continued to drill into his brain.

"Just because I'm not a footballer like Ben or a golfer like John he thinks I'm no good at anything."

*I'll show him. I'll show him.*

These words were often repeated through tear filled eyes in the loneliness of his bed in the dead of night.

It was all so long ago but the wound still hurt. It fuelled his determination to prove himself and to rise above the level of vulnerability that his father preached about. He would be more than just a survivor. He would conquer the world that tormented his father – the world of big business. He'd show them all.

He put all thoughts of Tom Stone out of his mind and concentrated on the day ahead.

———————◆•◆•◆———————

Ben Brant felt annoyed with himself, when he realised that he had allowed his mind to drift. He could see the darkening clouds through the small-panelled windows and wondered if it was the clap of thunder that had brought him back to the real world. He had been thinking of the joy that was his and Ciara's, now that they were moving with their two children to their new house in the County Wicklow village of Kilcoole. Sure, it was a modest, semi-detached house, and they had a large mortgage and all the problems that went with that, but they had their health and each other, and that was all he had ever wanted. Well, maybe just a little bit more than that. Maybe, in some small way, he hoped he could help to defend the human dignity of the workers that were being submerged by the tidal wave of corporate globalism that seemed to be engulfing the planet. He shifted uneasily in his chair as he tried to relieve his aching back, and resolved once more to take Ciara's advice and lose the excess weight that she claimed was its cause. But that would have to wait. Right now it was other peoples' problems that had priority. He unconsciously interlocked his fingers behind his head, as he straightened his back, and ritually patted down his unruly greying mop. He then focused on the speaker opposite and the start of the day's litany of woes.

Ben was sitting in the canteen, at a tubular-legged and white, plastic-topped table, with the shop steward and the workers' committee of Techno-Products Limited. Dining, however, was far from his mind, as the rain now lashed against the window panes. The atmosphere inside matched the weather outside. It seemed appropriate to the occasion. He had experienced this gloom and doom too often in the past. Ever since he had been appointed Branch Secretary of the No.1 Branch of the General Workers Union, he had worked tirelessly to improve the pay and conditions of his members. Meetings, nowadays, were generally more to do with preserving jobs than with improving them. It seemed to him that the Celtic Tiger was well and truly deceased. A lot of meetings with management were similar to the one he had just left.

"It has been decided 'at corporate level' that the Irish operation is now uncompetitive and, in the group interest, there is no option but to transfer the manufacturing process to India."

He now listened to what was the usual response of the shocked workers as he watched their anxious faces across the shiny, tea-stained surface that would have witnessed many happier moments.

"We won't let it happen."

"We'll sit in and make them rethink."

"Surely the government can do something. After all, didn't it pay out massive grants to get Techno here in the first place?"

Ben knew it was pointless. He would, of course, do all he could. He would make a lot of noise. He would give media interviews. He would talk to the Minister. She would talk to the corporate masters. But at the end of the day, it would happen. It always did. The best Ben could hope to achieve was worthwhile redundancy payments. The companies that the government was attracting into Ireland were global. The world was their playing field. They located wherever the economic advantages were. Shareholder interests were paramount. Nothing else mattered. The decisions that shattered so many lives were made thousands of miles away. The Irish management—these men and women that he would negotiate with—would have had little or no input into that decision. They themselves were probably similarly affected. Their final compensation would depend on how successful they were in keeping redundancy and closure costs to a minimum, and in avoiding bad publicity. Ben had sympathy with them too, although he couldn't show it. He was so glad he had taken his father's advice and kept out of the system. His only regret was that he couldn't change it.

He looked around with sadness. This once-happy venue, where hundreds of decent people sat daily to eat their lunches and socialise, as they did in thousands of similar worker canteens all over the country, would soon be no more, as the multinationals punished the success of local economies by moving to take advantage of less costly labour elsewhere on the globe.

---

"Jaysus, will it ever stop?" John Brant had to hold his head close to the windscreen in an effort to make out the road. The rain teemed down. The broken wiper didn't help his mood, as he steered his fifteen-year-old Ford Escort through the potholed gateway of Brantoil's yard. He turned the key and sat there motionless, oblivious to time and surroundings as the rain turned to sleet and pounded the roof and side-window. He wished he was somewhere else—anywhere else. Today was his birthday; he was twenty-five. But who knew, or cared, apart from himself? Life was passing him by and he was scared.

As the baby of the family, he had been doted on by his parents and his older brothers. Ben, in particular, was like a second father to him. Ed kept him in pocket money but was rarely around. He had always responded to their encouragement. He knew they were proud of his athletic achievements, particularly the rugby international caps he won as a schoolboy. To them he was an achiever; nothing was beyond him. Even when he quit university after the first year, they supported him. Maybe they were relieved to see him succeed their father at the helm of the family firm, Brantoil. Maybe because it meant that they didn't have to. Although he was only twenty then, he knew that they expected great things of him. He was determined to try. He had promised his dad. It was his duty. Although, left to himself, he would have tried to earn a living as a golf professional.

That was five years ago, and he had tried to carry out that promise. The momentum created by his father had maintained the profits for a while, but that had petered out. When the competitors exerted pressure, he couldn't respond. How could he? He knew nothing about running a business. He tried to remember what his father had done, but what had worked then did not seem to be working now. He knew he was heading for trouble. He had married but was now on the verge of separation. His mortgage repayments were in arrears, his credit cards were maxed, and his overdraft limit exceeded.

The rain and sleet continued. He couldn't sit here all day. He'd make a run for it. He reached the door of his office. He was soaked. "Fuck it," he muttered when he realised he had left the office key in the car, and had to repeat the drenching. He strolled back this time; he couldn't get any wetter. He hung his coat on the hook behind the door and shook his head to clear the loose rain. The movement caused a sharp pain in the back of his head. "Jaysus," he gasped, as he suffered the after-affects of the previous night with the lads. He'd stick to Guinness in the future, he resolved, once again. He searched for the kettle. A coffee would help. As he passed the window he saw, through the downpour, that many of the delivery trucks were still in the yard. *What the fuck?* he thought as he checked his watch. *Eleven o'clock.* He knew that he was late. He was late most mornings, recently. He was finding it more and more difficult to face the sheer boredom of the office, but generally it didn't matter; the delivery trucks would be long gone on their rounds when he arrived. He sped across the yard to the order office, dodging the pools and streams as he ran.

He flung open the door. "What the fuck?" he uttered as a dart hit the door-frame to the side of his head.

"Oh, sorry, Boss. I didn't see you coming." It was Jimmy Magee, a long-term employee who was supposed to be running the order office.

"Why aren't you manning the phones? What are all the fuckin' trucks doin' in the yard?"

"There's nothing happening, Boss. We can hear them ring— that is, if they ever do—although it's not often that happens these days. We've not had a call in the last half-hour."

John was still standing in the doorway. His long, reddish hair was now blackened with the rain and stuck to his head, and he was soaked through to the skin. Coming up to Christmas was always a busy time, and with the sudden drop in temperature and the storm raging outside, he would have expected to be inundated with orders.

"It's been like this now for a couple of weeks. In fact, this is the third successive week that we're down on last year. Come in and close the door before you catch your end." Jimmy offered him a towel from the gents.

John knew that sales were bad. He was being beaten on price. He had cut his margin to the minimum but still couldn't compete. He had never been put under price pressure before. He copied his father's approach, doing regular research to keep abreast of his customer wants, and he tried to meet those wants better than any of his competitors. This was the system he inherited, and it was the system that had secured the lion's share of the south County Dublin market. It had always worked for his dad, and in fact, had enabled him to get better prices than most of his competitors. Competition on price was something he was not used to.

The phone rang. John grabbed it. In his anxiety he tripped over the wire and landed on the floor. The ringing stopped.

"Was dat for me? Oh … sorry Boss." It was one of the young lads who had been in a back office.

"Jaysus, John, we're not that desperate."

Jimmy helped him to his feet.

It rang again.

"Find out if they're shopping around. Ask them if they've got other prices."

Jimmy did as he was asked.

"Yes, Boss," he said, as he switched to another call coming through. "They're all more or less the same. It's Anglo Oil. They now seem to be our main competitor. They're quoting prices that are almost the same as what they charge us."

Anglo Oil. This was his supplier. It was not Anglo's policy to sell direct. It sold through distributors, and Brantoil had the exclusive franchise for south County Dublin. The price being mentioned was what Brantoil was actually paying Anglo Oil. He could not understand how this could be right. With operating costs to cover he could not compete.

John phoned the order office of Anglo Oil and, giving a false name and address, asked for a quote. Yes! They would deliver within twenty-four hours and at that price. He hung up and telephoned their sales director to complain at this aggression. There obviously was some mistake. He would check into it, but had John given any further consideration to his offer to buy over Brantoil? So this was it: as had happened when his father had been running the business, Anglo Oil would try to get their way, one way or another.

Well, they could think again. They obviously didn't realise that his brother was the Ed Brant of Global Oil. If they thought they could undercut him into submission, they were wrong. He had never had the occasion to call on Ed for help in the past, but he would now. He knew that Ed would be only too delighted.

———◆•◆•◆———

Ed Brant was reviewing the business reports ahead of the weekly management meeting. The managers would account for their individual departments, but Ed liked to be ahead of them—to have his questions prepared and to keep them on edge. That way he kept them stretched, always striving to meet ever-increasing expectations. He could never allow them to relax into a comfort zone where mediocrity and complacency could become the order of the day.

*Funny the difference a couple of hours can make.* He walked through the lobby separating his office from the boardroom. The panoramic views of the bay, normally available from its windows, were now shrouded in mist, as the storm that his driver had warned of was now very much present. The day had darkened, and the sail-boats that he had admired from his balcony only a short time before were now just barely discernable, as they tossed wildly and struggled with their moorings. Even the light green carpet and cream-coloured walls of the boardroom had taken on a sombre shade, as if the storm was permeating the building with some form of foreboding. He seated himself at the head of the large, oval-shaped, mahogany table that had witnessed the strategic planning of the company for decades. Although he had sat there on numerous occasions since taking up his position as Chief Executive, today he was conscious that he was under the gaze of the cynical founder, now critically supervising proceedings from his privileged position on the boardroom wall. For the first time, he found it unsettling, and made a mental note to replace that damned portrait with a framed copy of the company Mission Statement. That would be far more appropriate.

His senior managers were arriving for the weekly business review meeting and acknowledged Ed with what he considered to be subdued enthusiasm. Nobody likes being held to account, he concluded.

"Ed, your brother, John, is on the telephone. Mary asked me to deal with it, but he's insistent. He wants to talk to you. I think you should take it."

It was Patricia. Brant looked at her, trying to make eye contact, but, as usual these days, she avoided any intimacy, and was already walking to take the seat at the other end of the table. He had just been about to call the meeting to order but he knew that, despite her frostiness, she would always act professionally in the office and would not have involved him unless she considered it important and unavoidable. He didn't mind. Tactically, he had always found it useful to keep meeting participants waiting and on edge.

He retraced his steps to his office. The storm was now raging, and water streamed down the lobby windows as he passed through. He pressed the speaker-button, enabling him to stand and look out of the window as he listened to his brother.

Ed could never really understand John. He had always seen him as carefree, as someone who would have earned his living from some active role, maybe as a professional footballer or as a golf professional. Instead, he had surprised Ed by opting to give up his student life to run the family business upon the death of their father. It would stifle Ed. It was a small oil distributorship. Global Oil, in its Irish operation, had thirty-five distributorships and owned twenty-two. Brantoil was small-scale stuff, against what Ed was doing. But, he guessed, somebody had to do it, and if John wanted to take up the easy option instead of carving out his own niche, well great. It meant he, or Ben, didn't have to worry about it. They hadn't talked in an age. John had never phoned him in the office before. He wondered what would prompt him to call now and to be so insistent.

It didn't take long to find out. There were no pleasantries.

"Ed, I need your help."

"Sure. What can I do?"

"That bollix, O'Raghallaigh, he needs sorting out."

Ed winced at John's language. He was used to strong language, but its gratuitous use by his young brother on the telephone surprised him. He was glad that he had elected to take the call in his office and not in the boardroom. Although the deep luxury pile of the carpeting throughout the executive suite was designed to deaden noise and preserve confidentiality, he wouldn't have wanted Patricia to hear John's tone. It would have been too stark a reminder of his balcony outburst. He knew that John was referring to Jim O'Raghallaigh, the Managing Director of Anglo Oil. He knew him vaguely from his college days and had heard his father talk of him in the past, although never really with the same level of exasperation.

O'Raghallaigh and he were different animals, with different interests, and different social circles that never seemed to overlap. They had both graduated with degrees in business in the same year, but then they went their separate ways. Ed went on to qualify as an accountant, while O'Raghallaigh, as far as he knew, studied human resource management and industrial psychology. It was several years later before he again heard of O'Raghallaigh. At that stage he seemed to be gaining a reputation for himself as a capable 'company doctor,' running the management consultancy division of an international firm of accountants. He was head hunted by Anglo Oil in the early nineties and then, of course, he had become a regular target of their father in his tirade against the evils of multinationalism.

"What's the problem, John, and what can I do?"

John explained what was happening on the pricing.

"Ed, he's doing to me what he tried to do to Dad. He's trying to force a sale."

"And what can I do?"

"You can fuckin' supply us," he shouted. "I'm not looking for a special deal; just give us the prices we had from Anglo Oil before they started this crap."

John was his brother and the company was his Dad's. Ed wanted to help him more than he knew. But he couldn't do what John was asking. Brantoil was contracted to Anglo, and, although what it was now doing was unprincipled, it was not illegal. 'Non-compete' clauses are outlawed by the European Union. He knew that if Global delivered to Brantoil, a contracted customer of Anglo, it would be sued. He was also concerned, however, that his bosses in Global Oil Inc. would see it as a personal conflict of interest.

"John, calm down and listen," he said. "It's not that simple. Anglo Oil has you under contract and they will injunct us if we supply you. Apart from that, I'm still theoretically a one-third owner of Brantoil, and Global would have my guts for garters if I got involved in what they considered to be a conflict of interest."

"Bollix to that," John shouted. "I'm just looking for supply until they realise that I have options. When they know that I'm not selling, they'll come crawling back. They always do."

"I'm sorry, John. I really am. But we can't supply you. Not yet, anyway. Let me think about what you can do, and I'll get back to you. I promise."

'Fuck it, Ed," he responded. "This is our family business, our father's business. You were there when he told us what they tried to do in the past. Well, what they couldn't do to Dad they're doing to me and you're letting them. I need your help. You're the only one who can sort them out. You've got to help."

"John, I can't discuss it any more. I've got a meeting going here that I've got to get to. I'll think about what you can do and get back to you."

"Thanks for nothing," John said, slamming down the phone.

The storm continued to rage and seemed to emphasise Brantoil's plight with a peal of thunder. Ed Brant remained motionless for several minutes. Feelings of fatigue and irrelevance engulfed him. Then, with his father's words of scorn echoing in his ears, he turned and slowly walked back to join his management team in the boardroom.

Tom Bergin, the General Manager, was talking as Ed re-entered the room.

"The market has got more competitive, but we're holding our own."

"Tell me about the heating oil business," Ed interrupted. "Is there price pressure?"

"None that we can't handle. We have a cost advantage in most areas of the country. The most aggressive competitor is Anglo Oil. They don't participate in the industry understanding on prices."

"What understandings are you talking about?"

Bergin immediately avoided his gaze. There was an embarrassed silence. Ed Brant noticed that Patricia was the only one who didn't suddenly have something to examine in the meeting papers. She caught his eye.

"They seem to be particularly aggressive in this part of the county. I've had their handbill put into my mail-box on two occasions since—eh, well, in the last couple of months," she said. "Their pricing is very keen."

For a moment their eyes met and Ed was sure that, at least momentarily, they were both connected by the thoughts of his stupid outburst on the balcony. However, the moment was lost. She quickly looked away.

She was so different from the others around the table, so different from anyone else he had ever met. He turned towards her. He couldn't explain it, but there was always a sort of serenity about her that gave him confidence and helped every situation. Regardless of the pressure, she never seemed to get hassled. Her soft American accent, with the slightest suggestion of an Irish lilt, was like music to his ears, and when she spoke he found himself totally enraptured. She was seated with her back to the window, her delicate femininity silhouetted against the sky. The rain had stopped and the sun was now beginning to break through the dark clouds. The emerging light, while putting her face in shade, created a halo effect that highlighted and emphasised the softness of her long auburn hair, and just allowed him to make out the movement of her lips.

He suddenly realised that Tom Bergin was speaking. Ed hoped the others hadn't noticed his momentary distraction from the business at hand. Tom, who seemed to have recovered his composure, was waffling on about prices in general. As much as he was tempted, Ed had more sense than to pressure Bergin with the previous line of questioning. Price collusion is illegal. Obviously, he had stumbled into an area that, as Chief Executive, he would be better off not knowing about. As much as he wanted to, he couldn't avoid glancing at the wall portrait. Stoneyface seemed to be looking into his brain.

Ed quickly got his mind back into gear. He interrupted Bergin's flow.

"Where in the country have we got the greatest cost advantage on Anglo Oil?"

Bergin thought for a while.

"In the Dublin area. We've got the biggest and most efficient terminal in the country in Dublin. They've got to haul their oil from New Ross."

Ed adjourned the meeting but asked Tom and Patricia to stay back.

"Tom, you've got four weeks to take all of Anglo Oil's high margin business in the Dublin area. I don't want to start a price war, so target Anglo Oil and let the industry know that, as market leader, we're sorting out the price-cutter. Get them into a position where their parent company, Anglo Oil U.K.,will be glad to get out of the market."

Bergin shifted uneasily on his chair. His suave appearance again seemed to degenerate. He rubbed his bearded chin, while his eyes seemed to blink incessantly. Ed never could understand how it was that Bergin could negotiate the deals that were his hallmark. He wasn't a poker player. He was of the previous generation—one of Tom Stone's lieutenants. Ed had already decided to replace those old dinosaurs one by one. If he was ever going to change the culture of the company to one with modern dynamics, he would first have to change the recruiters. Charlie Connors, the Director of Human Resources, would have to be the first to go, and then— then he would shift Bergin.

He suddenly thought of the morning's headlines and again became conscious of Ol' Stoneyface's unrelenting stare. He remembered Bergin's earlier awkwardness at the reference to price fixing. He wondered if Bergin relied on more than his negotiating skills to secure business. If that was the case, Ed knew that he would need to be careful that he never officially knew about it. In business, knowledge is responsibility. If Bergin was at it, and was discovered, then Ed would deny all knowledge and Bergin would carry the can. Regardless of the bottom line benefits, it was accepted that, in those circumstances, in the corporate interest, someone would have to be sacrificed, and that someone was rarely the Chief Executive. However, for his own protection, Ed resolved that he would have to be more diligent in scrutinising Bergin's expenses. Consultants and public relations expenditures would get his close attention.

"So that we understand exactly what you mean, Ed," Patricia interjected. "You feel that Tom has now got the brand image to the level that we can be aggressive in the Dublin area and that Anglo is a weak competitor. If we can exploit this opportunity the year-end bonuses should be attractive."

If that helped Bergin to do what needed to be done, Brant was happy to agree.

"Yes, Patricia," he responded. "You could say that's what I mean."

"And what's my role?" she asked.

"When we've taken fifty percent of their business, we'll buy the rest at fifty percent of its present value. I've got to attend a meeting of the Strategy Coordination Committee in New York next week, and I'd like to take the opportunity to get tentative approval for the acquisition. So can you please do the sums, and let's see what we can afford to pay to get a respectable return?"

"Of course," she answered. "And what return would you expect?"

"If you don't come up with at least thirty percent before tax, we'll delay the purchase and take a bigger slice of their business."

"Through predatory pricing?"

"Through whatever it takes. That's my job—and yours, Patricia."

"It doesn't mention morality or legality in our job descriptions but, nonetheless I'm sure it's implied."

Ed hated the tone of the exchange. Patricia was the last person he wanted to antagonise, but she was clearly still annoyed and was in no way conciliatory. He wondered what Bergin, his wimpish General Manager, was thinking as he listened to the Chief Execitive being challenged by his Executive Assistant.

"Patricia, leave this. You don't understand, I've no option. It's—er, it's more than business. You don't know the background."

"I'll do the calculations."

She stood up and left the room, followed by Tom Bergin.

"Have a nice day to you too," said Ed as he rose under the gaze of ol' Stoneyface.

———————— ·•◆•· ————————

Patricia knew that Tom Bergin was deeply troubled as they left the boardroom.

"How about a coffee, Tom?" she asked as she steered him in the direction of the coffee-making machine that was placed centrally in the general office.

She noticed his hesitation. Was it a reluctance to be seen with her, the Executive Assistant and, ostensibly, the confidante of the boss, Ed Brant, or was he just not interested? She watched him closely. His eyes darted furtively over the lines of desks, all occupied by young men and women busily attending to the fortunes of Global Oil.

"Better still," she said. "The coffee that Sheila in Catering makes is better. Come into my office and we'll ask her to make us a pot. I'd like to discuss this Anglo deal with you."

Bergin followed her to her office, which meant retracing their steps past the boardroom. Ed was still there. She could see him through the open door. He seemed to be examining the portrait of the founder, Tom Stone. *Good!* she thought, *maybe some of the geniality of the much-revered founder will rub off on him.* She noticed Bergin's deadpan expression. If he noticed Ed Brant he didn't let on. He seemed to shuffle along as though exhausted. His obviously well-tailored suit seemed several sizes too big for him.

"Tom, tell me, are you okay?" She touched his hand as she spoke. It was cold yet sweaty.

He looked at her for several seconds, as if trying to understand the question—or, she guessed, whether he could trust her.

"I'm just a bit tired. I haven't been sleeping too well."

"Tom, forgive me for asking, but have you lost a lot of weight lately?"

He ignored the question, but the folds of surplus material as he sat was answer enough.

He sat there without a word as she phoned for the coffee.

The rain had started again, and seemed to be blended with hail stones that pounded the window pane and created a welcome distraction.

"I always heard that the rain in Ireland was soft. Do you think the Good Lord has got things confused lately?" She hoped to lighten the atmosphere. "Maybe it's the end of the world!"

"I think it's the end of my world," he responded without a trace of humour. "I don't know what's happening to me; I can't seem to concentrate. I used be so organised, but now I keep forgetting things. I feel as if everything is getting on top of me. Brant doesn't help. I had such a good understanding with Tom Stone. He was such a great man, so different. I can't afford to lose my job. I married late and still have a young family."

Patricia struggled to hear the last few words. His voice was now almost a whisper, barely audible over the clatter of tea cups on a trolley. The indomitable Sheila had arrived with a gusto that drowned out all sounds except that made by the sleet that now furiously battered the window panes.

"Deya hear dat rain? Isn't it a terrible day?"

She seemed to take forever to lay out the cups and saucers and pour the coffees while delivering a detailed commentary on Irish weather. The sleet continued to batter the windows, and Patricia just hoped that this dual distraction would not divert Tom from his reflective insights.

*How could he?* she thought as Sheila sorted the cups. *How could he be so hard on an old man that was so close to retirement?*

What she was seeing and hearing was so different from the man that she had loved and lived with for six months. Yes, she had got very close to him—maybe too close too soon. Thinking about it now, she wondered how they could have been so foolish as to think that they could maintain a secret romance and still act out a normal professional relationship in the office. Yet when he asked her to share his new penthouse apartment, it seemed to be the most natural thing in the world. They had a love that was different and would survive, regardless. She should have known. She had seen corporate executives in the United States change under the pressures of a job that demanded exclusive loyalty to the interests of shareholders when, quite often, those interests were in total conflict with their own sense of morality. Their defense mechanism was almost to develop a dual personality: the corporate one to be switched on upon arrival at the office, and the other softer, human, considerate one reserved for their families and personal situations. Ed didn't seem to know that script. He struggled with the conflict, but more and more, the corporate persona seemed to win through. What was it that drove him so hard? What was it that forced him to stifle everything that she had fallen in love with in favour of this rough macho style where his true feelings were smothered and his beliefs relegated to a secondary level? She was used to a work environment composed of corporate executive automatons but she couldn't stand by and see the man she loved, or thought she loved, turn into one.

"Enjoy your coffees, an' if there's anything else ye want, Luv, well ye know where I am."

Sheila left, totally oblivious to the scale of the interruption she had caused. Patricia just hoped that the coffee delivery had not interrupted Tom's concentration and confidence.

"I don't think there's any question of you being let go, Tom; things are going so well in the company. You're the General Manager; you must at least share the credit with Ed."

"No, Patricia, you probably don't see it the way I do, but he's like a new broom. He wants his own people around him and the old guard will be pushed out sooner or later. He's told me to let Charlie Connors go. Charlie has been here as long as I have, and has been the Director of Human Resources for the best part of ten years. He's a friend, and I've got to tell him he's finished. I'll probably be next."

Patricia really felt for him as he seemed to age in front of her.

"Tom, I think you should take some time off and see your doctor. I reckon you're suffering from stress."

He acknowledged her with what she saw were tearful eyes, although he was obvious in trying to hide his distress.

"I can't; you heard his instructions and the tone he used to me. He doesn't expect me to be able to deliver on that Anglo Oil raid, and when I don't, it'll be his excuse to fire me."

Tom Bergin rose from his chair. He looked like a broken man.

"Thanks for listening to me, Patricia. I've got to talk to Charlie. Thanks for the coffee...and the chat."

He shuffled out of her office.

She noted that he hadn't touched his coffee. The darkness of the day seemed to invade the room and possess her usually vibrant spirit.

She walked to the window, as was her wont, and stared with unseeing eyes at the greyness beyond. Although she was glad that she had been there as a sympathetic colleague, she realised that her efforts at softening the impact of Ed's words had failed miserably. Tom Bergin, she knew, was on the verge of a nervous breakdown. She hoped that he would heed her words and seek medical help. She couldn't do anything further, since even if things were different between herself and Ed, she had to respect Tom's confidence. She wished she could do something to help. She knew Ed Brant was just trying to raise the standards and motivate the team, but increasingly, she noticed that his words of encouragement sounded more like threats, and morality seemed to be more and more relegated to a subordinate consideration, if it featured at all. She had spent two years in the corporate office in New York before coming to Ireland and knew Ed's boss, Dino Papandreou, Senior Vice President of Petroleum Operations. He operated on the basis of fear. Conformance was not an option; it was mandatory. It was not a question of bonuses being cut for non-achievement; it was a question of survival. Papandreou didn't suffer fools, or indeed even independent spirits. She hoped that too much of this was not rubbing off on Ed Brant, but she recognised the same blinding ambition that seemed to drive for results regardless of the human consequences.

"Jaysus, Mary, and Joseph, did ya hear dat?" It was Sheila, returning to remove the coffee cups. Her entry had been prefaced by another clap of thunder that only competed with the noise she was creating in putting the crockery back onto her trolley.

Patricia smiled an acknowledgement but didn't comment. She was thinking over the events of the previous few hours. She had talked to his brother, John, before asking Ed to take the call. He had explained what Anglo seemed to be doing, and while she suspected the difficulty was probably of John's own making, and needed to be resolved by direct discussion between himself and Jim O'Raghallaigh, Ed was, after all, his brother, and she did as he asked and got Ed to speak to him. She never suspected that he would respond in the way that he did. What he had instructed Tom Bergin to do was clearly illegal, and for Bergin was clearly a very slippery slope. Predatory pricing is not permitted, nor indeed is collusion with other competitors. She understood how Ed could take Anglo's tactics as an attack on his family, but for the Chief Executive to be encouraging illegal activity was what created and gave momentum to vicious and immoral corporate cultures. It was the type of reaction that she would have expected from the ruthless Papandreou in New York, but not from Ed Brant in Dublin. She hoped she misunderstood and that Papandreou's tentacles were not stretching across the Atlantic.

The rain continued to fall, and she was sure she heard a further roll of thunder far out over the bay.

⸺◆⸺

*Funny the difference a week can make,* Patricia thought as she entered the boardroom, noting the contrast with the gloom and doom of the previous meeting. She glanced at the end wall and wondered how Ed Brant would react when he discovered that she had ignored his instruction to remove the portrait of the founder, Tom Stone.

"I'm trying to bring Global Oil Ireland into the twenty-first century," he had told her. "And looking at that old goat every week is unnerving. Replace Ol' Stoneyface with a framed version of the Mission Statement. Make it a coloured version," he added.

She knew that Brant was not then in the mood to discuss it rationally, but scrapping the image of the founder would, she knew, be seen by the staff as insulting to everything they had accomplished in the past. Whatever discomfort Ed Brant felt under the gaze of "Ol' Stoneyface," as he disparagingly called him, was small as against the damage it would do to morale. No, she decided, she'd handle whatever reaction he had, but she wouldn't participate in undermining morale without a fight.

While Ol' Stoneyface continued to watch over the proceedings, and to hold the new Chairman unblinkingly in his frosty expression of disapproval, the patriarch was now bathed in winter sunshine that flooded the room, and his unflinching stare, without the support of the weather props of the previous week, had lost most of its menace. She acknowledged Brant's smile as he entered, and felt relieved when she caught him winking at the portrait, as he took his seat at the head of the boardroom table. *Yes,* she reckoned, *the intruding sunshine and the blue, almost cloudless, sky that was clearly visible to all meeting participants has clearly lifted all spirits. All but Tom Bergin's, that is. He still looks depressed.* He had his back to the window and probably wasn't affected by the sunshine as all others clearly were, she concluded.

"Well, Tom, I suppose it's too early to report on the Anglo Oil project?" Ed asked him, having dealt with almost all other agenda items.

Patricia really felt for him. He seemed to have aged over the week. She had, herself, unobtrusively talked to his sales managers and couldn't find anything that Tom had done to mount any sort of aggressive marketing campaign directed at Anglo Oil. In fact, she had learned that Anglo Oil would probably be a most difficult competitor. Its manager, the guy with the Irish name that she couldn't remember, apparently had such a grip on his business that it was unlikely that Tom Bergin would make any inroads. She quickly looked away to save him embarrassment but pictured his ritualistic beard tugging and blinking.

"Yes, Ed, we've saturated the south of the county with handbills. I'm—eh, very confident that we'll pick up a lot of their customers."

"I thought we agreed not to do a blanket campaign. For Chrissake, Tom, that'll start a bloody price war."

Patricia knew that Tom was lying. The problem for him was that he had just told the wrong lie. He had obviously forgotten Ed's instructions that he was to specifically target Anglo and to alert all other competitors that he was just "sorting out the price-cutter." That was specifically what she had a problem with; it was price collusion and was illegal.

She looked at Bergin. He looked startled. Like a hare in headlights.

"That makes sense," she interjected, in an effort to save him from the inevitable onslaught. "With all the tribunal publicity, it's safer to do the blanket blitz but be selective about who we take. That way we can avoid antagonising any particular competitor."

"Good thinking! Okay, well done, Tom. Tell me, has Anglo had any difficulties with supplies?"

"No—er, eh, none that I've heard of."

*Wrong again*, thought Patricia. Even with the very tentative enquiries of Tom's staff, she had heard about Anglo's stock run-out and the fact that they had to borrow oil from Esso. She wondered why Tom would not have heard about it; his staff spoke openly of it.

"Why do you ask, Ed? Have you heard something? Are there problems with their supply lines?"

She was conscious of a definite period of hesitation before he answered.

"Well, er, the Niger Delta region of Nigeria are having problems that I thought might affect Anglo."

Patricia met his gaze. She knew that he knew.

*What's going on here?* she felt like asking. *I know and you know that the problems in Nigeria are nothing to do with Anglo Oil except in a very general way, and certainly would take months to affect the heating oil market in Ireland.* Before coming to Europe, Patricia had spent several months in the Corporate Affairs Division of Global Oil and the logistics of every competing oil company was the basic course of study. This knowledge was fundamental in assessing the competitive advantages of competitors, although the main emphasis was in assessing their weaknesses. She knew the fundamentals of Global Oil and those of Anglo.

She recalled the presentation done by Norman Kem, the head of the Corporate Affairs Department in New York before she took up her assignment in Dublin.

She knew that Anglo Oil was, in industry terms, a "mini." It purchased its oil on the bulk European market and relied on rented facilities from other oil companies. Headquartered in the U.K., it sold heating oils through franchised distributors. Its marketing strategy was very successful. It undercut its competitors, and, while that produced lower margins, its sales through each outlet were far higher. Periodically, it pushed to increase its sales in an area, or to consolidate its position by buying a distributorship that it had been supplying on contract.

Patricia guessed that it was presently on such a splurge and had targeted John and Brantoil. If that was the case, she knew that it had made a major mistake. In the world of oil, Anglo was small fry and could never withstand sustained pressure, applied vindictively, by a determined aggressor using the resources of the largest oil company in the world. That was the purpose of all the protective legislation outlawing unfair trading, to which Ed Brant seemed to be totally oblivious.

She knew that Ed would be as knowledgeable on the international oil scene as she was. Any executive in his position would have been schooled by Global ahead of his appointment. So why had he intimated that the recent problems in Nigeria would have affected Anglo's supply, when clearly it would not, and certainly not within the timescale of a week or so? Obviously, he expected Anglo to have difficulties. But how would he know?

She tried to see his expression but couldn't really see his eyes. The sun was reflecting off the polished surface of the table and made it difficult. No, she thought, surely not. Surely he would not use Global internationally to settle a family feud. She looked at him again. He seemed to know her thoughts and was smiling. Was that a knowing smile? Damn, she wished she could see his eyes.

Global's influence reached far and wide. At some point in Anglo Oil's supply chain, Anglo would be dependent, either directly or indirectly, on Global or a contracted partner. Ed could have talked to his colleagues in upstream to put pressure on Anglo Oil's source of supply. She had no doubt he would find willing accomplices in the murky world of international oil. Global Oil was a unified operation that thought globally but acted locally.

She let the subject drop. She knew that if Ed was using subterfuge because of a lack of confidence in Tom Bergin's ability to mount a successful marketing plan, then he certainly would not admit to it in front of the management group. She hoped she was wrong. She would have to wait and see.

Ed Brant adjourned the meeting. The sun had passed to the west and Ol' Stoneyface was back in his frame. She couldn't help but wonder what he would have thought.

———◆•◆•◆———

"Ya look well in the papers this mornin', Boss."

Ed looked up in acknowledgement and nodded to the eyes in the rear view mirror as they proceeded along Dun Laoghaire's seafront on their way into Global House.

"Keep your eyes on the road or we'll both be in the papers tomorrow."

He was right, though. The pre-released photograph of Ed, smiling benignly at the world, looked very well. It had been taken a year previously when he had first taken over as Chief Executive. It was in full colour and on the front page of the Irish Times. He glanced quickly at the other papers. Yes, ah—he also graced the Irish Independent. He remembered the occasion well. The public relations executive had been adamant. She wanted a full-length picture of "the youthful new heavy hitter in the world of black gold."

"The papers will be more supportive if we make it easier for them. But that's not the only benefit," she had said. "They will want a picture and it's better that we provide it, rather than have them snatching a quick shot that might not show us in the best light. That way we keep control of our image. Here, sit on the edge of the boardroom table."

She had spent ages in getting him to pose just as she wanted it.

"Fold your arms—no, unfold them."

"Look to the right—no, to the left."

Eventually she was happy that the best option had been selected.

"We'll airbrush it a bit if your complexion is not as we want it," she said without a hint of apology.

Well, here it was; the first outing of the new friendly corporate image of Global Oil in Ireland. It certainly lived up to expectations. He wondered what Ben and John would think. He wondered what his father would have thought.

His eyes shifted to the headline: 'Global Oil Chief Warns of Oil Shortages'

The text went on to selectively quote from an interview that Brant had given on global oil supply. As industry leader, the media had asked him for his comments on rumours which were circulating about Anglo Oil's supply difficulties. He had avoided talking about Anglo Oil directly but referred to the fact that supply was tight due to the threatened invasion of Iraq, and the likely cutback in the availability of crude oil due to events in the Niger Delta region of Nigeria. Three major oil companies operating there, he had said, were likely to have to shut down operations because of violence in the region.

This seemed to have been accepted, by the editorial comment, as the reason for Anglo Oil's supply difficulties. Ed breathed a sigh of relief. He had recalled Patricia's sceptical look when he had mentioned it at the management meeting in the boardroom. She had never referred to the subject again. He was glad. He couldn't have told her the truth. She would not have understood. How could she? He didn't understand it himself. He knew he had to help John – to help his Dad's firm? So what else could he do? What would his Dad have done? - a Brant using the muscle of a multinational to settle a score! No, his Dad would have been appalled. But he would also have been appalled if he had done nothing. No! he wasn't proud of what he was doing, but no matter what he did, he would have been wrong. Sure wasn't that the story of his life. In his Dad's eyes he was always wrong.

He looked again at the photograph. The effect of the airbrushing was hardly noticeable, but that wasn't what took his attention. The disapproving look of Ol' Stoneyface was clearly visible in the background, his eyes boring into the back of his head, from that damned portrait that he had told Patricia to scrap. Was he losing control? First Bergin ignoring his instructions on firing Connors and then, again, on focusing the attack on Anglo's customer-base rather than on the market in general. Then there was the portrait. He remembered specifically telling Patricia to get rid of it. He would have to assert his authority. He could just fire Bergin, but that would leave Connors, and Connors was a bigger problem. He was out there recruiting people like himself—like Ol' Stoneyface. No, he decided he would personally fire Connors; but he'd offer him a generous retirement package. His departure would make the others understand that the old days of the country club were over. It was a new era.

"Looks pretty good, boss, eh? What do ya think?' asked his driver as he opened the car door at Global House.

Brant automatically looked again at his picture.

"And despite the forecast, I think it'll stay dry."

———◆◆◆———

Patricia Harvey looked quizzically at Tom Bergin. He seemed to have escaped from his almost permanent state of despair to one of euphoria. She had visited his office to enquire after his health, and to discreetly encourage him to carry out Ed's instructions with regard to Anglo Oil. She didn't know whether he understood that she had saved him from Ed's anger at the last meeting, but any continued blatant disregard for instructions would definitely result in his dismissal for insubordination. Ed was a senior executive of a multinational corporation, and that's the way he would have been trained to operate. She knew that Ed was having problems in dealing with Tom Stone's legacy, and his patience was running thin. He would probably welcome the opportunity of changing the management figures that he had inherited from Stone's regime. She recalled that even Stone's portrait was targeted. Tom now seemed oblivious to his predicament. He had certainly changed his mood from that of their previous conversation.

"Can you believe it?" he asked as Patricia entered his office. "I called Ed this morning to tell him that I had been able to help his brother, John, with supply. He was delighted, and then he went on to tell me that Charlie Connors had elected to take early retirement. Such a relief; I had no idea that Charlie wanted to retire. Imagine the embarrassment to him, and to me, and the futility of it all, if I had acted immediately on what Ed wanted and I'd fired him. This way," he said with obvious delight, "Ed gets what he wanted and nobody gets hurt."

Patricia said nothing for a moment, but she wondered.

"How did you help John?"

"It was a fallout from the difficulties that Anglo Oil are having because of the problems in Nigeria that Ed was talking about. It's apparently got worse. Anglo cannot get any supply and they've had to release all of their contracted customers. Otherwise, they themselves could be sued. A lot of their major customers have approached us for supply. I had a call from John Brant this morning. He was delighted when I told him that we could supply Brantoil, and so was I, obviously. Ed was really thrilled when I told him. It looks as if all is now back on the rails—everything that Ed wanted has been achieved in a couple of hours. I can sleep again."

Patricia Harvey now sat absolutely enthralled. No matter how often she came to this spot, she was enveloped with this same feeling of wonderment. Far below and around, the sunlight converted the darkest green into a myriad of softer shades and left a brilliant sheen on the still water, near the shore and then again at the distant horizon. The clouds superimposed a patchwork of shadows, extending beyond the water and embracing shoreline, to highlight patches of the Bray headland, the Wicklow hills, and the majestic Sugarloaf peaks beyond. From her refuge point on Killiney Hill, overlooking the bay and Dalkey Island, she wondered if this wasn't the most heavenly place on earth. The December day was dull but calm, and the stillness and quiet filled her very being. Nature, at least, was at peace, interrupted only occasionally by the gentle nudging of a golden retriever that obviously lived nearby and seemed to always sense her presence. He, or she—Patricia was never sure—was now sitting and offering its paw, eyeing her with a dewy-eyed pleading. Blondie, Patricia had christened him, or her, and was glad that if she was a he his masculinity was not offended. He seemed quite happy to respond when she called.

Patricia had found, over the months since her arrival in Ireland, that she needed a contact with nature to preserve her sense of reality and to escape from the highly-pressured hours working for Ed Brant. For a while her rooftop "Garden of Eden" provided the solace that she craved, and which she had hoped would bring some measure of tranquillity to Ed. Somehow, however, she doubted it. She wondered if he ever went out on the balcony now, or if he was sharing its joys with someone else. For her now, whenever possible, early morning or during the day, whenever she could, she would walk the steep pathway to this special rock on the hill and let the artificiality of business life dissipate. Here, the heavenly beauty that surrounded her, and the adoring gaze and lively antics of Blondie, would allow her to recharge her batteries, and face the next challenge that the crusading nature of her boss, would inevitably create.

She enjoyed Ireland, and although Ed was not one for compliments, she knew that he appreciated her efforts. She had been so afraid after they parted, that their working relationship would be impossible. She had maintained her space and only went to see Ed when strictly necessary for business, and even then, whenever practical, she made sure she was accompanied. That way, business stayed business, and some degree of normality returned to their relationship. Her job had become almost an extension of his. She had become involved in all aspects of his work and understood his objectives to the extent that she could, and did ensure that all divisions of the company were aligned. Over time, she had assumed the responsibility of referring to Ed only what he needed to see. Other matters she handled under his name and with his authority.

As she marvelled at the scene before and around her, which transformed itself with the movement of the clouds as she watched, she wondered whether her mother had enjoyed this beauty all those years previously. Although she was too young at the time to understand, she knew that her mother once had a similar role with Ed's father, Paddy Brant, in his family-owned firm, Brantoil, almost thirty years ago before emigrating to America and settling in Texas. Patricia had grown up there. She had graduated in business at the University of Houston, joined Global Oil Inc., and was offered the training opportunity of relocating to the company's Irish subsidiary, as the Executive Assistant to its Chief Executive. It was only afterwards that she realised the extraordinary coincidence of her position. Her mother had never mentioned Brantoil, but had she lived, Patricia knew she would have enjoyed the repetition of history: her daughter's support role to another Brant.

Ed's reaction when she told him was, she thought, strange. Although he was very clearly driven by trying to achieve his father's expectations of him, he didn't seem at all keen to talk about him, or her mother, or their working relationship all those years previously. In fact, any subject that in any way touched on his father seemed to be taboo. She deeply regretted pushing him the way she did on the balcony that morning. She knew she should never have mentioned his father, but the aggression in his reaction was something she would never have believed possible. She could forgive him that, and she had, but what she could never forgive or forget was what he had said about her father. The memories of that awful morning came flooding back—the look in his eyes, the tone of his voice, those piercing words. If he had problems with his own father why did he have to take them out on the world – on her, on her mother, on the father she never knew? No, that was something else. That was something she would never forget or forgive. *The bastard—why did he have to say that about my father?*

She continued to gaze out over the ocean but its wonders, visible now only through tear filled eyes, were lost on her. *The bastard!* she thought, at the memories of her mother's struggle to raise her. *The bastard!* The clouds continued to roll by, and the surrounding trees rustled a serenade in the gentle sea breeze, as she sat and brooded, and Blondie chased the flies.

# CHAPTER 2

Global certainly made its up-and-coming executives feel important. A chauffeur-driven car had been arranged to meet Aer Lingus flight EI 104, direct out of Dublin to JFK International Airport, and to take Ed Brant to his suite at the Waldorf-Astoria. Ed considered the first-class air ticket to be a ridiculous extravagance, but it was a corporate charge, and Global was the biggest oil company in the world, so why should he argue? He had taken full advantage of the pampering and comfort, and felt rested but anxious, as he was driven through the heavy Manhattan traffic for the first time into the exciting world of international business.

With barely enough time to shower and change, and none to explore the offerings of this world famous hotel that he would, over time, come to regard as his New York abode, the same driver arrived to take him to meet his mentor and boss, Dino Papandreou, President of Petroleum Operations of Global Oil Incorporated and the acknowledged powerhouse behind the rapid expansion of its global empire. His huge, oak-panelled office suite, occupying almost the entire thirty-first floor, and fronting onto Fifth Avenue

with panoramic views of Central Park, was truly awesome to
Ed Brant and certainly in keeping with the prestige of the lofty
corporate position that Papandreou occupied.

*One day*, he thought, *one day*, as he rode the elevator to that
palace in the sky, concluding on arrival that, apart from an
aeroplane, he had never before in his life been as high, so close to
heaven, so within reach of that paradise that he was determined
to one day make his own.

Papandreou's secretary was there to meet him on his arrival at
the thirty-first floor and, very courteously but efficiently, brought
him straight to the boss. There the business-like atmosphere
was maintained. There were few preliminaries with Dino
Papandreou.

"Hello, Ed, good to see you. Come in, take a seat. What's goin'
on in your patch of the world? Well, no, save that for tomorrow
evening. I guess I'm a bit pushed for time now. I've gotta meet
some half-assed politicians in forty-five. Thought I'd just catch up
on this acquisition project you have in mind. Tell me about that.
You will join me for dinner tomorrow, eh? We can talk about the
rest then. My driver will pick you up at seven-forty-five. Sound
okay to you?"

No reply was called for, and Ed just nodded assent and followed
Papandreou's arm gesture towards the black, leather-upholstered
armchairs, in the distinctly informal and more comfortable section
of his office.

"Guess it's after quittin' time. Want to join me in a glass to take
the edge off?" Papandreou said as he produced a bottle of Johnnie
Walker Blue Label from a cabinet near his desk.

"No thanks, Dino, I'll stick with the water for the moment."

Brant wasn't exactly sure of the time, and he resisted the urge
to check in case it would be construed as a critical gesture, but
he certainly didn't think that he was in hard liquor time. Under
normal circumstances, an executive proposing a multi-million

dollar investment would have professionally-prepared handouts on the strategic fit and the economics of the project. He had not expected to be thrown in at the deep end of what, he thought, was to be an informal, how-ya-doin type of meeting. He was totally unprepared, but Papandreou went straight to the bottom line and seemed happy. Brant was amazed at the speed with which he was able to grasp the essentials. He asked few questions—almost as if he already knew the detail. In the context of the type of expenditures he was used to dealing with, it was probably small change, but Brant was stunned; a hundred million dollars had to be big in anybody's world.

"Okay, Ed," he said. "You seem to have negotiated a very good deal, and it will be a good fit with Global Ireland. That squeeze you put on their supply lines helped, I bet?"

Ed waited with alarm. *How did Papandreou find that out?* He waited for the admonishment that was inevitable. The chief representative of Global in Ireland resorting to illegal tactics to furter a personal dispute. *How could I have been so stupid?* So near to his goal of accomplishment and yet so far. He had no doubt that he was about to be fired. Global could never trust him again?

"You gotta use your advantages. Well done." Papandreou said with a wink.

Ed Brant said nothing, he couldn't.

"I've no doubt that it will deliver all of the benefits you've included in the economics and that'll give us a very acceptable return. But you and I know that you're going to do even better than that. Don't we, Ed? When you include the savings you'll get through eliminating the surplus heads, you should be able to improve the internal rate of return by three or four points. I look forward to seeing how you get on."

In this, Ed Brant was very aware that Papandreou had done several things: first, "you" was delivered with a lot of emphasis. He was letting Ed know that it was his project and he was expected to deliver. Also, while he was approving the project, he was also putting him under extreme pressure to extract the last ounce of economic benefit. More importantly, however, he was being told that Papandreou knew what was happening in Ireland and was not beyond using illegal tactics to further a corporate goal.

His philosophy became even clearer when Papandreou leaned forward and captured Ed's attention in an unblinkered stare.

"Ed, guess you'll be sittin' in on the Strategy Coordination Committee meeting tomorrow for the first time. Well, eh—let me fill you in on some of the rules. What you will hear is totally confidential and under no circumstances is it to be discussed outside of the meeting room. That way we can all more or less think out loud and arrive at the best strategy to bring the company forward. Any problems with that?"

Ed assumed the question was rhetorical and said nothing. It wasn't. Papandreou's stare demanded a response.

"Of course, Dino, that goes without saying."

"Okay then, let me fill you in on the current topic. Some members are a bit pissed over the fact that Global has not exactly been a favourite of the Iraqi government in the 'Oil for Food' programme. They reckon our exclusion has affected the profits in their patches and, as a result, their bonuses and stock options. Well, believe me, it's not a problem. That scheme is riddled with payoffs and will be used by our government when the time comes to pressure the U.N. and, if necessary, to replace Annan with someone more amenable."

Ed Brant thought he was hearing things. He had read about the United Nations' scheme to allow Saddam Hussein to export limited crude oil in order to get funds for humanitarian supplies, otherwise prohibited by the sanctions. Could this be what he was talking about?

Papandreou seemed to read his thoughts, as he refilled his glass with another double measure.

"Yes," he continued. "Kofi Annan is a wimp, and we need to get a Secretary-General more amenable to U.S. foreign policy. The Oil for Food programme has given our people the excuse. It won't be long before our troops move in to root out Saddam and those goddam warmongers."

Brant was genuinely confused as to where the conversation was going. He wasn't left like that for long. Papandreou again fixed him in his cat-like stare.

"I kept Global out of that fuckin' fiasco because I knew that any company, with that smell, couldn't play any part in the President's plan for the Iraqi oil after the invasion. It worked like a goddam dream. Global has been selected, along with Halliburton, to get the industry up and running when the dust settles."

Papandreou was beaming, displaying several gold-capped teeth. He mopped his bald head, which glistened both with excitement and, Ed guessed, the effects of the alcohol, which he seemed to be downing in copious quantities. He paused as he held Brant in the unnerving stare, it seemed, in order to allow the magnitude of his achievement sink into Brant's slow brain.

"Do you hear what I'm sayin'?" he almost shouted. "Global is on the trail of billions, and I do mean billions. Christ, I gotta go. Those fuckin' politicians; I need to keep them on track. We'll discuss it further at the meeting tomorrow. I'll deal with any questions you have then. See you at the meeting, Ed. Have a good evening."

With that he was gone.

Ed Brant put the Anglo Oil papers back into his briefcase. He was beginning to understand why Papandreou didn't get too excited about his mere one-hundred-million-dollar project.

Ed Brant had arrived in the big league.

He rode the elevator down, alone, and strolled down Fifth Avenue towards the Waldorf-Astoria. The cold of the December evening helped to clear his head and his aching chest.

As he sat through the discussions of the Strategy Coordination Committee, Ed Brant began to realise that global companies don't just accept the political order of things; if that order does not suit their economic objectives, they set about changing the order. He looked around at the anxious faces of those seated at the table: twenty or so multi-millionaires who made their money by directing the fortunes of this huge corporation, all celebrated names within the oil industry, and now he was one of them. As he listened to a succession of speakers—presently Papandreou, who had just taken the podium—it became evident that he and all others at the meeting were very much a part of the preparations for a regime change in Iraq. It was clear that the sole motivation of that invasion was to install a more U.S.-friendly regime, which would ensure ongoing access to Iraqi oil and create upward pressure on the market price of crude oil. The morality of the war effort wasn't mentioned by any of the speakers, nor was the risk to the lives of thousands of people. The focus was exclusively the huge financial gains for Global. What he had been worried about in Ireland was nothing compared to what he was being drawn into in New York.

He looked again at the faces around the table. Was it anxiety or concentration? He didn't know the characters well enough to decide. Nobody expressed any dissent, so presumably all were in favour. He was the newest, and by far the youngest, and represented the smallest of Global's operations around the world. *No! It's not my place to question what has already been decided. In any event, why should I? Jesus, though, are they really going to start a war?*

Although Ed was exhilarated by the pace of events and the earth-shattering and history-making strategies being discussed, of which he was now a part, a few beers and a nice dinner alone in a small restaurant where he could sort out his thoughts would have been his preferred evening. Unfortunately, this was not to be. As arranged, Papandreou's driver collected him at the Waldorf, where he was staying, to take him to the exclusive 21 Club on West 52nd Street, where the dinner reservation had been made. Ed didn't realise that the restaurant was so close. He would have enjoyed the walk. As it was, he felt that he was no sooner in the limousine than the driver was pulling in and telling him that they had arrived.

"Have a good night, sir."

It was the uniformed doorman, who competed with the driver to open the car door and then fawned over him as if he was their most important customer. Ed had heard of the restaurant. Who hadn't? It regularly featured in newspaper reports, where stars and starlets regularly met to enjoy its thirty-eight-dollar hamburger lunches. He had never been there before and was beginning to look forward to the experience. He passed what seemed to be a welcoming line of colourful jockey figures guarding the entrance and stairs, and was escorted by the manager to the Remington Room on the Third Floor. He was glad to have arrived ahead of Papandreou. It enabled him absorb the surroundings and adjust his demeanour to its splendour. *Yes*, he thought, as he looked around and soaked up the atmosphere. *This is what it's about. A fella could get used to this.* On its timber-lined walls was a most remarkable collection of original gouache paintings, depicting scenes of American history. The room, which could easily have accommodated thirty or so diners, was empty except for him. Only one table was set, for two. *Jesus! Was it possible that Global had reserved the whole room? If so, what possible justification could there be for the cost of such opulent privacy?*

Papandreou arrived with considerable fanfare.

"Howyadoin' Ed? Whatyahavin'? The usual for me, Tom."

It all seemed to run into one, but Tom, the maitre'd, seemed accustomed to Papandreou's bluster and nodded politely.

He was determined to keep a clear head, deciding to stick with the red wine. Although Dino had presumably selected the 21 Club for the quality of its surroundings as well as its food, it was obvious to Ed, who tried to make polite conversation, that his comments on the quality of the wall art or the general ambiance of the room were lost. His only interest seemed to be in getting on with his own agenda, and after his Bourbon on the rocks, food was item number two. He was oblivious to everything except the menu, which he now studied with the intensity of a starving man. Ed had had the opportunity of making his selection before Papandreou arrived and was ready to order the Foie Gras to be followed by the Roasted Halibut. Now, as Papandreou focused on the menu, Ed was able to focus on him.

It was hard to gauge his age, but he had to be a man in his late fifties, Ed guessed. As he bent his head, Ed couldn't but notice his bull-like neck that would have done justice to any front row forward. His crown glistened, and its starkness was in contrast to the darkened stubble above his thick ears.

"Maine Crab Cake to be followed by the Crushed Coriander Lamb Rack," he exclaimed in a way that, for a moment, Brant felt that he himself was the waiter.

He had no reason to fear; the real Head Waiter, being at his shoulder, responded with due aplomb.

"And will the gentleman have Mister Papandreou's usual preference for red Burgundy?" he asked obsequiously.

Ed couldn't help noticing Papandreou's immediate reactive lifting of the head. He reckoned the question was rhetorical and nodded assent.

"Then I would suggest the usual Nuit St. George." He left with a flourish and returned within minutes.

Papandreou had started on general industry matters but stopped to allow the waiter to pour the wine. His eyes closed as he savoured the aroma. He then rolled the liquid around his tongue for what seemed an age. His brow creased with the weight of the decision. Brant couldn't help but contrast the intensity of this care with the apparent cursory consideration given to the one-hundred-million-dollar project the previous day. Eventually he nodded. The waiter, as if reprieved, with his left arm stiffly behind his back, filled both glasses.

Papandreou continued as if nothing had happened, and Ed Brant was then the focus of his undivided attention, only interrupted by the regular attention of the waiter. His look was one that demanded eye contact. Ed tried to respond. Behind gold-rimmed glasses Papandreou had the coldest, most penetrating pair of light blue, unblinking eyes that Ed had ever had to endure. As a relief from his stare, he searched in vain for the eyebrows. He hadn't any, nor were eyelashes evident. Ed Brant then realised that his host had started on the real purpose of the dinner date.

"The Chairman and I are most impressed with what you have done in Ireland."

This was his opening statement. He then proceeded to list the achievements of Global Ireland since Ed had come in as Chief Executive. He covered everything from sales volumes and market share to profitability by market channel. He knew the operating cost, how many people were employed, and the latest market research results on brand acceptance. He then went on to congratulate Ed on the tactics he employed to weaken and soften Anglo Oil before he had made the purchase bid.

"I was very impressed that you saw fit to leave that part out of your presentation. Those innovative strategies are critical for business, but we can't boast about them. Have you heard about the difficulties those morons in Enron have created for themselves and their company, by not only talking about their price fixing and market manipulating tactics, but actually recording what they said?"

"No," Ed responded. "I haven't."

"Well, I'm sure you will soon. The tapes are due to be released. The regulatory authorities in California have them. I've listened to them and they're something else. The state will be suing not just Enron, but the other electricity companies as well for literally billions of dollars. They were caught because of a few blabbermouth traders. 'Burn, Baby, Burn' those guys were shouting when a major transmission line bringing electricity into California was caught in a forest fire and they saw the energy price skyrocket. A company hasn't a chance with that type of loose cannon on the payroll."

In all of this, Papandreou was only critical of the traders who were recorded talking about their corporate strategy. He seemed to approve of Enron's strategy. But why wouldn't he? It was very similar to the one that he had earlier that day expounded at the corporate meeting. His attitude suggested that, as far as he was concerned, Ed Brant had proven himself to be a true corporate disciple, and could be trusted with these confidences. Ed wasn't sure it was a compliment.

Again the flow was interrupted when the waiter served the appetisers.

"I need some help in this Middle Eastern strategy," Papandreou stated. "I might be asking you to extend your area of operations beyond Ireland. The President will be ordering the troops into Iraq in mid-March. After that things should happen very fast. See if you can free yourself up, so that you can take on a more challenging role than you have in Ireland. It will be a great career move for you."

Ed Brant was very conscious of the enormity of the confidence that Papandreou was placing on his shoulders with that simple statement. But, he thought, wasn't that exactly what he wanted— to be part of the top elite? It was delivered with absolutely no expectation of debate, not to mention refusal.

"I'll be delighted to do whatever I can," he said, as he joined Papandreou in a second vintage port.

It was obvious that Papandreou had reached the end of his agenda and had little interest in social chit-chat.

"How's the family? Kids still doin' well?," he enquired, while looking over Ed's shoulder to the headwaiter.

"I don't have kids. I'm not married."

"You're not? Could've sworn you were. Me neither; never had time."

As if on cue, the head waiter returned to advise the arrival of his car just as he had finished his third port. Ed was relieved that there was no protest when he declined the lift, electing to walk the short distance to the hotel. He really needed to clear his head.

"Jesus it's cold," he thought as he left the 21 Club and walked down West 52$^{nd}$ Street. He was glad he had come prepared, and turned up his collar and tightened his scarf as he felt a blast of colder air when he turned right onto Fifth Avenue. It was close to midnight, but the buzz of the City that Never Sleeps, and the freezing temperature, cleared his head, and he tried to put the last two days into perspective.

Although he had not heard about the incriminating Enron tapes that Papandreou had mentioned, he had certainly heard about Enron and their manipulation of the Californian energy market. The fact that Papandreou only commented on the juvenile discussions of Enron's West Coast traders brought home to him how unscrupulous big business really is. There was no concern expressed about the millions of Californians who had experienced price rises of almost eight hundred percent—that is, when they had electricity. Frequently they did not. Nor for the impact on the state's economy, which had been as much as forty five billion dollars in 2000 and 2001 in higher electricity costs, lost business due to blackouts, and a slowdown in economic growth.

As he passed St. Patrick's Cathedral and turned down West 50th Street towards Park Avenue and the Waldorf-Astoria, he wondered what Papandreou's reaction would have been if he had raised this, or drawn his attention to the many thousands of Enron employees whose retirement savings were tied up in Enron stock, which was now worthless. Or how those same workers had been denied access to their retirement accounts at a time when the executives and directors saw the company collapsing and had dumped over a billion dollars of their own stock on the market. By the time the workers could get to their stock, which many were relying on for their retirement pensions, it was worthless. Their losses were just fractionally short of the gains on the sales made by those executives with inside information.

No, Ed Brant didn't think Papandreou would have appreciated this point of view, nor the concern he had for Global's role in that scam. Global was not in electricity generation, but he knew that the company was a main supplier of natural gas on which these generating plants were fuelled. Natural gas prices had also skyrocketed in California at the same time. There had to be a connection. Was that a rehearsal for Iraq?

The stately magnificence of the Empire State Building, bedecked in the red and green of the festive season, seemed to dominate the skyline. He stopped in his tracks. His tortuous deliberations were momentarily suppressed as his thoughts were driven back to those carefree days of his childhood when, at this time of the year, his father would take him into the Wicklow hills to cut a sapling. The smell of pine seemed to fill his nostrils as the memories of those happy days filled his brain. The childish joy of it all; of helping to decorate the tree and the pride that was his when, to his father's applause, he would switch on the tree-lights. How easy it was then to get his acclaim for those childish antics and how difficult later on when he really needed his Dad's recognition.

He arrived at his hotel just as the first snow flakes started to fall.

————◆•◆•◆————

Patricia sat opposite Ed in his Dublin office. He had called her in on the pretext of getting an update on the Anglo Oil contract.

*Her hair looks different. Ah yes—she has it pinned up. My God, she looks great today, but I think I'd prefer it down. Should I tell her?* Her light green suit blended perfectly with the white leather of the armchair and the rich, dark green of the carpet, and seemed to highlight her tanned complexion and her clear, green eyes. *She looks more relaxed than at any time since our break-up. But what does that mean? Am I forgiven, even without an apology, or has she just moved on? Jesus, I wish I knew.* They had always acted professionally in the office, otherwise it would have been impossible. *Should I risk talking to her now about our relationship? If I do, and she freezes me out, it would make working together almost impossible. It's difficult enough to stay objective as is.*

"Ed, you wanted to see me?"

"Yes. Eh … eh—how has it been with you, Patricia?"

"You mean while you were away?"

*Is she deliberately misinterpreting or is she on a different wavelength?*

"Well, as you know, Anglo has no oil and their customers are moving to other suppliers, so I thought it appropriate to get the contract legalities into motion. It'll be ready for your signature by this afternoon. That is what you were asking, eh, Ed?"

"Well, no—I mean, er, yes—eh, will we have a problem with the Competition Authority? This acquisition will give us over thirty per cent of the market!"

"Don't worry Ed, I'm sure that won't be a problem. I knew that Tom Bergin has some good contacts in political circles. He has been able to get some significant concessions in the past. I discussed the issue with him and he offered to see what he could do. As a result, he was able to get an interview for me with the Minister. I've been to see him. He was very informed. He himself was concerned that Ireland would not be able to secure replacement oil supplies if Anglo Oil liquidated. He was happy that Global, who he knew was the only oil company with secure Saudi supplies, was the best option. While he did indicate that the Competition Authority might raise objections, we at least have his support and he promised that he would talk to them. True to his word, the formal approval came through, and we're now in a position to acquire the shares of Anglo Oil Ireland."

*Jesus, what a woman. I hope to God I can get it back on the rails. I was such a fool to talk to her the way I did. I just hope I haven't blown it.*

While he marvelled at Patricia's initiative, Bergin really worried him. Ed knew that he hadn't the ability, or the social skills, to be so damn influential. How did he do it? *I must remember to closely examine his departmental expenditures. He obviously has some leverage other than personality.*

"When we integrate the two operations what reduction in headcount can we achieve?" he asked.

"With Charlie Connors gone, I know Tom Bergin is personally handling the staffing issues. If you like, I'll ask Tom to update you. I'll be passing by his office."

Patricia rose and walked slowly towards the door.

"Okay, thanks Patricia." He knew, as he watched her leave, that he had missed a perfect opportunity to reconcile with the only real love he ever known.

He pulled his mind back to the issues at hand. Yes, Tom Bergin would indeed have to handle the staffing implications. It would be interesting to see if he was as successful with the unions as he was with government officials. If he screwed up on this one, though, that would be it. He would have to go.

Ed didn't have long to wait. Bergin arrived to report on the staffing situation. Although anxious to hear what he had to say,

Ed didn't want to extend the conversation beyond what was necessary. Bergin sat in the guest chair, directly in front of his desk, and sat bolt upright as he spoke.

"I've consulted with all of the operational management, and we've put together an organisation chart as we see it, following the merger of both companies."

Ed noticed the disclaimer of personal responsibility.

"Jesus, Tom, this is nothing more than an amalgamation of both sets of employees and management. It's the fuckin' easy option, and I'm in no mood for easy options."

Bergin took on his rabbit-in-the-headlights look and overworked his beard.

Ed waited for some response but got none.

"Tom. You've got a little more than five years to go before retirement. This is the biggest deal we will ever be able to do in Ireland. We've got corporate approval because I assured them we could take the business and avoid the staff cost. We've got governmental approval for no other reason than Patricia Harvey was able to convince the Minister that we were the best option in a tight supply situation. We've got one shot at creating a streamlined, competitive organisation that will over-deliver on what we have promised. That's the only way that you and I are going to make our bonuses and stock options. Tom, go back, look again at your chart, and start by delivering to me."

Ed didn't think that Tom Bergin had quite appreciated his mood. He pushed his glasses back on his balding head and tugged at his beard. For the first time since Ed Brant had arrived, he thought he was about to be challenged. If Bergin had this in mind he quickly dropped it. Without another word, he stood up and left Ed's office. He returned later that afternoon. He had regained his composure, but he stood near the door as he spoke.

"Ed, I'm sorry that I misunderstood what you had in mind. I thought that we would just initially merge and then, over time, weed out the surplus. I'd certainly recommend that because we're not going to get an easy ride from the union. Your brother, Ben, will be representing the unionised employees of both companies. Maybe you can influence him, but I've talked to Charlie Connors and he says that Ben is one of the toughest union officials that he has ever dealt with. In any event, what I've done is to prepare two charts: one that I think is the best we can realistically hope to achieve now, and the other, what might be achievable over time."

Ed smiled to himself at the suggestion that he could influence Ben. To think that Ben would go soft, just because it was Ed he was dealing with, was not to know him. Ben's reaction to their father's words of wisdom was diametrically opposed to Ed's. Ben would never be part of the system. It was his ambition to tear it apart. Ed knew that Ben would see him as a challenge and put his head down. If Bergin had come up with two options, he knew that Ben would see several more and would have a strategy to deal with each one. There was no point in postponing the inevitable, but he regretted that he had been so hasty with Connors. He couldn't see Bergin being a match for Ben.

However, he would "get on with it," as his father would have told him. He would go with the most severe cut and stick with it. Ben wouldn't like it, but he would have to accept it in the end. Sure, wasn't it happening all over the country? What was the big deal anyway? The newspapers were full of closures every day, and the workers involved would get their compensation. What else could they want?

"Organise a general meeting of the combined staffs," he directed his ashen-faced General Manager.

———◆———

John Brant had felt devastated by his brother's refusal for Global to supply. He couldn't understand Ed, but then he never could. He was gratified, however, when he learned that Anglo Oil itself were being put under price pressure by Global. This would certainly distract them from pressuring him. He half suspected that this was Ed's response to his request, and provided that it did not ruin the market by making it overly price conscious, he was happy. That is, until the delivery problems started. At first he thought that it was directed at Brantoil specifically until, talking to other distributors in the Distributor Association, he learned that all the others were experiencing similar problems. He knew that there would be no point in adopting an aggressive tone to Jim O'Raghallaigh. Like his Sales Manager, O'Raghallaigh would probably pretend that he wasn't aware of the problem, would promise to investigate and call back, but probably wouldn't. He was very surprised when his secretary told him that O'Raghallaigh was on the line.

"John, how are you?" O'Raghallaigh sounded tentative.

"Not good. We're inundated with orders but have no oil."

"That's what I'm on about, John. I don't know whether you've read it in the papers, but there's some sort of fighting going on in Nigeria where our suppliers get all of their crude oil. Production, we're told, has been shut in. Which means there's no crude oil at all being shipped."

"Jaysus, Jim, are you telling me that you, an oil company, have no fuckin'oil?"

"That's about it. Normally, in a situation like this we can borrow from other companies and repay them later. For some reason, all supply has gone tight. I think it may have something to do with all the talk about the Americans going into Iraq."

"Jim, I can't just accept that. We've a fuckin' contract with you for supply. You better do it, or you'll be hearing from our solicitor."

"John, we've had our differences, but I'm really sorry about this. That's why I phoned. I've no option but to formally call force majeure on the contract. We can't supply, so you're free to get supply anywhere you can. I'll be sending over the paperwork."

John was reeling. This had never happened before in the industry in Ireland. If Anglo Oil had no product, then what about other companies?

He decided to talk to his colleagues in the association before putting in a call to Global again. This time he'd phone their General Manager, a guy called Tom Bergin. Other Anglo customers had found him to be very helpful—more helpful than he had found his brother to be. He was so glad he phoned the association first. It was from it that he first heard the rumour that Global was in the process of taking over Anglo Oil.

———————◆◆◆——————

"Have a seat, Patricia. How are you?" Ed Brant smiled as he waved Patricia Harvey to a comfortable armchair in the informal section of his expansive office. "I want you to progress this Anglo deal while I'm in the States. I thought we'd talk over some of the details. Would you like a coffee?"

"Great! I'd be delighted—on both counts," Patricia responded, as she took the seat offered. She waited as Ed continued to read a legal agreement until his secretary entered with the coffees. He then rounded his desk to join her.

"You've done a great job in handling the legalities, Patricia. I'd really like you to stay with it until we put Anglo to bed totally."

"Of course. I'll be glad to do anything I can, but—" She stopped as the intercom buzzed.

"Yes, what is it Mary?" Ed asked without crossing to knock off the loudspeaker.

"Your brother, John, is on the phone. Ed, as usual, he's very insistent."

Ed remembered the tone of their previous conversation but he guessed that the news of the Global bid for Anglo would change everything. He reckoned that eliminating Anglo Oil and their manager, Jim O'Raghallaigh, would make up for his initial refusal to supply.

"Okay, put him through," he said without rising from his seat. John's voice came clearly over the speaker-phone.

"Ed, maybe you're not such an ol' bollix after all. Getting rid of that bastard after all he did to Brantoil and Dad is fantastic. I just want to say, well done."

"Well, John, we were lucky. They had some problems with their suppliers that put them on the market. Only for that we couldn't have done it."

"Well, you did it, Ed, and that's all that matters. Thanks."

Ed was delighted with the call. He hated John thinking that he would not help. John seemed happy. They were reconciled and Ed didn't have to tell him the full story. It was a good ending.

"That's my younger brother, John. He, eh—has a way with words," he explained to Patricia as he added cream to his coffee. "Now where were we?"

"You were just about to tell me what you wanted me to do now with Anglo."

"Oh, right. Well, as you would understand, to make this work we have to get rid of most of the Anglo employees. The problem is that I can't trust Bergin to put the boot in. He hasn't got the bottle. I need you to keep an eye on the situation."

"As a sort of spy?"

"No, as my Executive Assistant."

"And what's Tom Bergin? Only your General Manager. I think that—" The sentence was left unfinished as the intercom buzzed again.

"What is it?" shouted Ed, in a tone reflecting his annoyance at the interruption.

"Your other brother, Ben," responded his secretary. "He's also very insistent."

"Okay," responded Ed, secretly welcoming the respite from Patricia's obvious disgust and anger. "Put him through."

"Ed, what the fuck do you think you're doing?" Ben's voice resounded around the large office. He had just heard that Global had called a general meeting of all staff.

"I don't want to hear of any bloody rationalisation plan second-hand. I represent the workers in both companies. If you've got something to say you better say it to me."

"Hello, Ben, nice to talk to you, too. We're in the process of buying Anglo Oil, as you've obviously heard, and we're informing the staffs. If we propose something that affects unionised staff, and they want the union involved, well, then we'll be happy to meet you. What we're doing now is nothing to do with the union."

"Listen, Ed, I've been around. I know that multinationals don't merge two companies and keep the workers of both. Global is like a fuckin' vulture hovering over the industry to see what easy pickings there are. You weren't long about capitalising on Anglo Oil's supply problems. For all I know you probably caused them!"

"Without our support that company would have gone under, and all of your members would be unemployed with just statutory redundancy terms in their pockets. At least now there's a prospect of some jobs."

"So you do have a proposal?"

"Well, Ben, I'll tell you. We have two options: one is to do what we are doing, to buy the company, keep up to a dozen of the staff and do a good package for those that are going. The other option is for us to stand back, to let the company go under, and then take the assets at bricks and mortar value."

Ed let that sink in and then asked, "Which is it to be?"

"John was right" he said. "I don't know where you were when Dad was talking to us about multinationals. You're exactly what he was talking about."

"Ben, we'll put an offer to the staff. It will be a generous one. They'll have a certain time to accept. After that it will be withdrawn, and the only compensation will be their statutory entitlement. You know me. I won't back off. I'd advise you to recommend it to your members."

"You'll be hearing," he said and rung off.

"It looks as if all the Brants have a way with words," Patricia said, taking advantage of Ed's embarrassed expression. "Do you want to leave our conversation for another day?"

"Yes," Ed responded. "I think that might be a good idea."

Patricia left. Ed noticed she hadn't touched her coffee.

———◆•◆•◆———

The darkness was ink black. The rustling sound of the canes, that was so enchanting previously, was now just eerie. The lapping of the water, that he had found so relaxing, was now threatening. *Funny how light can make a difference.* Ed Brant was standing on his balcony. It was another sleepless night. He switched on the discreetly positioned ground lights, which so often in the past had created a magic atmosphere for those moonlit dinners and treasured moments on the balcony, that he and Patricia had shared in the past. The light appeared but the magic did not. How could he have thought those thoughts, and had those feelings, that this was a special place? The canes continued to rustle in the breeze, and the water continued to flow, but now it was just noise. Noise that he could do without. He needed to think. *What was happening? Where was he going?*

He thought back on the strategy presentation that Papandreou had made in New York, marvelling at the confidence with which he seemed able to project its result. The principle of taking over the Iraqi oilfields was not something that he and the committee members had any input into. It had already been decided at the very highest level within Global Oil Inc. and the U.S. government.

The debate that had gone into that decision had taken place elsewhere and was now history. The agenda then was exclusively post-invasion. The committee, and certainly not its most junior member, Ed Brant, had no responsibility for what went before. Yet that nagging feeling of disgust was tearing him apart.

The implication of stock building and the subterfuge surrounding the pricing really sank in as he watched the daily e-mail briefing of world market prices. The strategy depended upon filling storage when prices were at their lowest, hoarding when prices were rising, and selling the product when prices were considered to be at their highest. There had been debate on the factors that would influence the price movements in both directions, but Ed had got the distinct impression, from the confidence with which Papandreou spoke, that this price swing would also not be left to chance. It would be arranged, through manipulation of the market, by others in Global Oil Inc.

He walked over to the wall and looked out over the lights of the city and the yachts in the bay. Closer in was suburbia, illuminated as if reflecting the night-sky. He wondered who would have lights on at this time. *Were other people as troubled and as lonely?*

*Was this how those executives in Enron felt? Did they get themselves caught up in something that they couldn't control?* Ed got the feeling that he was about to witness, and be part of, another Enron-type scam. This time it would be Global in the starring role. The casualties would not be employees who would lose their retirement pensions; they would be Iraqi people and "coalition" soldiers who would lose their lives. No one at the meeting expressed any dissent, and Brant wondered if this was due to real support or because any one-man protest at the exploitation of the Iraqi tragedy would be a resignation speech and would serve no purpose – it wouldn't change anything.

Still he was convinced—or maybe he just wanted to be convinced—that Global was not starting the war. If the company did not cooperate with the U.S. government in the postwar management of the Iraqi oil, then some other favoured company would. Global was not about to do something that Halliburton and many others were not doing on reconstruction. Papandreou had pointed out forcefully that commercial entities had a responsibility to their shareholders to maximise profits. He had quoted Milton Friedman, the eminent economist: "corporate executives must make as much money as possible for their shareholders. This is a moral imperative. Executives who choose social and environmental goals over profits, who try to act morally, are in fact immoral." With this no one could argue and, after all, this was the only official part of the strategy.

The price manipulation on the scale planned, however, did worry Ed. The market price of crude oil, like any other commodity, responded to the perception of supply and demand. Shortages, real or imagined, drove prices up, and surplus, balance, or stability tended to bring prices down. A powerful, global, well-connected company like Global Oil Inc. could get the market to respond in almost any way it wished. The impact of a ten-dollar increase in the price of a barrel of crude oil on forecasted economic growth would be very small, but the benefits to the oil industry, the producing nations, and indeed even the consuming nations in higher taxes would be enormous.

He marvelled at the pinkish glow that appeared in the sky to the east. He hadn't noticed it arrive to announce the start of another day. *Good God, I haven't finished the previous one.* He had a busy day ahead and he hadn't slept.

He wondered where Patricia was. Was she sleeping? Her crystal-clear thinking would have been of great help. But when he thought about it, her conscience would not. *She would not see it as I do. With her it would be either black or white and, in this case, I've no doubt she'd see it as black.*

Yes, he wasn't happy, but maybe he could live with that degree of unhappiness. The thought of the cash bonus and stock option that would result didn't really excite him. No, it was the possibility of a further boost in his career progression. He wasn't a failure, and even though his father wouldn't see it, the world would. That thought certainly helped his conscience. He was determined to give full attention to making the strategy work, and decided that he would tell Papandreou of his interest in extending his area of responsibility, as soon as he had wrapped up the Anglo Oil deal.

He shivered as the breeze became a sea-wind and the first signs of dawn appeared on the horizon.

———————◆————————

# CHAPTER 3

It was really a spur-of-the-moment and last minute decision that prompted Ed Brant to personally attend the general meeting of both staffs. Tom Bergin, he knew, would probably get there in the end. The problem was that it would take time and, with the pressures of the Iraqi strategy, time was one thing he did not have. He was fully aware that his attendance would underline the seriousness and urgency of the situation, but he also knew that it could inflame it by provoking Ben and some of the hardliners. It was risky, but he reckoned that, perhaps, he could shortcut some of the inevitable rituals of trade union negotiations and get down to the core issues. How many? Who was going? And at what cost? He would try to project an image of toughness and determination, but also one of fairness. He knew the inevitable outcome. Wasn't it happening every day all over the country?

He was very conscious of an air of hostility as he arrived in his chauffeured, S600 Mercedes and entered the lobby of Jury's Hotel on Dublin's Quays, where the meeting was to be held. It was cold but bright outside, the sun desperately trying to escape from the drifting clouds. As he emerged from the Merc, standing for a moment to straighten his back and his tie, he became suddenly conscious of the provocative ostentatiousness of the huge, gleaming car in the circumstances of the gathering. His driver also, obviously felt similarly threatened as, having opened the rear door for his boss, he ran back, almost unashamedly, around the car to move it off.

"Okay, Boss, I'll get it outa here. I can be back within five minutes of yer call. And Boss, don't hang around. Some of those yobbos are around the door and they don't look too happy."

His arrival caused a stir amongst the groups that had congregated around the entrance to the hotel, the foyer itself, and the door to the meeting room. Anglo Oil employees, Ed surmised, as he passed, noticing their furtive glances. They obviously recognised him, no doubt from the newspaper picture. He thought again of Ol'Stoneyface and wondered what he would do. *Jesus, he wouldn't be here in the first place, and maybe I shouldn't be either.* A feeling of panic descended. For a split second he felt for his mobile. He would have phoned his driver if it wasn't for Tom Bergin coming out of the meeting room.

"Good morning, Ed. You're right on time. I'm glad. I wouldn't want to keep them waiting. The mood is not great."

He could sense the tenseness and air of expectancy as he entered the room and took his place at the podium. It was not usual for the Chief Executive to appear at such a gathering and this point was not lost on the employees. Bergin introduced him as the Chief Executive of Global Oil.

"Mister Brant wanted to talk to you all personally so that no one has to rely on rumours."

Ed could feel the air of anticipation as those that had been outside filed back in, noisily, and took up their positions at the back of the large meeting room. He looked down over a sea of white, anxious, unfriendly faces. He waited for a few minutes.

The talking and coughing and noise of the chairs being moved subsided. His throat was as dry and as rough as sandpaper. When he spoke he didn't recognise the sound of his own voice. *Why the hell didn't I leave it to Bergin?*

He noticed a half-full glass of water on the podium, obviously left by the last speaker. *But I'm the first*, he remembered after he had emptied the glass. *Jesus, I wonder how long that has been there.* However, it worked. He felt a bit better and it improved as he went on. He got into a stride and almost forgot about the hostility that had enveloped the room.

He had made some notes in the car on the way, which he now furtively scanned. He talked about the threatened invasion of Iraq and explained how important its oil was to Europe. He also talked about the situation in Nigeria where, due to ongoing violence between the military and insurgents, the oilfields in the Niger Delta region had been shut in. This, he lied, was where Anglo Oil's supplier got its crude oil and, as a result of this and the overall market situation, Anglo Oil had not enough oil to service its customers.

"We have offered to take Anglo Oil over, otherwise they face liquidation and all jobs will be lost."

Brant hadn't noticed Jim O'Raghallaigh, the Anglo Oil General Manager, although he was near the front.

"How can Global get product if Anglo Oil can't, and how can you get enough to supply both companies?" he asked.

The interest was palpable.

"Hello Jim, nice to see you again," Brant said with as much sincerity as he could muster. "As you probably know, Global is owned by Global Oil Inc., which happens to be the biggest oil company in the world. We have an exclusive arrangement with Saudi Arabia for crude oil. You will know that they are, by far, the largest producers and probably the only one that has the capacity to increase production."

"If that's the case," O'Raghallaigh responded, "why can't Global just supply Anglo Oil on loan until the Nigerian situation resolves itself? Isn't it normal for oil companies to help each other out, operationally, from time to time?"

Of course he was right. "Loan Assistance," as it was called, is quite usual within the industry. Obviously this would not suit Global's purpose in this instance.

"Yes, Jim," Brant said. "In normal circumstances that would be the case, but these are not normal circumstances. We don't know that the Nigerian situation will resolve itself in the short-term, and if Iraqi production is cut as a result of the invasion, the supply situation for Anglo Oil can only get worse. We couldn't give product on loan if there was any uncertainty on the time of its repayment. You must understand that, Jim."

O'Raghallaigh sat down and didn't respond.

"Is the agreement to buy concluded?" asked a man in the front row, whom Brant didn't recognise, but afterwards he was told he was Mick Dunne, the Anglo Oil shop steward.

"Subject to a number of contingencies, one of which is a satisfactory agreement with the union on the merger of the two companies. If that doesn't happen, and happen fast, we'll walk away. Anglo Oil will liquidate and all employees will be out of a job with only statutory redundancy pay. That's the reality."

Ed Brant had pretty much done all that he had set out to achieve and was relieved that the meeting seemed to be coming to an end without any further embarrassment. There did not seem to be any more anxious spokespeople but, just as he was about to turn the meeting back to Tom Bergin to get into the details of the proposed organization and the severance package, an elderly man, whom Ed immediately recognised as Ned Murphy, stood up. Ned was an operational supervisor with Global and was the first and only Global employee to speak. He never had a lot to say, but was well-respected, and Ed guessed would carry a lot of influence with the other Global employees.

"Mr. Brant, you've told us that you're takin' over Anglo Oil. You've said that they will go out of business if this doesn't happen. That's fair enough, but what are we doin' here? What's it got to do with the employees of Global? Have you somethin' else to tell us?"

Ed hoped the perspiration on his forehead didn't show. The Anglo Oil people had something to gain from the take-over—either a job or a bundle of cash. The Global employees could only lose. After all, Global had no supply concerns. Ed Brant, their Chief Executive, had just told them.

The silence was deafening. Ed saw Tom Bergin grimace. He looked anxious but he couldn't avoid the question. This is what all the Global employees wanted to hear.

"Well, Ned, we all know that when one company takes over another they don't just continue as before. They merge, one into the other. Some jobs are lost. Its unfortunate, but you couldn't have two people doing the one job. Tom Bergin will put a very fair redundancy package to you, and it's open to volunteers from both companies."

"And if you don't get volunteers?" he asked.

"We'll leave it open for ten days, then we'll have no option but to make it compulsory."

"That's what I thought you'd say," he said.

With that he left the room, to be followed by most of those present.

Ed Brant wondered if he had blown it. Should he have left it to Tom and the other professionals to deal with Ben and the committees? He had no way of knowing, and there was no way of going back now.

He called his driver. He felt sick and it showed. His driver had more sense than to enquire as to how the meeting went. It was obvious from his boss's expression.

"Where to, Boss, back to the office?"

"No, just drive around for a while; I need to think."

They were out on the N11 driving south, and passed through the scenic Glen O' the Downs before the silence was shattered by the distinctive sound of Ed's mobile.

He had removed his jacket and fumbled with the pockets trying to locate it. Just as he did the melody stopped. The 'missed call' register told him that it was his secretary. He returned the call.

"Oh Ed, I'm sorry to bother you, but I thought that you might want to know, Mister Papandreou has been on from New York looking for you. He phoned twice. He seemed anxious. I thought you might want him so I gave him your mobile number. I hope that was okay!"

"Yes, Mary that's fine, thanks," he said, wondering what Papandreou could possibly want that warranted him phoning Dublin at ten a.m—five a.m., New York time.

He hadn't to wonder for long. The phone rang again. In his anxiety he dropped it, and it slid under the front seat.

"Fuck it," he muttered as he listened to its ring from somewhere under the driver.

He felt for it and found it wedged between the gearbox casing and the seat-frame. To avoid losing the call he pressed one of the dial buttons. He must also have pressed the loud-speaker, as suddenly, from under the driver's seat, the booming, eastern-tinged, American accent of Papandreou filled the car.

"You there, Ed? You dead or somethin'? Goddam phones."

Ed's driver reached down with his left hand and was able to retrieve the phone. He passed it back to Ed who, at this stage, was on the floor of the car as it sped along the motorway, frantically trying to extract his arm, which had become wedged under the seat.

"Sorry, Dino," he said, as he managed to hold the phone with his free arm. "I just couldn't talk where I was."

"You okay, now?" It wasn't really a question. Papandreou continued to talk regardless.

"You been keeping your eye on the NYMEX? Bet you have! Well, it's about to tumble, so I hope you've secured all the commercial storage in Rotterdam and anywhere else you could get it. The President is about to give Saddam an ultimatum. That means that in forty-eight hours our boys will move in and the price will slide. When it gets to rock bottom, fill every goddam bucket you can find. We'll have a window of about eight months before the price will move up again to where we'll want to sell. Do you see any problems?"

Ed didn't think that his immediate problem of trying to extricate his arm was on Papandreou's agenda, so his silence was taken as a negative. It was a number of days since he'd checked the NYMEX, the industry term for the New York Mercantile Exchange, where the market price of crude oil is posted daily. He racked his memory. At the time of the meeting in New York the price had been thirty-three dollars a barrel. He remembered that, because it was the highest price in more than two years, and was attributed to the strike in Venezuela. He knew at the time that influences would be brought to bear to bring this price down, but ever since it seemed to be rising and not dropping. He had thought that a recent announcement by OPEC, the cartel made up of the oil producing states, that it was increasing production could have been part of Papandreou's strategy to bring the price down, but, if it was the strategy, it clearly wasn't working. Instead of falling the price continued to rise, and was now at its highest in more than twelve years. The strategy depended on the price dropping, so that they could hoard the oil when the price was at its lowest.

"Great, Ed, I knew I could count on you. Let me know when you have it all in place. I want you to spend some time in Saudi and Moscow. Come over to New York next week and we'll talk further."

"Sure, I'll be glad to." Ed had freed his arm and was struggling to climb back onto his seat while continuing to hold the phone and sound casual.

"By the way, well done on Anglo Oil. It's still goin' according to plan, isn't it?"

Ed almost vomited. He wasn't sure whether Papandreou's congratulations were sincere or whether he was aware of the union difficulties and was just exerting another bit of subtle pressure.

"Ah yes, no problem." He wasn't to know that at that exact time his brother, Ben Brant, was preparing to serve him with strike notice.

Papandreou was gone. The driver looked at the dishevelled figure in the back.

"Will I take you home, Boss, or to the office?"

They headed out to the Dalkey penthouse, where Ed Brant would try to catch up on another night's lost sleep.

————————◆•◆•◆————————

Ben Brant's back still ached. Ciara was still on to him about his weight, but he wondered: *Could it be his posture?* Day after day he sat at this or other tables, listening to people whose lives were being destroyed. *Wouldn't that affect the way you sat? How could anyone sit upright when your heart is so heavy?* Today was worse than most. In fact, today was one of the worst days in his life. Generally the daily tragedies were remote; he could be objective. They were caused by inanimate bodies, owned by faceless shareholders, and affected unknown workers. He only had to face a few, but he was always conscious that they represented countless others whose dreams were being shattered. Ciara and he would often talk about some that made the headlines, and count their blessings that they and their kids were safe from the ravages of the multinationals. How he'd ever be able to talk about this one he didn't know. *How could the son of his own father and mother, who sat around the same dinner table and listened to the same words of warning, turn into one of those ruthless capitalists whose only interest was their sacred 'bottom line'? How could he do this to me, his own brother?*

Ben had never been close to Ed. He was seven years older and had left their home before Ed was even a teenager. Nonetheless, he couldn't understand how two brothers could be so different. Ben knew he had been very much influenced by his father's view of life, but Ed, who would have listened to the same thoughts, had grown, in Ben's mind, into the type of multinational tycoon that his father abhorred. He lived in Dalkey, socialised with the jet set, and was a member of the exclusive Powerscourt Golf Club, where the entrance fee, Ben knew, was more than twice the annual earnings of some of his workers.

He had never had to confront Ed professionally in the past, as Global paid the standard industry rates and got the standard level of industry productivity. On the minor issues that periodically arose, Ben always got his assistant to deal with Charlie Connors, a decent man. Although Ben would never compromise to suit Ed, it was professionally important that he never left himself open to any criticism. However, there was no way he could avoid the present issue. He had never, in his career, experienced such militancy amongst his members. He looked out over the sea of anxious faces, where some of the women were crying openly, and some of the men were close to it. They were in the largest meeting room of Liberty Hall, the headquarters of the Irish General Workers Union, a bleak and cheerless room surrounded by glass that merged with the greyness of the mist that shrouded the sky and overlooked the dark green, soupy waters of the Liffey far below.

Speaker after speaker was essentially saying the same thing.

"My wife and family are in bits over this."

"After twenty-five years, I get a letter in the post, which my wife opens, to be told that if I don't accept their offer by March 31, I'll get paltry compensation."

"One way or the other, after March 31 only ten of us will have jobs."

"They're planning on giving our jobs to that contractor who delivers for Anglo Oil."

"I've just taken out a huge mortgage on a house. We'll have to sell it. How can I tell my wife that we're back where we started?"

"They've even done the dirt on the management of Anglo Oil. I heard that that manager chap, O'Raghallaigh, has also been let go. What chance has the ordinary worker?"

Ben knew that they knew that the "bollix" they constantly referred to was Ed, his brother. He was thankful that they felt capable of expressing themselves, as they did, despite this. It was a vote of confidence in him and in his integrity. He adjourned the meeting with the promise that he would do everything possible to help them. He went into his small, cramped, untidy office, which was just off the meeting room. He stood for an age at the window just staring, unseeingly, at the darkening day.

Although he had seen such desperation so often in the past, he knew there was little he could do. The redundancy offer of five weeks pay per year of service was generous in industry terms, and while he would try to get some improvement, his main focus would be on the preservation of jobs. He knew that the merger would give Global more than thirty percent of the market, so the company was bound to come under government pressure to resolve any industrial action that would leave so many filling stations without petrol. He would bank on this and serve strike notice.

Ben Brant understood the power of political pressure. He contacted his friend, Pat Roberts, the leader of the Labour Party.

"Pat, Global is proposing to shed up to fifty jobs. Now, I know some of them will end up with one or other of the private oil haulage companies, but you can bet your life not all of them. We're not accepting it and have served strike notice. I thought you'd like to know."

"Do you know whether they have gone through the process of getting Competition Authority approval?"

"I know their Chief Executive well; he's my brother, and I'd bet all the 'Ts' are crossed and the 'Is' dotted. He's like that."

"I take it you can't talk directly to him."

"Well, relationships are fine, but under the circumstances I don't think it would be appropriate. If it got out that he and I were having cosy chats, it wouldn't help the situation."

"Yes, I can see that. Tell me about Bush's ultimatum to Iraq. Is that going to affect supply?"

"It must. As far as I'm aware, Iraq, under the Oil for Food programme, has been producing something in the order of ten percent of OPEC's production."

"Great! That gives me something to pressure the Minister with. Leave it with me, Ben, and I'll see what I can do."

———◆•◆•◆———

Ed Brant looked again at his Rolex and paced up and down the pathway, through the shrubbery, on his rooftop balcony.

*Seven-fifteen*, he noted as he searched for the approach of the Mercedes.

*I should have told him to come earlier. Jesus, I hate this hanging around.*

He tried to console himself. The calmness of the new day helped. He watched the early morning sun, emerging low in the sky to the east, reflecting on the still water.

*It could be worse, I suppose*, he admitted, as he aimlessly walked around to the other side of the balcony, his eyes following the skyline to the tree-topped craggy cliff, with its fortress-like ruin, overlooking his apartment and Dublin Bay.

*Funny*, he thought, *that cliff-face used to be so familiar.* As he looked at its imposing presence he remembered, as a child, that he'd climb it without ropes or gear or even climbing expertise of any kind. It was now a favourite for the fully-kitted-out experts. *How did I ever survive?* he wondered as he remembered those happy days of his youth when fun and adventure, over those hills and through those woodlands, was the scale of his life's challenge.

He looked again at the empty driveway. There was no point in phoning; the driver was due at eight and was never late. He'd be on his way now. A phone call couldn't help him through traffic.

He hated periods of waiting; periods when the hands he dealt needed time to settle; periods when others needed time to catch up with where he was. This was one of those times. He had so many balls in the air, and all he could do was sit and wait. First, *that damned Anglo Oil. That is becoming a bigger problem than it's worth. I suppose I could have pressured O'Raghallaigh without taking his company out. But then, despite what Ben thinks, I only did what I did to protect our father's legacy.* Ben's words of scorn, however played on his mind. *What's happening to me? What have I turned into?* It frightened him. He seemed to be developing another personality, becoming a corporate desciple that acted in a way that was foreign to everything he really believed. *O'Raghallaigh seemed to be a bully that neeeded to be stopped but to annihilate him and his company, perhaps was an over-reaction. Yet it did make economic sense as an acquisition and it seemed to impress Papandreou. Sure aren't closures now  happening every day of the week in Ireland? No!* Now that I think about it, *Ben's perspective would be purely to oppose everything management proposed – that's what unions do. Yes, maybe I am being unduly sensitive. A company will always rationalise after an acquisition. An efficient operation always has fewer people on the payroll than it really needs. That way I can keep everyone stretched and it actually helps morale while boosting profits. Yes, I have a job to do. They can huff and puff but, at the end of the day, they'll go. That's just the way it is. Governments can't control multinationals, so what chance has a bunch of workers represented by a principled-ridden union official immersed in a personal crusade? Yes, I'll go full steam ahead and get Ben back on track by offering a redundancy settlement that is a little bit over the odds.*

Then there was that stock building programme. Sure enough, Papandreou's scenario seemed to be falling into place. Immediately following the ultimatum by President Bush, the price of crude oil dropped, as the market reacted to the ending of uncertainty and the general perception that the Iraqi conflict would be short in duration. Then, when the military action commenced, the price came down even further and continued to fall. Ed had already tentatively booked huge storage in Rotterdam. As soon as he reckoned the price to have bottomed, he would set about filling those tanks with the cheap oil.

*Why hang around here?* he thought, as that hilltop ruin again came into focus and seemed to beckon. His driver could pick him up there just as easily as he could here. Anyway, he needed the exercise. He hadn't been to the gym this morning. In fact, he hadn't been for quite a few mornings. It wasn't that Patricia was right, it was just that, well, he hadn't been sleeping too well and found it more difficult to get up. That wasn't working either. He just had so much on his mind that he would rather get up than lie in bed thinking. *Right, I'll walk up the hill. It won't be too strenuous and it'll help me focus on what needs to be done.*

The cool fresh air and warm sunshine was exhilarating and, as he walked briskly up the Burmer Road to the base of the hill, things began to look better.

There had been that hint from Papandreou about the next step in his rise to the top. That mention of Saudi Arabia and Moscow was exciting. He had no idea what that was about, but by God it sounded good. He knew that the nominations for the prestigious Global Award for Management Excellence were due to be made. That was the ultimate accolade, the Global Oil passport to the lush pastures of international corporate management, where millions in cash bonuses and stock options were almost assured.

Yes, things weren't as bad as they had looked only a half-hour ago. *If only I could get back with Patricia.* He knew that he had seriously screwed up on the one relationship that had meant something to him. But he couldn't rush that one. He knew that Patricia thought he was totally naïve in his approach. That wouldn't worry him too much if it hadn't been for that stupid row. *I haven't got where I am, even now, by being soft. The tough, direct approach to any problem gets the best results and gets them faster. It hurts people occasionally but they get over it. It's my job to get results and it's on that basis that Papandreou will judge me. Not on bloody popularity.*

*No*, he thought as he threaded his way through the woods heading towards the summit. *Maybe on balance it's just as well that Patricia and I are not too close right now. There are still a number of things that I have to do that she wouldn't approve of; it would be just constant agro.*

He thought of Tom Bergin's reaction when he had instructed him to send the redundancy letters to the home addresses. Patricia would have been horrified. He had no doubt that it would be controversial, but he also knew that when the spouses were involved in a decision about whether they should accept a certain cash offer or take their chances, they would accept the certainty. Everyone has bills to pay. *No, I can do without the weight of Patricia's conscience right now—plenty of time for that later.* As for O'Raghallaigh, well, he didn't know exactly what problems he had created for John and his Dad before him, but whatever they were, this humiliation would be his contribution to the family feud. O'Raghallaigh was obviously not a union member so he would have to fight his own battles. He would have no option but to accept the offer and, with their boss gone, the others would be more receptive. *Yes, I know what I'm doing. It's only a question of time and holding my nerve.*

He had reached the summit. He remembered it well, this scene of many of his youthful escapades that seemed to have happened so long ago. On the seaward side of the hill, looking down, he recognised the rocky patch amongst the shrubbery from where he used to watch the landed gentry that lived further down on the hill, secure in the mistaken belief that their garden antics were private. He made his way down and sat for a moment as those memories flooded back.

These vivid images were interrupted as he became aware of a movement in the bushes behind him. He instinctively felt for his mobile phone. Corporate executives are trained in personal security. He heard it again, closer and more vigorous. There was definitely something. He pressed the "names" and "search" buttons as his eyes scanned the shrubbery and bushes around him.

*Jesus. It's just a fucking dog!*

"Hello, hello, Ed, is that you? What did you say? What dog are you talking about? It's not Anglo? It hasn't gone sour? Has it?"

He recognised the voice. He must have pressed Tom Bergin's preset button. The dog, a golden retriever, was now playfully pulling at his trouser leg. Thank God it wasn't Papandreou's number he had dialled. He threw a stick to distract the dog. It worked. The retriever knew his trade and went after the stick.

"What are you talking about, Tom? I didn't say anything about a dog. I asked you how it is going. How many acceptances so far?"

He could imagine Bergin's frightened expression as he tugged at his beard and his eyes blinked uncontrollably. He wondered if he was still in bed.

"I'm afraid, apart from Jim O'Raghallaigh, there's no one. It looks as if the union is really taking a hard line. I've asked for a meeting, but they say there will be no meeting until we withdraw what they call our ultimatum."

"What can we do?" Brant asked.

"Ed, I don't know. I think they'll go ahead with the strike. The only good thing I suppose is that, with this Iraqi thing, competition won't be too predatory. The sales managers believe that we could take a closure of a few days without it hurting us too much."

This was not what Ed Brant wanted to hear. Apart from the damage to Global's market position, he did not want all of his customers' tanks to be empty when prices were dropping and margins were good. If the strike went on for any length of time they would have to be filling them out of higher-priced supplies. This would seriously reduce the benefit of the Papandreou strategy, and would leave him looking silly with the corporation. There was too much at stake.

He said nothing to Bergin. What was the point? He'd ring his brother Ben and talk sense to him.

Ben seemed sleepy. He left Ed in no doubt that he was interrupting a lie-in.

"Ed, do you know the time? What are you callin' me at this hour for?"

Suddenly Ed felt ridiculous. Sitting on a rock on Killiney Hill dressed in a business suit, that he had to protect from a dog, that was intent on getting his full attention. He held the phone with his left hand while trying to keep the dog amused with the other.

"Ed, let's face it, you and I have never been that close, but we are brothers, and I hate to see you do to yourself what you're now doing. Do you know, in all my years in the union, I've never experienced the level of downright hostility that you've created?"

"Ben, I've been upfront. I haven't beaten about the bush. I've put out our best offer, which is as good as has ever been paid in the industry. If Global doesn't buy Anglo Oil it will go under. They've no oil, and with the Iraqi invasion on top of the problem in Nigeria, it's not likely that they will be able to get any in the near future. As I told you before, we're the only thing standing between your members and statutory redundancy."

"Ed, you're probably brilliant at high finance and corporate strategy, but you've a lot to learn about human nature. Accepting your offer is probably the most logical thing for the members to do, but that's not the issue any longer. Anglo Oil has an extraordinary culture. They're all very proud of what they've achieved, management and employees, all together. It would be bad enough for them to be taken over, but to be taken over by Global is adding insult to injury. And then for you to go about it the way you did was like pouring your petrol on a fire. You should have made your proposal through me, like I told you, and you should not have gone out of your way to humiliate Jim O'Raghallaigh and his management team. I don't know how we are going to get out of this one. I really don't."

Ed hoped his panic was not coming through in his tone.

"You know the problems O'Raghallaigh created for Dad, and John tells me that he's still at it."

"No, Ed, I don't, but I do know that that man is revered inside Anglo Oil, and someday I'd like to hear his side of the story. That's unlikely now, though. I couldn't ever see him having a civil conversation with a Brant again. Unless, of course, you meet him in court."

Ed thought it best to ignore that comment.

"Ben, why don't you withdraw your strike notice? If you and I get together I'm sure we can solve this."

"You need to start listening. I can't withdraw a strike notice without the vote of the members. Even if I could, you would have an unofficial stoppage on your hands."

"If they go out they'll be out for a long time. We won't be improving our offer."

"It's not a question of 'if.' They will be out on Monday, and let me tell you this, Ed, I know the government won't like to have your five hundred stations without petrol. The opposition will be raising the roof about the size of your market share. It's likely the merger will be stopped."

With this Ben really got Ed's attention. He had assured Papandreou that the government approval would not be a problem.

"Listen, I'm sure if we meet up on this we can find a solution."

"Ed, you know I can't meet with you on this. We're on opposite sides. I couldn't expose myself to even a suggestion that we're discussing this issue behind closed doors, or that I'd be in any way influenced by our relationship. No, I think we have to let it take its course. Talking will eventually solve it—that's the way with every dispute—but feelings are running at a very high level right now. I'll talk to the shop stewards and the committees and see if I can find a way forward."

"Thanks, Ben, I appreciate that."

"No need to thank me; it's my job. But do one thing for me."

"Sure, Ben, what's that?"

"Nothing," he said. "Do absolutely nothing. Leave it to Connors."

"Well, eh, Charlie Connors is not with Global. He, eh, opted for early retirement."

"Ed, don't use that corporate spin on me. I know what it means. He outlived his usefulness, or you got a cheaper edition. I hope you know what you were doing. Charlie Connors had a chance. I'd say you've none."

Ed Brant called his driver and asked him to bring the Mercedes to the car park at the base of the hill.

As it started, the day again looked bleak.

"Will you fuck off?" he said as the golden retriever retrieved the last stick he'd thrown.

———————◆◦◆◦◆———————

Patricia Harvey sat opposite Tom Bergin. She had made a routine of periodically calling in to his office to see how he was and to offer encouragement, but, on this occasion, he had asked for her help. She hated his office. The décor was dated and dull, and it depressed her. He was not a small man but always seemed lost behind his large mahogany, leather-topped desk. The back of his black leather chair seemed to tower over his head as it was framed by the dark red velour of the old world drapes behind him. The intrusion of the gilded-framed Mission Statement on the wall glinted like a lighthouse in the dullness, but did nothing to lift the whole setting out of another age. She wondered whether all of this was his choice, or if had he inherited it. To the rest of Global House, it was like a forgotten oasis.

What Tom was describing was as depressing as the room. She could hardly believe what she was hearing. She sensed that Tom Bergin was being careful in what he was saying, but the picture he had painted was clear enough. Ed Brant had himself attended the joint meeting of the employees to personally tell them that if they didn't volunteer to go, they would be effectively fired. As if this was not enough, he had instructed Bergin to put this in writing to each employee, together with the redundancy terms, and to mail it to their home address. She herself had no experience in industrial relations but would have thought that Ed's talents were certainly not in that direction. Feelings were running high, and she knew that Ed didn't have the empathy or the patience to handle the sensitivities of people who were being told that they might not have a job. In fact, he wasn't even adept at handling his own family, and she vividly remembered her own hurt at his suggestion that she would be prepared to effectively spy on this pathetic old man who seemed to be aging before her eyes. It still rankled her. She accepted that organised corporate intelligence was necessary to protect shareholder interest—every global company had to monitor the loyalty of foreign nationals within the management structure—but this was different. This was bullying an old man. It was to escape  this corporate cannibalism that had prompted her to accept Papandreou's offer for her to relocate to Ireland. She remembered the feelings that she  shared with Ed only six months ago. Had he changed or had she? She wasn't sure, yet the feelings she had, and maybe still had, she knew, were then very, very, real.

She looked at Tom. His physical appearance had reverted to what it had been that day at the meeting. She had absolutely no doubt that he was in trouble. Her heart opened to him. He had aged beyond his years, all in a matter of a few months. The very thought that anyone would spy on him disgusted her. It was help he needed, not more pressure. But it was only pressure that Ed seemed able to contribute to the whole project.

Even with her limited experience, she knew it was a major mistake to lump the manager in with the rest of the employees. This was bound to antagonise. She knew that the people of Anglo Oil held Jim O'Raghallaigh in very high regard and this could be seen as an effort to humiliate him. It wouldn't help, and she guessed that they might need O'Raghallaigh's support before they were finished. Ed had dismissed this concern when she put it to him. He seemed adamant. Maybe it had been too close to their balcony row for him to accept her advice, but, for whatever reason, he made it very clear that he didn't want any special treatment for O'Raghallaigh.

She knew that Tom needed to arrange an urgent meeting with the union, but she had no idea how he could get any resolution in the face of the militancy that their boss's entrenched attitude had brought about. She had made numerous trips to the coffee-making machine that morning in an effort to chat up the staff and assess the mood. This approach had always worked for her in the past, when as a new arrival to Global Ireland, indeed to Ireland itself, she wanted to socialise and understand the Irish. Not now; even the moderates unashamedly avoided her. Maybe she'd get more from the operational staff at the terminal. She decided to try it. She'd nothing to lose.

---

Tom Bergin sat in the passenger seat, staring straight ahead, as Patricia drove to Global's huge oil import and storage terminal on Alexandra Road in the heart of Dublin's dockland. He had readily, if unenthusiastically, agreed to accompany her when she suggested the trip.

He was almost fatalistic about his own future.

"I should have been more assertive with Ed when he told me he was going to the meeting. I could have predicted the outcome. And then sending those letters to the home addresses. Well, what would you expect?"

Patricia glanced at him but it was obvious that he wasn't looking for a response. As they drove through the railway crossing at Merrion and onto the Beach Road he seemed to be more relaxed, or maybe more resigned. His confidence seemed to pick up again as he talked.

"Jim O'Raghallaigh called in this morning," he told her. "The conversation was businesslike. He delivered his acceptance of the redundancy terms and asked that the cash be transmitted direct to his bank account."

"Did he say what he intended to do?"

"Yes, he said that he intended resuming his career as a management consultant, but that this time, he would work for himself. He would never again leave his destiny in the hands of others. He seems a decent sort of fellow. We shook hands and he wished me good luck. Would you believe that? He's the one that we fired, and he wishes me good luck."

He had seemed totally oblivious to everything except his own thoughts, until they arrived at the East Link Toll Bridge. As Patricia slowed and joined the queue of cars at the toll station, he sat bolt upright with a suddenness that caused her to slam on the brakes, much to the consternation of the driver behind.

"Jesus, Mary, and Joseph," he exclaimed. "There he is."

"Who?"

"Jim O'Raghallaigh! There he is in the car ahead. What's he doing here? He lives in Blackrock. Why would he be crossing the toll bridge? Jesus, I hope he's not going where we're going."

"Surely not, Tom," she said, with more hope than certainty. "It would be most unprofessional for him to agitate the employees now that he had accepted termination. You didn't think of mentioning that to him this morning?"

"No, Patricia. Like everything else these days, I never thought of it."

"Don't worry, Tom. It's not your fault. It shouldn't have been necessary to tell a departing executive not to visit any of the company's premises or contact its people. I would have thought that normal protocol and convention would have prevented O'Raghallaigh from doing that. The last thing Anglo Oil needed at this time was for emotions to be stirred up by its former General Manager. I think Jim would have been very aware of that."

They moved through the toll station and on through the roundabout leading to the oil terminals. Their worst fears were realised when O'Raghallaigh turned right down Alexandra Road straight to the Anglo Oil head office and parking compound. Even worse, it seemed that every Anglo Oil truck was parked up and a large crowd of Anglo employees were standing around. This brought home, very forcibly, that no deliveries were being made, and the urgency of bringing the stalemate to a conclusion before there was irreparable loss to Anglo Oil's customer base. Global could end up getting nothing but its fixed assets.

As Jim O'Raghallaigh's car entered the compound, they were amazed to see him greeted with spontaneous applause by the assembled crowd. Patricia couldn't help but think that it provided such a contrast with their own Chief Executive, who at that time was enclosed in his ivory tower back in Global House. They drove on past the Anglo parking compound and into the Global terminal. There was nobody around except the gantry workers busily loading several oil tankers. Tom seemed to have perked up and confidently jumped out of the car and led the way to the canteen. He knew that was the usual place for drivers to wait while their trucks were being loaded.

A very animated conversation stopped abruptly as they entered the room. Patricia knew that she was in a very male environment.

"Howerya fellas?" Tom said, acknowledging the five or six that were present.

There were only grunts in a reluctant response.

"Okay, lads," he continued. "I know you're sore over what has happened; we've got to move forward. There's no point in everyone being hurt with a stoppage. We've come here to listen if there's anything you want to tell us."

The silence was impenetrable, and the length of time before anyone spoke seemed interminable. Patricia knew that it would be Tom's show. She was glad he was here. She marvelled at the level of confidence that had come into his voice.

John Kerry, whom Tom knew was a committee member and recognised spokesperson for the drivers, broke the silence.

"Well, Tom and Miss," he said, acknowledging Patricia. "Fair dues, at least you've come down. It's more than we can say for our lord and master, Mr. Brant."

"Ed Brant has to run the company. That's his job. It's ours to solve this problem and that's why we're here."

"That's the problem. Mister High and Bloody Mighty Brant thinks that all he has to do is write a letter home telling us we've no jobs and our wives will do the persuading. Well, he can think again, and I don't mind you telling him that I said that."

"It's so different from Anglo Oil," interjected Eddie Barnes, the shop steward. "Even though he's been shafted himself, their General Manager is coming down to their yard today to console his people. If only we had someone like him this problem would be solved in a jiffy."

"It would never have arisen," said John Kerry.

"What do you mean?" asked Tom, obviously anxious to prolong the discussion.

"It's all in the approach. Jim O'Raghallaigh let go the same number of drivers in Anglo Oil two years ago. There was no hassle. He went about it the right way and respected the men. They respected him back. Our guy threatens us and then tries to intimidate our wives. What the fuck did he expect? Oh! Sorry, Miss."

"Well, at the end of the day it's got to be resolved through discussion. There's no point in avoiding one another. Why won't you meet us?"

"We'd be very happy to meet you, Tom, but let's face it, Brant calls the shots. That was very obvious at the last meeting. He did all the talking and he made the threat. We won't meet with him until he withdraws his threat and apologises for bullying our wives."

"Fellas, I hear what you say, but you're talking about the Chief Executive. You can't humiliate him like that. You're asking for the impossible."

"So is he," responded Barnes.

———————————◆•◆•◆———————————

The bright sunny spring morning, and the regatta-type gathering of yachts in the bay, got less than a glance from Ed Brant as he strode, purposely, across the lobby from his own executive office suite to the boardroom. It was time for the weekly management review meeting, and he was keen to get this one up and running. The psychological pressures he normally exerted by being last to arrive were far from his mind. He was, in fact, early. His mind had been almost totally preoccupied with the threatened strike and he was behind on the normal operational detail. Papandreou phoned each Monday, and he needed to be briefed before the call. Multinational corporations expected their executives to be on top of their game, regardless, and with the prospect of promotion so close, he wanted to be sure not to disappoint.

Obviously, expecting him to be late, none of the senior managers were there when he entered the boardroom. This too was good. The subordinate managers were less likely to play politics, and, in their bosses' absence were generally more forthcoming with information that might reflect on their managers. They were standing in a group at the end of the room.

"It'll be morning prayers soon," he heard one of them say as he entered the room.

The laughter this generated was quickly stifled, with nudges alerting the group that the boss had entered the room.

"Morning all," he offered, with more cheer than he really felt.

There were just some muted, half-hearted responses.

In an effort to encourage some informative banter, Brant pretended to busy himself in sorting his meeting papers. The awkward silence continued as the managers moved to the table.

Tom Bergin entered, accompanied by Patricia, and they took their places in their usual seats.

He noted that Tom looked, as he had come to expect, morose and pale. Patricia's initial cheeriness seemed to subside. He tried to catch her eyes with a welcoming glance. She was looking away.

He followed the direction of her interest.

"Jesus, Ol'Stoneyface is gone," he muttered involuntarily.

Ed looked at the wall with dismay. He had just wanted that watchful stare obliterated. The privileged position that Tom Stone had held with such domineering authority for so long was now, unapologetically, occupied by the gilded frame of a Mission Statement, proclaiming the company's newly-found values. Unfortunately, the portrait had been far larger, and the sun-bleached wallpaper seemed to be proclaiming to all present that the culture, as represented by those granite-like features and now jettisoned forever, was bigger than the new morality, clearly enumerated, one through ten, on a beautiful, golden-framed Mission Statement proudly displaying the logo of Global Oil Incorporated, the largest oil company on the globe. *Still,* he thought, *the ol'goat is gone, and now I can really set about establishing a new and dynamic culture with a new breed of hard-headed managers.* That, he knew, would help him reach the dizzy corporate heights that he now felt destined to achieve. He looked across at Bergin. *You'll have to be the next; your whole image is reminiscent of the culture that has to be replaced.*

Patricia's posture puzzled him. Obviously he had been mistaken when he had felt that she was disregarding his instruction to remove the portrait and to keep an eye on Bergin. She clearly hadn't forgotten the portrait, and it certainly wasn't her fault that the wallpaper was faded. Also, it wasn't lost on him that, despite their heated exchange, she was keeping close to Bergin. Yes, he knew it was more than just corporate loyalty; Patricia still had those feelings. He wished they were alone so they could really talk; he'd apologise. But why was she not acknowledging his glance of appreciation? Surely she, of all people, would understand the pressures he was under and what he was trying to do. He'd let the moment pass and thank her later. In the meantime, he appreciated the opportunity to be himself at these damned meetings and not have to constantly compete with a ghost of the past. *Yes, despite the temporary problem with Patricia, I'm getting there, bit by bit, one step at a time*. He could almost hear his father's words of encouragement, and he knew the way forward.

He had just completed his review of the monthly operating results when his secretary told him that Papandreou was on the phone. As he had all of the detail and numbers in front of him, he decided to adjourn the meeting and take the call where he sat. The meeting attendees filed out and, although he tried, he couldn't catch Patricia's eye. She seemed to be deliberately avoiding him again. *Jesus, what is her problem?*

He had mixed emotions as he took the call. Global Oil Ireland had had another excellent month, but the operating cost trend was still worrying. It continued to rise well beyond the rate of inflation. Brant knew that they badly needed to get that damned productivity deal through on the back of the Anglo Oil acquisition. There had been no further progress since his conversation with Ben, and March 31 was fast approaching. The last thing he needed was a strike.

"Hello, Dino," he said, hopefully sounding enthusiastic. "Nice to hear from you. Thanks for ringing."

Papandreou was business-like.

"I just want to brief you on a few things before you hear them elsewhere. You need to be prepared."

"I appreciate it. What's on your mind?"

"As I told you, the price started to fall as soon as the President made his announcement. This downward pressure on prices will continue as our forces move northwards into Iraq."

"Yeah, I understand that, but last week the price moved up again."

"There will be some temporary blips. Last week, for instance, the pipeline was hit and, as a result, the crude exports out of Iraq were down seventy five percent on the previous week. This is being worked on and will be fixed. Don't let aberrations like that fool you, and for Chrissake don't lose your nerve and start buying in before the price has bottomed out. We don't want to leave any dollars on the table. Not that I think you would, but watch your people."

"Have the Coalition forces got control of the oil wells yet?"

"At this stage, more than six hundred wells are in the area controlled by the Coalition. I'm told that there are still six wells on fire, but work is continuing to put them out."

"So, all in all, things are going according to plan?"

"You betcha. The boys are doing exactly as they said. By the end of the month, or early April, our forces will have taken Baghdad, and at that stage, eighty to ninety percent of Iraq's southern oilfield production and the export facilities will be under Coalition control. It'll then be up to us to get our people in place and get the production up to its potential of six million barrels a day that we promised the government."

"What about Kirkuk?" Ed asked, more to appear informed than out of any real interest. Kirkuk, he knew, was the hub of Iraq's northern oilfields.

"Good question, Ed. That's my real concern. Kirkuk is being left to the Kurdish guerilla forces in the north. I think they'll wrestle the fields from Saddam's forces all right, but I suspect we'll have a problem with them before we're finished. So much for that," he said. "How're things at your end?"

"I've just finished reviewing the monthly report. You should have it by e-mail within the hour."

"Give me the highlights," he persisted.

"Well, we've once again beaten budget. We should make over twenty million this year before any bonanza on our stocking strategy."

"Great. Well done, Ed. Tell me what's your tax rate over there in Ireland now?"

"Corporation tax is now down to twelve and a half percent," Brant responded, wondering what the point was.

"Very good," Papandreou said enthusiastically. "I'll talk to the accountants about lowering your transfer price. We want to make the money where tax is lowest. No point in giving it to a goddam government. They don't know how to spend it."

"Tell me," he continued. "Have you put Anglo Oil to bed yet?"

"More or less," Ed lied. "We just have to sort out some union problems."

"Will you bring it in within the numbers we discussed?"

"Yes, we will," he answered, with more confidence than he felt.

"Good! See if you can hurry it up. Light a fire under that fella, Bergin. I hadn't meant to tell you this, but I've nominated you for the Global Award for Management Excellence. The result will be announced at a dinner the week after next when you're over. I think it's on the thirty-first. I'm very optimistic. The other Vice-Presidents will have put forward names from their divisions, but I think what you've done in Ireland should swing it for us this year. It's important there are no loose ends, that's why I want you to have that Anglo Oil deal squared away."

Ed Brant was lost for words.

He continued. "One other thing: that damned Enron. The FERC are all over us. They're due to issue a report on that goddamn Californian thing I was telling you about. The report will be out before the month-end. A bunch of companies will be named, and it's rumored that some will be prohibited from selling energy in competitive markets anywhere in the United States again. Can you believe that?"

Ed didn't tell him that he could. He just hoped Global didn't feature in the report of the FERC, which he knew to be the Federal Energy Regulatory Commission, a body that couldn't be influenced. Try as he did, he couldn't keep his eyes from furtively taking in the wall at the far end of the room. Ol'Stoneyface's image was gone, but his spirit was still present in that huge shaded square on the wall that seemed to dominate the room and absorb every word spoken.

He quickly bundled his papers, anxious for the security of his own office. It didn't help his state of mind.

If Papandreou had intended to motivate him with his telephone call, it had the opposite affect. He had mixed emotions, or maybe was just plain confused about how he felt. On the one hand, it seemed that he was now regarded as a confidante of the Senior Vice-President of Petroleum Operations, which was what he had always wanted. After all, he thought, to get to the top he needed to be on the inside track, and that was where he now was. On the other hand, the reality was not what he had expected. He didn't really want to be a part of a global corporation that, more and more, seemed to regard war as a legitimate business strategy. Each day when he read the headlines, he only saw the death and destruction that was being brought down upon the unfortunate Iraqis and Coalition soldiers. All Papandreou seemed to be conscious of was the number of oilfields secured or on fire. Ed was not proud of his passive response, yet he had come this far and couldn't see himself quitting on an issue of principle. Principles, after all, were for his brother Ben, not for him. At least, that's the way he had always seen it.

That damned Stone. He had none of these wimpish thoughts before he had met him that day in reception. He tried to put him out of his mind. He'd get Bergin to have the boardroom redecorated. Even Tom Bergin should be able to do that.

The operating results for Global Ireland were excellent and the only worry was Anglo Oil. He was now almost regretting ever having started on it. A strike would be a disaster, and very embarrassing if it was on while he was being presented with an award in New York for management excellence. He knew that every Chief Executive within the Global empire would give a right arm to be in his position, but somehow the gloss had gone. Recognition by the sort of people that his father abhorred, which he now seemed to be one of, was not what it had seemed when he started in Global, which seemed to be a lifetime ago.

Despite these misgivings, Ed Brant really admired Papandreou's business sense. He didn't miss a thing. Already he was planning to manipulate the cost of bringing oil into Ireland in order to reduce the corporation's tax charge. It made sense for a multinational corporation to make its profits where the taxes were lowest. This it could easily do, because each subsidiary bought from another within the group, and transfer prices were set with the lowest ultimate tax charge in mind. Nothing is left to chance; governments are there to be manipulated and national boundaries don't really matter to the global corporation.

Ed Brant knew that, like it or not, he was now in the big league—a location that did not allow for the immersion of the spirit in the wondrous creations of nature that were spread out panoramically behind him and were at that very moment being absorbed by his Executive Assistant, as she sat and wondered and played with Blondie, high on her hilltop retreat.

———————◆◆◆———————

Ben Brant was looking out of the window of his sixth-floor, sparsely furnished office in the union's headquarters at Liberty Hall, on the banks of the River Liffey, when his brother was talking to his New

York-based boss. He too was mulling over what might have been. He knew that Ed was facing a very serious problem. Industrial disputes about pay or conditions were bad enough, but when issues of principle got in the way it usually spelt disaster. He suspected it was part of the Irish psyche: an instinctive reaction against a perception of injustice, even to the extent of self-destruction.

He worried that unless the strike could somehow be averted, it would be the end of his younger brother's illustrious career. It was self-inflicted, he knew, but that was no consolation. As always, he felt responsible for his siblings. He was highly embarrassed that a Brant would be so callous. Again, as was his habit, he excused it by putting it down to inexperience and not malice. He hoped he was right. He knew their father would turn in his grave at the notion that a Brant was eliminating the livelihood of so many families in the interest of corporate greed. As much as he agonised over the problem, he saw no possible way out for Ed. Even if a meeting was agreed to, how could he negotiate with his brother under the scrutiny of his members, who inevitably would now be looking for some signs of partiality? It was an impossible situation.

It was about then that his assistant told him that Tom Bergin of Global wanted to see him. He was in reception. His initial reaction was to refuse. Bergin should know that meetings in these circumstances, between an employer and a trade union official without a shop steward being present, were inappropriate. Both could be compromised professionally. Yet Bergin had been around as long as he had. He would know that and was risking his reputation. He decided to see him.

Ben had never met Tom Bergin before. Shop stewards don't generally meet general managers—certainly not general managers of Bergin's vintage. General managers of oil companies were in a class of their own, and they certainly don't come any bigger than the General Manager of Global Oil. He had heard of him, of course; Tom Bergin had been around since time immemorial.

He had a reputation for decency and fairness, and was considered by the industry to have been the real driving force behind his company's spectacular growth in the marketplace—before, of course, it was taken over by Global Oil Inc.

Ben was shocked at the sight of the pathetic old man who entered his office. He seemed to have shrunk in size as his suit, although obviously well tailored and of quality material, seemed several sizes too large. He came in with a shuffling gait, tugging at a goatee beard that had seen better grooming. His eyes blinked incessantly and he spoke almost inaudibly.

"Come in, come in, Tom." Ben rushed to him with an extended hand, but also with the thought that if Bergin fell he'd catch him. "Delighted to meet you after all these years. Sorry I can't entertain you in the manner that I'm sure you're accustomed, but you know, I'm just a humble union official. We can't afford the luxuries of big business."

His attempt at humour was lost on Bergin. He just smiled wanly and offered a cold, clammy, limp hand.

"Can I offer you coffee or tea, or can I get you water or something?"

Bergin didn't seem to hear the offer. Instead of taking the hard wooden chair to which Ben had gestured, he moved to look out of the grime-covered window overlooking the Liffey and the industrial life of Dublin.

"I went there last week."

Ben searched the busy riverside scene for the object of Bergin's comment. Nothing seemed obvious.

"Where was that, Tom?" he asked, with as much gentleness as he could muster.

"The oil terminal. It's been years since I ran it for Mister Stone. It hasn't changed much. But I suppose you know it well. Do you spend much time down there?"

Ben glanced at the object of Bergin's comments. Almost on the horizon was the oil zone, where the huge Global Oil storage tanks, with their distinctive logo of the globe, were clearly visible.

"No, not too much in recent times, but it looks as if all that's going to change shortly."

"That's why I'm here. I was passing, and thought that maybe we could have a friendly, unofficial conversation about how to get out of the hole that we seem to have dug for ourselves."

Ben decided to ignore the insinuation of joint responsibility for where they were.

"You know better than that, Tom. I can't negotiate with you without the shop steward being present. The situation would be delicate under normal circumstances. As it stands it would be dynamite for the two of us."

"Yeah, I understand that, Ben. I'm not looking to negotiate. In fact, despite my title, I don't have the authority to negotiate. I'm just looking to see if there is anything any of us can do to avert this impending disaster."

"Feelings are running very high."

"Yes, I know. At the terminal I had brief words with Eddie Barron and John Kerry."

"What did they say?"

"Not much. I'm afraid they are very anti-Ed. Jim O'Raghallaigh didn't help. He had come down to say goodbye to his people. Ours were inclined to contrast this with Ed's attendance at the combined meeting."

"I've told Ed to stay out of it from here on in and to leave it to you. Tell me, Tom, has O'Raghallaigh accepted your offer?"

"Yes, he told me last week, the day I went to the terminal. He says he's going back into the business he left—management consultancy. Although this time he's going to work for himself. I think he'll do well."

"Do you think he could help us on this problem?"

"Do you mean as some type of conciliator or mediator?"

"Yes. Our members in both companies trust him and he did a brilliant job in negotiating a rationalization plan in Anglo Oil before you fellas entered the picture. So he should understand where you're coming from too. I think I could get the men to accept him. What about you?"

"Ben, we're having an honest, upfront conversation. I won't bullshit you. I don't have the authority to agree. I do know that Ed has something against Jim O'Raghallaigh. I just don't know if he'd accept him."

"Tom, why don't you go back and discuss it with Ed. Tell him that you've talked with me and the union will accept Jim O'Raghallaigh as a mediator, provided he has the authority to settle and Global pays his fee."

Tom Bergin left to travel to Global House, wondering how he would summon up the courage to tell Ed that he'd been to see Ben and that he had agreed to propose Jim O'Raghallaigh as a mediator.

Ben Brant telephoned his brother.

———————◆•◆•◆———————

John Brant felt ridiculous. Gelling his hair was for a Saturday night and shaving was something rare. To do both, and at the same time, didn't happen often. The last time he wore a suit was for his father's funeral. He hated suits and the formality that went with them. He thought that he should also wear a tie. That started to choke, so he loosened it and unbuttoned his shirt collar. To soften the formality of it all, he had pulled the end of his shirt out of his trouser top, letting it hang loose. He hoped he now looked like a businessman. It was as far as he was prepared to go from his normal attire. He sat in a massive leather armchair in front of an equally impressive dark mahogany desk, inhaling the smell of lavender polish and disgusting opulence.

*I hope the bollix that lives here has it paid for*, he thought. *He won't be getting too much out of me for this consultation.*

With that, the portly frame of Larry Rudder, his father's long-time accountant and financial advisor, entered with a flourish.

"It's not good, John," said Larry pointing out the obvious. "This is the third month that Brantoil has made losses. Your sales are down and so are your margins. The only thing that's up is your operating cost. What's happened?"

"It's temporary, Larry. Anglo Oil cut the hell out of prices back last December. Global then came in and undercut them. Between them they fucked up the market. It's never really recovered."

"But haven't I read that Global has taken them over?"

"They're in the process of doing that, but the price-cutting by the two of them has caused the problem."

"I don't know whether that's the problem, John. I've looked at your margins. They don't seem to have fallen, yet your sales revenue is down. It looks as if you've just lost business."

"Of course I've lost fuckin' business! Anglo Oil had this low-price philosophy. They had built up this low-price image and wanted all of their distributors to sell on price and undercut competition. Their price to us was lower; the idea was that we would both share the price discount. We never agreed with that fuckin' policy and didn't pass it on, so we actually did well. We had a higher margin than anyone else. Now that they're gone we've had to increase our prices to maintain the same margin. Global's price to us is higher than Anglo's was."

"Do I understand you right, John? What you're telling me is that there is now price competition in your area for the first time, and you've actually increased your prices?"

"Yes, as I explained, we've had to. We believe in service, not in this fuckin' low-price crap."

'Well, tell me about your costs. If your sales are down your costs should also be down. They're not."

"Well, we've taken on a new manager."

"Why did you do that? I thought you managed the business yourself!"

"To be honest with you, Larry, I've lost interest. It's too difficult. I thought I'd give it a go because it was my Dad's business. But everything is against us, even our fuckin' supplier. Just because we don't agree with their pricing policy, they don't help with advertising or other marketing costs. I think they're jealous of Brantoil and would like to have taken us over."

"Have you talked to your brothers about how you feel?"

"In a way, but they're too busy to listen. Ed's running Global Oil when he's not trying to take over the fuckin' world. Ben's the opposite; he's trying to save the world. I'm really on my own; that's why I came to see you."

"Well, John, I'm glad you did. I hope you don't mind me saying this, but you're not a businessman. Its 'horses for courses,' and this is not your course. Your reasons for taking over the running of the family business are admirable. You wanted to carry on the family tradition. But, John, it's not your forte, and you'll run it into the ground. It won't be long before the bank manager is knocking on your door."

"What should I do?"

"Tell your brothers you want out and sell your share while its still worth something."

"Could I sell my one-third interest?"

"Yes, you can. I was the executor of your late father's estate, and I recall that any one of the brothers can sell without reference to the others. I always thought it was a strange omission. I'll make some discreet enquiries and see if there would be much interest."

———◆◆◆———

Ed Brant could read Tom Bergin like a book. He saw him as a good 'good news' messenger. When Bergin asked to see him, he said nothing about Patricia. Now when he came into the office, accompanied by her, Brant knew it wasn't routine. He was on edge. Patricia, he noticed, was being involved more and more by the managers when they felt they needed support. They probably thought that they'd get a better reception that way. It wasn't that he was any easier on Patricia. Well, of course he was; he loved her, but he tried to make sure that didn't show when the others were around. With her approach, since their rooftop bust up, it wasn't hard. She still froze him out. Anyway, apart from a relationship, anyone would be easier on Patricia. She seemed to bring out the best in everyone. He loved her direct approach and the fact that she always seemed to be two steps ahead of the rest. Patricia brought it home to him how principled she was—a rarity in modern-day business. She had shown how much she disagreed with removing the portrait, yet she did. Also, there was the issue with Bergin. Although she was definitely upset when he had asked her to keep an eye on Bergin, here again, she was doing exactly as he had asked. If only he had others like her.

He could sense the trepidation in Bergin's voice as he put forward the suggestion of hiring Jim O'Raghallaigh as mediator. Ben had told him of their conversation. Ed's initial reaction had been that he wanted nothing to do with the guy who had harassed his father, but Ben was prepared to give him the benefit of the doubt and, if he could help to get them out of the mess they were in, then so should Ed.

"Get him on the phone, Tom. You can do the talking. We'll use the squawk box so we all can hear. We need to get a feel for his mood."

Bergin dialled O'Raghallaigh's home number. He got through immediately

"Hello, Jim. I didn't think we would be talkin' so soon. We've got a proposal we would like to discuss with you. I think it'll be of interest. Would you be able to call into Global House tomorrow at, say, ten? Ed Brant, our Chief Executive, and I would like to talk to you?"

"What's it about?"

"I would prefer not to discuss it on the telephone; that's why I'm asking you in."

"Tom, there's nothing that Ed Brant could put to me that would be of interest. I've left Anglo Oil and that decision is final. I only hope that you treat my people with more respect, humanity, and compassion than you treated me."

Tom was clearly shaken by the directness of O'Raghallaigh's rejection. The usual signs of distress appeared.

There was an awkward silence until Patricia intervened.

"Hello Jim, this is Patricia Harvey. I work directly for Ed Brant. It's your people that we want to talk to you about. We've got a stalemate with the union right now. If this strike goes ahead, your people will be left with no jobs and no redundancy except the statutory compensation, and you know what that's worth. We thought that maybe you could help us avoid that."

Brant could detect an immediate change in O'Raghallaigh's tone.

"Okay," he said. "I'll meet you, but it won't be in your office. I'll see you at ten in the Royal Marine Hotel in Dun Laoghaire."

With that he rang off.

"He's a cocky bastard," Ed Brant said. "But anyway, he's agreed. We'll go to Dun Laoghaire. He'll pay for our inconvenience without knowing it. I would have been fairly generous in a fee if he hadn't been so damn obnoxious."

Ed was surprised at Patricia's response.

"He's every right to be sore after the way we treated him and his company. I just hope that his loyalty to his people and his interest in their welfare is sufficiently strong for him to put aside his obvious disdain for us. We need him far more than he needs us."

Without another word, both she and Bergin stood up and left the office.

———————•◆•———————

Patricia Harvey was upset. Tom Bergin had, on his own initiative, opened the possibility of breaking the deadlock with the union and avoiding the strike, but there wasn't a word or gesture of appreciation from Ed. Instead, he had just further pressured him by leaving the sensitive phone call to Tom without any support, or even a suggestion as to how to smoothen the feathers that he himself had so unceremoniously ruffled. She knew that Ed totally devalued Tom and his contribution. She was not prepared to risk the old man being exposed to further humiliation through the possibility of Ed, either deliberately or otherwise, asking her to accompany him in his car while leaving Tom to make his own way to the Royal Marine. If she was with Tom, Ed could hardly single her out to travel with him. She also had another, more personal, reason. She was not yet confident that she was emotionally ready to be alone with Ed in anything other than a strictly business environment.

"Good morning, Tom," she enthused as she entered his dull and dreary office early the next morning. "I must say I was really impressed with that stroke you pulled with Ed's brother. I don't know how you did it, but if we can get more of your magic today, I think we've got a chance."

"It's very kind of you to say that, Patricia, but we both know that without your help yesterday it would have been a disaster. I ran this company under Tom Stone for years, but that man upstairs totally unnerves me. I can't seem to think when he's around."

"I think you misunderstand things, Tom," she said kindly. "Ed is himself under immense pressure, and that sometimes just seems to come out in his tone. I think you'll find he's like that with everyone. It's nothing personal. It's just his way."

"I wish I could believe that, Patricia. Thanks for trying. He was like that certainly with Charlie Connors, until Charlie had enough and left. Now he's after me. He wants to get rid of the old brigade—anything and everything that reminds him of our founder. A real gentleman."

Patricia followed the direction of his gaze. That glinting frame, which had so ostentatiously intruded on the atmosphere of his office during her previous visit, was now gone. The Mission Statement, on which the precepts of Global Oil were so eloquently enumerated for reverence by the staff and for admiration by others, had been replaced by a portrait of that beacon of yesteryears, the much-revered and renowned Mr. Tom Stone.

"Tom, it was you. You did it. Did Ed ask you to remove that portrait from the boardroom wall?"

"No, certainly not! If he had, that would have been the last straw. I would have gone with Charlie. I couldn't leave Mister Stone to be insulted and ridiculed by what now passes for principled management. That portrait is appreciated here, while that rubbish that the ad agency produced, called a Mission Statement and printed off by the dozen, maybe means something to those now sitting around the boardroom table. I switched the two. I didn't think anyone would notice."

"You know, Tom, I think I would have enjoyed working for you and Mister Stone."

"You know, Patricia, I think we would have enjoyed having you. You remind me a lot of him when he was young. Like you, he was full of compassion and idealism. Come on and let's meet Jim O'Raghallaigh. From what I hear, we'll enjoy him too."

Patricia almost linked him as they walked to his car. They noticed that the gleaming Mercedes S 600 was still in the car-park.

"Patricia, I'll go ahead in case Ed is delayed. I think you should drive him in your car. That vulgar display of multinationalism might be provocative to a man who has just been made redundant, and whose friends are now facing the same boat."

Patricia knew he was right.

"Yes, Tom; I think that makes a lot of sense. We'll meet up with you at the Royal Marine."

She walked back into the building to ensure that Ed Brant would not exacerbate an already bad situation by his usual habit of arriving late for meetings.

———————————◆•◆•◆———————————

It was a few minutes after ten when Patricia and Ed Brant arrived at the Royal Marine. Patricia had left the radio on in the car at a fairly high volume level. There was a discussion in progress on the morality of the war in Iraq, in which Ed seemed particularly interested. This suited her purpose ideally. There was no opportunity to get personal.

As they passed the desk, Ed interrupted a conversation the receptionist was having with a guest to ask for the private room number reserved in either the name of O'Raghallaigh or Global.

"It's probably in our name," he whispered to Patricia. "These guys take every opportunity to pass costs on to us."

"No, sir," the receptionist answered with the utmost constraint. "If it's Jim O'Raghallaigh you're looking for, I saw him go into the lounge not more that ten minutes ago. He has just been joined by another gentleman."

The lounge that she directed them to was a large bright room of old world ambience, with small polished mahogany tables, each with four comfortable chairs mostly occupied by men and women of mature years.

"Jesus, he's in a bloody retirement home already," Ed remarked as they searched the room for the familiar face of Tom Bergin.

Beside a window overlooking the beautifully manicured lawns, bristling here and there with shrubbery and plants displaying a myriad shades of green interspersed with lilacs, pinks and blues, Tom was engaged in what seemed to be friendly banter with Jim O'Raghallaigh and some of the 'mature inmates'. As they made their way over, Patricia couldn't avoid taking in the beauty of the gardens and thinking back on those blissful days and nights in the Garden of Eden. She stole a glance at Ed, wondering if he was sharing her thoughts. She needn't have wondered. He was striding purposefully across, like a gladiator in the Coliseum, seemingly oblivious to everything except the two men seated at the table, who looked like anything but adversaries.

"Told you we couldn't trust that damn Bergin," Ed muttered just before they got within earshot. "Glad I didn't tell him our bottom line. He'd sell us down the river."

"We would not be here if it wasn't for Tom. We'd be back in Global House looking forward to a strike with no visible end."

Tom Bergin jumped to his feet as soon as he saw the two of them approach. Immediately, as if on cue, Patricia noticed the nervous gestures reappear. He only stopped the beard tugging momentarily to introduce her to O'Raghallaigh. She was impressed with the warmth of his smile and the firmness of his handshake. Ed had told her of their acquaintance during their college days, and, in somewhat derogatory terms, had built up an image that she found hard to reconcile with the ruggedly handsome, confident, and relaxed Jim O'Raghallaigh that stood before her. He held her hand for what she felt was longer than the usual handshake, but she didn't mind one bit. This contrasted with the almost cursory "Hello, Ed," and she wondered whether his warmth to her was genuine or part of a strategy to unsettle Ed. If it was part of a macho-type game, she had to admit, if only to herself, that it was certainly working.

They were, pretty much, in the centre of the social event that they seemed to be intruding on, and she was surprised that they had not positioned themselves in a corner where privacy would be assured. He had already ordered coffee and tea. She knew that Ed would find his obvious, self-confident composure very disconcerting. Ed Brant was not used to someone else taking control at a meeting he attended.

"Can we get out of this old folks home to where we can talk?" he said, looking around with undisguised disdain. His tone and posture made it quite clear that it wasn't a question.

"Can't do that; I'm the host here. These are all my friends, pensioners of Anglo Oil. I treat them to a social morning every year. They expect me to socialise, so I can only give you fifteen minutes. You've taken five. So I suggest you get on with whatever it is you want to say. You've got a proposal of some sort that you want to put to me."

Before Ed could respond, Patricia had jumped in.

"Jim, we know you're sore and we're sorry. Can we, for the sake of saving what you built up in Anglo Oil, try to put personal animosities aside and be business-like?"

"You mentioned the Anglo Oil people. What have you in mind?" he asked.

Much to Patricia's relief, Ed seemed to decide that he would leave it to his two subordinates.

She started.

"We're buying Anglo Oil. Without us, it'll fold. There's no available oil on the market, and the indications are it'll only get worse. Our source of Saudi Arabian crude oil is secure and we're the only company in that position. Global Oil is the only option they've got. Negotiations have gotten off to a bad start and feelings are running high. We've been served with strike notice that will take effect on Monday. If they go out, very few will probably have jobs to come back to. We think you can help."

"Go on," he said.

Tom Bergin seemed to come alive.

"I've talked to the union," he said. "If you are prepared to act, they will accept you as a mediator. Of course, we'd need to agree on terms."

"What's the deal?" he asked, looking at Ed.

"We're prepared to pay a reasonable fee if you can get union agreement to the rationalization and productivity plan we put to them," Ed said. "We want you to act as a sort of facilitator of the discussions."

Again, he looked at Ed.

"As I understand your proposal, the merger will give you a surplus of ten staff, or nine now without me. You also want to get rid of your drivers and employ a haulage contractor. How many drivers do you have?"

"Thirty-five," Ed responded.

"Okay," he said. "So, all in-all, you want to get rid of forty-four people and your offer is five weeks pay for each year of service?" he asked.

Ed nodded.

"What's the average pay and service?"

"Thirty-five thousand a year and just short of fifteen years."

"What's you best offer?"

"That's it."

"I haven't time for bullshit. Nobody puts out their best offer first day. I'm not negotiating with you. I'm trying to decide whether you're wasting my time."

"Okay," Ed said. "We would go to six weeks."

"And statutory redundancy?"

"Yes, okay."

He took out his calculator and within a few moments said, "That's a total of almost 2.8 million with statutory."

Ed nodded agreement with his calculations.

"Have you negotiated a deal with a haulage contractor?" he said.

"Tentatively," Ed said. "Nothing's signed."

"That's not what I asked. Have you agreed or not?"

"No, we're still negotiating."

"What productivity levels are you looking for?"

Ed was tempted to ask him its relevance but was curious to see where he was going.

"We're looking for ten percent improvement," he answered.

"Okay," O'Raghallaigh said, looking directly into Ed Brant's eyes. "Here's the deal. Take it or leave it. I'll negotiate both the rationalization and a productivity agreement that will give you a fifteen percent improvement in standards. It'll cost you three and a half million euro, including my fee."

"You're joking! You're looking for a fee of seven hundred thousand?"

'Yes," he said. "And I want the full amount deposited with my solicitor ahead of any discussions. The whole amount will be returned to you intact if I don't deliver the agreement in four weeks."

Ed glanced at Tom Bergin, who looked ashen.

"How can you be so sure you would get this done?" He asked.

"Sorry for disturbing you. How are you, Jim? Are you keeping okay?"

It was a couple of the guests who had come over from a neighboring table. They looked fit and well but were certainly octogenarian.

"Ah, Tom and Maisie. So good to see you," Jim responded as he rose to kiss Maisie on the cheek. "You two are obviously doing well! The family okay?"

"All great, Jim. We're sorry for disturbing you, but we have to go now and didn't want to without saying hello to you."

"No problem. I'm very glad you did. Now, look after one another, and you know where I am if you need me."

"God bless you, Jim," Maisie said as they moved off.

O'Raghallaigh said nothing for a few moments as he looked after the retreating couple. He then seemed to remember Brant's question.

"Well," he said. "When companies like Global are trying to influence people by making deposits into their offshore bank accounts, people like me are building up deposits in an emotional bank account with people like Tom and Maisie. It doesn't cost anything except treating people decently. When you need something, they owe you, and they know that they can trust you to be fair. It makes life very easy and rewarding."

"An emotional bank account. What the hell is that?"

"Well, Ed, I don't expect you to understand, but it's the amount of trust that you build up in a relationship. It's done by saying what you mean and meaning what you say."

"How can you have any emotional bank account with Global people? You don't know them and they don't know you." It was Patricia's interruption to head off what she saw as the inevitably aggressive response by Ed.

"Do you see that group over by the pillar?" he said, indicating five or six men who were obviously drinking more than coffee or tea. Noticing the attention they were getting, every one of them smiled and waved.

"Well, some time ago, I had to dramatically improve the cost structure of Anglo. I had no option but to let twenty go. Their compensation was barely more than their statutory entitlement, but as our profitability improved we voluntarily put more into their pension fund. They're here today. We can look them in the eye and say 'We're your friend,' and they'll know we are."

He stopped again to acknowledge another group.

"Ireland is a small place. Your people will know how I handled a similar problem in Anglo Oil, and how I've managed my people generally. They also know, incidentally, how you treated me, and that's a huge withdrawal from your emotional bank account with them. It's how you treat the one who reveals how you regard the ninety-nine, because everyone is, ultimately, a one."

"It sounds like very weak management to me."

"Leo Roskin once said, 'Only the weak are cruel; gentleness can only be expected from the strong.' Think about it."

"I don't have time for a philosophy lesson, and I don't have four weeks," snapped Ed. "Can you do it any faster?"

"I could have it done by Friday week."

"You've got a deal. I want Patricia involved in all talks."

"I wouldn't have it any other way," he responded, looking directly into her eyes as he stood up and stretched out his arm. "Right now I've got to get back to my guests."

Ed shook his hand. It was obvious to him that as far as O'Raghallaigh was concerned, the meeting was over and he was being summarily dismissed. He again resented O'Raghallaigh's arrogance. Ed Brant was the Chief Executive of a subsidiary of the largest oil company in the world, and O'Raghallaigh was unemployed. Did he not understand his position? However, Brant needed him now, and he knew his time would come. "What goes around comes around," his father used to tell them.

"Can you stay back, Tom? I need to get some factual detail on your people. We'll find a seat out in the gardens. You'll enjoy that while we work. I've got the pensioners' lunch first and then we'll get to it. You're welcome to stay as my guest at the lunch."

"I'd be honoured." Bergin replied.

With that he turned to chat with an elderly couple that were at the next table. The meeting was clearly over. Patricia glanced at her watch. It was ten-twenty. They had been about five minutes late, so the three-and-a-half-million euro deal, which would earn O'Raghallaigh nearly three quarters of a million, took fifteen minutes.

She was impressed. Like her boss, Ed Brant, this man Jim O'Raghallaigh didn't hang around. But would he get the job done? She'd have to wait and see, but somehow she thought he would.

---

Ed Brant was boiling. He had never been so dismissively treated in all of his professional life. He looked at Patricia to see her reaction to O'Raghallaigh's rudeness. She didn't seem to be at all perturbed herself, but seemed to sense an explosive situation. As he had seen her do so often in the past with his subordinates, she rescued O'Ragallaigh, or perhaps himself, from a degenerating exchange.

She touched his arm and said quietly, "Leave it, Ed. You could win the battle and lose the war. Let's take some time to consider where we are."

She steered him out of the lounge.

"I know how you feel. I know that the chemistry between you and O'Raghallaigh is influenced by what happened in the past. In some strange way I feel involved. I know Jim wasn't there at the time, but the bad relationship goes right back to the start-up days of Brantoil, when your dad and my mother were battling it out with Anglo Oil. It looks as if our generation is taking up where they left off. I think we should break the chain; there's no sense to it."

Ed looked at her. He saw her in a completely new light. No longer was she just the attractive, Global expatriate that he had fallen in love with, who had been sent to Europe by the company to be oriented to a foreign culture. She was emerging as more than all of that. She was a real friend, like he had never known before. He could see that she had feelings for their shared heritage. She seemed genuinely concerned for him and he appreciated that. It was really a long time since he had seen anyone from Global Oil with a motive other than personal advancement disguised as the esteemed 'corporate interest.' He felt even closer to her.

They walked through the reception area, heading back towards the car park, in silence, each deep in thought.

"Did you not find Jim?" It was the receptionist whom Ed had rudely interrupted on the way in. "He definitely went in. I'll be glad to page him for you, sir."

"No, thanks, that won't be necessary. We did meet him. Thanks."

He noticed Patricia glancing towards him, noticing his change of tone. She said nothing, nor did he. He had been caught momentarily off guard. That damn O'Raghallaigh had unsettled him.

Although he still felt humiliated by O'Raghallaigh's attitude, he could now see that Patricia was right in what she was saying. He had treated O'Raghallaigh badly. He had done much to destroy both him and his company. In fairness, he accepted, O'Raghallaigh had every right to feel sore. He himself would probably have been more aggressive had their roles been reversed. It was his damned self-confidence that rankled him. How could anyone in his situation be so arrogant? But perhaps it was that trait that maybe, just maybe, would enable him to get the job done. The fee he was looking for was outrageous, but the overall figure was well within the budget that he had discussed with Papandreou. O'Raghallaigh would get nothing if he didn't deliver. Yes, for the first time since that damned meeting with all of the people, he saw a light at the end of the tunnel. He just hoped that he could get it done in time. He was glad he had the foresight to insist that Patricia be involved. She seemed to have a talent of helping every situation.

"Do you feel like lunch?" he asked her.

He noticed her hesitation. He had the apartment in mind. The morning was chilly, but sunny and pleasant. She loved the balcony; he could arrange a takeaway for lunch.

"If it's a snack and a take-away coffee, and the venue has the most wonderful view in the world, I'll gladly accept," she said.

His heart flipped with visions of the afternoon with her in her Garden of Eden. He looked at her enquiringly.

"No, Ed," she answered softly. "I'm not yet ready for Eden again. I've found another hideaway. I know a place in Dalkey, on the way to my hilltop hideaway, that does excellent sandwiches. I'll pay."

He didn't know what she was talking about, but it didn't sound like his apartment. However, he was lifted by the gentleness of her tone—something that hadn't been there in recent times. Anyway, he thought, time alone with her, anywhere, would give him the opportunity of repairing the damage he had done on that fateful morning.

They drove to the village of Dalkey to pick up their lunch and proceeded up the Burmer Road, where he had gone only two days previously on his early morning walk. They stopped in the carpark at the base of the hill, and having changed her shoes, she strode effortlessly up the steep sloping trail, her long auburn hair swirling in the light breeze. Ed's mood improved, and for the first time in an age, he felt exhilarated by the freshness of the woodlands as he followed her petite figure to her hilltop retreat. She didn't seem to notice his regular stops, at strategic points, to admire the scenery of the bay and beyond, and to catch his breath and allow the tightness in his chest to subside.

"What did you make of that 'emotional bank account' stuff that O'Raghallaigh went on about?" he asked her, as they sat on the rocks and looked out over the glasslike expanse of Dublin Bay. "It sounded a bit airy fairy to me, I must say."

She unwrapped the sandwiches as she considered his question.

"Well, Ed, I must admit, I haven't heard too much of that in the macho world of Global Oil, but I do think it makes a lot of sense. I don't think he was saying anything more than that if you treat people decently and with respect, they will respond similarly."

"At the level I operate, that would be seen as weakness and you'd be devoured by your rivals, both within and outside of the organization," he retorted.

"I think you misunderstand what I'm saying, Ed. How can anyone take advantage of you taking the trouble to understand their point of view? How can anyone object to you delivering on your promises? Or apologising when you know you're wrong? Or being courteous to subordinates, or accepting their feedback graciously? It doesn't seem any different to what my mother taught me back in Texas. I thought it was the Irishness in her. Jim calls it a deposit in an emotional bank account. I guess it's the same thing and has the same result."

Ed placed his sandwich on the wrapper on the ground beside him, as he struggled with the coffee container.

He could see that what Patricia was saying pretty much described her own approach, and was one of the million elements of her personality that he had found so irresistible. But, although it was okay for her, it would certainly not work for him. She didn't have to manage a multi-million-pound organization, or compete in a world where you are as good as your next success. If he tried to adopt a softly, softly management style he knew that the words of his dad would certainly prove true. He would be 'devoured' by those corporate vultures who looked for opportunities for advancement in the exploitation of the weaknesses of others. The proof was before their eyes. It was O'Raghallaigh who was out of a job, and it was his company that was being swallowed up. No, he concluded, he had gotten to where he was, and would get to the highest rung in the Global Oil ladder by being tough and ensuring that all around him understood who the boss was. Patricia wouldn't really understand that. She never had the responsibility for the bottom line of a corporation.

The atmosphere was good, and they were getting along just fine. He'd drop that subject. It was too contentious. Much to her amusement, he continued to struggle with the lid of the coffee carton.

"As my mother used say, 'tis plain as the nose on your face, that 'tis far from picnics that you were reared.' Here, give it to me and I'll open it for you."

Just as she spoke—or maybe because of the amusement in her voice—he made another last effort. He pulled too hard or squeezed the carton too tightly. It all ended up on the grass.

"Fuckin' hell," he said involuntarily. "Oh, I'm really sorry, Patricia."

He needn't have worried. Patricia was almost hysterical with laughter.

Ed recalled when she arrived first. She was heralded as an up-and-coming executive, bright but with common sense; qualities that were not always found in combination. When he was asked by New York to take her on, he had suspected she was the daughter of a non-executive board member, or a friend of someone else with corporate influence, and was being sent to Europe to be broadened before being given some lucrative role back in the United States. He'd seen it before. Some succeeded; others fell flat on their face and couldn't cut it in Europe. He remembered their first meeting. She was singularly attractive, despite being attired in one of those mannish suits that businesswomen wear. He could never figure out whether they were intended to mask the fact that the woman was a woman, or whether they were supposed to be feminine in a masculine sort of way. Whatever the reason, it certainly suited Patricia, and he found it difficult to focus on her business chatter as her reddish hair, pale green eyes, and tanned good looks competed for his attention. It was afterwards that he felt that maybe he had not given proper attention to what she was telling him about her mother and his father working together in Brantoil many years previously. Maybe he'd been a bit abrupt. He knew she wanted to chat about her mother's role in Brantoil all of those years ago, but she'd never raised it with him again. He'd ask John to see what he could find out from some of the ol' timers in Brantoil, who would have been there at the time. That'd be an opportunity to start from scratch and put the past behind them.

He drank what was left of his coffee and noticed that she was still quietly laughing at his predicament. As he watched, he knew that they were slowly getting back what they had. He wondered and pondered whether he should once again apologise for his crassness in upsetting that wonderful relationship, which every day had been developing to a new level.

"Patricia, eh—"

"No, Ed, don't. You hurt me beyond description. I need time to sort my head out."

She had tears in her eyes. They looked at each other for several seconds without saying anything. Suddenly her expression changed once again. She started to laugh, gently at first, then heartily. She wasn't looking at him any more. He followed her gaze.

"Jesus, not again, that effin dog. Don't worry, Patricia, I'll get rid of it."

The golden retriever that had driven him off the hill on the previous occasion, and that had tried so hard to shred his trouser leg, suddenly appeared out of nowhere and was enjoying the rest of his lunch. This time, Ed decided he'd take positive action. He looked for a stick, not to throw but to clear the area of this, and any other, predators. He avoided another catastrophe in the nick of time. The tail-wagging brute suddenly spied Patricia and obviously decided that she was better company.

"Ah, Blondie," she cried, while at the same time excitedly tickling the animal under his chin; he reckoned Patricia had ignored its gender before christening him "Blondie."

As if on cue, Blondie went down on his hunkers and crawled towards Patricia while turning over on his back to have his belly rubbed.

"Ah, isn't he so cute? How could you be cross with him?" she said in a tone of gentle admonishment, while at the same time looking at the weapon in Ed's hand.

Suddenly it occurred to him that there was a lesson in all of this. The way to forgiveness by Patricia was a softly, softly approach in all of his dealings with her. If necessary, at the end of the day, as a last resort, he would do a certain amount of crawling, if that was what was required; but he was a bit away from that resort right now.

As she played with Blondie against the backdrop of the sunkissed waters of the bay and the cloudless sky, he watched, and was once again totally enthralled with her unblemished perfection. More than anything else in the world, he knew that he wanted her. She was so different from anyone he had ever met. The fact that she worked for him was a difficulty. Maybe he could afford to adopt a softer approach with her without compromising his authority within the company. He could be himself with her; he didn't need executive armour. Yes, he would definitely make time for her and, over time, work his way back into her affections. It could be as it once was.

As he looked at her deriving so much pleasure from the scenery around them, and the gentleness and playfulness of Blondie, he wondered what it was about her that had him so captivated. He began to realise that there are unique and beautiful people, with ambitions and desires, who were in no way driven by wealth or power or by the traditional trappings of success. People like Patricia were in love with nature. They saw beauty in the birds and the bees, in the hills and the trees, and they just used his world of corporate wealth as a means to that end. How he'd love to stop and explore her world with her. But he had come so far, and the ultimate goal of reaching his father's expectations was so close. Patricia would wait. He knew she would. Funny, though, he thought, how two people who were essentially sharing the same daily work experiences could have so completely different motivations. Patricia attributed hers to her mother, and he to his father. He thought of both of them for a while. They were so different. Their work-lives must have been so interesting.

They drove back to the office, each preoccupied with their own thoughts, but Ed felt he had been changed, in some way, forever.

---

Tom Bergin was more relaxed than he had felt in ages. He felt as if he was among friends. These were people to whom he could relate, people he could trust. It was getting towards the end. He had enjoyed his lunch and his conversation with his host, Jim O'Raghallaigh. Some of the waiting staff were now busily removing the dessert dishes; others were filling the coffee cups. A hush descended on the gathering.

"Ladies and Gentlemen, you know I'm not one for speeches. But there are some things that have to be said, so in this case I don't mind. I've been asked to talk for all of you, and for all of those who, for one reason or another, can't be here. I want to acknowledge and to thank Anglo and Jim for everything they have done, and continue to do, for every one of us. This is a sad occasion for all of us—to see a great company that we all built up over a lifetime humbled by greed and corruption. We're pensioners, and thanks again to Jim we won't be affected, but our hearts go out to all those existing employees whose lives are about to be turned upside down, when they are told that their jobs are gone and their lives' work has counted for nothing. That's all I want to say. Thank you all very much for listening to an old man."

The speaker sat down to rapturous applause.

Another old man stood up.

"I won't be adding to that; Paddy has said it for us all. Let's give our general manager three cheers, and so he'll know we all mean it, let's raise the roof."

And raise the roof they almost did. The noise from these old people reminded Tom Bergin of the Irish supporters when their team scores at a World Cup qualifying game. It doesn't happen often, so there's a lot of pent-up emotion when it does.

He was sitting next to Jim O'Raghallaigh at the lunch table, and was engulfed by the throngs which suddenly appeared to shake his hand and add their thanks. It was a highly emotional experience for Tom Bergin.

They both now sat out in the beautiful gardens of the Royal Marine Hotel. The spring-time sunshine was warm, the wooden seat was sheltered from the breeze.

"Jim, I've never witnessed anything like the emotion over the last hour. It was extraordinary, and I'm delighted that I was there to see it. It's renewed my faith in human nature—well, to some extent anyway."

"Yeah, it's nice to see your efforts appreciated."

"Your close relationship with your people will be a disadvantage when they discover that you are the one who will be doing Ed Brant's dirty work."

"I never said that I would do that. I said that I would get an agreement—not, as you put it, 'do Ed Brant's dirty work.' That would be a win-lose agreement. Brant wins and everyone else loses."

"That's exactly what will happen if we put forty-four people out of a job."

"Tom, let's change tack. I honestly don't know what the solution will be, but I can assure you of one thing. Unless both sides win, there will be no deal. I'll walk away and return Brant's cheque."

"You'd walk away from seven hundred thousand euro?"

"I wouldn't want to, but I would rather that than con one side and not be able to look them in the eyes again. Life is too short!"

"I still can't see how you can resolve this, because of the circumstances, and what's gone on already."

"You misunderstand. I won't be resolving anything. They've got to do that themselves. The most I can do is to make sure that they deal with the real issues. Most of the time in negotiations, I find neither side listens to the other, so that the real issues are never addressed."

"That sounds too simple."

"Well, it's not difficult. It's amazing what you can learn when you listen. I mean really listen. Listen to understand the other's viewpoint. Most people listen to respond. They can never get a lasting agreement because they never really deal with the other's real concerns."

"Ah, I understand. So you listen to understand, and then you put forward some sort of compromise to, in some way, meet the concerns of both."

"No, Tom. I listen with my eyes, with my ears, and with my heart. When I'm as certain as one can be, that I really, really understand the other side and they understand me, I see if I can find a solution that gives both sides what they need and a little bit more."

"So that's how you did it in Anglo Oil?"

"Yes, it's the only way to get a lasting agreement. Otherwise, you think you've got an agreement, but you really haven't. As soon as one side realises that they've been duped, with a cosmetic or superficial solution, their suppressed feelings and resentment towards you, towards their company, and towards their jobs, will be such that in the end you'll both have lost."

"You really care about these things, don't you?"

"I care about people more than anything else. I firmly believe that my job, as General Manager of Anglo Oil, was to increase the standard of living and the quality of life of all of Anglo Oil's stakeholders, be they shareholders or employees, customers or suppliers. Some people—and I would venture to suggest that Ed Brant is one of them—believe that the best interest of all stakeholders is mutually exclusive. I believe the opposite. Life should be based on interdependent relationships, not on independence and confrontation."

"Jim, it's a privilege to be working with you on this. I thought those principles were dead and gone."

'Thanks, Tom! I really appreciate you saying that, and I'm delighted to work with you. I knew you'd agree. What I've said, and what I believe, is no different to what you and Tom Stone practiced in your company before it was taken over by Global. Come on, let's you and I get down to business. I need to know about every single Global Oil employee; we need to know what each one of them really, really, wants."

<hr>

Two days later, in a rented room in Jury's Hotel beside the river Liffey, Jim O'Raghallaigh sat at the end of a horseshoe-shaped table, flanked on one side by Patricia Harvey and Tom Bergin. Ben Brant sat on the other side, along with Eddie Barnes, the shop steward, and Mick Dunne, his counterpart from Anglo Oil, and union committee members from both companies.

O'Raghallaigh, in a very relaxed manner, started by saying that he had a few things to put to the meeting before discussions commenced.

"First, I want you all to know that Global will pay me a lot of money if an agreement is reached and nothing if it's not. You need to know this so that we're all upfront. Secondly, I won't be recommending any agreement; you'll be making up your own minds. But I might recommend against one, particularly if there are losers. In other words, I want us to accommodate everyone, or it's no deal. Thirdly, we're going to do this a little bit different to the norm. Tom Bergin will present the case for the companies, and Ben Brant will do likewise for the employees. Each will explain their views in great detail. The company will do it first, and the union side can ask whatever questions they need to ask in order to get a thorough understanding. Ben will then present his understanding of what the company has said, so that we can ensure there is absolutely no misunderstanding. It will then be the union's turn to present its case and the company will ask the questions. Tom Bergin will then summarise his understanding of the union's position. Only when we're all satisfied that both positions are totally understood will we look to see where we agree and where we disagree."

He stopped and searched the audience.

"Does anyone have any problem with this approach?"

There was no dissent. Tom Bergin stood up and confidently presented his company's proposal and justification.

The negotiating process had begun. Its outcome would have a major bearing on so many lives, not the least of which was that of Ed Brant, who at that moment was standing, anxiously, at his office window, watching the sky darken as storm clouds were blown in from the southeast. Was this an ominous sign? He wondered.

---

Freezing temperatures, clear blue skies, and shrieks of laughter circling the ice from the skaters, young and not so young, did nothing to influence the sombre mood of Papandreou and two of his top aides, as they sat around the conference table, high above the carnival atmosphere in Central Park. The ant-like figures, far below, would have been indistinguishable through the leaf-stripped trees off Olmsted Way, even if the worried executives had been interested. Skaters and strollers were far from the minds of men who were part of an ambitious plan to change the political structures of the Middle East, secure the energy needs of the United States into the foreseeable future, and consolidate and expand their own considerable fortunes.

Conflicting reports were reaching Dino Papandreou. He was not used to inefficiency or incompetence, and his frustrations were clearly evident to the other two in the room.

"Where is that goddam Iraqi?"

He went to the window as if one of the ant-like creatures so far below would be recognisable as Salam Kashmola, Papandreou's 'ear' in Iraq, whom he had summoned to New York to add to his encrypted reports that had caused such concern.

"We need to know what is really happening in that god-forsaken desert on which the very future of Global is so dependent."

He and his aides had just listened to a routine update from the military representatives, and were alarmed at the increasing divergence between what they were saying, and what his own on-site intelligence was telling him about the events and likely outcome in Iraq. It appeared that the Washington officials were either totally misinformed or were deliberately putting a politically-motivated spin on the situation.

He looked at his watch. This was the third time in ten minutes. His aides had never seen him so agitated, but then again, perhaps the stakes had never been so high.

Anyone else would, and the gullible public in their hundreds of millions did, accept the jubilant reports emanating daily from the offices of the Central Intelligence Agency and promoted with such glitzy enthusiasm, night after night, by Fox News. But

Papandreou and his two companions knew more than most. They were very aware of the Agency's limitations. Papandreou himself had been the CIA's senior Middle East operative until the Agency was debilitated under the Carter presidency in the 1970's. The two others had been his field operatives. At that time, in the age of emerging satellite surveillance capabilities, Carter's appointee to the Agency, Stansfield Turner, considered that moles and their clandestine activities, known as 'humint' or human on the ground intelligence, to be part of another outdated era. As a result, the Agency was gutted of all experienced operatives. Papandreou had gone into the oil business and his two companions had formed a special investigative unit that had worked, almost exclusively, for him in his new capacity. Since that act of national folly, the United States was dependent on Saudi Arabia for most Middle Eastern intelligence. Papandreou knew that the Saudis were not capable of defending their own interests against their own religious fundamentalists, let alone the vital interests of the United States, and so never relied on the intelligence reports until he was able to verify them from his own sources—his own 'ears'. Salam Kashmola was a well-established mole within the Sunni Muslim community in Iraq and, as such, was invaluable.

The two military officers, who had left the meeting room, had come from the Pentagon, and confirmed all official statements that the war would be over in a matter of weeks. In fact, they advised confidentially, that the President himself was preparing to announce the end of major combat operations in some spectacular fashion on May 1. When that happened, Papandreou's people were expected to be ready to move in. He was ready. He had elaborate plans drawn up on that basis.

"The goddam arrangement could not have been simpler: the army would, as a priority, take control of the oil fields; the Houston company, Halliburton, would attend to any damage; and then we would take over and run the goddam Iraqi oil industry. Why hasn't that happened?" he asked nobody in particular.

He walked again to the window and looked out over Central Park as if willing his visitor's arrival. Visibility had reduced considerably. Snow had started to fall. Although he couldn't see them, the skaters were still active, though most of the spectators were drifting away.

Based on the presumption of a stable post-invasion political situation, Papandreou knew that, with modern technology and adequate funding, there was little doubt that Iraqis pre-war production could be more than doubled over a relatively short time frame. Iraq had the third largest oil reserves in the world, despite the fact that only around ten percent of the country had been explored. In addition to the prospect of new finds, it was believed that production from the existing fields could be substantially improved through the introduction of modern extraction techniques, which, due to the embargos, had never been applied in Iraq. This was Global Oil's challenge.

He had been assured that the government's intelligence on Iraq was first-rate, checked and double checked, and totally reliable. So when the President announced the end to major combat operations, that would be the start of a new Iraq under American control, where the oil industry could be developed without undue risk or interruption. He became alarmed, therefore, when his Iraqi 'ear' reported that not only was the Iraqi resistance not defeated, but in fact, it had always been their strategy to counter the invasion of the Coalition forces through guerrilla tactics. They expected Saddam Hussein to be killed or captured, so he would not personally feature, but this would not be the end, it would be the beginning. Other leaders, like the rebel cleric Moqtada al-Sadr, would emerge to lead the Shia sect out of the impoverished state that they were kept in under Saddam. They—initially, at any rate—would have common cause with the ruling Sunni tribe, and extremists from both sides intended to destabilise the country and sabotage the oil infrastructure.

Suddenly the room was lit with flashing amber light, and what looked like a regular television screen immediately came alive with the face of a bearded, dark-skinned man, whose general unkempt appearance looked totally out of place in the palatial ambience of Global Towers. He wouldn't have known, of course, that he had entered Global Towers, the heart of the biggest oil company in the world. Although the oak-panelled walls and moss green carpeting was similar to what was throughout the rest of his executive suite, this conference room was seldom used. It needed iris and thumbprint identification for access directly from Papandreou's office area. Similar security checks were applied in the private elevator, which carried specially-vetted and secretive visitors from the nondescript entrance on a laneway off Fifth Avenue. The conference table was sized for fifteen people, but rarely if ever saw more than three. Today was an exception. The two military visitors had gone, and the video screen and alarm now confirmed the arrival of Salam Kashmola, former CIA operative of Iraqi nationality and now Papandreou's Iraqi 'ear', for whom he had been so impatiently waiting. He had summoned Kashmola from Iraq to explain in person the real scenario that was developing in his country.

"At last, and now perhaps, we'll get to the real situation."

He pressed the button that activated the lift and brought Salam Kashmola to the thirty-first floor, with information that could literally change the world.

Kashmola came out of the lift looking like a refugee scrambling out of a truck at the Channel Tunnel. He shook the snow from his coat with little regard for the deep pile carpet that seemed as much removed from his normal habitat as Fifth Avenue was from the war-torn streets of Baghdad. He took the seat proffered by Papandreou, and sat without any acknowledgement of the other two present. His beard continued to glisten with the snowdrops that it carried.

Papandreou leaned forward and, with a tone of extreme gravitas, opened the conversation.

"Welcome, Salam. I need your help in understanding what you think will happen in your country. As you know, after the military operations, Global Oil has been selected by our government to bring the oil production to its maximum level in order to fund the reconstruction and help create a modern democracy for the Iraqi people."

Salam Kashmola was deadly serious.

"Rumour has it that it is the intention of the Coalition forces to do a deep purge of Baath Party members from their jobs in government ministries, schools, and universities, and to disband completely the Iraqi military. If that is true, the results will be disastrous. All of a sudden you will have hundreds of thousands of Baathists and still-armed soldiers who will go underground. It will create a ready-made army of deadly enemies."

Papandreou seemed oblivious to the far-reaching and national implications of this statement. He seemed only interested in its effect on the oil industry.

"Do you believe that they will concentrate on military targets, or will Global Oil personnel be at risk?"

"Iraqi insurgents will attack everyone they consider to be a collaborator—a term they apply to those who would work with the interim government, whether they are Iraqi nationals or not. Westerners will, in particular, be targeted in order to derail international support."

"Good God! You do think that we'll be targeted?"

"The minority Sunnis and the majority Shiite Muslims are watching each other, and are united in their determination that the Kurds, who are considered collaborators, will not get preferential treatment. The oil infrastructure will very likely remain a terrorist target and, if one ethnic group is favoured, it could trigger a civil war. If it's thought that the benefits are to be retained by the occupiers, there will be a jihad of unimaginable proportions."

"For Chrissake, military operations are only expected to last six to eight weeks; surely any jihhad will be forestalled or at least terminated with the installation of an Iraqi government?"

"No, the problem is that the West just sees the invasion as the removal of a dictator. They don't know what they have unleashed. The insurgents see it as far more than that. They see the war as one of liberation, not just of Iraq but also of Islam itself. Members of the former Baathist regime will lead it. The militants will then turn the resistance into an international jihadist movement. Iraq will become a magnet for fanatical Muslims from around the world. There they will train before carrying the jihad to the land of the infidel. The West just see the invasion as the removal of a dictator, and the insurgents see it as a war for the liberation of Islam."

"A war for the liberation of Islam."

Papandreou repeated Kashmola's words as he rose from the table and walked to the window. The snow had now turned into a blizzard. Large, beautiful snowflakes framed his large bulk against the window. His aides, who knew him so well, were not surprised when he elected not to debate this strange Iraqi's comments. Kasmola was one of Papandreou's trusted people and he knew his business. He had no reason to doubt him. It was crystal clear that CIA intelligence had got it disastrously wrong. To think now that the official view, at one time, was that the invasion would be met with rapturous applause seemed incredible in its naivete. That misunderstanding would have its repercussions, and it wouldn't be long before the politicians would be looking for scapegoats. *They can look elsewhere. While oil is fundamental to the vital national interest, they still need me.* In any event, he knew that he had covered his tracks, and anyone would have difficulty in connecting him to the

Iraqi strategy that now seemed destined to end in a humiliating failure.

Although no one had admitted it officially, Papandreou knew that the U.S. occupation and Global's business in Iraq, was to have been permanent. But the justification for this permanency was that the attainable production levels in Iraq would allow for the total displacement of Saudi crude. This assumed complete and unimpeded control, similar to what Aramco had in Saudi Arabia. Anything less, and certainly a hostile environment involving sabotage and terrorist attacks on oil personnel of the intensity described by Kashmola, would be nothing short of a disaster.

Papandreou stood at the window, with his back to the others, for what seemed like an age. Eventually he turned and spoke to Kashmola, dismissively, in a language that the others did not understand. Kashmola stood, very respectfully, and listened. He then quickly put the bulky envelope, that Papandreou had given to him, into an inside pocket. After Papandreou had manipulated several buttons on the monitor, he entered the lift and disappeared as quietly as he had come. There had been no introductions or cross conversations. In this conference room, a strict need-to-know rule applied.

"Okay, you've heard Kashmola. He's pretty much confirmed what we thought; that goddam war will go on forever, regardless of what Washington thinks. Looking to Iraq to replace our Saudi supply is beginning to look like a frying pan and goddam fire scenario. Let's go over that Saudi situation again."

It didn't take long. They were all experts on that part of the world; they had to be. They had each spent their early careers there, and it provided the very lifeblood to what had become the reason for their existence. It was the main source of crude oil to Global Oil Inc.

Saudi Arabia, the traditional and second-largest supplier to the United States, was in medium to long-term decline as the world's most important producer. Their high level of production, despite the rapid depletion of its reserves, was driven by their desperate need for oil revenues. The increasing demand for its oil from China and India, left little chance of conservation measures being put in place to extend this life span. This accelerated depletion of reserves, and the facilitation of their newfound friends in the East, left the United States feeling vulnerable. It was this reason that prompted it to look to Iraq as an alternative.

"I need to get a real update on that Saudi situation, sooner rather than later, but this time I won't be relying on that neutered Intelligence Agency for our information."

---

Patricia Harvey was exhausted as she made her way up to her vantage point on Killiney Hill, overlooking the bay and the beautiful coastline that was now so familiar to her. It was a cloudy but calm day, and the tranquillity of the setting was just what she needed, as she reached her spot and sat on her rock. She closed her eyes to play the mind games that she had come to enjoy. She would imagine the scene before her in all its splendour, and then open her eyes to compare the detail. She seldom won. Seldom would even its imagined beauty exceed the full magic of reality. Today, however, she found it difficult to clear her head. She had sat through two full days of intense negotiations. No, the term 'negotiations,' she felt, would not do justice to the process that Jim O'Raghallaigh had taken them through. It was more of an orchestration, where, when O'Raghallaigh was satisfied that each side thoroughly understood the concerns of the other, he painstakingly got each of them to focus on those concerns. Time and time again he brought people back to the point at issue.

"There will be no losers," he stated emphatically, again and again. "We'll keep at it until everyone gains."

She understood now why he had looked to include the productivity agreement in his remit. In his role as General Manager of Anglo Oil, he himself had outsourced his delivery function. He just didn't throw his people to the wolves. He had helped them to set up a cooperative called "Transoil." This was owned by its members, his former employees, but managed by a professional manager under the guidance of an elected and rotating group of the members. Altogether, it was considered to be a model for cooperative ventures and had been nominated for a European award.

O'Raghallaigh had told her that he knew that Transoil had the best operating standards in the industry, and would have no difficulty in delivering the fifteen percent improvement in productivity that he had committed to Ed Brant. But also, and more importantly, he knew all the people personally. They had been his employees, and he knew their aspirations. He knew that when the transfer was made originally, some of the older men would have preferred to retire. Unfortunately, that was not an option he could provide at the time. Anglo Oil was in bad circumstances and could not afford to make cash available for redundancy compensation. He now saw an opportunity of rectifying that situation. Between both companies, he hoped to be able to allow to retire those who wanted that option, and to be able provide positions with Transoil for those who wanted to continue working.

The total financial package, which was unanimously accepted in a vote of the joint body of employees, was well within the budget that O'Raghallaigh had agreed with Ed Brant.

"Ah, Blondie! Where have you been?" Her daydreaming was brought to an end by the warm feel of Blondie's tongue on her ear. Game for a chase, she walked down the trail to her car with Blondie at her heels. In the distance, on the seaward side of the hill, she could see a lone figure on the balcony of one of the apartment blocks. Her heart missed a beat. It was Ed. She stopped and watched, secure in the knowledge that from his position she would not be visible amongst the trees and against the dark green of the hill. He seemed very alone.

As she watched the motionless figure, silhouetted against the billowy white and the fathomless blue of the sky, she could feel his torment, his isolation, in his absolute compulsion to advance the fortunes of the faceless owners of a corporation, to achieve some personal, undefinable sense of accomplishment, some measure of personal worth, which she knew would always just move beyond his reach. Yes, she could feel his misery. But she was glad. She had tried to help him and he had turned on her. She had tried to help him because she had loved him. She had tried to explain that, in the order of things, compared with her scale of values, his ambitions were like a raindrop struggling to be formed in those clouds above his head. It may or may not happen, but, in a lifetime, would it matter? She had tried to help him and he had hit her with the torment of her life: she had never known her father.

She couldn't help but contrast Ed with the man to whom she had listened over the last two days. Jim O'Raghallaigh always seemed to operate within the constraints of decency. The impact on people seemed to be the deciding factor, on whether or not a course of action was viable. With Ed it was economics. He seemed to be able to detach himself from the human consequences of his decisions, his actions, and his words. Human misery could be justified in terms of the common good or the impact on the bottom line or, as she had found out to her cost, his inexplicable obsession with the ambitions of his dead father. Yet, for all that she found disdainful, she believed that beneath the bravado and machismo there was something irresistibly endearing about him. He acted ever so tough, but always seemed true to his principles, although often misguided, and to have a logical justification for everything he did. She had seen the same defensive mechanism at work with other executives in the United States. The profit-driven culture of modern corporations seems to force ordinary decent people to compartmentalise their lives, so that the beliefs and principles that the executives teach their children and apply to their private lives, have no place in the office. There, ruthlessness seems to be the order of the day. She knew that most of this outward appearance of arrogance that Ed Brant portrayed, was just a cover for insecurity and the loneliness of his job.

Blondie was getting impatient as he stood back on the hill and yelped for her attention. She threw another stick.

She wondered whether she should use her mobile to tell him she was there. Should she surprise him and just call? She knew he would ask her to come up to the apartment if she phoned. But where would that get them? She was sure she didn't want to be back in his competitive world, where the goal posts were constantly moving. She couldn't listen to an apology; it was too soon, the hurt was too raw. They weren't even his goal posts, they were his father's. How funny the world was. She knew nothing about her father, and Ed knew too much about his. He was constantly trying to please a ghost.

She suddenly remembered that Jim O'Raghallaigh had offered to buy dinner for the team. Tom Bergin had another engagement, and Ben Brant was keen to get home to Ciara, his kids, and their new home. Wasn't she glad she hadn't made that phone call? She could imagine Ed's reaction. She would have had to tell him.

Patricia, the love of his life, and Jim O'Raghallaigh, his arch-enemy, were to dine alone. No! She was glad she had avoided that one.

---

The view from the 40-foot roof-top restaurant on Dun Laoghaire's sea-front was breathtaking as Jim and Patricia took their place at the table. The sea was calm and the sky clear. The reflection of the full moon and myriad of lights illuminated the many sailing boats moored in the harbour, while beyond the speckled outline of the Howth peninsula was silhouetted against the moonlit sky. O'Raghallaigh had asked for and procured a table by the window, allowing the full splendour of the vista to be enjoyed.

"We were lucky to get this table," Patricia said, looking around at the crowded restaurant.

"Paul will generally look after me if he can. He used work for Anglo. I was able to help him get a job here when he left. Pity Tom and Ben couldn't join us," he said, as he examined the menu. "I think both have been under immense pressure and I would have enjoyed chatting to them."

"Sorry for your disappointment in having just me to chat up," Patricia responded with a grin.

"Oh I didn't mean that, it's just that anytime I meet Ben it's across a negotiating table. Although we've been on opposite sides, I've often felt more in tune with his position than the corporate one that I was charged with pursuing. I'd like to get to know him better in a social context. You'd never think that he and Ed Brant were brothers, they're so different. Do you have a preference for red or white?" he asked, examining the menu.

The wine arrived within minutes, and both savoured the quality Merlot while searching the menu for their choice of food.

Patricia knew that Jim was right. In fact, she had often wondered how the three Brant brothers had all turned out so differently and seemed to be so confrontational. They were all passionate about what they were doing—even "young John," as Ben had referred to his younger brother. She saw that he was clearly exasperated in trying to do a job he was not cut out for. Ben was unable to help. Ed could, but didn't seem to recognise John's call for help. She wondered why their father, who seemed to be paranoid about them being exploited, had never tried to mould them into a team where they would support one another. They'd make a perfect unit, she thought, if only someone could get them together. She had always regretted having no brothers or sisters and envied those of her friends who did. Here was a family who didn't know their blessings. Such a waste, she thought.

"I don't think that it's so much that they are different, it's more the different pressures they have to respond to," Patricia said defensively, although she surprised herself at her anxiety to defend her absent boss. "Being a high-level executive in a global corporation leaves little room for displaying personal views. It's always the corporate view that must be projected."

Jim smiled at her protective spirit as the waiter took their orders. He topped her glass.

"I understand corporate pressures, but unless they draw the line, executives will be engulfed and swept along in the mainstream of the company's culture. This, as you know, is generally not one that's founded on moral principles. The all-important profit motive and resultant executive compensation plans become the main driving forces. Executive career-paths are really slippery slopes, where the golden rule is unambiguous; conform and perform, or be jettisoned along the way."

Patricia had never thought about it in such stark terms but knew that Jim was right. She had experienced those pressures herself in the New York office before she left for Ireland, when Dino Papandreou had described her job assignment. However, she had no intention of getting involved in discussing her boss or his failings, but wondered herself as to why she still felt so protective of him. She thought she had gotten over him and what they had together. She felt embarrassed, and was glad when the waiter's interruption allowed for a change of subject.

"Tell me, why are you so antagonistic to the Brants?"

The directness of her question surprised even herself, but O'Raghallaigh seemed to take it in stride.

"Oh, I would hate to think that you saw it as antagonistic; I'd be happier with exasperated. I found the Brants in Brantoil very difficult to deal with."

"They believe that you were trying to force them out of business, to buy Brantoil on the cheap."

"In the same way that they bought Anglo? No," he said, without waiting for an answer. "It's a long story, but briefly, at the time when I moved into Anglo Oil it was like many companies in Ireland: sluggish and confused as to how it saw itself in the marketplace. It had a low price image, a bit like Dunnes Stores, but unfortunately, the market saw the reason for its low price as being low quality. It had the worst of all worlds. With the low price it had low margins, and with the poor quality image, it had low sales. As a team, we all worked very hard to translate the low price image into one of value, where we could improve Anglo's profit margins."

He paused to top their glasses again, although they had hardly touched them. Patricia could see that it was an emotional memory. So much of him, she reckoned, had gone into this time in his life.

"We spent a lot of time talking to our distributors. It was critical that all outlets projected this value image that we had created. In the main, we were successful, except in the Dublin area. Here our biggest distributor, Brantoil, continued to operate its own policy—service with high prices. Undoubtedly, they were good operators, but I knew that they would considerably improve their profitability if they followed the Anglo Oil policy of low price. I had great difficulty in dealing with Paddy Brant, the founder. I thought it was probably on account of my age. I thought that when he retired, his son, John, who took over the business, would be more receptive to progressive ideas. It was the opposite. He was totally entrenched in the old ways. It had now got to a stage where it badly affected the relationship between myself and John.

I couldn't understand the reason for the antagonism. I had had dealings with John's brother, Ben, and apart from a professional difference in opinion had always got on well with him. I had absolutely no feelings of antagonism towards any of the Brants and still don't, despite everything."

"I'm sorry," she said with feeling. "You obviously had great feelings for your company. Were you disappointed that Global did not offer you a position with the merged entity?"

"No, not really," he said hesitatingly, but she could see that there was a lot of emotion behind his private thoughts.

He nodded towards the sea as the moon was emerging from behind a light cloud, throwing an eerie half-light on the water.

"I had no illusions about that. I know that any company taking over another will want to stamp its own personality and install its own culture. They generally don't want any symbols of the old regime around. Anyway, I wouldn't have stayed. I couldn't work for a company like Global. They ambushed Anglo, first with their price pressure and then by turning off our supply. I'm okay. I'll go back into private practice as a consultant. It's my people that I felt sorry for—the trauma they were put through. But it's worked out for them now, and that's all I care about."

"You certainly looked after them. I must say I am most impressed with your loyalty."

"Those people supported me with their bodies and souls. They are my friends. When I joined Anglo I knew that I had to fundamentally change its culture. I invited the staff to join with me in writing a mission statement—a constitution for the company that not only would set out the interests of the shareholders but would give equal emphasis to the interest of the employees. I signed that statement and publicly committed myself to be the guarantor of those pledges. I worked very hard to gain their trust and confidence, and now there is no way I could stand back and see them thrown to the wolves."

Both declined the offer of a selection from the dessert trolley and waited, while the waiter poured the coffees, and took the order for after-dinner drinks. They sipped their coffees while taking in the moonlit splendour of the harbour below.

*Such a contrast with everything I have seen in Global both here and in the United States*, she thought—*a company and a company executive with a sense of loyalty and a morality.*

Jim interrupted her reflections.

"I didn't realise that you were born in Ireland. Ben told me that your mother actually worked for the Brant family firm, Brantoil."

"Yes," she said. "My mother moved to the United States after my father died, shortly after I was born. I think she wanted to start anew."

"So you never knew your father?"

"No; that's probably the main reason I applied for relocation to Ireland through Global Oil. It was only when I got here that I realised that Ed Brant was the son of Paddy Brant, the founder of Brantoil, for whom my mother worked here in Ireland thirty years ago."

"So you're really reliving history."

"Yes, and it's a wonderful experience," she said with feeling. "I really hope that I can find out more about my Dad while I'm here—what was he like? Where did he come from? Has he family here? And," she added, hesitatingly, "how did he die?"

"That shouldn't be too difficult," Jim assured her. "Thirty years is not too long ago. There are probably still people in Brantoil who were there at the time your mother was. I have some friends in Brantoil, despite the fact that John Brant would consider me to be his greatest protagonist. Would you like me to make some discreet enquiries?"

"I think I would," she answered.

"You're hesitant?"

"I know it's irrational," she answered. "I've come all the way to Ireland to trace my heritage and, when you offer to help, I get scared. I always sensed that my mother was reluctant to talk about it, and I guess I'm afraid of what I'll find. I'd hate to find out something that would destroy the romantic notion I have of the kind of person my dad was."

"I understand," he said kindly. "But if you need a friend, you've got one," he said, squeezing her hand gently.

"I can see that," she responded. "And I very much appreciate it."

"You know, I'm sorta glad neither Tom nor Ben could make it."

"Me too," she answered.

"Actually, I knew they couldn't make it before I asked them," he said, putting emphasis on the word "they."

She looked at the moon and the stars, and wondered.

# CHAPTER 4

*No! It isn't possible; it couldn't be, but it is. It's Dino Papandreou, the Senior Vice President of Petroleum Operations of Global Oil, in flowing robes. His unmistakable portly frame, his short legs, his bull neck, his glistening forehead, and those staring browless eyes are all his. I hope he doesn't see me, dressed like this—like him—in a thobe. But he does. He's turning towards me. I think he's about to kiss me on the lips. But no, thank God, he just leans forward and rubs his nose off mine. He smiles that mirthless, sardonic smile of his and, hand-in-hand, we walk slowly, almost aimlessly, down Fifth Avenue. He chats about camels and desert sands. I interject, "Let's get out of these blankets." He raises his finger to his lips; he hasn't finished talking about camels and it's rude to interrupt. We walk on...we meet my father...he shakes my shoulder...he is smiling approvingly...he seems pleased...he shakes me again...*

"Sorry, sir, we expect some minor turbulence; could you please fasten your seatbelt?" It was a female voice.

"Jesus, where am I?" Ed Brant woke in a sweat.

"You've been sleeping, sir. I think you've been dreaming."

She was dressed in green. The air hostess, on Aer Lingus flight EI 104 to Dublin out of JFK, smiled quizzically as she removed the dinner tray and attempted to pull his seatbelt together.

"Gee, right, thanks. I must have dozed."

He looked around, concerned that maybe he had caused a scene—made a fool of himself. The seat beside him was empty. Across the aisle, some passengers were watching the in-flight movie, but most were sleeping.

"Thank God," he breathed, although feeling refreshed.

"You haven't touched your dinner. Can I get you something, sir?"

He hadn't noticed the dinner tray.

"No thanks, I—eh, I'm not hungry."

"Maybe later? Just ask if you want something."

"This first-class travel has some benefits after all," he thought, as he lowered the back on his armchair-type seat and stretched his legs. His head still hurt. He didn't usually dream; not since he was a boy. If he did he would always be aware that he had dreamt, but then would never be able to remember the dream. Not this time. His recall was crystal clear.

*Jesus,* he thought, *it is ludicrous, but that's exactly what it would have been like if we had carried out Kem's recommendation in Riyadh. What is so out of place in New York is so normal in Saudi Arabia.*

The sessions in New York had been intensive until today, when a small group from the Global Office in the United Kingdom had prevailed upon him to skip the scheduled lunch and celebrate with them in the bar. This accounted for him falling asleep and for the bizarre dream. He was now wide awake, and as he relaxed his mind went over the events of the previous two days.

While most of his time had been spent with Papandreou and his aides, he had spent a half day with members of the Corporate Affairs Department of Global Oil, being oriented into the culture of Saudi life. As with most multinational companies, Global had its own experts on the different countries and regions of the world in which it did, or intended to, operate. It is staffed mostly with former diplomats. It is their responsibility to ensure that Global invests only in countries providing a friendly political and economic environment, and to monitor developments so that the company can speedily react against adverse changes and capitalise on opportunities.

Norman G. Kem, the Head of the Department, a former ambassador to Iran and an acknowledged expert on the Middle East, spoke initially in general terms about some of the cultural differences to be experienced in Saudi Arabia.

The presentation covered all normal human interaction but concentrated on those matters most important to avoiding gratuitous offence. Brant was intrigued at the level of detail, as Kem warned that it is the position of the Saudi host to set the subject of conversation at the outset. The visitor should not change the subject of conversation except by logical opportunity or invitation. Ominously, he had advised that it was better for Westerners to be inconspicuous, and when possible, to dress and act like the Arabs, even to the extent of holding your male companion's hand; and to stroll casually rather than walk briskly, as we're inclined to do in the West.

Ed opened his eyes and smiled in acknowledgement as the hostess was about to cover him with a blanket. For the first time, he looked around at the other passengers in the first-class cabin. None were of obvious Arabic origin, he noted with disappointment, as he would have toyed with the idea of chatting them up at the compulsory Shannon stopover. He had found the whole Arabic orientation session intriguing and was keen to test its practicality.

When Kem was satisfied that Ed would not abort the visit before it started, by insulting some royally connected airport official, he went on to explain the historical backdrop to the present-day Kingdom of Saudi Arabia.

"You will have something to eat now, Mister Brant?" It was his hostess with the disarming smile.

He realised he was famished. He had skipped breakfast and lunch. He hadn't eaten since dinner the previous evening and then, with all the excitement, he hadn't really eaten even then.

He ordered a meal gratefully.

"Can I put away that case for you? It would give you more room!"

He looked at his feet as she reached down and lifted the leather carrying case. He had almost forgotten. Life had certainly sped up. At his feet, secure in the case, was the tangible evidence of his arrival in the big time, and of how high he had risen within the corporation in such a short period of time. It was the much-coveted Global Oil trophy for *Global Excellence*, sought after by senior managers from, literally, all over the globe. Winners, traditionally, were singled out for rapid promotion within the corporation and were included in an unofficial Achievers Club, securing considerable financial awards and stock options, and which, very significantly, was confided in and entrusted with the most sensitive of confidential information on all aspects of the corporation's activities all over the world.

Ed had attended his first meeting of the prestigious club, where the main subject under debate was, of course, the lack of progress in Iraq. The Committee was most disturbed that the local support anticipated was not forthcoming, and the level and intensity of the hostility was seen as a major setback. Papandreou informed the Committee of what Salam Kashmola had outlined regarding the nature of the Iraqi resistance.

The great concern was that the political relationship with Saudi Arabia would irretrievably break down before the U.S. could secure the Iraqi oilfields, and before Global could replace the Saudi source with oil from the Iraqi fields. Ed understood from the Kem presentation that the United States was now very dependent for its energy on the reserves of the Islamic world, and on Saudi Arabia in particular. If the flow of oil from Saudi Arabia was seriously interrupted, or control passed to a hostile regime, it would take military, and not monetary, policy to keep the U.S. economy growing.

The hostess arrived with the dinner tray. He declined the wine. He had overindulged the previous night at the presentation dinner. That had been an event he would never forget.

Much to his surprise, the new non-executive Chairman of the board, Tim O'Reilly, had presented him with the award for Management Excellence. Papandreou had, as part of the congratulatory tribute, announced details of Ed's record in Ireland, and of the recent "elimination through acquisition, of a low price competitor, at a steal of a price that had been strategically influenced." He went on to say that he had selected Ed Brant to be his personal emissary on a fact-finding mission to the Middle East, so that they could once and for all find out what the heck was happening in "that god-forsaken desert."

The audience greeted this announcement with polite applause, but Ed could sense the elevation in his perceived status within the Global hierarchy.

That was not his only surprise. At a meeting attended by some of the more senior members of the Achievers Club, Papandreou confirmed a disconcertingly detailed knowledge of the Anglo Oil negotiations and of Jim O'Raghallaigh's involvement, although he gave Brant the credit for hiring a street-wise negotiator with coal dust under his fingernails. He went on to say:

"We won't talk right now, but Ed, I'll be looking for you to join my team operating out of New York. I think you've earned it. You'll need someone to run the shop when you're out of Ireland. Why don't we look at that guy with the Irish name, O'Ra—something or other? He looks as if he might fit in. What do you think?"

As was becoming his habit with these shock announcements, Ed Brant had just nodded assent. *How the hell does he know so much? Surely he hasn't got one of his 'ears' in Ireland. But how else could he know about O'Raghallaigh?*

He was still wide-awake when the pilot announced that they were approaching Dublin Airport.

———————◆·◆·◆———————

Reflecting afterwards, Ed thought the idea of a Brant employing O'Raghallaigh was highly ironic but still made a lot of sense. Although he had no previous personal experience of O'Raghallaigh, he was vaguely aware that his father had difficulties in dealing with him in the past. Objectively, however, he had to admit that although O'Raghallaigh had annoyed him intensely in the Royal Marine; he was impressed with the way he had delivered on everything he had promised. Ed recalled his conversation with Ben prior to that meeting, and had been very surprised at the regard that Ben had developed for O'Raghallaigh through their previous industrial relations encounters. Yes, the more he thought about it the more sense it made. He could think of no one better than O'Raghallaigh to knit the two companies together and, as it was Papandreou's idea, if things went wrong, well, he would get the credit for getting rid of a goddam incompetent—a thought he entertained with relish. *But I wish to God I knew how the hell Papandreou knew about him, and what else he knows.*

O'Raghallaigh seemed only mildly surprised when Ed contacted him and asked him to meet both Papandreou and himself. He decided against telling O'Raghallaigh about the purpose of the meeting. Ed guessed that he probably assumed it had to do with his new role as a consultant. Given the amount of money he had paid him for the Anglo Oil job, he didn't expect, nor did he get, any demur—even when he told him that the venue would be the Churchill Hotel in London's West End.

Papandreou had business in London, and Ed had to travel through London to get a B.A. flight to Kuwait City, where Global Oil had an office. From there he would travel by company helicopter to the northeast coast of Saudi Arabia. Both were over-nighting in the Churchill, and Papandreou suggested that he interview O'Raghallaigh over dinner at the hotel.

The Churchill, a Hyatt Regency five-star hotel nestling on the picturesque gardens of Portman Square in London's West End, is attractive to visitors from all over the world, provided they are monied and don't mind spending it on worldly comforts—or, of course, if they are on the payroll of a multinational company. It is close to many of London's main attractions, offers luxurious accommodation, and boasts one of the best, if not the very best, Italian restaurant in the city of London.

Ed Brant sat in the opulent splendour of its Regency Club Lounge on the eighth floor, reserved for members and their guests. As he waited for Papandreou, he wondered which of the attractions would have prompted him to select this as against any of the other five-star hotels in London. The tourist attractions and shopping he had pretty much eliminated. He couldn't see Papandreou being too much into the British Museum, or even Buckingham Palace, and certainly couldn't see him being interested in the fashions of Oxford Street. Luxurious comfort would be a possibility but then again he could get that in countless other hotels. No, it had to be its restaurant; remembering the dedication that he applied to his food in Manhattan's 21 Club, the Locanda Locatelli restaurant recently opened by the renowned Italian chef, Michelin star winner Giorgio Locatelli, and widely regarded as one of the very best Italians in London. He wondered whether O'Raghallaigh would be suitably impressed, or if his social conscience would prevent him from enjoying its comforts. He hadn't long to wait.

O'Raghallaigh arrived and chatted amiably. The tensions of the Royal Marine seemed to be in the past, and Ed was relieved that in front of his boss, at least, the atmosphere would be cordial.

As they chatted about nothing in particular, awaiting the arrival of their host, Ed noticed Papandreou at the other end of the room in close conversation with a brilliantly white-robed Arab. The manicured moustache and goatee beard, dark bushy eyebrows, olive skin, and sallow complexion were all features that Ed would expect from citizens from that part of the world, but what set this Arab apart from the norm was his superior, almost regal, bearing. Ed Brant had no doubt that this desert knight, with whom his boss was engaged in a deep conversation, had to be a member of the House of Saud, the extensive royal family of Saudi Arabia. He looked forward to meeting with this gentleman to test some of the idiosyncrasies that Norman Kem in Global's Corporate Affairs Department in New York had told him to expect. However, this was not to be. He was disappointed. Papandreou and the Arab royal parted before Papandreou came to join O'Raghallaigh and himself, with noisy bombast but without any reference at all, to either his lateness or that intriguing encounter. Was it just a chance meeting with a casual acquaintance? Somehow Ed didn't think so, but that conversation certainly seemed to compete with the food as the main reason for Papandreou's stay at the Churchill.

"Well, Jim, sure glad you could make it to London. Ed has told me of the fine job you did back in Ireland in cutting out the chaff from our operation there and from that little company we bought."

Ed quickly looked at O'Raghallaigh, sensing that this was not the ideal introductory note. O'Raghallaigh, apart from hesitating for a while, seemed unfazed.

"Well, I wanted to spend a weekend over here with a friend so its nice to have a sponsor. As to the people we had to let go from both Anglo and Global, there was absolutely no compulsion.

They were happy to go. None of them wanted to stay and work for Global."

Ed could see Papandreou's eyes narrow and that intensity come into his stare.

"Well, whatever the reason, you got 'em off the payroll, and that's what matters. I always say, if some goddam employees are not happy, get rid of 'em. It's the only way to improve morale."

Ed could clearly see a confrontation developing, similar to what had happened between him and O'Raghallaigh at their meeting in the Royal Marine Hotel; only this time there was no Patricia around to get it back on the rails. Fortunately, the waiter, getting himself into the front line of Papandreou's ire, saved the situation.

"Will you and your guests be dining, Mister Papandreou?" he asked, obsequiously.

"Of course we will; get us a table with Locatelli," he snapped.

"Oh, I'm sorry, sir—eh, the Locanda Locatelli is booked weeks in advance. Perhaps I can get you a table in the Terrace. We serve delicious international dishes there, and I can get you a nice table overlooking the square."

Papandreou looked as if he had been struck. His eyes narrowed and his neck, already overhanging his collar, seemed to bulge and redden.

"Goddam foreigners," he muttered, in a tone of dismissal. "Listen, you go tell Giorgio that Papandreou wants his usual table. It'll be for three, and we should be in by nine."

The waiter was glad to escape.

"Goddam foreigners," he said, to an audience that extended beyond his immediate company. "It's getting to be as bad as the States. You been to the States?" The question was directed at O'Raghallaigh.

"Yes, I have. In fact, I lived there for a short period after I graduated."

"Good, very good. How would you describe the States?"

Ed was relieved that the previous confrontation scenario seemed to have been avoided by the unfortunate waiter. It now looked as if Papandreou was leading into the business at hand—the job offer to O'Raghallaigh.

"How would I describe the U.S.? Well, I suppose the best description I ever saw was in a cartoon featured by the Economist magazine some years ago. In depicting an image of the United States, it showed a picture of North America from which arrows pointed to different parts of the world, with the captions: Huntin', Surfin', Fishin', Fightin' Exploitin'."

Papandreou raised his eyebrows at what he assumed was a light-hearted response, and followed up:

"Surely as an oilman, you agree with U.S. foreign policy?"

O'Raghallaigh turned serious.

"Some time after the al-Qaeda terrorists attacked the twin towers and the Pentagon, the symbols of U.S. military and economic power, the leader of 273 million American people stated:

'How do I respond when I see that in some Islamic countries there is vitriolic hatred for America? I'll tell you how I respond: I'm amazed. I just can't believe it, because I know how good we are.'

I don't for a moment think that these utterances truly reflect the level of thought behind your foreign policy, but the U.S. must move beyond the simplistic argument that 'they hate us because they're jealous of our freedom and our wealth.' This is simply not the case. You've got to understand not only the despair but also the fervour that drives people to willingly sacrifice their own lives for a cause they ardently espouse. If Western politicians remain ignorant of the causes and carry on as before, there will be repetitions."

"Well, what do you think are the causes?"

"Global corporations, not unlike Global Oil, relentless in their search for profits, are locked into a relationship of mutual dependence with the politicians. Contemporary politics is conducted and presented in a way that is intended to shape public opinion, to facilitate the unquenchable thirst of these corporations to exploit the resources of the world. This would be fine if all were to benefit. But that doesn't happen, does it?"

He stopped to give Papandreou an opportunity to respond. It wasn't taken up. Papandreou's eyes were transfixed. O'Raghallaigh continued.

"No! It is almost to the exclusive benefit of their already rich shareholders. These corporations are aided and abetted in their global conquest by global media networks, who present this rampage in a way intended to shape public opinion through disinformation and censorship. This is done deliberately so that the public never get to know, or understand, the real motivation behind political actions, or have the opportunity to counter sectional interests through moral pressure. This blatant plundering of resources and the smothering of reality and truth causes frustrations that erupt in violence."

Papandreou leaned forward in his chair, and with a tone Brant had not previously heard, spat out, "We're in a war against terrorists, for Chrissake. Surely you understand that it would not be in the national interest to have a too open news coverage! The U.S. will not be the only superpower forever. While we are, we must use our strength and the opportunity to change the world to one in which Western civilisation is not threatened by weapons of mass destruction, or indeed by oil embargos or other acts of goddam terrorism."

O'Raghallaigh wasn't at all fazed by Papandreou's bullying.

"I think you well understand that, when I talk about disinformation and censorship, I'm not talking about the circumstances you're referring to. I'm talking about a basic distortion of reality in order to mislead your own citizens, not the enemy. In any event," he went on, "we cannot accept a situation where superpowers can change the world order to further their own economic or ideological interests. The U.S. justification for war, as evidenced by the desperation of the Bush administration to link the 9/11 attack with Iraq, and its insistence on the moral right of a pre-emptive strike, moved the U.S. out of the realm of international law and asserted the principal of unilateral action, based on perceived interests, justified by military capacity, without regard to the moral justification or the dire consequences. In other words, 'might is right.' Saddam used exactly the same reasoning when he invaded Kuwait."

"Do you not believe a country has the right to defend itself?"

"Yes, I do. Not just the right, but also the moral and legal responsibility to defend its citizens. But Iraq didn't attack the U.S. We have all witnessed the efforts to justify this illegality, this abuse of power. If it was not based on known lies, it was at least in callous disregard for the truth, disrespect for the United Nations and other members of the world community, resulting in the appalling loss of human life and the creation of the best circumstances for the recruitment into international terrorism that have ever existed."

Papandreou switched to an officious, if not patriotic, tone.

"The U.S. and Great Britain had to enforce the resolutions of a wimpish U.N. Clearly, as a body, it was not prepared to act."

O'Raghallaigh was equally assertive:

"The U.S. President referred to a 'crusade,' and spoke as if he had some godly revelation that he was born to root out evil in the world. The U.N. is the democratic institution existing to monitor and maintain world peace. It is not acceptable for any one country, no matter how powerful, to unilaterally and selectively enforce any of its resolutions. That is a function it cannot delegate."

Papandreou looked pained.

"You sound as if you're very anti-U.S.!"

"It's unfortunate that that is the complexion put on any dissent with the U.S. foreign policy. No! I am very much pro-U.S., but also very much against the foreign policy of your present government. Terrorism is an abomination, but lightly disguised wars of revenge waged in the heat of the moment, or to combat a single-minded and ruthless fanaticism by becoming equally fanatical and ruthless, will not further the cause of justice or bring about a meaningful democracy. It can only prolong the cycle of violence."

The waiter appeared at Papandreou's shoulder.

"Your table for three is ready, sir," he said sheepishly.

"Oh, I'm sorry. I can't make it. I did say I'm here with a friend. I've arranged to have dinner with her." O'Raghallaigh got to his feet and courteously wished the others a good evening.

The meeting ended without Papandreou ever raising the proposition of O'Raghallaigh joining Global. When O'Raghallaigh had gone, Ed asked him why not.

"He's a shit-head," Papandreou responded.

———◆———

# CHAPTER 5

*Was it only a week since that afternoon on Killiney Hill? Maybe a little bit more, but it seems much longer than that.* Ed Brant had only a half day in the office between arriving back from the committee meeting in New York and flying to London to meet with Papandreou and O'Raghallaigh in the Churchill. He desperately wanted to see Patricia before he went, to put all that unpleasantness behind them and start again. She was not there. She had taken a long weekend. He wouldn't get another chance now for ten days, until he got back from Saudi. He couldn't understand his feelings. He had not felt like this about any woman for a long time. No! He had never felt like this before. She was always in his head. He'd would almost give up this mad pursuit of a dream for her. But would he? That would be silly. He was so close, and then he would have all the time in the world. He'd take her back to the United States when he got that promotion and was based there. Yes, that was the rainbow's end, and he almost had it in his grasp.

Right now he had to deal with this Saudi business, to find out if Global was vulnerable and, if so, what the timescale was. Would the U.S. military have time to secure the Iraqi oil fields before there was any dislocation to the Saudi supply of crude oil? There was also that trip to Moscow that Papandreou had mentioned once, but not again. He wondered what that was about. Global didn't have any dealings with the Russians of which he was aware. Maybe they were about to, as an alternative to the volatile Middle East. Funny how things change; here he was thinking that Russia, the traditional enemy, would be more stable for supply than the traditional ally, Saudi Arabia. *Exciting times, and here I am right in the middle of it. I wish you could see me now, Dad. If only I hadn't screwed up with Patricia, life would be perfect. There I go again, back to Patricia. But I really can't help it. She's so different: beautiful not only in looks but also in spirit. She has such an adventurous outlook and sensitivity that's irresistible. When I think of it, she joined the Global Oil Corporation, a mammoth company, in its Houston headquarters and came to Ireland as an expatriate. She obviously shares my aspiration for success within a corporate environment. I wish I could be like her, though, and be able to switch off and take time to be enchanted by the wonders of nature, and have that empathy and feeling that I used to have.* Quite often, during the presentations on Iraq and Saudi Arabia, his mind had wandered; he imagined Patricia on her rock, overlooking the bay, and wondered if she was thinking of him.

His taxi drew up at London's Heathrow. Before boarding British Airways flight BAO133 direct to Kuwait City, he would telephone Dublin and talk to her. But what could he say on the phone? No! He'd do it properly when he got back. He'd take her out to dinner, buy her an expensive present. That would work. Isn't that what all women like—thoughtfulness and romance? In the meantime, he would just use the facilities in the VIP executive lounge in the airport to e-mail the management team back in Dublin. Under normal procedures, the senior managers would assume his authority for their area of responsibility, so an e-mail just confirming the delegation was all that was necessary under company rules. Still, he wanted an excuse to talk to Patricia. He would telephone her on the pretext that he wanted her to retain the services of O'Raghallaigh, to oversee the integration of the two companies and the outsourcing of Global's distribution function. Somehow, he felt reassured that O'Raghallaigh, rather than he, would be handling that matter. With O'Raghallaigh, he felt it would go routinely; with anyone else, even himself—or maybe especially with himself—it could be another disaster.

"Damn it," he muttered as he remembered that Patricia was on a long weekend. He'd just e-mail.

*That woman is having such an effect on me I can't think straight.*

He still hadn't had the opportunity of checking Bergin's expenditures, and if he was making payments to officials in order to influence decisions, well then, what else was he doing? He would have known of O'Raghallaigh's role in the negotiations; wasn't he there throughout? And wasn't he deeply resentful that the old guard had had its day? Is he the one? Was this his way of trying to protect his ass—by acting as a spy for Papandreou. Was Bergin Papandreou's 'ear' in Ireland? If he was, he would have to deal with him, but in his own time and in his own way. In the meantime, although he certainly didn't want to flatter Bergin by asking him to deputise for the Chief Executive during his absence, it would be one way of throwing him off guard. Besides, he had no option. If he appointed Patricia, she'd think that it was just another way of getting her to watch Bergin. He remembered the frostiness that had caused before. He'd have to rely on Bergin to run the company while he was away. He'd just have to hope that he was wrong about him.

He boarded the aircraft and tried to concentrate on his agenda and itinerary for the ten days he was due to spend in the land of Islam. He was disappointed that there was no first-class available as he settled in to the six-hour flight and looked forward to meeting some of the Global personnel who were biding their time in neighbouring Kuwait.

As the U.S. army secured the Iraqi wells, the Global Kuwaiti-based team would move in and optimise the output once Halliburton had attended to any damage sustained during the fighting. In the meantime, these well-trained specialists would be interacting with a huge number of foreign expatriates, as well as the Kuwaitis, and Ed knew that they would be a good source for local information before he travelled on to al-Khobbar, in the heartland of Saudi oil production on the Persian Gulf. For the duration of his visit he would travel on a Global-owned helicopter, which was to be at his disposal for the scheduled ten days of the visit.

From the briefing, provided by Norman Kem in New York, he realised that to gain any understanding of what was really happening in Saudi, he would have to develop some unorthodox sources. Some information could be got from expatriates, ordinary Saudis, and hopefully, lower-level government officials who would be receptive to inducements. Ed was aware that these were the conventional conduits, and there was the danger that he would only be confirming erroneous or misleading information already with Papandreou. Internal news coverage was censored and was less than useless. Freedom of the press was meaningless, as journalists and academics, who managed to get visas, generally spent their time in five-star hotels in Riyadh, or Jeddah, or wandering around sterile malls. He decided to deliberately avoid the usual locations for Westerners in the hope that, by visiting the oil rich northeast, he would meet some informed, non-Global expatriates, officials, or, with luck, some disillusioned member of the extensive royal family.

The small state of Kuwait, where he was scheduled to spend the first twenty-four hours, lies at the northwest corner of the Arabian Gulf, and is bordered on the east by the blue waters of the Gulf, and to the south and southeast by the yellow sands of the Kingdom of Saudi Arabia. To the north is Iraq. Like all Arab Gulf countries, Kuwait is an Islamic state. The population is around two million, of which expatriates make up more than sixty percent. Because of their influence, it is, to a limited extent, more tolerant of Western culture than its neighbours and, as such, would be a more hospitable place to spend time awaiting the call of the military from neighbouring Iraq.

As he had hoped, the Global people were glad to be of assistance; the fact that he was reporting directly to Papandreou helped. They had prepared a formal presentation, revealing their extensive knowledge of the Gulf States, and had arranged for him to meet several Kuwaitis and other resident expatriates. By the time of his departure the next evening, he felt he had a good understanding of what to expect, as the Global Oil helicopter took him north to al-Khobbar in the Kingdom of Saudi Arabia.

Western residents of Saudi Arabia exist in a world of their own, making their homes in walled-off compounds away from the country's citizens. The compounds in the oil-rich eastern province of al-Khobbar offer a lifestyle of opulence and exclusivity, as they cocoon their expatriate residents from the realities of everyday Saudi life.

Outside the walled-in compounds there exists a great cultural conflict: the Saudis want a better lifestyle, want the benefits of Western technology, but don't want to become replicas of their Western counterparts. Every aspect of the nation's life is circumscribed by a strict adherence to the Muslim call to prayer, five times a day, each one emphasizing the clear reality that no Islamic country can be Westernised.

Within the Oasis compound, the luxury, three-story, Mediterranean-design villa for visiting Global Oil executives is very firmly in the glamour club of expatriate homes. Even though he doubted that he would have the time, on this occasion, to really enjoy its facilities, Ed couldn't help but admire the marble floors, the beautiful rugs, the wood panelling and rich fabrics and wonder how many billions of dollars its facilities had enabled Global extract from deals consummated within its walls. Politicians and high-level executives were, the world over, susceptible to the attractions of tax-free opulence, and the Oasis Club was clearly designed to provide just that.

He wasn't there very long when he became conscious of the security precautions in place. Mounted on the four-metre high, reinforced concrete walls surrounding the compound were closed-circuit television cameras supporting armed mobile patrols. The only entrance was through a gate manned by armed guards twenty-four hours a day. A Kuwaiti, who had no English, piloted the helicopter, and Ed wondered whether the guards had been notified of his arrival or was their casual disinterest, as it landed within the compound, an indication of a low standard of security actually employed.

He didn't mention this concern, but from discussions with the other, more permanent Oasis Club residents, Ed could sense that the feeling of safety, both physical and psychological, seemed to be undermined rather than strengthened by the need for a compound wall and the other elaborate security measures. Residents stayed within the fortress-like compound when possible, and when they did venture out into the real Saudi Arabia they were now permitted to carry guns. This seemed to confirm that the safety concerns expressed were more than paranoiac. The government could not, or maybe would not, protect them outside the compounds. More disconcerting was the suggestion of instances of collusion between terrorists and security forces. Some of the concerns expressed painted a graphic picture of life for the expatriate.

"Some Americans are trying to blend in, growing beards and wearing thobes—the traditional ankle-length garments worn by most Saudi males."

One senior executive working for Aramco, the state owned oil company, said quite tellingly:

"A suit and tie is tantamount to wearing a bull's-eye."

"A lot of Saudis assume that if you're white you're American, and Americans aren't very popular here. They avoid getting close—they don't want to get caught in the crossfire."

It became obvious to Ed that the security situation was much worse than was being reported, but he still needed to get into the heartland to really feel the pulse of this bastion of Islam.

---

Ed had met very few Sunni Muslims, but one important one was Prince Sultan bin Saad bin Jiluwi, who was the landlord of the Oasis complex. As a member of the extensive royal family, Ed was sure that he would have a unique perspective on the situation, and could be of particular help on the deteriorating relationship with the United States, which was the essence of his brief in the region. If he could get him to talk openly, it would provide a unique insight. He was not to be disappointed.

The introductions came through Sebastian Cooper, manager of the company managing the Oasis complex. The promptness of the invitation led Ed to believe that his own position, and relative importance within Global Oil, had been greatly exaggerated. Royalty in Saudi Arabia, particularly at the lower strata of the family, operate on the basis of favours exchanged, and Global, Ed guessed, would have had a reputation for responding handsomely if the information gleaned was worthwhile.

"The Prince's hospitality will be extended at his desert abode," the invitation proclaimed. This turned out to be a marquee-type accommodation in the desert, close to the foothills of the al Aramah Mountains. Brant travelled out in the Global helicopter accompanied by Sebastian Cooper, who explained that because of his position he met many visiting dignitaries passing through the

Oasis complex. Many of the Saudi princes offered themselves as 'facilitators' for visiting businessmen. Among the most active was Prince Sultan bin Saad bin Jiluwi, who made a point of meeting oil company executives and traders, who regularly visited Aramco in the oil heartland of al-Khobbar. He himself was enormously wealthy and seemed to have influence in Riyadh. He could certainly get things done.

As a Bedouin chief, Prince bin Jiluwi was a member of the extensive royal family, although, on which side of the political divide within that extensive family was not known. Cooper intimated to Ed that he was being especially honoured by the Prince in being received in the lifestyle of his forefathers. Ed reckoned the price would just be that much higher.

As the helicopter approached, Ed could barely make out the outline of a gigantic marquee that, in the bright sunshine, blended into the yellow sands of the desert. Extending outwards for more than thirty metres, and contrasting against this sea of gold, like the giant tongue of a lizard, was a dark crimson carpet to welcome and direct guests to the otherwise inauspicious entrance. The pilot had obviously not been on this trip previously, as he circled the oasis awaiting hand directions from the ground as to where he was to land. When no one appeared, he brought the machine down at the end of the carpet trail. Whether this was the correct procedure or not he would never know, as witnessing the virtual sand storm that the blades created, and the resultant golden sheen left on those sections of the carpet that were still visible, he was ultra-efficient in taking off and disappearing into the swirling sand.

Cooper led as they tentatively approached the entrance strewn with rugs of exotic eastern design, and framed by two motionless, bearded six footers, clad in traditional thobes of snowy white. Ed wondered if the submerging of the welcoming carpet beneath the desert sands was a violation of some sacred rule of etiquette that Kem had omitted to mention.

"As-salem alaikum," broke the silence. Ed almost laughed. It was Cooper announcing their arrival.

Immediately from within the marquee came the deep-throated response, "Wa alaikum as-salam."

Cooper gestured that they should remove their shoes and enter. The Prince met them, just inside, and greeted him with the customary kiss on the nose. Ed was beginning to appreciate the orientation course that had prepared him. Much to his relief, no mention was made of the passing sandstorm.

The opulent splendour of the interior engulfed them. They were in world of satins and silks, of rugs and soft furnishings, all basking in the soft light of countless oil lamps, discreetly positioned and coloured, to project an atmosphere to rival the most lavish of five-star hotels. There, they were to be pampered with a standard of cuisine, and attended on by the most obsequious of service unimaginable by Western standards. Apart from the absence of wine, nowhere had Ed Brant ever experienced the standards enjoyed by this Saudi prince in his temporary desert abode.

Ed impatiently noted that the conversation during dinner was superficial, but remembering the Saudi social etiquette on which he had been coached, he was careful to allow his host to set the pace and tone. Eventually, the Prince indicated that they should walk and admire his fifty or so white camels, which stood motionless in the sand about fifty yards from the entrance to the marquee. Rather than risk offence by refusing, Ed strolled with him. He again silently thanked Kem for the forewarning when the Prince casually took, and continued to hold, his hand as they nonchalantly strolled along the now spotless carpet. The sun had set and the full moon, in an almost cloudless sky, was rising out of the desert so that the camels, still motionless, were eerily silhouetted against the darkening sky. The night was balmy and, as they strolled in the moonlight with the soft sand yielding under the deep pile of the carpet with each step, he felt the warmth of the Prince's hand in his and thought of the waste. *Why couldn't it be Patricia who was here? Why couldn't it be the warmth of her hand in mine? And why couldn't those desert sands be the blue seas that she loved so much?*

As soon as they were out of earshot of the group, Ed, while being very careful to avoid offence, as warned by Kem, carefully steered the conversation to the subject of the changing political climate. The Prince went to great lengths to assure him of his Western sympathies, and while acknowledging the royal family divide that others had only speculated on, stated that he was unquestionably on the side of the status quo. Despite this, Prince bin Jiluwi's sympathies were anything but pro-Western.

"September 11th need never have happened," he said. "The Arab world is desperate for change. No one listens. The West says our rulers are corrupt, yet continues to support them because they connive at the plundering of our natural resources by global companies and facilitate vested interests. The voice of our people is ignored. Is it surprising that some are responsive to the leadership of Osama bin Laden? Who else offers anything? The United States? It talks of democracy, but wants it only on its terms, and as it defines it. The demand for our crude oil will soon outstrip our ability to supply. If we, as Saudis, democratically elected our own government, would that government be free to sell our crude oil to the Chinese or Indians, or would the U.S. apply their new-found definition of democracy—that the freedom of a sovereign state does not include freedom to act contrary to American interests? For the West, democracy means believing in exactly the same things it believes. Is that real democracy?"

They had walked up close to the camels, which stirred uneasily as the Prince said something in Arabic. He raised his arm as if to soothe them, releasing Ed's hand in the movement. Ed saw this as the opportunity. He widened the space between them and ponderously gesticulated, as if it were necessary to emphasise the question. Much to his relief it seemed to work. If bin Jiluwi noticed, he showed no sign. He spoke with the same ardour, and Ed made sure to keep his hands busy and moving.

He followed up the reference the Prince had made to Osama bin Laden as they turned to stroll back to the marquee.

"I have never yet met a Saudi who truly admires Western society. We use your technology and admire your facilities, but we see you as decadent. We despise your culture. No one in Saudi Arabia has condemned absolutely what Osama bin Laden has done. His sons work for the bin Laden organisation: family ties are strong. He is not seen as a terrorist but as a highly religious man."

"How can anyone see an acknowledged terrorist as a highly religious man?" Ed asked, hoping that his rising agitation at the insufferable arrogance of this man would not stifle the flow that was really getting to the issues that would affect Global's future. "Surely the Koran forbids such violence?"

Prince bin Jiluwi turned and looked directly into his eyes. Ed saw him for the first time. That manicured moustache, those dark bushy eyebrows and sallow complexion that framed those piercing eyes that were vaguely familiar. *All of these white-robed Arabs look the same,* he concluded; *his father has probably sired dozens like him.*

Without shifting his eyes from Ed's, even for a second, he brought a deadly seriousness into his tone.

"Whoever kills a human being, except as punishment for murder or other villainy in the land, shall be regarded as having killed all mankind."

There was a deliberate emphasis on the word "except."

"Osama bin Laden," he continued, "has no difficulty in convincing fellow Muslims that the foreign policy of the West has caused "murder and other villainy" in the Arab lands, and as such not only are they permitted by the Koran, but they have a Koranic duty to respond in kind. You must remember that these young followers are stifled by corrupt regimes that are supported and maintained in power by the United States."

He stopped, inviting Brant to respond—an invitation that was not taken up. Ed found the whole monologue intriguing. He had never given any thought to the motivation of terrorists, except that they were deranged. Bin Jiluwi went on:

"During the war against the Soviet Union, Pakistani military intelligence requested the presence of a Saudi prince to lead the jihad in Afghanistan. The Saudi leaders recommended Osama bin Laden. Now I believe, that up to twenty five thousand of the Saudi militants, who fought with bin Laden against the Soviets, and then against the Americans in Afghanistan, are supporting the Sunni insurgents in neighbouring Iraq.

*Jesus*, Brant thought, *and only a week or so ago the brains of Global Oil were calling the Iraqi resistance "sporadic."*

"Osama bin Laden offered his services to repel Iraq when Saddam invaded Kuwait in 1990. The House of Saud refused this offer, and instead, with the approval of the religious, invited in the Americans. More than a half million American troops arrived on Saudi soil. This was seen as an extreme provocation. Infidels defiling our country. And it brought bin Laden into direct opposition to the House of Saud."

"Do you believe that the House of Saud is in danger of being toppled?"

"Abdulaziz al-Murqrin, who is bin Laden's chief strategist, has warned the royal family. 'Our war with you will not end until God's will is enforced, and the crusaders are expelled from the land of Muslims, leaving you as easy prey.'"

Ed asked what a change in government in Saudi Arabia might mean as far as the West was concerned.

His reply said more than the words he used. Never for a moment did he concede, or even suggest, that there was a possibility of anyone other than bin Laden taking over if, or in terms of the certainty he seemed to be implying, when the present royal family was deposed.

"Osama bin Laden has said that 'the sale of Saudi oil to the U.S. at paltry prices is the biggest theft ever witnessed by mankind in the history of the world.' He compared this 'paltry price' with the large taxes that the consuming countries impose on our finite natural resource."

By now they had arrived back at the marquee, and the Prince motioned for them to stand inside as the global helicopter hovered overhead, and began to stir the sand in its descent. Cooper joined them. Ed wondered where he had been.

"Saw you two getting on so well that I didn't want to be a gooseberry." He whispered with a mischievous grin. "Besides, for the regulars there's the medicinal Scotch that always appears when the outside guests are not present. It beats holding hands."

Although Brant was very conscious of the Saudis' dire need to keep up the price of crude oil, and that the atmosphere of impending strife was exactly what was needed to achieve that, he found it impossible to believe that, despite their power and resources, either Global Oil or the Saudi government were capable of deliberately creating the conditions of near panic on the scale that he had witnessed and now heard. On the other hand, he remembered Papandreou's confidence about the outcome, and wasn't Prince Sultan bin Saad bin Jiluwi a member of the royal family? He obviously felt threatened—or did he? Could he be part of the threat? Ed Brant just didn't know what to believe except that Saudi Arabia, no less than Iraq, was not a healthy place to be in. And neither seemed to be a place to stake the future of Global Oil Inc.

For the present, however, he was glad to get back to the security of the Global villa in the Oasis compound.

On reflecting on what he had learned over the previous days since his arrival in Saudi, Ed was worried; perhaps he was being overly influenced by the insecurity of the expatriates and the startling revelations of his desert host. In order to get a broader understanding of the Saudi psyche, he decided to spend a couple of days out in the area of the giant Ghawar oil field. There, by talking to not only the field management, but also to the many field operatives, he felt that he could get an unsanitised version of the anti-Western or, more particularly, the anti-U.S. passion that seemed to be taking hold on the ground. The fact that he was Irish, and not American or British, would help the flow.

Right from the start, the contrast with the carpeted oasis of the previous evening could not have been greater. It was an area of feverish activity, where from the air, as the helicopter approached, the oil-stained sands looked more like charcoal or volcanic ash. There was a clearly-defined parking area, already occupied by several helicopters, some of which had their rotary blades rotating in preparation for takeoff. The differences to Prince bin Jiluwi's desert dwelling continued. Apart from the heat haze, that rose off the tarry surface, these sands were firmly consolidated with traffic and spillages and could no longer angrily respond to the whirring intruders from the air.

Ed had sent prior advice of his arrival, and the Global Oil connection was an assurance of hospitable attention. He was allowed to roam freely, and talk with anyone who had the inclination to talk to him.

The views were fairly consistent. The religious fundamentalists control much of education, which is why many Saudi children leave school knowing the Koran and nothing else. That makes them almost unemployable. More than two-thirds of the population is under the age of 30, and perhaps a third of them are unemployed. They spend their time in the mosques being "indoctrinated for jihad and righteous murder." Many of the Kingdom's brightest, best-educated, and in theory, best prepared for work, are reluctant to do any. Two out of every three doctorates earned in Saudi Arabia are in Islamic studies. Young Saudis are being educated to be ardent followers of Osama bin Laden and the like, or to take part in a world that will exist only if the Wahhabi Jihadists, and their Muslim brother allies, can succeed in turning back the clock by a couple of centuries.

After a number of hours, Brant arrived at the site office where he had scheduled a meeting with the well manager, Saeef Baqr.

Saeef hadn't talked for too long before Ed took an instant liking for him. He was a man's man with, as Ed's mother used say, "a lived-in face." His dark, suntanned complexion was topped with longish black hair tinged with grey. This was parted naturally over his deeply-lined forehead, and seemed to frame two coal-black eyes, that were windows to some great sadness. He seemed to be a man in his early sixties, an Iraqi by birth who had fled the Saddam Hussein regime, and had worked for Aramco for the previous five years. He had travelled extensively throughout the Kingdom. Saeef, a Shiite Muslim, was considered to be a moderate leader of the Shiite community in Saudi Arabia's North-Eastern Province, the central location of the oil industry. He took a keen interest in the events in his homeland and had obvious political ambitions. He was very forthright in expressing his views.

"This rage against the West and against the House of Saud is everywhere. The belief is that all oil money has corrupted the ruling family beyond redemption, and that the Saudi leaders have defiled the faith by allowing the U.S. troops into the Kingdom. On the streets, they are reviled for failing to protect fellow Muslims in Palestine and Iraq, and for standing by helplessly as Islam is humiliated."

Brant asked Saeef Baqr whether the violence in his homeland was sporadic or organised, and whether he felt that the United

States would succeed in its ambition of establishing a freely elected, democratic government in Iraq.

Those dark pools of sadness seemed to envelop Brant as this introspective Iraqi searched his soul. His response was alarming.

"Since the 1920s the Sunni Arab minority has ruled Iraq through brutal oppression, lording it over my community, the Shiite Arab majority, and the Kurdish minority. It was this Sunni minority regime, and not just Saddam Hussein, that was toppled by the American-led invasion. With the exception of one case, Moqtada al-Sadr's renegade army, all violence is the rearguard action of this Sunni minority that is desperately trying to cling to power.

"The U.S. mistakenly believes that it can impose its system and definition of democracy on an Islamic state and form an administration with friendly Iraqis, whom the natives see as Westernised collaborators. With the transfer of power to this interim government, the attacks have focused on its officials and sites. The Sunnis see clearly that if any form of government is imposed, it will mean that, at the very least, they will be required to share power with the other religious and ethnic groups, or be faced with a dreaded Shiite-controlled government. They will accept neither."

He stopped for a few moments. What he was describing was causing him great distress. Brant wasn't to know it then, but what he was about to hear would have profound implications for him and for Global Oil.

"Unlike in Iraq, the Shiite population in Saudi Arabia is a small minority. It is concentrated in the oil region of the Eastern Province and forms the majority of Aramco workers. We are poor and oppressed. The groundswell of emotion that would follow the installation of a Shiite government in Iraq will spill over into the Shiite community in Saudi Arabia. If that happens in the very heartland of the Saudi oil industry, both Iraq and Saudi Arabia will be conflagrated."

Ed Brant was relieved to get back to his haven in the Oasis Club and away from all of this madness.

He decided to telephone Papandreou on the secure line so that he could take any further instructions before heading home to the solace of the Garden of Eden, which by now, even without Patricia being there, seemed a very attractive alternative to this desert fortress.

------◆·◆·◆------

Papandreou's tone became more and more tense as he was briefed on the revelations of the previous week. Ed could clearly visualise the glistening forehead and rimless glasses that only accentuated those humourless, dispassionate eyes.

"What are you tellin' me, Brant? That we're sort of in the mangle? That no matter what way we turn, we're squashed? That couldn't be. How could it? I know those technocrats in Intelligence don't know their ass from their elbow. I know it's not like the old days when we got it on the ground—not from some goddam satellite dish somewhere out in space. But surely even the pencil pushers, that are callin' the shots in Washington these days, couldn't have gotten it that wrong. Let's go over it again."

Without waiting for Ed to reply, Papandreou continued.

"I know we're in big trouble in Iraq. But you're saying that the Sunnis won't accept any political solution other than their reinstatement as a single-party government. The United States cannot do that, so if we support the majority Shiites, which we must, and if they end up in power, which they will, then that will result in a civil war. So much for our noble gesture in liberating that godforsaken desert from Saddam."

Papandreou's voice faded somewhat, and when he spoke again there was a hollow echo. Brant could visualise the scene, thousands of miles away, as those browless eyes looked unseeingly out over

Central Park. Papandreou was obviously using his squawk box as he walked around his spacious office, deep in thought.

"Now turning to Saudi Arabia. You're telling me that the House of Saud is for the chop, that it's only a question of time before Osama bin Laden ousts King Fahd and Prince Abdullah, and when that happens we'll have dry fuckin' hoses. Even if that goddam terrorist doesn't make it, you're telling me that those goddam Chinese and Indians will suck the place dry—unless we can block them. We need an alternative, and we need it fast. The Saudi reserves are short-lived anyway—which is why we went into that fuckin' Iraq in the first place."

Ed could tell that he was now back at his desk. He pictured him with his eyes closed, concentrating. Those short stubby arms raised and his hands joined behind his head. Each of his statements was punctuated by a pause, during which Brant was unsure whether or not he was supposed to comment.

"Now you're adding another goddamn complication. When the Shiites take power in Iraq, their brethren in northeastern Saudi will be encouraged to start some goddamn secessionist movement and look for a form of confederation, if not bloody integration, with the Shiite Iraq. This will start another goddamn civil war in Saudi Arabia, right slap bang in the heart of the oil-producing region.

"Now tell me, Ed, in case I'm missing something—is there any real possibility that we can continue to draw oil, beyond the very short-term, from this region?"

There was no mistaking the note of sarcasm in his voice. Yes, he expected some sort of an answer.

"Well, it's pretty clear that the royal family is not popular. They're considered to be corrupt and inept, and the puppets of the United States. The only thing that would keep them in power is an extremely high oil price—one that will enable them to buy loyalty as they have done in the past."

"Hell will freeze over before the administration will okay that. I know our Washington friends are close to big business, but apart from the oil industry big business wants low oil prices. Hell, the folks in Washington are our greatest advocates and supporters, but if those goddamn Arabs have been funding those hate schools around the globe with our petrodollars, we couldn't ask them to support the kind of high prices that the Saudis need. We need another strategy, and fast."

Ed surprised himself at the feeling of resentment that was welling up inside. Papandreou's tone was dismissive. After all, it was he who had unearthed the complete folly of the Global strategy. He would have expected a more appreciative tone.

"Dino, I'm just reporting the facts as I see them. You're drawing the conclusions, but to answer your question, no, I don't see any long-term security of supply in either Saudi or Iraq."

Papandreou didn't seem to notice his annoyance.

"Okay, this is what I want you to do. Take an unmarked chopper and have a look at the level of security the Saudis are employing on the Gulf fields. Global's vital interests are at stake, and we need to know how safe they are."

"Okay, Dino. Will do," he heard himself saying.

"I've arranged for a special meeting of the main board to be convened in New York in ten days. The main agenda item will be the Strategy Coordinating Committee's report on the conclusions drawn from your trip. I'll need you to report on what you see from your chopper trip. Oh, eh, and well done. See you in New York."

With that he was gone.

*Jesus, if only I could be back on the hill. I'd gladly put up with ravaging Blondie.* He checked his watch. *I wonder what Patricia is doing. Jesus, I wish she was here.*

This initial stage, at any rate, of his fact-finding trip to the Middle East was coming to an end. He wasn't sorry to see the last of those golden sands as he settled into his first class seat in British Airways flight BAO156, non-stop to London's Heathrow.

It was the most real experience he'd had in ten days.

------◆·◆·◆------

Patricia Harvey was thinking of Ed, but not in a romantic context. As was her daily routine, she was sipping coffee with her superior and friend, Tom Bergin. The portrait of Tom Stone still watched her from his office wall, but she thought the stony-faced grimace, that Ed had been so intolerant of, seemed more reassuring, more benign, more approving. He was amongst friends, and it seemed to show.

She, no less than Tom Bergin, had been surprised to receive the e-mail from Ed Brant. He had been expecting to be fired, not appointed as Acting Chief Executive. Patricia too wondered why. Had she convinced Ed that all Tom needed was encouragement to bolster his self-confidence? She hoped that was the case. Without the pressure of Ed Brant, Tom was confident, and a good, competent executive—old-style definitely, but conscientious and considerate of his staff. She looked at him now. The dull, glazed, expressionless look that had dominated his appearance only a few weeks previously had gone out of his eyes. He was still thin— painfully, unnaturally thin—but he obviously now had a new-tailored suit, made so his weight loss was not so noticeable. His beard looked well-groomed, and she noticed the twitching and blinking and beard-tugging habits, if not gone completely, were certainly not as pronounced as they were. Funny the difference an e-mail, expressing a bit of confidence in him, had done.

Patricia wondered if he knew, or suspected, that she had a relationship with Ed. He never in any way even hinted that he knew or suspected, and never embarrassed her by asking her questions on subjects that, as Ed's Executive Assistant, she would have had access to confidential information. Indeed, most of their conversations were where he was confiding in her.

Today was a little different. Maybe it was his newfound confidence, but he was venturing on an area that he had not done previously. He was speculating on why Ed was in the Middle East. He was used to his boss making increasingly frequent trips to New York—but Saudi Arabia? Well, that was new. Although he knew that a huge proportion, if not all, of Global's worldwide product demand was fed from Saudi Arabia, most locations would have no direct dealings with the Kingdom. The crude oil was brought by huge tankers to Global's state-of-the-art refineries in Europe. After being refined, the products like petrol, diesel, and heating oil were then shipped by smaller tankers to the European markets where Global had marketing operations. Global Ireland, even then, didn't directly handle the products of refined Saudi crude oil. Ireland was supplied from the huge refinery at Milford Haven, on the west coast of the United Kingdom, under a product exchange agreement that Global had with Texaco. So why Ed Brant was going to Saudi Arabia was beyond him. Patricia didn't enlighten him. She couldn't have even if she wished. She didn't know herself. Information with New York was one-way traffic.

"I'm glad he wasn't here to see those people leave. I think there would have been scenes and a lot of unpleasantness. It was a pity, but for the best." He spoke with emotion.

Patricia couldn't disagree. She was really sorry that Ed, who was so brilliant in so many areas, seemed to have a blind spot when it came to people.

"Yes, it's a pity. It would have meant so much to so many, that the Chief Executive would be around when the last farewells were being said to departing staff. You know, just to acknowledge the long service that some of these people had given to Global. In some cases more than forty years."

It was a point not lost on the media. She wondered what Ed's reaction would be when he learned of the negative coverage the merger got from the national press, precipitated by the half-page notice that the Anglo Oil employees had inserted to thank their company for their wonderful careers.

She had got to know a lot of them personally since her arrival, and was herself surprised at the depth of feeling. The fact that Ed Brant was not available to speak on behalf of Global was presented cynically by the press, as was the interview given by Ned Murphy, the longest-serving member of Global's staff, who had elected to take the redundancy package. When asked how he felt after such long service, he said that he felt lucky that Global had survived to give him a lifetime of employment. His only regret was that it never valued its employees and never asked for their opinions, despite regularly paying many thousands of euro for consultants to ask for employee opinions and then report them as their own. This demeaning approach was evident again when the Chief Executive of Global wasn't even around to shake their hands and wish them good luck.

"Can you believe it?" he was reported as saying. "When I walked out of the Global terminal, it was Jim O'Raghallaigh, the General Manager of Anglo Oil, the company we'd just ravished, who shook my hand and wished me the best. My own manager was sunning himself in some exotic resort on the Persian Gulf. We weren't even worth saying goodbye to."

"You know, Patricia," Tom said with emotion. "Ed Brant never made any reference to the individuals who opted to go or to stay. He is a man totally preoccupied with his own thoughts, which seem to be thousands of miles away. When he did get around to the developments in Ireland, his questions were all to do with the final cost of the redundancy package, the proposed new organisation structure, the unit delivery cost following the outsourcing of the distribution function, and the reaction of the customers. There were no questions regarding whether or not valuable, experienced people had elected to go, or the impact on morale."

Patricia was too quick to defend her former lover.

"Tom, you've never been the number-one man in a multinational corporation, so you really don't understand the pressures. The corporate board are only interested in those issues—the hard issues, as they describe them. The soft issues are dealt with by local management."

She was sorry she excused Ed's indifference the way she did. She didn't really think that way herself, and she knew she disappointed Tom with the comment.

He looked at her with some surprise and sadness.

"Still, you just can't help but compare the two men and wonder why they are so different."

"Jim is exceptional," she said, without hesitation and with feeling.

"Oh, I meant Ben, his brother," Bergin said, giving her a quizzical look.

She rose to leave and to cover their mutual embarrassment. The steely eyes of the founder met her's again as she turned towards the door.

"Tom, tell me about Mister Stone" she asked, "what was he like? Was he your friend as well as being your boss?"

Bergin's eyes took on the now familiar glaze as he reactively turned to look at the subject of her question.

"Yes he was, and still is, very much my friend" He and I... and Paddy...Paddy Brant that is...were inseparable in our youth. But that was a long time ago. We all worked very hard to create employment for ourselves and for our people in an Ireland that, in those days, didn't offer too many opportunities."

"How long ago was that? Was it at the start? Were you involved then? Did you... did you know my mother? All of her questions ran into one.

She answered his blank stare with "did you know Maureen Harvey?"

Tom Bergin became transfixed. After what, to Patricia, seemed an age, he rose slowly from his chair and stumbled around the desk to where she was standing. He put his hands on her shoulders and looked into her eyes.

"Good God. Mo Harvey! You're Mo's little girl?"

# CHAPTER 6

It was with great anticipation that Ed Brant went into the office on his return from Saudi Arabia. Apart from the e-mail he had sent from Heathrow, appointing Bergin as his stand-in during his absence, he had not been in touch since he had left for Saudi Arabia. But he had confidence in Patricia, and knew that if needed, he would have been contacted. The uncertainty of future supplies would certainly dampen the enthusiasm of the competitors, and it was very unlikely that any would try to take advantage while Global was completing the integration of Anglo Oil into the system. Tom Bergin's area was his main concern. He hoped there were no sales or marketing problems.

For the first time in weeks, Ed really felt that they had achieved something. The timing of the corporate Management Excellence Award was opportune. News would have filtered through. In fact, its presentation to him by the Chairman would probably have been featured, with photos, in the current issue of Global Times. He expected that the staff, as well as the management, would be generous in their congratulations and would participate in the sense of achievement that, only now, he was beginning to feel.

"Mornin' Helen," he shouted with uncharacteristic cheerfulness as he pushed open the glass doors of the reception area.

"Mornin'," responded a young, blond fellow sitting behind the desk sipping a cup of coffee or tea.

"Helen doesn't work here any more," he said as he pushed a 'visitors' book' in Ed's direction. "Please sign in here. Have you an appointment with someone?"

Completely taken aback, Ed ignored this young fellow and entered the lift for the executive floor.

His secretary was awaiting the lift as he stepped out.

"Good morning, Ed," she said quietly. "Did you have a good trip?"

"Yes, thanks, Mary! Where's Helen, and who is that young fella at reception?"

"I'm afraid Helen is gone. She opted to take the redundancy package. Joe was formerly with Anglo Oil. He was a dispatcher at their depot. He's got a few rough edges, but he'll be all right."

"Well, I'm not impressed. I'll talk to Bergin, but in the meantime, will you take him in hand and keep an eye on how he treats customers?"

"Ed, I'm going too. I just stayed back so that I could tell you directly. I've decided to leave. I've got another job."

Ed stood in disbelief. Mary leaving? She had been with the company, well ... forever. He couldn't imagine operating without her reassuring presence.

"What happened, Mary?" he spluttered.

"I've been here thirty years," she said. "It's not the same anymore. I don't enjoy coming in in the mornings as I used to."

She realised just what she said, and to whom she had said it. With an embarrassed "sorry," she turned and was gone.

Ed knew he should have acted on instinct and told her how important her contribution was. He also knew that he had to sort out his thoughts. He would talk to her later, maybe even take her to dinner!

He convened a meeting of the management group.

The boardroom had been completely repainted and the offending darker patch surrounding the gleaming Mission Statement was now gone. *The ghosts of the past have finally been exorcised. Now, at last, we can move into the twenty-first century.*

He looked around the table. There was a full presence. Bergin seemed to be glowing. New suit too, Ed noticed.

Patricia was in her usual position. The day was cloudy with the sun fighting for survival, so although her back was to its light, he could see her face. She seemed to have a dazed expression and was deadly white. She returned his look with a wan smile, the first since their row.

*Thank God, she seems to be softening. I knew she would if I gave her space. I won't push it. She'll come to me in her own time.*

He thought back to the unprofessional image of the reception area. He just knew Bergin would screw up. Imagine that young guy presenting the image of Global Oil to the world. He faced Tom Bergin.

"What the hell is happening?" he asked.

"Everything you planned," Tom Bergin responded with a confidence that Ed had never seen before. "We've got the numbers down by forty four, and we've got a productivity agreement that gives us a fifteen percent improvement, and its well within the budget of the three and a half million that you approved."

"What about the business?"

"Well we've had a rough ride with the media, but we're lucky with the timing. Customers don't feel they have a choice and, with the security of our Saudi supplies, they feel they'll be better off with Global. All in all, I reckon we'll retain the bulk of Anglo Oil's business."

"Has there been media concern on supply?"

"Mainly about the effect on price, but the Minister's office has been on. They want to meet the Chief Executives of all of the oil companies. I have my own contacts in the Minister's office and, through them, I've been able to find out that the Minister is mainly concerned with supply, and particularly Saudi supply."

"What did you tell them?"

"That you had gone to the Gulf to personally check out the situation, and that you would contact them on your return."

"Okay, what is our stock situation like?"

"It's as you instructed, Ed; I've got it down to ten days supply. We can't go any lower. As you know, we've got to report our month-end stocks to the Department each month. It's causing concern. They're associating our low stocks with the overall situation in Iraq and Venezuela, and they want to know how these problems can affect us with our Saudi supply. We haven't given any answer, but I expect when they know you're back, they'll be looking for an early meeting with you."

"What's crude oil at now on the New York exchange?"

Bergin tapped into his laptop computer.

"Okay, it says near-month crude oil futures dropped another 5% to $28.85 per barrel. It'll probably drop lower as the Americans bring the production up to full capacity," he added.

Ed was tempted to inform the team of his discussion with Saeef Baqr, and his predictions of immediate and ongoing turmoil in Iraq, and in the area generally. This, however, was not part of the Irish agenda, and without the rest, would be meaningless. As far as the team was concerned, Global's supply source was Saudi Arabia and would continue to be. As was usual, Brant had signed a confidentiality agreement with Papandreou to keep corporate issues separate, and not disclose them to anyone, including his own management team.

"How much rental storage have you been able to buy in?"

"We're now just about two hundred thousand tonnes, one hundred and twenty in Rotterdam, and the rest between the U.K. and Germany. Then we've kept our operating stocks at thirty thousand below normal."

"Good. I reckon the price of crude will rise to about $50, so that gives us a premium of about $20 a barrel, which is about $150 a tonne. Carrying costs will depend on how long we hold it, but we've a huge margin. We can't lose. We should net twenty to twenty-five million euro before tax."

The others nodded agreement.

"Okay, let's see if we can fill it at today's quote for Brent crude in Northwest Europe. Tom, start looking around for the best refining deal you can get. I think with the shortage of refining capacity in the United States, the margin on refined products will widen, so it might be in our interest to sell it as products."

He adjourned the meeting.

No mention had been made of the Management Excellence Award, and Patricia had not said a word.

————◆•◆•◆————

In considering what response he should make to the government officials, Ed was fully aware that oil companies were not required to hold strategic stocks themselves, but were expected to hold a prudent level of operating stocks. It was obvious, from the contact by the Minister's office, that some official had noticed from Global's monthly return that its stock levels were at an exceptionally low level, and was probably concerned that now, with over thirty percent of the Irish market, Global was experiencing supply difficulties which would have national implications.

He didn't want any hassle from the government, so he thought it prudent to return their call.

He had always found the officials of the Department of Energy to be very conscientious and competent and, while these had been attributes he had admired in the past, he was a little apprehensive on this occasion. He had received every assistance in avoiding Competition Authority problems with the Anglo Oil acquisition, and was embarrassed that they would associate the low level of operational stocks reported with a perceived difficulty in supplying the combined businesses. He recalled the Minister confidently accepting his assurance at the time, that Global's Saudi source of supply was unaffected by the problems elsewhere in the world. It would not help Global's relationship with the government if the opposition, particularly Pat Robert, the leader of the Labour Party, thought the company had a problem. For some reason, he had been particularly vociferous in his opposition to the merger, and in his criticism of the government for letting it through.

Instead of dealing with the issue by phone, Ed elected to visit the officials in their office in Dublin. He thought the courtesy would help. His temporary secretary made an appointment with the top civil servant. He knew Matthew Brennan, Secretary General of the Energy Department. He had had previous dealings with him, but generally only of a courtesy nature. It was hard to judge his age—fiftyish, Ed guessed. He was one of these people with honesty almost engraved on a craggy face that sheltered under a mop of dark brown wavy hair. He had been a heavy smoker, before smoking was banned in offices and all public places, but was still often seen with an unlit pipe in the corner of his mouth. "Helps the concentration," he would explain in the remnants of his West Cork accent. His subordinates knew different. When that pipe appeared they should disappear. It was generally the harbinger of a 'bollicking' for whatever unfortunate didn't recognise the signals. Ed was taken up to his office on the top floor of the departmental office block. Brennan remained seated behind a huge desk that bore the ink stains and scratches of another era. Apart from the desk and a couple of chairs, and what seemed like dozens of files in various states of usage, there was nothing else in the room—nothing, that is, except that infamous pipe, which seemed a natural extension of the mouth that caressed it.

Matthew Brennan got straight to the point. As was usual, every word he uttered, he attributed to the Minister.

"The Minister himself asked me to check with you as to why your operational stocks have been abnormally low over the past two months and, last month, were at an all-time low of only ten days' supply. We would have thought that you would have made arrangements to ensure high stocks, particularly in view of the uncertainty in the world, not to mention the assistance given to you recently by the Minister."

Ed was a little taken aback at the absence of introductory small talk but reckoned an equally assertive response was called for.

"I understand any concern the Minister might have, and I have come over here to personally assure you that we have no supply problems. The dip in our stock figures is just a slight aberration in our system. I reviewed the situation only this morning, and our operations people are on top of it. This month you'll find that we will almost have full tanks."

There was no respite. In fact, the Cork dimension to Brennan's accent seemed to take over, and the speed of the dialogue increased exponentially.

"That's good. As you know," he said, "we keep in touch with the situation through the IEA. They tell us that OPEC have committed to making good any loss in supply due to Iraq, and that there will be no need to draw on our strategic reserves. Do you see any problem on the horizon?"

"Well, OPEC have increased their official production quotas by one million barrels a day to twenty-four and a half million. We know that they are actually producing at a higher level; they need the revenues. So it looks as if they intend to prevent any crisis, except perhaps in the price of crude."

"Price could obviously become a major concern, but right now it's secondary to supply. Do you see any problems that could affect supply in the future?"

"Yes, there are many. You've got unprecedented demand coming out of China and India; you've got Venezuelan production still affected by their prolonged strike; you've got the U.S. diverting supplies to build up their commercial stocks; you've got the problems in the Niger Delta Region which have cut Nigeria's output by about forty percent, and then you have Iraq. Last week its oil exports were down by a massive seventy five percent on the previous week."

Brennan's stare was unflinching, and the sound of the dry sucking seemed to punctuate his words. The pipe remained firmly in place.

"Jaysus, it sounds catastrophic! Is Saudi Arabia affected? I understand you visited that country last week. It was that news that set our alarm bells ringing."

"My visit was routine. I needed to see their situation first-hand."

"I hope you were reassured. Do you anticipate problems? We detect, and our colleagues in Foreign Affairs have confirmed, a growing anti-Americanism in the Kingdom. Is it likely to affect your supply?"

"I can't see into the future, but yes, I was concerned at the atmospherics. However, the greatest security we have on supply is that all of the producing states, Saudi in particular, desperately need the oil revenue, and regardless of politics, they need Western markets."

He removed the pipe and surreptitiously looked around the office. When he was satisfied it was clear, he continued.

"I shouldn't say this, even though I know the confidence will be respected, but our Foreign Affairs colleagues are concerned as to whether the House of Saud will survive. If some bloody fundamentalist group, headed by the likes of bin Laden, got into power, then pragmatism may not apply, and the oil may stop coming in this direction. Even a temporary dislocation could be a disaster for this country."

"Isn't that what you've got the International Energy Agency for—to deal with such crisis situations and share available supplies? In any event, I could not see the Americans letting a vital interest be affected to that degree. Apart from that, I don't see what we, as a commercial enterprise can do, except hope sense will prevail and the oil continues to flow."

He adopted a shocked expression.

"As a sovereign government, we can't live in hope. We have to act. Does Global have any contacts with the Russians?"

Ed was taken aback by the question. He was aware that Papandreou had had talks with Mikhail Khodorkovsky, the major shareholder of Yukos, the largest oil company in Russia. He had been told this in strict confidence, and had suspected that it was in some way connected with Papandreou's request that he visit Russia. Apart from the once, however, he had not referred to it again.

Ed thought he'd explore further.

"Well, yes, we've had some talks. In fact, I'll be going to Moscow shortly. We're at an exploratory stage in our negotiations. Any help you can give us will be appreciated."

"I was thinking of perhaps getting the Irish National Petroleum Corporation to visit them. But maybe that's duplication. Maybe it would even be seen as competition and put the price up. Yes, we can certainly make the introductions at official level. Let's know when you're going and what you want us to do."

Ed promised to do that, and hoped that admitting what he knew to be highly sensitive information would not cause problem for whatever Papandreou was trying to do. He was, however, getting a little bit tired of finding out Papandreou's Global strategy by chance encounter.

Despite the grilling, Ed really respected a man who was completely unfazed by the size of Global Oil, and despite his eccentricity, Brennan was capable of handling the nation's affairs in any company. He would be a very useful ally.

---

John Brant was dreading the visit to the bank. He could sell and he knew it, but finances—well, they just baffled him. He had concluded long before his session with his financial advisor, Larry Rudder, that he wanted to quit. The losses had continued, and he was spending less and less time in the office. The company had exceeded its overdraft facility, and now the bank was exerting pressure, both on the company and on him personally. Business was certainly not his forte, and the possibility, put forward by Larry, of selling his share of the company certainly seemed to be the solution that would address his increasing financial problems. Unfortunately, he was relying on Larry to produce a potential buyer and, so far, this had not happened.

He was confident coming in, but that was slipping. *What have I to lose? It was going down the tubes anyway. Unless I can get this geezer to give me a long-term loan. If that happens, maybe things will improve. Jaysus, I'm glad I took the time again to dress the part.* The suit hadn't been out since his meeting with Larry Rudder. For all the good it did then. *Maybe it needed to be pressed. I should have had my hair cut before I came in—these "suits" like conformity.* Still, he did shave, and although he would have liked a bit more, there was just enough gel left in the jar to keep his hair in place.

"Have you approached the oil companies? asked Andrew Chapman, Manager of the Bank of Ireland, where Brantoil banked and where John himself had his overdraft?

"No, I haven't. The problem is that I only own one third of the company. As you know, Ed, my brother, who is the top man in Global Oil, also owns a third and, naturally enough, would hardly agree to allow a competitor to supply us, so none would be interested in investing."

"Have you considered asking your brother, Ed, to get Global to buy Brantoil?"

"He's in the States at the moment, and I hear he's off to Russia after that. I haven't been able to talk to him."

Chapman looked at him quizzically. "Does he not have a mobile?"

John said nothing. How do you tell a stranger that your brother is too busy to talk to you? Apart from that, he had caught his own reflection in the glass door of the bookcase behind Chapman. He looked a real geek. There was Chapman in front of him, with his own reflected image alongside, as if they were buddies at a convention or something. Chapman looked like Chapman; baldy head and glasses. He didn't know who he looked like; certainly no one any of his friends would recognise or want to know. He began to feel a bit giggly. What was the point? This was not for him, and his brothers didn't give a shit.

"John, we've done business with you and your father before you, and with your company, Brantoil, for as long as I've been with the bank. But you've got financial problems that I don't believe will disappear. Even the company is now in the red for the first time in my experience. You've been advised to sell, but you're now telling me that there's no market interest in your share. You've got very little option but to get your brothers to agree to sell the company as a unit without any restriction on supply. Otherwise, I'm afraid that the next time we talk, we'll be into legalities. I'd hate that to happen."

"Well, Dad, at least you know I've tried," he said quietly as he left the bank.

He dialled Ben. Maybe he could persuade Ed to join them for a game of golf when he would sound them both out on the sale possibility. He wouldn't let on, of course, but it was the entrance fee to the golf club that had provoked the call by the bank. Still, he was beyond caring. He'd done his best to carry on the family tradition, more than his two brothers had done. He'd even invite O'Raghallaigh along to make up the four-ball. He seemed to have more pull with both of his brothers now than he had. He smiled sardonically. *What would Dad have thought?*

---

Even though the outcome was far more than Ben Brant had hoped for, even in his most optimistic moments, he had a tinge of regret that he had to manipulate Ed. He hated himself for the way he did it—by forcing Ed to eat humble pie and hire O'Raghallaigh as a consultant. He knew that Ed, temperamentally, was not suited to emotionally-charged industrial relations scenes, and he would have exacerbated an already bad situation. On the other hand, he marvelled at the way Jim O'Raghallaigh had handled both sides, the way he got them to listen to one another, and then to work to find a solution that was better than compromise. It was a pity, for Ed's sake, that he had not been present to see a master at work. He resolved that, somehow, he would get the two of them together in a relaxed atmosphere, and perhaps they could find a way to work together without the need for a referee. He was convinced that Ed would benefit enormously from the cool, clear logic that O'Raghallaigh seemed to bring to all situations.

The opportunity presented itself sooner than he expected. His brother, John, called him on his mobile. Ben was driving along the motorway at the time and couldn't take the call just then. He hated not being available to his younger brother. It was not often he called, so when he did, it meant he had a problem. At the first opportunity he pulled into a filling station forecourt and called John back.

"Listen Ben," he started. "I've got the opportunity of membership of the Glen of the Downs Golf Club. It's not often that membership vacancies arise so I'm thinking of taking it up. It costs a few quid though, and before spending that sort of money I'd like to try the course and get your opinion. What do you think? Would you be on?"

Ben had played golf socially but never had the time, the inclination, or indeed the money to join a club and play with any regularity. His opinion on the comparative quality of the course would be next to useless. He was, however, amazed at the request. He knew that Glen of the Downs, like the other County Wicklow clubs of Powerscourt and Druids Glen, cost a small fortune to join, and then there was a high annual membership fee. He didn't think that Brantoil would be making the sort of money that would allow John that level of lifestyle. Certainly the periodic profit statements that he got, as a one-third shareholder, generally showed less than a break-even position after paying John a less-than-reasonable salary. He was curious to know the source of John's good fortune, whatever about the golf. Without waiting for a reply, John continued:

"I'd really like you to come. I was thinking of asking Ed and also Jim O'Raghallaigh, if he's available."

That sold it. Ben promptly accepted. John seemed delighted and promised to phone back with the tee-time, as soon as he had contacted Ed and O'Raghallaigh.

His tone was more subdued when he did phone back.

"Surprise, surprise," he said sarcastically. "Guess what; it'll have to be a three-ball. Ed is too busy preparing for some fuckin' meeting he's got in New York. He says he can't make it this time, to call him again. It'll be a long time before that fuckin' happens."

———◆•◆•◆———

Ed Brant felt exhilarated as he walked briskly down Fifth Avenue. The morning was chilly but sunny, and despite a forecast on the Weather Channel of tornado conditions in the Gulf moving north, there was certainly no sign of it, as the early morning New Yorkers set about their business. Life was good.

*Today is special*, he mused as he strode along. *If only Dad could see me now. Here I am, by far the youngest member of the Strategy Coordination Committee of Global Oil Inc., its newest member, and today I'm going to address the committee on its core strategy. Alright for a failure, eh, Dad?*

There was an added bounce to his stride as he recalled his rehearsals in front of the mirror in his hotel bedroom. Yes, he had really looked the part. That extra weight he was carrying suited him, but he realised he'd have to get back to his gym work and get some medication for that bloody heartburn. The two went together. He wondered if Patricia had forgotten what it was that had caused their row. Still, just in case, he'd go to the doctor back home as soon as he got the time.

He arrived at Global Towers. Was there a note of deference in the attitude of the other committee members, as they stood around the buffet breakfast table that was the usual prelude to these early morning meetings? This was very different. Although no one mentioned it specifically, it was obvious that his inclusion on the meeting agenda gave him a newly-acquired status as a Papandreou confidante. The others seemed to gravitate in his direction—seemed somehow to be more attentive to his views.

At eight a.m. exactly, they filed into the large meeting room. The seats were arranged theatre-style. It was obviously to be more of a presentation-type address than a round table discussion. *Christ, this is not what I expected.* The formality of the occasion unsettled him. Why, he didn't know. He had spoken in similar circumstances before. But maybe not to an audience that had the power of life or death as these guys had. *Jesus, I hope I don't make a bloody fool of myself. I should have prepared better. I should have prepared a script and some overhead slides at least. Though I did alright this morning. Yeah, this morning was okay. Just relax, Ed, for Chrissake. Everything will be alright. If only this bloody heartburn would ease up.* He looked around. Papandreou was not in the room. That only added to his sense of panic. After five or six minutes an audible hush occurred, as the doors opened and the great man made his way to the lectern. *I'd better sit up in one of the front seats, so that I'll be ready and won't have so far to walk. A glass of water will settle my nerves.*

Papandreou's stride was slow and deliberate. Ed had seen him address audiences previously. He was a past master at public speaking. He rarely used notes, and this occasion was no different. He stood there and just looked down on his audience. Every eye was focused. Every mind was concentrated. When at last he spoke, he was as a conductor, except it was not musical notes he was orchestrating, it was the emotions of almost thirty hardened businessmen. This was a keynote address. Every word would be carefully selected, every cadence and every pause deliberate, to give credence and urgency to his message. Within minutes he would have his audience totally captivated.

"I won't pull any punches in discussing the situation as we find it today." He stopped for emphasis and stared again at his audience.

"You will recall the strategy we discussed at the previous meeting, as approved by the main board." Again he gave that pause and that challenging look.

"We talked about price management, about leaving nothing to chance. We talked about the necessity of ensuring that periods of high crude oil prices on the world's markets, would be followed by periods of low or lower prices, so that the consumer nations will not be prompted to accelerate the search for alternative energy sources, or to permanently adopt conservation policies that will indent our future earnings capability. Periods of major profitability will be followed by brief periods of lower earnings, so that the consuming states revert to the comfort zone of complacency."

When he knew he had their full attention, he continued.

"As with all market-led pricing, the price of crude oil will respond to events, whether real or perceived. We understand all of these price prompters to the extent that we can control them. We can now turn them on or off, almost at will."

Ed couldn't believe that Papandreou would be openly advocating and admitting to market manipulation, but that's exactly what he was doing, and all those listening would be well aware that that was what had brought about the downfall of Enron. There was a stir amongst some members of the audience, but Papandreou didn't seem to notice.

"There are so many price drivers working for us now that we don't have to do too much ourselves. The producing states desperately need higher prices. Saudi Arabia has had very serious budget deficits. The very survival of the House of Saud is at stake. Their unemployment is running in the region of fifteen to twenty percent. They were expecting a budget deficit of ten billion dollars this year. Needless to say, they did not need too much encouragement to take the opportunity of turning this deficit into a surplus of approximately twelve billion."

He stopped, and Ed was sure that he was deliberately looking in his direction.

"We know that despite their own public statements and those of OPEC, they are restricting output to the level that they agreed with us. That's the reality, but that reality is also being helped with the anxiety they are causing through their domestic security policy and official statements. We all know that an atmosphere of supply insecurity is so vital in keeping the price high. All in all, they seem to be doing a first-class job, and coupled with our worldwide stock building policies, it looks as if we have the price situation well in hand. Unfortunately, those other elements of strategy that we have not had direct control of, are not working as well."

He paused again and scanned the audience with those challenging eyes. The morning sun glinted off his glasses, giving him a satanic look. His smile, undoubtedly intended to be embracing, just added to his demonic appearance.

"We forecasted fifty-dollar-a-barrel crude for the middle of 2004. This will be exceeded. At that stage, the military operations in Iraq were scheduled to have been well and truly completed, when enough Iraqi oil could have been released onto the market to dampen this high price, well before the Presidential election."

He reached again for his glass, but his eyes scanned the audience as he drank. He hesitated again, and it was obvious that the main point of the presentation was imminent. His voice rose by several decibels, his fists punched the air for emphasis, and a new passion came into his speech.

"I haven't told you anything new. This is the strategy we developed at our last meeting, which has since been approved by the board. Well, there is a new concern. Our own intelligence, and Ed Brant's recent visit, is enough to give us concern that maybe the military operation in Iraq will not be as smooth as the Pentagon has told us. I have to tell you, gentlemen, that, based on all of the information coming to me, I believe that Iraq is faced with civil war, and that its oil industry will not be operational for many years to come."

Papandreou stopped and scanned his audience. Brant had come to recognise this as a tactic to ensure undivided attention. He was about to drop one of his heart-stoppers.

"We were in the process of abandoning Saudi Arabia as our core source in favour of a Global Oil-controlled Iraqi oil industry.

Gentlemen, we now know that this will not be as easily achieved as we were led to believe by the administration."

He then proceeded as if he had not said anything of monumental proportions.

"We had made the decision in favour of Iraq in the belief that the Saudi regime would soon be overthrown, and replaced by Islamic fundamentalists sympathetic to Osama bin Laden. If we let this happen then we will find that their primary ambition is not domestic improvements, but to inflict as much damage as possible on the U.S. and on the Western economy. Gentlemen, with Iraq in chaos we can't sit back and wait for this to happen. We've got to get back with the State Department and the Pentagon to ensure that our traditional source of supply is secured."

Several members of the committee were on their feet. Papandreou ignored them. He used his microphone to effectively drown out the dissenters.

"So that we all have a clear understanding of the nature of our options, I asked my local sources to report to me on the security of the Saudi Arabian oil infrastructure. I also asked your colleague, Ed Brant, to do a similar exercise on his recent visit. His conclusions were very similar. Before we get into that, does anyone have any questions?"

David Coleman, the Chief Executive of Global Oil U.K., was first to speak.

"Unfortunately, I missed the previous meeting; otherwise I would have had a lot to say then on the strategy you've just outlined. I was aware, of course, of the strategy on stock building. That's fair enough; that's prudent management. If you expect the price to rise, well, you buy as much as you can before it does. But we're not just doing that, are we? We're actually manipulating the market to make it rise! Is that not illegal? Is that not what Enron is being prosecuted for? Secondly, what about the moral aspect?

What about the effect of this oil price on the global economy, and the thousands of jobs that will be lost as a result?"

Ed could sense the tension in the room and the change in tone in Papandreou's voice. It a reminded him of the session he had with himself and Jim O'Raghallaigh in the Churchill Hotel in London, just prior to his trip to Saudi Arabia, when O'Raghallaigh had also put forward some moral considerations. He had an involuntary flashback to that meeting—to the princely Arab that Papandreou had been talking to before he joined himself and O'Raghallaigh. He had thought that his desert host, Prince bin Jiluwi, looked familiar. Was it? - could it possibly have been, the same man? Papandreou was replying to Coleman.

"David. I'm sorry you didn't attend the last meeting, but you'll understand that we can't cover that ground again. However, let me reassure you that advanced economies such as ours—that is, the U.S. and the U.K.—are far less sensitive to oil costs now than they were at the time of the last crisis. I'm not saying, of course, that energy costs don't matter any more. What I am saying is, that it's far less crucial to their economic performance than it was thirty years ago. Even on the basis of inflation alone, the comparable price would have to be about eighty dollars. We're not talking about anything like that."

With a gesture of resignation, David Coleman sat down.

Tom Roden, the President of Global Oil, North American Petroleum Operations, who was sitting next to Ed Brant, was the next to speak.

"Dino, you didn't fully answer David. I was at that last meeting. I didn't quite pick up what I'm picking up now. I now see price manipulation, but not just that. I see an alignment with the military to the extent that we're almost part of the invasion of Iraq, for the purposes of controlling the supply and the price of crude oil. I don't think it was ever put forward as a strategy in such stark terms. We're a commercial organisation, not an arm of the government."

Papandreou was obviously fuming. He was almost shouting.

"I'm not about to redo the last meeting. The strategy I outlined was as approved by resolution of the main board. That is history and is not open to debate by this committee. We're here to consider new information, and whether we need to make a further recommendation to the main board, to alert the company to the fact that Iraq may take longer than expected, and that, in the meantime, our supplies from Saudi Arabia may be in jeopardy because of the deteriorating situation in that country."

Obviously, realising that he was losing his audience, he resumed his tone of reasoned logic, but it now took on a note of condescension.

"But Tom, let me put the whole matter in perspective for you. We're not invading Iraq, as you have put it. Rather, as a commercial enterprise, we're taking advantage of its fallout. That's our job. That's our responsibility to our shareholders. Yes, it is serious business. We're talking about billions of dollars, and we're talking about our bonuses and stock options."

Seeing that he had regained the high ground, Papandreou again stopped for emphasis, and then—

"Even in your operation in North America the numbers are staggering. America consumes about twenty million barrels of oil every day. A ten-dollar increase in price amounts to seventy five billion dollars. It's not significant in economic terms. We don't import all of our oil. As you know, about forty percent comes from our own oil wells. So that means thirty billion of the increase goes to the U.S. oil companies that own these wells. Your operation happens to manage eighteen percent of those wells, so in a full year your bottom line would improve by about five and a half billion dollars before tax. Yes, Tom, it's big league stuff, and we're all in the kitchen."

He again paused to symbolically embrace the entire group with outstretched arms.

"That level of earnings is unprecedented for this company and any other oil company. We're the ones who are making it happen, and we're the ones who will benefit through cash bonuses and stock options, based on those unprecedented numbers."

He stopped again, challenging his audience.

"Any other comments?" he asked.

"Good," he said, and without really waiting for a response. "We'll get on with the rest of the presentation."

"I'll ask Ed Brant, whom you all know, and a guest, Tim Savage, a former CIA operative and military strategist, to very briefly outline the options open to the U.S. to protect this vital interest."

The weather had changed. Ed could see that storm clouds were gathering as he passed the windows on his way to the lectern. Storm clouds were also evident in the room. There was a lot of muttering from the usually compliant committee members. He took the place where the great man had stood only seconds before.

It was then his mobile rang.

Ed stood there in disbelief. *Surely it's not mine; it can't be. I turned it off. Or did I?* It continued to ring. The sound had been drowned by the muttering and movement in the room. Not any more. A hush had descended. He grappled with his jacket buttons to get into the damn phone. *Play it cool*, he told himself. He found the phone, and with a calmness he didn't feel, prepared to turn it off. He saw the screen. *Jesus, it's Patricia.* She had never phoned him since their break-up. *What'll I do? I can't talk to her, not now. But I just can't cut her off.*

"Hello, Ed." He heard that low, sensual, Irish-American lilt that burrowed into his soul.

"Jesus, Patricia, I can't talk to you. Not now." Before he realised what he was doing he had pressed the red button. The phone went dead. He pressed the off button and replaced the phone in his pocket. He desperately tried to regain his composure. He looked down over the sea of faces. The previous solemnity was now well and truly disolved. Papandreou's eyes were boring into him. His chest ached. *Continue as if nothing has happened,* he told himself. *Jesus, why didn't I prepare a formal presentation?* He looked around. Fortunately there was a map of the Middle East hanging on the wall—obviously the remnants of a previous session in the room. With relief he used that as his crutch.

"Well, gentlemen, I'm no expert, but I did look at the oil fields recently from the standpoint of a terrorist attack. I had the use of a helicopter and free access. I was able to view the entire area."

Ed felt his composure return. He moved to the map with a pointer that had been left on the rostrum.

"More than half of the Saudi oil reserves are in eight fields within a very concentrated area of the Persian Gulf. You can see it here," he said, pointing to the Gulf coast region of eastern Saudi Arabia. "They include the giant Ghawar field, the world's largest with about half of Saudi Arabia's total, and Safiniya, the world's largest offshore oilfield. The Saudi oil is piped from these locations through the huge processing facility here at Abqaiq, and then on to one of two terminals, Ras al-Ju'aymah or Ras Tanura. From there the oil is pumped out to offshore loading platforms in the deep water of the Gulf for shipment to the United States, Europe, and Asia."

He stole a glance at the sea of faces. The signs of merriment had certainly gone and were replaced by what he interpreted as perplexity. *What is this all about?* He could read their thoughts. *Vulnerability!* He was supposed to be talking about the region's vulnerability.

"The real vulnerability seems to be at Abqaiq, which handles two-thirds of the country's oil output. If this facility was disabled for any period of time, it would mean a loss of approximately one third of America's daily consumption of crude oil. It would be a disaster, particularly with the Iraqi production still curtailed."

Yeah, even Papandreou looks interested.

"The facilities themselves are heavily guarded, but the concentration of the main infrastructure in such a confined area, makes the entire Saudi oil industry vulnerable to a spectacular attack of September 11 proportions. As I said at the start, the fact that I, and presumably anyone else, can get within striking distance of the world's most important energy supply source is a most alarming security gap."

Ed had concluded and awaited questions with a good deal of apprehension. There were none. He looked out over the audience and sensed a level of disgust and hostility like never before.

Tim Savage took the microphone. His southern drawl seemed to resonate and dampen the mutinous spirit that had enveloped the room.

"The threat to the Saudi oil infrastructure is more likely to come from inside the country than without. The September 11th bombers were mostly Saudi nationals, led by a member of one of the most influential of Saudi families. Yeah, I know the Saudis own the oil facilities in their country, but let's not forget that their protection is in the vital interest of those consuming nations that are dependent on the continued availability of the oil at a reasonable price. If the Saudis cannot be relied upon to maintain a proper level of security over an issue of such vital concern to the U.S. and the industrialised countries of the West, then we have a moral right—indeed an obligation, a duty—to intervene.

"Inland Saudi Arabia is of no interest and largely uninhabited. Apart from the holy cities of Mecca and Medina, it's nothing but sand. Those cities were taken from the Jordanians less than a century ago and can be handed back. The Coalition forces would just have to concentrate on the defense of a very defendable stretch of coastline that is no longer than about four hundred miles. I'm talking about this narrow strip of coastal Saudi Arabia stretching from the Iraqi border down through Kuwait to Qatar."

Savage, in true Papandreou style, paused for a few seconds. In the charged atmosphere, it seemed like minutes. He wanted to allow the impact of what he was saying to percolate his audience. He eventually continued. His words, delivered at almost a shout, were interspersed with pauses to provide emphasis.

"That area holds about forty percent of the world's oil reserves."

The audience was clearly shocked. Ed knew he had been used. His observations were not important. What was important was that he had been able to get so close to the oil installations. This was being used as the justification for war.

Tom Roden tipped him on the shoulder.

"I think you and I should talk. I'll be having a drink later with David Coleman: I'd like to talk to you after that."

"Why, Tom? What about?"

"We're all on the banks of our own Rubicons. It'll be a foolish man who tries to cross."

As Papandreou had said, they were all in the kitchen. Ed Brant was feeling the heat.

———◆———

The walk back to the Waldorf was a different experience. Ed Brant's mood had changed. That feeling of optimism—the feeling that he had really arrived in the big time, that had put a bounce in his step only five hours previously—had noticeably gone as he retraced those steps along Fifth Avenue. Even nature seemed to be in sympathy with his doleful mood. That blue sky and sunshine, which had done much to lift his spirits that morning, were now replaced with darkening clouds and a gloomliness that seemed to ominously suggest that his world had somehow changed forever.

He had decided to skip the arranged lunch after the meeting ended, and to walk back to the Waldorf to sort out his head. It was spinning. *What was happening? What was the real purpose of his trip to Saudi Arabia? Was it to check up on bin Jiluwi?* Ed was now convinced that that Arab sheik was on Papandreou's payroll and had the job of scaring the living daylights out of visiting oil traders and the like. Through him, Global could maintain apprehension regarding the continuing availability of oil and, in that way, keep the price up. Sure, didn't Papandreou admit that in his presentation? If that was the case it was certainly effective. But what about the Iraqi national, Saeef Baqr, that he had met on that unscheduled visit to the Ghawer oil field? *No! He had to be genuine. Papandreou was definitely concerned when I told him of the possibility of a spillover of the Iraqi violence into the oil region of Saudi Arabia. It was after I told him about that conversation, that he instructed me to survey the security arrangements of the Saudi oil infrastructure. I wonder was bin Jiluwi instructed to facilitate the aerial survey, or was the fact that I was not intercepted a real lapse in security?* The thought lingered like a leech. *Could the unmarked helicopter have been seen as a potential terrorist attack and shot down? Did Papandreou recklessly put my life at risk in order to help him muster support for his strategy change? Would he do such a thing? Would big business?* The answer frightened him. Sure, wasn't the whole purpose to start another war?—so what value would be put on one life ... his life?

*If Papandreou has his 'ears' in the Saudi desert, well, then he certainly has them in Ireland. It has to be Bergin. Who else would have the level of detail that seemed to be filtering back. I'll have to be careful with that bastard—but then maybe I can use him. Two can play that game, Mister Papandreou!*

He had reached East 51st Street. The reassuring spires of St. Patrick's Cathedral loomed ahead. Unthinkingly, he drifted inside and took a back pew. He hadn't been in a church for years. He found it comforting and safe. There were some worshippers, but mainly tourists. He looked at those in the pews ahead, sitting motionless. He wondered why they were there. Were they troubled like him? *But why should I feel such guilt?*

The only two in the meeting room who didn't seem to have any misgivings about what was happening were Tim Savage and Papandreou. Savage he could understand. As a former CIA agent he came from a world of subterfuge. To Papandreou, intrigue seemed to be second nature. David Coleman and Tom Roden, the two most senior executives of the group, were clearly unhappy, and Brant would have given anything to have been a fly on the wall wherever they were having their chat. But the rest of the group he couldn't fathom. They clearly were not enthused, to say the least, at the prospect of being associated with such a drastic solution to Papandreou's perception of a problem, but they were still not prepared to put their jobs, stock options, and bonuses on the line by objecting. There had been a clear change in atmosphere when Papandreu talked about the huge profits that Global would earn this year, and the 'unprecedented' cash bonuses and stock options that would flow from it. *I'm sure it was much the same in the Enron boardroom when those guys planned the manipulation of the Californian electricity prices. None of them spoke up. I'd say they regret it now.*

He looked to the roof, hundreds of feet above where he sat, no doubt witness to countless world-shaping occasions. *In fairness, the circumstances were very different. In Enron's case it was pure and simply corporate greed. Global's motivation in all of this was patriotic, to support the vital interest of the United States. This was fundamentally different. If Global, uniquely positioned to foresee a crisis, made a recommendation that the government took up, and then responded to a request to operate the oil fields, its executives were just doing their patriotic duty, while discharging their moral and legal responsibilities to their shareholders. The fact that the company would make billions of dollars for its shareholders was justification enough. Wasn't it the moral duty, and indeed, the legal responsibility of its directors to put the interests of the shareholders above all else? Wasn't that what that eminent economist that Papandreou had quoted, confirmed? If its executives made millions as a result, it was not a reason for guilt or objection.* Yes, he breathed easily again. He had his conscience sorted; he'd support Papandreou. *I wonder which side my father would have been on.* With Patricia he had no doubts. She would be strongly on the side of Coleman and Roden, and immoveable. But maybe he'd phone her and find out. *Jesus, Patricia!* He'd forgotten all about her phone call that he had so peremptorily cut off. He hurriedly left the hallowed portals of the cathedral, and within minutes was entering the elevator to his room on the sixth floor of the Waldorf Astoria.

———————◆•◆•◆———————

Ed Brant had heard that Papandreou was meeting David Coleman that evening for dinner. Remembering his own evening with Papandreou, he wondered if Coleman was about to get the 21 Club treatment. It would be Papandreou's style to pressure Coleman privately. Everyone knew he didn't tolerate dissenters. No doubt, Roden would be next. Recalling that penetrating stare, Ed didn't envy either of them. He himself had been asked to meet with Papandreou the following morning for a routine business review. Based on Papandreou's mood, he was very glad he had the evening clear, although he had excellent news to report on all divisions of the Irish operation. He'd also phone Patricia, but first he needed to collect his thoughts.

He looked at his watch—3:15. *I must have been the guts of two hours in the cathedral. It seemed like twenty minutes. It's eight back home. I'll have a quick lunch, collect my thoughts, and phone Patricia.* How he longed to hear her voice and feel the cool clarity of her thinking blowing the smoke from his brain. *I hope she understands. Why didn't I take the time to explain where I was when she phoned?* The memory of the occasion flooded back. *No! That was not a possibility.* He could hardly stifle a grin at the thought of Papandreo's reaction if his protégé started taking personal calls from his girlfriend during the middle of a presentation. *No, that definitely would not have been on. Patricia, of all people, will understand.*

She answered immediately.

"What's wrong, Ed?" He noticed the anxiety in her voice. No sign of the old tension or hurt. *Great,* he thought.

"Nothing at all, Patricia, just thought I'd call and apologise for earlier. Really, I just want to see how you are." He spoke tentatively.

"I'm fine.  Sorry if I got you at a bad time. I shouldn't have phoned, Ed. I should have known you'd be too busy."

"No, you just got me at a bad time." He was tempted to elaborate, but left it at "the meeting was on when your call came through."

"Oh! I'm sorry. I knew I shouldn't have called. It could have waited. How was your meeting?"

Ed knew that she would be very aware of the confidentiality agreement that all corporate executives are required to sign. He desperately wanted to confide in her, and would have if only he could have been sure that she would not again be disappointed in him. After all, if he couldn't keep corporate business to himself, how could she trust him with her secrets? Still, he needed her.

"Not great. There's a lot of tension. I sometimes think that I'd be better off with a lower profile job at home."

"I thought that you really enjoyed the international scene. I thought that you were now getting the recognition you so badly wanted."

"So did I, and I suppose I am, but sometimes—"

"And today was one of those days?"

"Yes, it was. The worst!"

"Well, Ed, my mother used always tell me that 'behind the clouds the sun is shining.' Tomorrow will be better."

"Funny, my dad had a similar saying. 'After the rain comes the rainbow.' You know, Patricia, they must have had a good relationship and we're good together. Let's fix this stupid row. I'm really sorry for the hurt I caused. Can we put it behind us and get back to where we were?"

The silence was deafening.

"Ed—"

"Yes, Patricia! What is it? Why did you ring me today?"

"Ed, I love you very much, but Ed, we have to talk. There's something I have to tell you, but not now. I can't—not on the phone."

He could hardly believe what he was hearing. The problem with Papandreou seemed irrelevant. Bergin "the snout" didn't matter anymore. The sun was again shining in his life. What an extraordinary girl. Five minutes on the phone with her and he was ready to deal with the world.

"I'll be home in two days. I can't wait."

<hr />

"Jesus, it must have been the greatest giveaway of all time."

"Yes, but it wasn't seen as a giveaway—more a transfer of wealth. You gotta remember that under the Communist system the Russian people already owned the wealth of the country. This merely transferred it into what was hoped would be more efficient, individual ownership."

Norman Kem looked down at Ed Brant. In the half-light of the theatre, Brant again seemed absorbed in learning about an area of the world in which previously he had only a passing interest. This time Kem was relying on Sergie Kholodov, a Russian national and economist who was contributing in perfect, if heavily-accented, English.

"The scale of the transfer to the private sector and the short timescale in which it was to be done created a massive problem— almost chaos. Nearly all of Russia's natural resources were to be passed over, as were apartments, office blocks, department stores, and restaurants in an economy in which, previously, no free-market conditions or property ownership was tolerated."

Although it would not have been apparent to Kem, Ed's attention was wavering. It had been one of those nights. His brief conversation with Patricia had triggered memories that had kept him awake into the early hours. If he had known that his scheduled meeting with Papandreou was off, he could have made good use of the morning to catch up on his sleep, instead of skipping breakfast and rushing down Fifth Avenue to arrive, struggling, to recover his breath, and hiding the pain of his heartburn.

"I'm afraid Mister Papandreou has had to postpone your meeting," his secretary informed him when he reached the thirty-first floor. "He's got Mister Coleman with him now. It was unexpected. He suggested that you contact Norman Kem. He said you know him. He's head of the Corporate Affairs Department. Mister Papandreou will then see you immediately after lunch. He's aware that your flight to Dublin leaves at 20:10 from JFK. He told me to assure you that he'll have you there in plenty of time. Can I get Mister Kem on the phone for you?" she offered.

Of course he had agreed. What else could he do? You don't tell the Senior Vice-President of Petroleum Operations that a phone call would have been in order, that he could have done with a few extra hours sleep. Within seconds he was talking to Kem.

"Hi, Ed," he started. "You're becoming one of my best customers. Dino tells me you're off to Russia. Very interesting place is Russia. When are you off?"

"To be honest, Norman, I don't know. Dino mentioned it some time ago, but not since. I thought he'd forgotten."

"No, not Dino. He's like an elephant, he never forgets. If he doesn't mention something there is a reason, but not that he's forgotten. Not for as long as I know him, and that's a long time. Anyway, he told me that you did a fantastic job for him in Saudi Arabia. I like to think that it was due to our briefing, but maybe not. He told me that your Russian trip was imminent, and asked me to fit you in for a briefing this morning. I've changed things around a bit, so if you want to drop down to the fifteenth floor, I'll be glad to update you on Mr Khodorkovsky, who happens to be our main interest in modern-day Russia."

"Okay, Norman, I appreciate you fitting me in. I'll be right down."

Within minutes Ed sat in what was, to all intents and purposes, a private cinema with a capacity of about ten. On this occasion the audience was one. At a top table sat a young, bright, blonde but nervous Sergie Kholodov, who in addition to being competent in his subject was proving himself to be adept with the light dimmer and the projector.

"It all really started with Mikhail Gorbachev in the early 1990s. He was moving to fundamentally restructure industry, to make it viable in a free market environment. Boris Yelstin then accelerated the pace, demolished the old system, and launched a massive programme of privatisation as the basis of a new democratic society. His successor and appointee, Vladimir Putin, is continuing, attempting to provide consolidation and stability after a disruptive first decade of post-communist government."

Ed could see that he was being taken through a prepared presentation, although he had been invited to interrupt at will. For the moment, however, still resentful at the intrusion into what would otherwise have been a restful morning, he was content to keep in touch with the monotone and bask in the subdued light of the room.

*What did she mean when she said she had something to say to me?* He hoped she wasn't going to apologise. That was really up to him. It was he that had reacted stupidly. She had just been concerned about his health. *Christ, why didn't I go to the bloody doctor? That's the first question she'll ask, and then there's this extra weight. I'll need to get rid of that.*

He realised Kem had stopped talking. The two were looking at him. Had they asked him a question? He had no idea.

"I don't know a lot about Russia. With the breakup of the Soviet Union, was it—eh, left with natural resources of any scale?" He hoped the answer hadn't already been provided.

"Russia is blessed with natural resources. Only Saudi Arabia has more crude oil. That's probably where it all went wrong. Everything was to be privatised." There was no awkward pause. The question must have been okay. *I'll have to concentrate.*

"I know that the enormity of the task would have been problematic but, in general terms, was the privatisation a success from the Russian government's point of view?"

Sergei took over.

"No! Under the Soviet system, these state companies had the responsibility for social services in their regions. The private owners tried to shed these extremely costly services that were in no way connected with the business. They pushed hospitals, schools and tramways into the hands of local authorities that had little competence or money to take up the slack. Payment of public sector wages and pensions were seriously in arrears and reduced to miserable levels. By the mid-1990s the Russian government was in dire financial straits."

"The mid-1990s? That must have been about the time that it was rumoured that the Communists were regaining control. I remember reading about it at the time."

"Yeah. This was on the brink of the '96 elections when everyone was certain that the communists were going to win. Yelstin was getting ready to run for a second term and needed funds to pay wages and pension arrears, which otherwise would have cost him the election."

"Sounds familiar! We have tribunals in Ireland investigating the same sort of thing. How did he get over that? Political donations in brown paper bags?"

Kem looked at Kholodov and smiled.

"It would have taken more than brown paper bags, or sacks for that matter. We're not talking about millions, we're talking about hundreds of millions of dollars. As much as five hundred million dollars was secretly funnelled into Yelstin's campaign coffers, and the nation's newly privatatised newspapers and television networks were pressured to promote him."

Apart from a fleeting mental flash of Tom Bergin, dressed as Santa Claus with a sack over his shoulder, knocking on a Minister's door, Brant found these disclosures fascinating and was now fully in tune with the excitement of his presenters.

"Who had that sort of money? Did it come from the West?"

"No, not at all. A consortium of Russia's biggest private banks came together with the money needed to get Yelstin re-elected. As collateral, the state put up shares in the oil holding companies. These shares were worth far more—in some cases as much as a hundred times the value of the loans. The arrangement was that if the money was not repaid one year later, the shares could be sold off by auction, by the same banks to which the loan was owed."

"Was it ever repaid?"

"In reality, no repayment was intended. When the loans became due, the rules relating to the sale of the securities were constructed by the banks so as to exclude serious competition. No foreigners were allowed to take part, and a series of investment conditions left the selection of the winner to the discretion of the bankers that administered the auctions."

Ed noted the similarities with Papandreou's scheme to manipulate the price of crude oil, but was sure that these two guys would not be aware of the Machiavellian plans that were developed on the thirty-first floor.

Kem had been talking. It was now Kholodov's turn. The lights were dimmed once again, and a number of young men appeared on the screen. There was nothing particularly distinctive about them. They looked like any ordinary bunch of executives in any boardroom, except for one thing: They were all so young. Most looked as if they were in their early thirties.

"The principal beneficiaries of privatisation was this group of young bankers. Most had been in their late twenties and early thirties when the Soviet Union had fallen apart, and they moved swiftly to seize the opportunities that the free market economy presented. They emerged having secured ownership of some of the world's most valuable petroleum, natural gas, and metal deposits, resulting in the greatest transfer of wealth the world has ever seen. By 1997 five of those individuals, who became known as the 'Oligarchs', were on Forbes Magazine's list of the world's richest billionaires."

"Pity Global Oil couldn't have taken a piece of the action," Ed ventured.

"Sure was, but then there were no opportunities for any Western interests. The Oligarchs closed them off."

It was then back to Kem.

"But every cloud has a silver lining. It consolidated one man with whom we believe we can do business—Mikhail Khodorkovsky."

The reference to the cloud brought Ed out of Russia and back to the previous evening. Patricia had said something about a cloud. Oh, yes, he remembered it was something her mother used say—

something about the sun shining above the clouds. Jesus, how he wished he was there with her. The others were waiting.

"Was Mikhail Khodorkovsky one of the Oligarchs involved?" he asked.

Kholodov walked to the screen and pointed out a man of about forty, with pleasant features, sallow complexion, close-cropped hair, and rimless glasses. A single, enlarged shot of him appeared on the screen.

"The most notorious 'Loan for Share' deal was done by Khodorkovsky. He ended up acquiring a controlling interest in Yukos Oil, Russia's largest oil company, for a mere 309 million dollars—slightly above the amount of the loan. It has since been valued at between eight and ten billion dollars."

'How did Yelstin survive this scandal? Surely there was uproar when the ordinary Russians saw their country's natural resources being so blatantly pirated by these bankers?"

"Media opposition was stifled. Anatoly Chubais, a St. Petersburg economist who masterminded the scheme, maintained that it was of little importance who won the auctions or how much they paid. The aims were to prevent a reversion to Communism and to push the state companies into private hands. That would eliminate their continued mismanagement under public ownership and encourage a new class of entrepreneurs who would build and invest in the development of a capitalist economy in Russia."

"So Yelstin was off the hook, and the controversy was just to do with the possible manipulation of the price through rigged auctions?"

"Well, it was a bit more than that! The popular perception is that, in addition to the auction being rigged and the purchase price being ridiculously understated, the cash, which was given as a loan to Yelstin in the first instance, was in fact government money. This was cash that the bank had retained through the delay of payments to state creditors. At that time there was no treasury and state funds were held in these private banks. This was confirmed by a subsequent investigation by the Audit Chamber, the Russian Parliament's financial watchdog."

"What does Khodorkovsky say?"

"In fairness, Khodorkovsky advances a different perception. He has maintained that the government, for completely understandable reasons, made the decision to sell off a large industry because it did not pay taxes. It was on the brink of the '96 elections when everyone was certain that the Communists were going to win. They had firmly announced that any companies that were sold off would be renationalised and without compensation. So no investor would have paid a single dollar for the company."

"What do you think is the truth?" Ed asked.

"Well, Khodorkovsky has received substantial, even disproportionately negative, publicity for practices that were widespread amongst all of the Oligarchs at that time. There seems little doubt that he may have a point when he says that there was little or no investor interest because of the risk of the Communists returning and confiscating the shares. You've also got to remember that, prior to this, there were no companies in Russia as we know them, so there was no company law for the Oligarchs to break, even though, by our standards, they operated immorally."

As if on cue the lights went out.

The distinctive husky voice of Sergei, uttering something in Russian, came out of the darkness. It left Ed in no doubt that, regardless of its appropriateness in the context of what was being said, this particular piece of drama was definitely not on the agenda.

While Sergei struggled with his controls, Ed thought he would relieve his embarrassment by continuing his questioning.

"How are the Oligarchs accepted by Putin? Is he likely to undo the deals that were done under Boris Yelstin?"

The reply came out of the darkness.

"Well, the financial power of the Oligarchs secured Yelstin's re-election. Yelstin appointed Putin, so there should be some allegiance between Putin and the Oligarchs. It's true to say, however, that they were at the height of their power under Yelstin and times have changed. In July 2000, Putin convened a now-famous meeting at the Kremlin in which he told the Oligarchs that they could retain their acquired businesses but would no longer be allowed to meddle in politics. I believe he meant what he said. The vast majority agreed, and they are still wealthy and influential with connections to various levels of government."

Sergei gave up. He had switched on the main lights. He looked at Kem in deep embarrassment.

"I've a lot more to show on the key Kremlin personalities and the protocol. It shouldn't take me too long to have this fixed," he said sheepishly.

Ed was not aware of the specific mission that Papandreou had in mind. It obviously had to do with developing some business links with Khodorkovsky, but he had thought that he was handling this personally, as it had not been officially discussed at the Strategy Coordination Committee meeting. Yet, based on what he had just heard at that meeting, Papandreou seemed to have several strategies operating at the one time, which he seemed to drip feed to the committee when it suited him. He guessed that Papandreou, even at this stage, could very well have had negotiations at an advanced stage with the Russians.

He would soon know. Much to Sergei's obvious relief, Kem's secretary came in to tell him that Papandreou would see him at 2.30 p.m. and that Tom Roden, the President of the North American Petroleum Operations, had invited him for lunch.

He now had a general understanding of what was happening in Russia, and this was all he needed at this stage. He thanked Norman Kem and Sergie Kholodov and set off to find the executive dining room and Tom Roden. But first he made a quick call to

Dublin. He needed to get an update on performance, as he had no doubt that Papandreou would get around to it at some stage when he met him in the afternoon. He also thought that he would say "hello" to Patricia. This, unfortunately, was not to be. She, he was told, was with Jim O'Raghallaigh. He'd no wish to get involved with him, so he looked for Tom Bergin.

Tom Bergin had excelled in negotiating the purchase of 100,000 tonnes of crude so far at a discount of $1 on the quoted price and on extended credit. Sales were up and the productivity agreement was achieving a twenty percent improvement on their previous delivery costs. *That man's newfound confidence will never cease to amaze me. If he thinks that his snitching has consolidated his position, he'd better think again. He'll go as soon as I can make it happen.*

---

At six feet five inches and weighing two hundred and eighty pounds, with a voice to match his physique, Tom Roden is, in all respects, a powerful man. A Texan by birth, still living in his native Houston, he has had a lifetime career with Global. Joining in the 1970s as a refining engineer, he quickly moved through production, pipelines, marketing, and human resources to spend five years in various postings in international operations. This meteoric rise within Global appeared to crash, when his boardroom backers seemed to lose out in a tussle, that saw his archrival, Dino Papandreou, get the top executive job. The wheeling and dealing that went into that appointment was not open to scrutiny, but when Roden was subsequently appointed to head up Global's North American Petroleum Operations, which to many was seen as an equally satisfying and prestigious position, it was generally taken as a conciliatory gesture to the younger, dynamic management strata within the company. In this role, he had a functional reporting relationship to Papandreou. This seemed to irritate both. He still had powerful support on the main board, and Ed resolved to steer clear of any interpersonal rivalries.

Roden was already seated in the dining room of Global's elite when Ed arrived. Shunning the more sought after, but discreet, seats at the windows, with their panoramic views of the city offered by its location on the fiftieth floor, Roden had a centre table. The position seemed to dominate, but this just matched his physical presence. It was also a signal that this wasn't really a social call. Roden obviously didn't want the allure of the city sights distracting this particular luncheon guest. He wanted to talk business.

"Howdy, Partner," he boomed as Brant crossed to his table. Ed was very conscious that this made him the centre of attention. Every head turned to find out who the 'partner' was. *Christ, I hope Papandreou is not entertaining Coleman here. I don't think he'd appreciate me lunching with this guy.* A furtive glance allayed his fears. The great man was nowhere to be seen.

Ed felt his hand being enveloped in one twice the size of his own. He sat down, deliberately answering in a subdued tone to try and lower the decibel level of their conversation. It seemed to work.

"Thanks for joining me, Ed. I thought I'd grab hold of you before I headed back to Houston to see if I can get some handle on what that goddam Greek is doin' to our company."

Ed was surprised at his directness. The "Greek" he referred to was, he guessed, Papandreou, who was obviously of Greek origin. He thought it better to continue to study the menu and say nothing.

Still suffering from his lack of sleep, and still a bit sore at having the potential of a lie-in hijacked by Kem and his Russian protégé, Ed was determined not to be bullied by this oversized Texan. *Such a bombastic bully. He obviously automatically assumes that I'm on his side.* He ignored the gratuitous insult to his boss, but in retaliation spent an inordinate amount of time on selecting his lunch from the extensive menu. He was famished, and only then realised that he had skipped breakfast and had nothing since the previous evening. *There's no way he's going to drag me into any high-level internal political wrangle, and certainly not on the side of the loser. I've my own career to think about, and that's going quite nicely without your help, and I want to keep it that way.* Eventually he looked across at Roden. He looked anything but pleased, but seemed to have his emotions under control. He continued to speak quietly. They proceeded through their meal. The conversation was casual until the waiter had cleared their plates. Ed ordered a coffee. Then the casualness evaporated.

"When I supported our role in Iraq, it was apolitical. We were goin' in to help the Iraqis get their oil industry up to speed. We were to be the guests of a liberated Iraqi nation, our new friends in that part of the world. Our involvement would help them and us. That was fine. It was patriotic, altruistic, and also good commerce. Now I'm told that the motive was not so pure—in fact, it was downright piracy. We went in there purely and simply to grab their oil. Now that we've stirred up a hornet's nest, and realise we've bitten off more than we can chew, we're lookin' to Saudi Arabia as an easier option. You seem to have that bastard's confidence, Ed. Tell me I'm wrong."

His voice had risen again. Ed looked around to see if they had an audience. Apart from some glances from those at the nearby tables, everyone seemed preoccupied with their meals and their own company.

"Tom, for Chrissake, I don't know why you don't direct these questions to Dino. I'm just the CEO of the Irish subsidiary, the smallest operation Global has. The Irish numbers will hardly show in the consolidated accounts; they—they'll get lost in the rounding. I'm not on the inside of anything. I went to Saudi Arabia because I was told to, and reported on what I found."

"Your report will very likely start another war."

*Thank God I took that time in Saint Patrick's to sort out my head.*

"That's ridiculous. Energy supply is an issue of vital concern to the United States and to all of the industrialised countries. Its availability cannot depend on the whim of a hostile government or on unequal competition from the likes of China. If Western governments decide to take pre-emptive military action to safeguard their civilization or lifestyle, then they're only discharging their electoral responsibility. They won't do that based on a report completed by a novice following a ten-day visit."

"Ed," he said very quietly, while looking directly into Brant's eyes. "A torrent starts as a single droplet. That committee meeting we attended, at which you and that CIA agent presented conclusions, was a molehill that Papandreou will build into a mountain. I've seen him do it before."

"Well, Tom, I can only say what I said before: If you have something to say, you need to take it up with Dino Papandreou or maybe the Chairman, but not with me. I'm too far down the league table to do anything, even if I wanted to."

"I take it from this that you agree with what's happenin'?" he asked.

"To the extent that I'm a member of the Strategy Coordination Committee, I accept the conclusions of that committee. It can't make a declaration of war."

"I'm sorry for you, Ed," he said. "You're even beginning to sound like Papandreou. I've seen it happen so often in the past. It's a process. First he creates you, then he mesmerises you, and finally he permeates your very being. At what stage are you? Get out now while you can, Ed, or like the others you'll be part of the driftwood."

———————◆———————

Riding the elevator to the thirty-first floor, whether ascending or descending as he now was from the executive dining room, was like a shot of adrenaline. The closer he got, the more he could taste, and feel, and even smell the power of its occupant. The excitement of being so close to his ultimate goal was almost overwhelming. The boardroom politics that he had endured over lunch were petty. He looked across at Tom Roden, towering above everyone else in the crowded elevator. *Pity, but that man's twisted logic will inevitably leave him, and not me, on the scrap heap. How he could think that he could possibly survive an attempted mutiny in Global Oil against the incumbent of its most powerful position, was beyond belief.* Although big business didn't operate as a democracy, the executives had had their input and, at the end of the day, all had to accept and support the decisions taken. The board was obviously supporting Papandreou, and Roden, despite his seniority, would be on a slippery slope if his dissent got back to the board. As in any corporation, there were those who would see it to be in their interest, to ensure that it did.

With unbelievable pleasure, he saw that he was the only one getting off at the great man's floor.

"Excuse me, please. This is my floor."

There was an immediate hush as all necks turned to see who was exiting at "the gates of heaven," as level thirty-one had become known. Brant couldn't help but steal a glance at Roden. He seemed to have paled under his tanned Texan skin as he watched Papandreou's disciple head for the target of his failed conspiracy.

Dino Papandreou was in pensive mood when Ed Brant entered his office. Without any apology for, nor even a mention, of the broken morning appointment, he gestured that they would sit in the comfortable red leather armchairs in the more informal end of his plush office. For three or four minutes Brant sat there in silence, as the powerful executive continued to tap out directions on the keyboard of his desktop computer. *No doubt changing the business world, and perhaps, some of its political structures in the process,* Ed speculated, as he watched enviously, the exercise of the power he wanted more than anything else in the world. Well, after Patricia, that is. *Christ, I wonder what she's doing now. He looked at his watch. 2:35. I wonder what she was doing with that pompous sod O'Raghallaigh when I called. Holding his feet to the fire, I hope. She'd need to. We paid that guy enough to handle the Anglo deal. I'd bet she's standing over him, as I'd be doing if I was there. God, it's a great comfort having someone you can really trust on your side in this murky business. This guy here could certainly do with a friend or two.*

"Something came up that I had to attend to," Papandreou offered, eventually.

He hesitated for a moment and then continued.

"I guess it's not a secret. In fact, the way things happen around here, I wouldn't be surprised if you've heard already. David Coleman is leaving us."

"Oh," Brant said, in genuine shock. "I'm sorry to hear that. I don't know him too well, although I suppose we're neighbours. He seems to have done a good job in the U.K. He'll be difficult to replace! Where is he going?"

"I really don't know, and I care even less," Papandreou said. "I fired his ass. The son-of-a-bitch."

This was another of Papandreou's missiles. Brant said nothing.

"He doesn't buy into our strategy. He's one of these goddam moralists who doesn't know who pays his salary. I had dinner with him last night and he spent the evening lecturing me on the evils of global corporations. Then this morning he was back to tell me that, according to the International Energy Agency, a sustained ten dollar increase in the price of crude oil cuts the output of the rich OECD countries by an average of 0.4 percent, leading to four hundred thousand job losses."

He stopped and gave Brant one of those stares that he had come to associate with a challenge. He then continued with a sardonic grin.

"Well, he was wrong. It's 4001. He forgot himself."

"Are you not concerned that he will talk to the media? Our Middle East strategies would make some headlines," Ed ventured.

"Coleman won't pick up his accrued bonuses for twenty-four months. He won't jeopardise that or his pension by acting foolishly. He also knows that he'd never again get a management position that would pay enough to buy his breakfast if he disclosed boardroom secrets. I'd see to that."

He continued. Ed felt his heart flip.

"Ed, I don't know yet what I'm going to do about filling his position in Global U.K. I'd ask you to take that job, only the Chairman and I have talked about you taking a bigger job over here. I expect another high-level resignation in the not-too-distant future. That's why I was anxious to look at that guy with the Irish name to replace you eventually. Pity he turned out to be another wimp."

Ed recalled the meeting in the Churchill and O'Raghallaigh's lecture on the immorality of the foreign policy of the United States.

"Pity, though, I need to free you up fast. You're too big for that little Irish operation. What about that bright young thing I sent over there for—eh, European experience. The Irish-American. What was her name? You know her. I sent her over there as your Executive Assistant. Yeah, she's doin' well. I'd like to move her up. Politically, it'd be good. As far as I can recall she came with the recommendation of the Chairman."

Ed Brant found it hard to breathe. His heartburn had really started to act up. Patricia to take over from him as Chief Executive in Ireland! And where would he be going? To the U.S.? To New York in some top-level corporate position? Or was Papandreou

233

dropping the hint that he was going to fire Tom Roden? If that was the case—and it seemed more likely—he'd be going to Houston in Texas, where the North American Petroleum Operations were based. That would leave Patricia in Dublin and him in Houston. Sure, he'd never even see her. He had planned to take her with him wherever he went, but as his wife. That was a plan he couldn't reveal to Papandreou. Corporations are suspicious of in-company romances, particularly at his level.

"That wouldn't work, Dino," he said, as casually as his aching chest would permit. "Eh, Harvey I think her name is—Patricia. Yes, she's coming along but she's a long way from the Chief Executive's role. No, I guess we'd have to find someone else." He hoped his unusual assertiveness in responding to the Senior Vice President didn't arouse suspicion. He needn't have worried; Papandreou never spent too long on the minions.

"Okay, I'll be spending some time in the U.K. myself. I want to make sure that that son-of-a-bitch doesn't try to create problems on his own patch. I'll have an opportunity to get to know the local people a bit better. Maybe I'll find another Ed Brant amongst the chaff."

With that Papandreou gestured that David Coleman was history, and he wanted to get on to another subject. But first he clicked the switch on his squawk box.

"Can you let me have some coffee?"

It wasn't a question. His secretary answered with a polite confirmation. Ed assumed he was included. Papandreou never asked him and never mentioned his name in talking to his secretary.

"I was very impressed with your report on Saudi, and also on your observations on the way that Iraq might go. As you know, I've got several outside sources that I use to cross-check critical information, but I always end up asking one of my own trusted staff to confirm before I draw a final conclusion. The stakes are far too high to do anything less.

Papandreo's reference to his 'ears' was a stark reminder to Brant that he had some unfinished business back in Ireland. *Yes, and your spy in my camp will be short-lived. As soon as I get back, Mister 'Stone-age' Bergin is for the chop. You don't need to cross-check me. I'm firmly focused on Roden's job, and you needn't worry about me straying off course. I'll do the reporting on the Irish operation.*

"Based on what you presented, we'll progress the idea of a Saudi strike with the Pentagon planners. I'll also talk with Washington about whether we can maybe make concessions to the oppressed Shiite majority in Iraq, in return for the support of the Shiite minority in Saudi Arabia. As you very astutely pointed out, they are dominant in the northeast—where the oil is located.

The fact that this is the only area that the military need occupy makes it very viable. I'll let you know in due course what they consider our options to be."

The conversation ceased, almost in mid sentence, as his secretary came in with the coffee. She proceeded to make space on the crowded table with one hand, while trying to hold a tray with the other. Papandreou was closer, but made no effort to help. Ed instinctively intervened, receiving a wan smile of acknowledgement as she proceeded to pour the two cups. He looked to see if she was embarrassed by the sudden silence, indicating that her boss mistrusted her with overhearing a confidential discussion. She seemed totally unfazed, obviously used to being humiliated as she handled Papandreou's menial chores. Papandreou remained silent until she left the room. He immediately reached for the coffee cup. *Obviously, human relations are not high on the list of qualifications for the top job,* Brant thought as he watched.

"Let's talk about Russia for a minute," Papandreou said. "Confidentially, as a third option, I have been wooing the Russians. Our exploration people believe that the former Soviet Union will be the source of the world's energy supply in the mid to long-term future. We need to get in on the ground floor."

"Slurp."

Ed glanced at Papandreou, whose head was horizontal, draining the dregs from his coffee cup. *Neither are social graces, but he must really have needed that coffee*, he thought.

"I was briefed this morning by Norman Kem and a Russian colleague of his."

"Good! I don't know whether it worked out the way it was planned, but a handful of individuals ended up with billions of dollars worth of Russian natural resources. I've been talking to one of them. He owns the biggest oil company in Russia. I think we can do a deal."

"Are you talking about supplying Khodorkovsky's company, Yukos?" Ed asked, naively.

"Yes, we are. We're talking to Yukos and also to one other company about a possible merger, or maybe an outright acquisition. There is a concern amongst the Oligarchs, though, that their profitability will be severely restricted by Putin. With American investment they feel that their position would be strengthened and their companies would be less likely to be taken back into public ownership. Also, with an external refining and marketing partner such as Global Oil, if Putin imposed penal taxes we could take the profits to a low tax regime, such as Ireland, through transfer pricing."

"I take it you have something in mind for me?"

"Well, yes I do. It's okay talking to these Oligarchs, but to put cash into Russia is another matter. BP had its ass kicked. They ended up writing off something like two hundred million dollars, but they've gone back for more. We don't want to take any chances but BP are no fools. If the odds were not in their favour, they would be gone. We need to be sure that the industry is now buttoned down in the private sector, that we're talking to the right people, that we don't suddenly wake some morning to find that our friend Putin has taken it back or that he himself has been deposed."

"From what Kholodov said this morning, it seems to me that Putin has got over any misgivings he had about the way the state assets were auctioned. It would seem that the Oligarchs are home and dry."

This seemed to trigger a reaction from Papandreou. Once again he leaned forward to fill his coffee cup.

"I hope you're right, Ed, and I think you are." Slurp. "But as I said before, I need to double and triple check. I know that BP's Chief Executive believes that nothing is guaranteed in Russia. He's reported to say that 'Russia is a country ruled by men, not by laws.' That's a bit disconcerting when you're considering massive investment. I know you're giving me your honest thoughts, but your opinions are just based on what you heard this morning. I've already had all of that from Kem directly. I need you to get your ass over there to do what you did in Saudi, and give me some independent thoughts."

"There's another problem I haven't mentioned." Again he paused, which Brant had come to expect as the prelude to something important, although his priority again seemed to be his coffee.

"Slurp."

He eventually took the cup down from his face.

"As you know, we've been working with the Saudis to get the price up. We need to keep it there until just before the Presidential election, when, having dumped our stocks onto the market at the high price, we'll reverse the process and keep our buddies in office by bringing it down—temporarily. But there's a problem." He stopped, and gave his now familiar, penetrating stare.

"We know that Putin wants low energy prices in Russia and is pressurising Yukos to increase output. Khodorkovsky will resist any political pressure, I think for the hell of it, but if he did relent it could ruin everything. If the market believes that the crisis is over, the price could fall overnight and we could be left with massive crude holdings all over the globe. It could be loss making, and—" Again he gave that stare. "We're talking mega bucks."

"Do you have any influence with the Kremlin?" Ed asked.

"No, not directly, but we do know that Crown Prince Abdullah, the head of the Saudi Royal Family, is planning a trip to Moscow. It's the first time since the 1930s that a Saudi leader has made an official visit to Russia, so something's up. We believe it's to encourage Putin to back off and leave Yukos and Khodorkovsky alone. The Russian exchequer, like the Saudis, desperately needs the revenue, so you wouldn't expect too much resistance; but with these darn politicians, you never can tell."

"Another thing—" The rest had to wait until he had drained the coffee pot into his cup. "That anti-U.S. sentiment that you picked up on your trip also has me worried. If the Saudis suspect that the United States' real intent in Iraq was its oil, it might make them jumpy and they could be thinking of some form of alliance with Russia. If that is the case, we need to know, and get the Pentagon moving on our new thinking, sooner rather than later."

"Well, I'll be glad to do whatever I can," Ed said with more confidence than he felt. "What timing do you have in mind?"

"As I said, I'll spend some time in the U.K. to ensure that Coleman's departure does not cause problems. I'll take one of the company jets across. Why don't you fly with me? We can drop you off in Dublin and me in London. The jet can then go back to Dublin and take you on to Moscow. You can keep it there, as you'll probably need to move about over there. What do you think?"

"Sounds good to me."

"Good, that's fixed then. Ask Corporate Services to arrange your visa and accommodation. Unfortunately, we don't yet have anything of the Oasis standard in Moscow. Maybe we will as the result of your trip."

The meeting was over. Ed made his way to the door as Papandreou was looking into his empty coffee cup.

———————◆•◆•◆———————

On leaving Papandreou's office, Ed met his secretary coming the other way with another coffee tray.

"Oh, Mister Brant," she said with a confident smile. "I didn't realise you were leaving so fast. Would you like another coffee? I'll get it for you as soon as I leave this with Mister Papandreou. Your office has been on—a Mister Bergin? Your brother, John, has also been on, eh, twice. I told them both that I'd ask you to call back. You're welcome to use my phone if you like. But, oh, eh, it's—not secure; only Mister Papandreou's is. I won't be a minute with your coffee," she said, and disappeared into the inner sanctum of the Almighty.

Ed looked after her. *What a change*, he thought. She was a bright, attractive, middle-aged woman who seemed to exude confidence. Yet only thirty minutes previously, when she had delivered the coffees, she had seemed to be completely servile. *Funny how the realms of power can affect an individual—although I suppose I don't exactly act any differently myself. I hope that I don't come across as a wimp.*

Ed sat at the secretary's desk and phoned Bergin. He was in no mood to talk to John. He was beginning to accept that Ben's conclusion was right, that John was the problem and not Anglo Oil or Jim O'Ragallaigh. He'd never grown up and still expected people to run after him. Well, he'd just have to learn to process his delivery problems, or whatever else it was, through the appropriate people in Global's office. Ed Brant was far too busy and important to be dealing with those trivial issues.

Bergin seemed anxious. He was, by nature, optimistic and all-conquering until put under pressure. It was then he generally fell apart.

"Ed," he said. "I think we have a problem. As I'm sure you know, the price of crude has gone through the roof. It's now at thirty-eight dollars and rising. The media is hyper. The opposition parties, especially Fine Gael, have got in on the act and the government is running scared. They want a meeting with you."

"What are the papers saying?"

"Well, I have yesterday's Sunday Tribune in front of me. The headline reads 'BLACK FOR US, BLACK GOLD FOR THEM.' It goes on to say that 'importers and distributors of petrol and other fuel in Ireland are raking in multi-million euro profits.'"

"Do they mention Global Oil?"

"No, not yet, but it's only a question of time. I've had numerous calls that I've avoided. But I can't duck forever."

"Have you been able to fill the rented storage?"

"Yes, I have. We got a great price. It averages just under twenty eight dollars with ninety-day terms."

"Well done, Tom," Ed said earnestly. "Did you have to make any long-term commitments?"

"None that we can't avoid; there's nothing in writing about future dealings."

"Where was your main source?"

"Russia. I've never met a bunch like the Russkis. You don't even have to put it in a brown paper bag like you do here."

"For Chrissake, Tom, not on the phone," Ed said swiftly. "You mentioned the government is being pressured. Is it our friend in the Labour Party that seems to have it in for us?"

"No. Not this time. Let me read what it says:

*'The Fine Gael spokesman for Trade and Employment is agitating for a code of conduct for petrol companies to provide greater transparency on the impact of external factors on petrol prices.'*

It's being floated that the market price of crude is actually set by the industry itself. Their Middle East correspondent is saying that if there's no war to do it for them, then the oil companies restrict output and hoard supply in order to get the price up. While the world suffers, the oil companies come in with record profits."

"We can do without that sort of debate," Ed replied. "Fortunately, the industry has a lot of friends in the American administration right now, so I don't expect that there will be any support coming from this side of the Atlantic. However, we do need help in some work that I have been asked to do with the Russians, and the Department said they'll assist. Let's keep them as sweet as we can."

"What can I tell them?"

"Well, the last thing we want to tell them is that we've got two hundred plus tonnes offshore that we're holding until the price rises. If they feel that there is a supply crisis, they can bring in an order imposing quotas on consumers and forcing oil companies to share all available supply. They've done that twice to my knowledge—in '73 during the oil embargo and again in '79 during the Iraqi invasion of Kuwait. We don't want to be sharing our good fortunes with Exxon or any of the others. I know what you can tell them. Say that the price is largely due to shortages in the U.S. and, that as a result of my recent visit, Saudi Arabia has agreed to increase production, and that their state oil company, Aramco, has hired eight super tankers to transport additional oil to the U.S. It will take about six weeks to get there but will have an immediate impact on the price and availability."

"Does that mean that the price has peaked? Should we start to offload some of the crude onto the market now before it does drop?"

"Absolutely not. The price will reach fifty dollars and maybe a bit more in the next month or so. I'm certain of that."

"Do you not think that the increase in Saudi production, and the easing of the supply into the United States, will ease prices?" he asked.

"Tom, believe me, I know what I'm talking about. There are many factors at work here, but they all lead me to believe that we have not seen the end of high crude prices. They will fluctuate marginally, but the trend for some time to come will be up. Hold your nerve and hold onto those offshore stocks."

"I read about a huge flotilla of Saudi super tankers heading for the United States. Is that what you are referring to? Did you negotiate that?"

"No, not at all, it's entirely coincidental—but it suits our purpose. As you say, it's been widely reported so the government will be aware of it."

"That should ease the overall pressures, but they'll be looking for assurances that Global Ireland will continue to be able to supply both our own and Anglo Oil customers. That's their main concern."

"Well, as I said, don't, under any circumstances, let them know about our offshore stocks. Make sure it's not included on our monthly report to the Department. They know that I've got an upcoming visit to Moscow. Tell them that's the purpose, and that any influence they can exert the better. Global Oil has its own contacts in the private sector, but some of the Russian crude is still operated by state companies. We know, that with the Irish presidency of the European Union coming up in 2004, Putin will be looking for Irish support in their bid to join the World Trade Organisation. A bit of cooperation might not go amiss. As far as I can gather from the briefing I've just had on Russia, almost everything there is under the counter. Let's see if we can get some benefit out of the fact that Bertie and the boys will be kings of Europe for six months."

"Ed, I'm not at all comfortable about this. If Global is behind the price rise, what else are they behind? Sounds to me a bit like that Enron affair, only bigger. You know those guys will end up in gaol."

The mention of Enron sent shivers down Brant's spine. He remembered Papandreou telling him that evidence of Enron's price fixing in California was discovered through company recordings of telephone conversations that their traders had amongst themselves. Most companies record all phone conversations for security purposes, and now that he thought about it, he recalled that Papandreou never used the internal system for his own confidential calls. Was this conversation being recorded? He remembered what Papandreou's secretary had said about that telephone. With a feeling of panic, he desperately tried to remember exactly what he had said.

"Tom, I'll be back in Dublin first thing tomorrow morning. We'll talk then," he said, and hung up the phone.

In his anxiety he had forgotten to take the opportunity to talk to Patricia. He had also been oblivious to the coffee tray. He stood up and walked to the elevator. The day hadn't started well and hadn't improved.

———◆•◆•◆———

# CHAPTER 7

The Global company Presidential jet was something to behold. The most striking feature was its size. It was a regular Boeing 767-300 aircraft, originally designed to carry 350 passengers but adapted now for long-haul executive use. With so much on his mind, Ed Brant hadn't given Papandreou's invitation further thought, but arriving at JFK International, he couldn't but feel proud at the sight of this huge airliner, resplendent in its green livery, with the world logo of Global emblazoned on its fuselage. It was one of twenty-five aircraft in the company fleet, but was by far the biggest and most lavishly adapted.

"Good evening, sir, welcome aboard."

He acknowledged the captain and crew, all immaculately attired and professionally mannered, as they stood in a welcoming group at the foot of the stairs leading on to the front of the huge aircraft.

"Mister Papandreou has not yet arrived. Can we offer you a tour of the aircraft's facilities?" the captain asked, as they shook hands.

"This will be your cabin until we cross the Atlantic, then you are most welcome to move into the Presidential suite if you feel it would be more comfortable."

It was the hostess. She was to conduct the tour while the pilot busied himself with his preparations for the Atlantic crossing.

They entered the cabin, a bedroom that would be considered fair-sized in any circumstances. The beige coloured carpeting yielded, bounce-like, to Ed as he crossed it to check the springs of the cream-quilted double bed. As he lay, to the lightly concealed amusement of the stewardess, he thought back to the days in Dun Laoghaire when he shared a room with Ben and envied his bed, which was far softer than his. *By God! If they could only see me now. Are you watching, Dad?* he thought, crossing his ankles.

Passing a coffee table, adorned with a vase of fresh flowers, the stewardess pointed out the door to his own en suite and took him through an adjoining door into his lounge. This, she apologetically explained, had to double as his private work area. All in all, he reckoned, the facilities and décor would have done justice to the executive suite of any of the five-star hotels in Manhattan.

Further along the corridor, the Presidential quarters were pointed out. He wasn't offered a tour but, as he passed, he got the unmistakable aroma of Java coffee. *The lord and master must now be in residence,* he concluded.

Further along, they passed a kitchen.

"Welcome, Monsieur Brant."

A very French-looking Frenchman, who sported a distinctive chef's hat, met them at the door. He was brilliant white from head to toe, the glow contrasting with the blackness of his moustache, goatee, and sallow complexion.

"We are looking forward very much to cooking dinner for you and Monsieur Papandreou and to doing very well with any special recipes you might like on the trip to Russia."

*Jesus, I'd forgotten all about Papandreou's offer of the executive jet for the trip to Moscow.* Based on what Bergin just said, he could visualise the Irish headlines if this jumbo arrived in Dublin Airport with him as its single passenger.

Next to the kitchen was an exquisitely furnished dining room, more reminiscent of the Remington Room in the 21 Club than an aeroplane. Its highly polished, dark oak dining table was surrounded by at least thirty ox-blood leather chairs. A smaller table, Ed noticed, was already set for two people with its centre, three-stemmed candelabra already lit. This room too was panelled in the same rich dark mahogany, and carpeted in the same beige, but with a slightly firmer, luxurious pile. The ceiling lights were recessed and shone out of a dark blue ceiling like a myriad of stars on a clear night.

*The cost of creating this ambiance!* he thought. He and Patricia had enjoyed real stars, and real atmosphere, and real life on his balcony before he had stupidly blown it away. He hadn't forgotten what she had said when he had last talked to her. He'd soon be home, and life would be back to where it was. *Blast it,* he remembered his commitment to take this bloody plane on to Moscow. *Papandreou wouldn't appreciate having this parked on the tarmac at Dublin while I patch up my love life.*

"That's a missile-jamming device, similar to what they have on Air Force One," explained the captain as they entered the cockpit. "An essential protective device when we're in the Middle East," he explained. "Sometimes we're not exactly seen as bringing benefit to some of those countries."

What he didn't say, but what Ed had heard previously on the grapevine, was that it would cost almost two hundred dollars a mile to fly—their trip to Moscow from Dublin would cost around 450 thousand dollars. He couldn't help but compare it with his father's old battered Ford Cortina, which was the standard he had risen to after a lifetime of hard work. He hadn't approved of what he considered to be the immorality of big business, but had never tasted its compensations. The life-style that Ed Brant was quickly growing accustomed to was not for the faint-hearted or, as Papandreou would say, for wimps.

Papandreou was already sipping a Scotch and soda while seated in the lounge section of the dining room, when Ed arrived at the appointed time for dinner. For the first time since they met, Papandreou was informally dressed in a pink designer shirt and navy slacks. His appearance was a surprise. Ed suddenly realised that he had come to see Papandreou as personally reflecting the business image of the company: austere and humourless, without a human dimension. He felt awkward in his business suit and tie, but Papandreou didn't seem to notice.

"What do you think of the aircraft, Ed?" he asked rhetorically. "It's my first time with the Boeing. Normally this is reserved for the Chairman or bigger groups. I usually use one of the Gulfstream jets. This was available and it's a long trip and, besides, I thought that you'd get a kick out of taking it to Russia."

"I can't get over the size of it. Is it not too big?"

He had no sooner said this, than he realised how naive it sounded. Papandreou did not spare him with his look. When he did speak, the Churchill tone to O'Raghallaigh was back in evidence.

"This is Global Oil Incorporated, the biggest oil company." He hesitated for emphasis. "And before we're finished, it'll be the biggest goddam corporation on the planet."

His eyes squinted as they bored through Ed's head.

"Tell me," he continued, as his voice rose by several decibels. "Why do you think those goddam terrorists picked the Twin Towers, or the Pentagon, or why do you think they tried for the White House? Why do you think Britain has Buckingham Palace, or the Catholic Church has Saint Peter's? Well I'll tell you," he continued without waiting for, or Ed supposed even expecting, an answer. "It's the goddam symbolic affect. They're symbols of power, of might, of—" he seemed momentarily lost for a word— "majesty. Global One is our symbol of power."

His brow was glistening with the effort, and what seemed to be genuine emotion.

"It's always half the argument. When we arrive anywhere in the world, the goddam politicians know that we're in town. We're the big boys. We can deliver anything, including their electorate."

"Well, I understand the effect it could have, and I'm certainly enjoying the experience, but now that you mention it, Dino, I don't think it's a good idea that I use this plane on my trip. I've just been talking to Tom Bergin. He tells me that the media back home is acting up on the price of fuel. They're accusing the oil industry of exploiting the Iraqi war. To arrive in Dublin airport in a personal jumbo is bound to make headlines on the day that I need to reassure the government that we're victims too. I very much appreciate your gesture, but I'll pass on the offer this time and take a commercial flight from Heathrow back to Dublin. Depending on what I find at home, I may have to reschedule my trip to Moscow at a later date, when I'll fly Aer Lingus."

"Good thinking, Ed," he said. "That ol' guy, Bergin, seems to know what he's about. It's great to have support that you can rely on to keep us out of trouble."

The reference to Bergin wasn't lost on Ed—*That slip of the tongue is all the proof I need. How would you know Bergin if it wasn't for the fact that, somehow, you were able to recruit him as your goddam 'ear'? That bloody Judas. Well, now I know, and that's it as far as he's concerned.*

Despite Papandreou's unintentional revelation about Bergin, Ed breathed a sigh of relief. Now he'd be able to spend some time in Dublin with Patricia. He didn't think he should push his luck by raising his concerns about the security of the internal telephone system at the Global Oil Manhattan headquarters. He'd worry about that later.

Over dinner, loosened no doubt by the copious quantities of Scotch on top of a bottle of his favourite Nuit St. George red Burgundy, Papandreou reminisced on his childhood in Greece, and the ten years he had spent as a mechanical engineer with several of the major oil companies in the Middle East. He had been a special assistant to the Shah at the time of revolution in Iran, and was lucky to escape with his life. Several attempts had been made to assassinate him, even when he had left after the Shah had been deposed and the Ayatollah installed. His fear was evident, and for the first time he seemed to have a human dimension and to be as vulnerable as everyone else. Inevitably, however, Ed could see his thoughts drifting back to Global's business or, perhaps, it was back to that damned drip-feed strategy of his.

"The deal with Yukos will be major," he began. "Quite apart from our Saudi Arabian ambitions, which incidentally were well received by the Pentagon, it's critical that we get into Russia. We're aware that most of the Seven Sisters, particularly Exxon Mobil, Royal Dutch Shell, BP, and TotalFinaElf, are all counting on Russia for their long-term strategic growth."

"Have they struck up any alliances with any of the newly privatised Russian companies?"

"Not yet, but it's bound to happen. The Russians have enough cash to tap the most lucrative fields, so they're only interested in taking on Western partners for the toughest projects and regions,where investment risks are extremely high."

"I'm surprised that they have the resources at this stage to do it alone," Ed said. "I suppose the present high price of crude is helping their independence."

"Yes," Papandreou answered pensively. "We're helping them to screw us."

"So does Yukos have any special advantage for us?"

"Yes, it's the biggest, and Khodorkovsky seems to know what he's about. They're part of the real world. They didn't have to be told twice how they could save billions in tax. We put a little scheme together for them. It was that help on tax that clinched the deal for us."

"How could we advise them on Russian tax law to the extent that they could save that much tax?" Ed asked incredulously.

He got that stare as Papandreou responded. "Global corporations are in it for real. No obstacle can be too big. You know what we're doing in Iraq, you know what we're planning for Saudi Arabia. Well, they needed a facility in the former Soviet Union to avoid being taxed out of existence, and if there's one country where favours can be bought, it's Russia. It's part of their system. The public servants could not live on what the state pays them, so they're dependent on what they can get for services rendered. Coming from Ireland, you must be familiar with the real world, if what I read about your tribunals is anything to go by. In your country, if I remember correctly, the evidence was that the brown envelope has to be as 'thick as a brick'. Well, in Russia we found that the Republic of Mordovia was very receptive to the idea of bringing in some innovative tax exemptions. Yukos just had to set up a company there and route the profits through it in their invoicing. Once we got the tax provisions in place, everything after that was child's play and perfectly legal. Yukos appreciated our help. A clerk in an office can now save them billions in tax. As a result, they have agreed to join with us in a joint venture with that other progressive Russian oil company, Sibneft."

"Everything seems to be covered. What do you want me to do over there?"

The captain, who came down to the dining room to personally tell them that a slight turbulence was expected, interrupted Papandreou's reply. Although he spoke in the plural, it was very clear that his concern was more for the great man than for his guest, who got no more than an offhand glance as he spoke.

"Thanks, captain," he condescendingly responded. "And the food was excellent." But before the captain could bask in the warmth of Papandreou's rare appreciation, he got that stare and was dismissed with "Where's that girl with the goddam coffee?"

"The stakes are too high to rely on conventional sources," Papandreou continued when they were again alone. "Look where we'd be if we had relied on the CIA intelligence on Iraq. You saved our bacon, and the board won't forget it. Just do the same in Moscow. See what you can find out discreetly. As I said, the Russkis seem to appreciate what we've done, but you never can tell. BP thought that they had a deal with Sidanco in '97. In fact, they signed it in 10 Downing Street in the presence of Tony Blair. You would think that was secure. They were taken for two hundred million. I can't afford to be wrong on this one. Not with that bastard Roden waiting in the wings."

Ed was surprised at the reference to Tom Roden and the venom with which Papandreou spoke. From the lunch conversation he had had with Roden, following the briefing session by Norman Kem, he knew that there was no love lost between them, but he'd no idea it was open hostility. He again decided that discretion was appropriate and said nothing.

There was silence for what seemed ages while Papandreou seemed deep in thought.

"On reflection," he said, "maybe you would get more if you didn't advertise the fact that you're a Global executive. If there is any anti-Americanism about, your Irish accent might help. Maybe you should represent yourself as one of those bankers that have recently bought up millions of barrels on the futures market."

"You mean banks are now speculating in the oil market?" Ed asked in disbelief.

"You bet," he said. "In the city, Barclays, Morgan Stanley, and Goldman Sachs are leading the charge into oil, but in addition, several secretive hedge funds are now wagering hundreds of millions of dollars every day in the oil market. ABN Amro has also built up an oil trading team."

"That amazes me," Ed said. "I would have considered those banks to be ultra-conservative and only dabble in certainties and what they know about."

"Don't underestimate their knowledge. They've bought in the expertise. In fact, I've lost good people to them. The banks I've mentioned don't do anything half-heartedly. Some of the packages they've offered have been in the million dollar range. With the stock market in the doldrums, the oil market has really captured their interest. I've heard them describe it as the 'new Nasdaq.'"

"Where do they store the product?" Ed asked, naively.

"In most cases they never go near it; it's only a paper transaction. They even have sophisticated computer programmes to track and anticipate the market and to trigger a sale of the paper when the price is likely to drop."

"Well, long term we can do without that sort of competition, but right now, I suppose they're helping the price!"

"Yeah, Alan believes that the recent surge has been due to non-oil speculators. My planning people tell me that they account for about seven to eight dollars of the increase. Of course I haven't told him about our activities. "

"Alan?"

"Yes, sorry. Alan Greenspan, the Chairman of the America's Federal Reserve Board," Papandreou said, dropping the name of the most venerated financial genius of the Western world as if he had just met him for breakfast.

He went on. "They complicate the market though, making it harder for us to steer it the way we want. Right now, however, the extra activity will add billions to our bottom line, so we'll leave the banker problem for sorting on another day."

As always, Ed Brant was glad to exchange Papandreou and his world-shaping schemes for the solace of the luxurious double bed as they sped above the clouds heading for Heathrow.

———————◆•◆•◆———————

Ed Brant was relieved that he had postponed his trip to Russia when he saw the volume of work piled on his desk at Global House. Mary, his long-term secretary, had gone and he was missing her already. Under normal circumstances, all routine mail would have been distributed, as appropriate, without ever getting to him, as indeed would ninety percent of phone calls and e-mails. Even non-routine, but important mail, that was not absolutely critical for his attention, would be summarised for his information, but rerouted to be dealt with by Patricia. Today he had everything. A pile of paper, lists of phone callers, and dozens of unacknowledged e-mails confronted him. He had never appreciated the volume of work that Patricia had routinely handled. He hadn't wanted to talk to her for the first time in a business context, but he had no option. His desk had to be cleared. He had important, career-building work to do in Moscow.

He immediately told Human Resources to rehire Mary at whatever salary it took to get her back, and then he dialled Patricia's internal line number. There was no reply. Funny, he thought, surely she knew he'd be back today and would have come into him, or at least be waiting for his call. He'd told her he was coming. He remembered distinctly. It was just after she had said that she loved him. How could he forget?

In the meantime, he attempted to prioritise the pile in front of him.

He hadn't made too much progress when Tom Bergin entered his office.

"I see you're doing a to-do list. Make sure you add your brother, John. He was going ballistic when he heard you were not back. He wouldn't talk to me or anyone else; he wanted you."

"Well, it couldn't be that urgent if he wasn't prepared to talk to the people who could help him. I'll put him on, but he won't be number one. How did you make out with the government?"

"The same; they're most impressed with that fleet of super tankers they think you organised out of Saudi for the U.S. They got a bit caustic when I deferred on whether you could do the same for Ireland. Be prepared, though, it's on their agenda."

"Thanks, Tom. I'll give the department a call now. I want to keep our relations cordial; I need their help with the Russians."

Ed noticed that Bergin spoke with a good deal of confidence, which in fact seemed to grow as the conversation progressed. The beard-tugging habit seemed to have gone and the blinking was certainly not as pronounced.

"As you know, I got our offshore stocks from the Russians. They seemed happy enough to deal with us when they realised that the product was destined for Ireland. The U.S. dimension to Global wasn't something that we sensed would help, so we projected ourselves as an Irish delegation rather than Global Oil."

"I know Putin didn't support Bush on the invasion, but did you feel that there's hostility on the business front?"

"I wasn't there long enough to get a reliable feel, but I do know that the Western oil companies are getting short shrift from the Kremlin."

"What do you mean?" Ed asked anxiously.

"Well, the word in the industry is that they are hell-bent on keeping Westerners out. The Kremlin annulled a tender from Exxon to exploit Artic deposits, and Amoco was unceremoniously dropped from a Siberian joint venture with Yukos Oil, despite the fact that, at that stage, it had spent hundreds of millions."

"Is it anti-U.S. or anti-Western?" Brant asked.

"The impression I got was that they don't want any Western involvement, unless the financial risks are high or the technology is more than they can handle. Then, out of preference, U.S. companies are at the bottom of the list. BP and Shell seem to be more acceptable."

"That's on the exploration side. Is there a similar bias on the sale of crude, where our main interest would be?"

"I really don't know. I asked that question to a Russian trader based in London. He confessed that Russia is still a very secretive country, where theories and conspiracies are the order of the day, and the truth is hard to find. There certainly have been deals done. The biggest I've heard of is about to be done with China. Their National Petroleum Company has agreed to a deal with Yukos Oil for supply through a specially constructed pipeline over a twenty-five-year period."

"So, based on your experience in dealing with them, you believe that American companies like Global are at a disadvantage?"

"Yes I do."

"Okay then, it looks as if we really need the cover of our friends in the Department—to sort of give us an official Irish hue."

"That would help. It did with us. Certainly I think if you go as Global you'll get short shrift."

Ed was about to ask his secretary to get the Department officials on the line when he realised he hadn't got a secretary anymore.

"Bloody secretaries," he snapped. "Can't rely on them being around when you really need them."

He immediately noticed Bergin's hand movement. It just stopped short of his beard, but those eyes were blinking as never before.

"Mary has always been most reliable. She has worked for us—eh, for Mister Stone, almost since we started."

Ed decided he'd let it go. He was far too busy to sort out this old timer now, but when he got back from Moscow—

He had looked up the number and was awaiting his call to be put through to Matthew Brennan, the Secretary-General of the Energy Department.

"Jesus, the bureaucracy, and these guys are supposed to serve the public. That's the third time I've been asked who I am and what I want. By the way, Tom, do you know where Patricia Harvey is? She doesn't seem to be in her office!"

Before Bergin could answer, Matthew Brennan came on the phone.

Brant noted that Brennan was his usual courteous self, but his voice had a distinct note of urgency that he hadn't noticed in previous encounters.

"The bloody crude oil price had risen since our last conversation and the opposition is on a roll. The more pressure on the Minister, the more on me, so I need your help."

"Sure, whatever I can do; but as you know, the price is governed by international markets."

Brennan continued as if Ed had said nothing.

"Pat Roberts has got in on the act, and is accusing the government of irresponsibility for the sale of Whitegate, the only oil refinery on the island of Ireland, for what he said was a pittance."

Ed was wary of Roberts, the leader of the Labour Party who for some unknown reason seemed to have Global Oil in his sights.

"He seems to miss the point that if there was a supply crisis it would be in the supply of crude oil, and not in refining capacity where there is a European surplus."

"That's been our position, but he maintains that with all the amalgamations taking place within your industry, the European refineries will be rationalised and the older ones closed down. The media, as is their wont, has turned this into headlines that would give the impression that Armageddon was about to descend, and that it is all the government's fault for not corralling you guys."

"We've got to tackle this as a team. There can't be an 'us-and-them situation.' That would be disastrous for Irish supply, if there is a crisis."

"Yeah, we agree. The Minister is most concerned that the industry would be seen to be cooperating with the government in securing supplies that would avoid the country having to use its national strategic reserves. The fact that there was no evidence of a shortage to date is not the issue. The Minister is aware that the U.S. is bolstering its reserves with Global's help, and with your personal involvement. This suggests that the U.S. is expecting supply difficulties, and the Minister expects—indeed insists—on the same level of support for the security of Ireland's fuel needs."

"Of course, as I said, we'll gladly do anything we can, although I don't know what we can do at this time."

"Well, we've moved it on. The Minister has personally contacted his counterpart in Moscow and has received every assurance of cooperation. It now just remains for you to say when you will be available to travel and we'll be glad to make all the necessary arrangements."

Brant was stunned. He was the one who generally forced situations. Here, however, in a couple of minutes, he had been adroitly manoeuvred into a position where he would be in the forefront of the government delegation. Brennan wasn't finished.

"If necessary, the Minister himself will be available to travel with you, as indeed will I, and a colleague from Foreign Affairs."

"Okay, let me get back to you as soon as I can travel," he heard himself saying.

There was a click as the line went dead. Ed stared blankly at the receiver in his hand.

"Sounds good; maybe you can negotiate a deal in the name of the Irish government but put it through Global."

It was Bergin. Ed had forgotten he was still sitting there.

257

"You know, Tom, you might have a point. What's this you were telling me about Patricia?"

"Oh, eh, Patricia. Yes, she's going through a stressful patch right now. I told her to take some time off."

"Stressful patch!—what do you mean? Where is she? Why didn't you call me?"

Ed was on his feet. His involuntary outburst was like a bomb blast in that section of Bergin's brain that contained his confidence. He became transfixed by Brant's glare. Eventually the question seemed to percolate his consciousness, and he spoke, almost in a whisper.

"You appointed me to stand in as Chief Executive while you were away. I didn't think you'd need to approve a few days off for one of the staff. She was upset. It...it was a personal matter. I suggested she should take some time off. She...she needed space."

"She discussed my business with you?" he said with incredulity.

Brant knew he had overreacted. If this guy knew about their relationship, well, he needed to keep him onside, for the moment at least. He didn't want him reporting it to Papandreou.

"No, not your business; it was eh, as I said, personal. She...she got some disturbing information. She'll only be gone for a week or so."

"Yeah, I'm sorry, Tom, I—eh, well, with Mary gone and this Russian trip, I was hoping Patricia could carry some of this," he said, gesturing to the pile of papers on his desk.

He had almost told the truth. He had almost told Bergin that he was going to ask Patricia to go with him to Moscow.

"I understand, Ed, no offence taken. It's a trying time... for all of us."

———◆◆◆———

# CHAPTER 8

Ed Brant looked across at the granite-like features of Matthew Brennan. The excited pitch of his voice danced a merry jig in his eyes, but hardly reached the rugged exterior of his face.

*Maybe the effort of holding that bloody pipe in his mouth has brought on some form of paralysis,* Ed thought, as he listened to the melodic sound of the West Cork accent coming through in the flow.

"Isn't it great, all the same, the Minister making the government jet available to us for the trip?"

Ed was non-committal. He didn't know yet whether or not it was great. At the last moment the Minister had decided he couldn't come. That part, at least, was great. It would not suit Ed's purpose to be restricted by an official designation. After all, his only reason for going was to talk to as many informed Russians as possible, in order to get under the veil of secrecy that Tom Bergin had encountered, and establish what genuine and secure business opportunities existed for Global Oil. An official government group would be restricted to official sources, and the Russians would, in all probability, monitor its movements. Brennan's company was a compromise; the availability of the government's brand new Bombardier Learjet 45 for the trip was a surprise.

"You know it can operate non-stop from Dublin to Moscow, and travel at over five hundred miles an hour with eight to nine passengers."

"Really?" Ed felt obliged to acknowledge some of the comments, although compared to his trans-Atlantic crossing in the Global Oil Boeing 767-300, he found it hard to muster any enthusiasm for the Learjet 45. *It's more like the life raft on an ocean going cruise liner,* he mused.

"Why does the government feel it needs its own plane?" he asked, mischievously, remembering Papandreou's justification for the Boeing.

Brennan looked at him as if he had seriously underestimated his worldliness.

"Surely you know. Every leader in the European Union has to have his own transport," he said, looking around. "And the bigger the better."

"You reckon it's a sort of symbolism, sort of reflecting the relative importance of the leader in the European hierarchy?"

"Yes, that's it exactly, and as we're taking over the Presidency of the European Union from January of next year, it's important that we maintain the prestige of the office."

"So that's why we have a jet of this size?" he asked, hardly able to conceal his amusement.

"Yes, I know it might look a bit ostentatious, but believe me, it helps to influence others."

Ed left it at that. The Lear jet had taken off and was circling before heading east over the Irish Sea in the direction of Moscow.

Far below glistened Dublin Bay, and those billowing sails and headlands that had meant so much to him and Patricia on the many occasions that they had watched from his roof top garden, from her Garden of Eden. He stretched to look behind, to look inland. Yes, there it was: her beloved Killiney Hill. He wondered if her Blondie was still prancing around there. Gosh! He wondered if she was there. He strained to see. No, they were now too high, and banking, to take that left turn that would take him on his way in the next stage of his climb to the summit.

"Does this plane have a phone I could use?"

"Of course," answered Brennan, in a tone which sounded as if Ed had offended his masculinity. He proffered the instrument without further comment.

Ed went to the back of the aircraft in an effort to gain some element of privacy. It was difficult. He dialled Patricia's mobile number. As it rang, he remembered Bergin's words that she was upset. He tried to recall his exact words. He couldn't. He thought back to his last telephone conversation with Patricia. Yes, she had mentioned that there was something she wanted to tell him. But what could it be that could have upset her to the extent that she needed time off. It clearly wasn't to do with their row; it was then that she had told him that she loved him. Bergin had said something about her getting some disturbing information. Maybe that was it. He had said that it was personal. *What could it be? Was it about her father? Yeah, that would be understandable. She had lived with a romantic image of her dad all those years and maybe she now found the reality to be very different.* That vague image of her mother working with his own father in Brantoil all those years ago came into his mind. He had never told Patricia that he could remember her mother. He himself didn't understand why; why he didn't want to talk to her about either of them. His thoughts were interrupted by her beautiful, sensuous accent and his heart flipped again.

"Hello, this is Patricia. Sorry I can't take your call right now, but—"

Her voicemail. He switched off the phone. Whatever the mystery of her stress, it would have to wait until his return. "The story of my life," he muttered silently. He felt strangely disturbed as he made his way back to join Brennan in the passenger area. Yes, he remembered her mother. He remembered her very well. The image crystallised in his mind. He was so young at the time. He remembered how he used call into his father's office after school. It was such a fun place. Patricia's mother was always there. So friendly, so loving. He remembered how they talked to each other – his dad and Patricia's mother. Not like at home. *Why couldn't he talk to my mother like that? Why were they always rowing? Why couldn't he have taken my mother on those business trips? Why always her mother?* The perspiration rolled down his face. His chest tightened. The relationships now became obvious. He knew that he had always tried to blot out the obvious. He quickly found the toilet and vomited violently. "Jesus no, don't let it be. Oh God!" He buried his face in his hands as the realization sank in. *Oh God, how could you let it happen? Of all the women in the world how could you let me fall in love with my own sister?* He thought of her. *Poor Patricia! That's obviously what she has discovered. No wonder she wants to hide.* He sat there motionless for what seemed an age. *What am I doing here? What's it all about?*

———————◆———————

It didn't seem like a week since he had agreed to travel to Moscow accompanied by Matthew Brennan. The government had only recently taken delivery of its new aircraft, and the trip, Ed assumed, was seen as a familiarization opportunity for the pilots and crew.

The flight time was around four hours, and with a three-hour time difference, they were due to arrive in Moscow at 2.00 p.m. local time. Global Oil had arranged accommodation for Ed at the five-star Moscow Hotel National, one of the top hotels in Russia. Matthew Brennan was staying at the home of his friend, who ran the Moscow office of Enterprise Ireland, the Irish government's agency for trade development. He indicated that he would be returning to Dublin the following day, having done all he could to ensure that Ed was facilitated in every way, in what he believed was a mission to secure crude oil supplies for Ireland. Ed was happy to go along with this agenda. He needed space to think. He needed to sort out his head. He also did not want Brennan to be aware of any real business in which he might get involved on behalf of Global Oil.

"We've made arrangements to visit the Russian Ministry of Foreign Affairs, known as MID, tomorrow morning at nine, to be followed at noon by a meeting with the First Deputy Energy Minister of the Russian Federation."

"Very good. I appreciate that," Ed acknowledged with sincerity.

"This evening, if you're free, we can have dinner with Tom Scott of Enterprise Ireland, and also an American lady, Samantha Travers—or Sam, as she's known. She acts as a consultant to foreign companies interested in doing business with the Russians. She's very knowledgeable on modern-day Russia. I think you'll find her interesting."

"Sounds good."

Ed was aware from his briefing by Norman Kem in New York, that in the early 1990's, the World Bank International Finance Corporation had sent hundreds of young professionals to the former Soviet Union to help with economic reform and privatisation planning. Many of these idealistic IFC staffers now found that their inside knowledge of post-Soviet capitalism, and personal ties to leading officials, was a marketable expertise. These young professionals were known as 'The IFC Mafia.' Sam Travers was, according to Brennan, one of the most successful. Ed looked forward to meeting her.

The shamrock-emblazoned government jet secured VIP treatment at Sheremetevo-2, Moscow's international gateway airport, and it wasn't long before Ed and Brennan were comfortably seated in the embassy's Mercedes S Series. The smartly uniformed driver was Russian, and made a valiant effort to comment on the sights of interest, as they made their way along a busy eight-lane boulevard, heading northeast towards the city centre, 28 km. away.

As they chatted and exchanged whatever titbits of information each had on the city and history of Moscow, the distinctive tones of his cell phone sounded from deep within his briefcase. Mindful of the previous mishap, when in his anxiety he had dropped the phone, he was deliberate in calmly and coolly opening the case and reaching inside.

"This will be my office," he said as he pressed the accept button.

Nothing happened. The melody continued to resound throughout the car.

"Jaysus, it's mine," shouted Brennan. "I didn't recognise the tone. I forgot to get my daughter to change the tone setting back after she borrowed it." He fumbled frantically to extract his phone from his inside pocket.

Ed Brant could have told him. But who would believe it could happen again? Sure enough, the phone jumped six inches out of his hand and landed exactly where Ed's had landed only a few weeks previously: between the driver's seat and the gear box housing. Brennan was frantic. He could see it but not reach it. It was the Minister calling.

"Jaysus," he uttered as the ringing stopped.

He got down on his hands and knees to retrieve the phone before it rang again. Ed could have told him. He'd have to stop the car and move the seat back. Too late; it rang again—only this time it seemed to ring with greater urgency.

"Jaysus!"

Ed took control of the situation. The driver didn't help. He just tapped out his disdain with his leather-gloved fingers on the leather-covered wheel.

"Here's a pencil, Matt." He reckoned the situation entitled him to dispense with formality. "See if you can press the accept button."

He did as directed.

"Now press the loudspeaker button."

An angry voice echoed around the car, "Are you there, Brennan? Christ, man, speak up. I can't hear you."

Ed could see the funny side. Brennan, with his arse in the air and his ear to the floor, could not.

"Sorry, Minister, it's just a bit difficult to talk right now."

"Okay, I just want to tell you that the Taoiseach has talked to Putin; your meeting tomorrow will be in the Kremlin. Make sure you keep your ear to the ground and come back with the goods, or I suppose in your case, the oil."

With that, the phone went dead. Brennan scrambled back into his seat to resume the sightseeing. He was sweating profusely and breathing heavily but otherwise acted as if nothing had happened. Ed couldn't resist.

"I suppose that's what's meant by keeping your ear to the ground?"

In the space of thirty minutes Ed had seen more Mercedes and BMWs than anywhere else in the world. In a few years, it seemed, Moscow had been transformed from a picturesque, medieval city into a sprawling, modern, western-style metropolis with new office and apartment complexes and garish advertising banners. The Soviet planners had blasted away old quarters of the city to erect massive hotels and force through multi-lane highways.

It wasn't long before they arrived at the hotel. Standing just across the road from the Kremlin and Red Square, the Hotel National was impressive. Its architecture captured his mood. His Moscow experience was, so far, made up by a series of contradictory events, from the most austere to the most ridiculous. Here was another. The facade was decorated with sculpted nymphs and ornate stone tracery, only to be topped with a mosaic from the Soviet era, featuring factory chimneys belching smoke, oil derricks, electricity pylons, railway engines, and tractors.

And it wasn't finished yet.

The embassy driver insisted on helping with the check-in. Although the reception staff seemed to have perfect English, the procedure was conducted in Russian. Watching from the side, it appeared to Ed from the driver's pleas, that despite flashing some rouble notes under the nose of the check-in staff, he was being disappointed.

"Sorry, I really wanted to get you Lenin's room but, unfortunately, it is already occupied."

He thought that Ed would appreciate occupying the same room—number 107—that Lenin lived in for a week before moving into the Kremlin in 1918.

Ed was secretly glad at his failure. The bedroom he did get was extremely large and tastefully luxurious in its furnishings. It had high ceilings and highly polished wooden floors covered in rugs, but most of all, it had a spectacular view of the Kremlin.

As he looked over the famous Square from his bedroom window, he realised that he had four hours before the arranged time for dinner at The Central House of Writers on Povarskaya ulitsa, one of Moscow's most exclusive restaurants. *Four hours*, he thought, *four hours of brooding. I need to get out. I need to clear my head before I meet these people.* He remembered seeing details of a guided walking tour advertised in the reception area on arrival. *I'll take advantage of the hotel's central location and see some of Moscow.*

On approaching Red Square with his guide, they passed a dour mass that he was informed was the Moskva Hotel, where Guy Burgess, the infamous British spy, lived until his death in 1963.

His guide was amused at the story explaining its asymmetrical façade; its architect submitted two variations to Stalin, who casually approved both, not realizing that he was supposed to choose between them. No one dared correct the mistake. Ed couldn't help but note the obvious similarity with Papandreou's management image.

The Moskva Hotel is within sight of the Resurrection Gate, at the northern end of Red Square, and Brant could see, framed within its arch, the wondrous St. Basil's Cathedral at the other end of the square. This gate, the guide informed him, is a replica of a sixteenth-century gateway that was pulled down in 1931 as part of Stalin's determination to make Red Square more accessible for tanks and marchers. He obviously was very focused; another quality he shared with Papandreou.

As they entered the vast cobbled expanse of Red Square, Ed was very conscious that this was the spiritual heart of both the capital and the nation. He clearly remembered watching television broadcasts of military parades on May Day and on the anniversary of the Revolution, when rows of grim-faced Soviet leaders observed the spectacle from outside Stalin's Mausoleum. They, in turn, were undoubtedly scrutinised by professional Kremlinologists in the West, trying to establish the current pecking order and line of succession.

Looking to the southern end of the Square, Ed stood in awe at the outline of St. Basil's Cathedral silhouetted against the skyline where Red Square slopes down towards the Moskva River. The sight of the fantastic cupolas of the Cathedral, quintessential symbol of Moscow, was, he thought, unforgettable, as were the many legends that his guide assured him were all true. One related to Napoleon, who was supposed to have been so impressed that he wanted to have the cathedral dismantled, brick by brick, and have it rebuilt in Paris. Stalin apparently also wanted it demolished, but his motivation was different. With him it was because it hindered the mass exit of the Russian army from Red square after military processions.

The impact of Red Square on Brant was only surpassed by the Kremlin itself, the most famous—or perhaps infamous—address in Russia. The Citadel of the Tsars, headquarters of the Soviet Union and now the residence of the Russian President and seat of his administration. But most important of all for Ed, it was the venue for his meeting with the First Deputy Energy Minister of the Russian Federation the following morning.

As he strolled back to his hotel, he felt better. Had the trip been arranged by the Global office, he had no doubt that he would have had no time for such a sight-seeing walkabout. That's the way big companies operated. He knew his father would not have approved. He remembered those terrible arguments when his mother used ask his father to slow down. "Take time along the way to smell the roses," she used  regularly say, but he never did, and spent more and more time away from home, no doubt with his girl-friend, Patricia's mother – "money doesn't grow on trees" was his usual excuse. It was the second time that Ed felt that he had any appreciation for what his mother had meant – for what she had been trying to teach his father. He was now becoming so aware of an aspect to life, indeed to living, that had almost passed him by—an aspect that was so much a part of Patricia's soul. The afternoon he spent with her on Killiney Hill was his first consciousness of the wonders of nature. It now seemed so long ago. *Did it mean the same to her? Jesus, why didn't I spend more time with her? On the hill, in the garden. Hell! Anywhere. As my Executive Assistant, I could quite legitimately have taken her with me on this trip. I wonder would she have come? She would really have enjoyed all of this, and having her here would have added so much more.* It wasn't long before the reality struck home and his sudden elation gave way once again to a numbing despondency. *God, it's all over! It can never be! Patricia and I can never be together but…how can we be apart?*

He felt frightened; very frightened by this new feeling of vulnerability to the attractions of a woman, a feeling that he wouldn't and couldn't resist. He would get her back. This would not be the last time that he would take time off from the hectic pursuit of corporate approval. From here on in, he would share her wondrous world, and the roses that his mother had talked of; that his father had rejected. His fright turned to alarm. *That can never be. It's all over!*

———————•·◆·•———————

Ed Brant arrived at the restaurant. It was a little after eight. It was not the typical Moscow restaurant. Here the food, the service, and the ambience were reputed to be on a par with the best in the world. The reception was warm and friendly, aided and abetted by flickering candles, a large open fireplace blazing a welcome, and discreet piano music that provided background and texture to the hubbub of the excited diners. It had the look and feel of Western opulence, and expense, that he was now well used to. *Brennan certainly knows how to live. I suppose I'm the justification tonight, but I wonder where he eats when the taxpayer's not paying the bill.* The youth of the patrons was striking, and it was obvious to Ed, peering through the half-light, that this was not a regular tourist haunt. Here he was rubbing shoulders with the newly arrived captains of Russian industry.

Over the dichotomy of the light classical music, and the hubbub of the guttural sound of the diners, floated the distinctive 'jaysus' and symphony of sound, that Ed had come to recognise as the unmistakable West Cork accent of Matthew Brennan. Following this melody through the soft lighting, which was further muted by cigar-smoke, he traced its source to a trio seated at a discreet corner table. Here a robust, ginger-haired, ruddy-complexioned, middle-aged, and very Irish diner faced two companions, one carrying the unmistakable mop of dark brown wavy hair, from whom the melody flowed, and the other, a youngish female, with long reddish hair, tied back in a pony tail. The resemblance to Patricia was uncanny. *Jesus, what's the point of it all now without her?* he wondered. His heart, which had started to pound within his breast cavity, now took on the ache he had grown so accustomed to, as his initial elation gave way to a feeling of hopelessness bordering on despair. *What's the point?* He asked himself as he followed the maitre'd, gingerly threading his way through the array of tables towards where he had spotted his host. His deepening melancholy, which was prompting him to turn on his heel and seek the solace of his empty hotel room, was temporarily interrupted when he became conscious that his every movement was being assiduously covered by two crewcut-haired diners, seated in a party of four at the neighbouring table. Four people, but only two—a loving couple—showed any evidence of dining. The other two, burly in the stereotype image of the Russian shot-putters, had their backs to the couple who had the inner seats. Brant glanced around. *No! it's me they're watching, unmistakably. What had Kem said about the Russian Mafia?* He couldn't recall, but felt very uneasy and helpless under this intense scrutiny, which continued unashamedly, until he reached his table and for some moments after.

The introductions by Brennan were brief. Trying to ignore the hostility of the neighbouring table, Ed silently listened to the casual banter of the two guests whom he had rightly concluded were Tom Scott of Enterprise Ireland and the IFC Mafia member, Sam Travers. The light-hearted exchanges were in stark contrast to the tone and intensity of his most recent dinner engagements in New York, and helped him to suppress the overwhelming feeling of life's irrelevance, that now seemed to be his permanent state since his startling realization of the cruel dilemma, that his father and her mother had unwittingly created for their children so many years later. *Of all the women in the world why did it have to be my own sister that I fell in love with? Why?*

He struggled to hide his emotional state from his guests. Apart from his neighbours, who continued to greet any approaching diner with the same scowling suspicion, the atmosphere confirmed his first impressions, and the company, together with the scope of the menu, would, in other circumstances, have been the basis of a very enjoyable first evening in Moscow.

Samantha was an MBA of Harvard University, who had been sent to Moscow by the World Bank as part of its support to President Yelstin in his efforts to privatise the economy. She had met and married a Russian oil executive, Sergei Mikhailovich, and stayed on as a consultant to Western companies that wished to operate in or invest in Russia. Her husband was an executive with Rosneft, the last state-owned oil company. Their combined incomes, she told them, enabled herself and her husband to enjoy a good lifestyle, and a fashionable house on the stately, and sought-after, Bryusov Lane. This was not far from Red Square, and in Soviet times was home to the Moscow cultural elite.

The conversation inevitably got around to life in Moscow. Ed commented on the welcome that he had received on entering the restaurant, which he said was certainly not what he had expected in Russia. As if to emphasise the point, the waitress and headwaiter arrived to take their order. Both were young and friendly, slim and attractive people with faultless English, although heavily accented. When they had left the table, Sam continued.

"Yes," she agreed. "Most people from our part of the world had a set image of Russians that we now see as blatantly false. The image of muscle-bound female shot-putters, sullen shop assistants, police informers, inedible food, and bloody-minded bureaucrats is outdated, as is the Russia of red flags, parades of ballistic missiles, and grim-faced octogenarian rulers set on dominating the world. The city that I know is ablaze with an infectious, creative vitality. These were a people who, under their Communist rulers, were forbidden to fraternise with Westerners, and were misled into believing that their society was the envy of the world. Muscovites felt the disillusionments of the 1990s more keenly than most Russians, although some prospered beyond their wildest dreams."

"Are you referring to the Oligarchs?" Ed queried, anxious to get the conversation round to the purpose of his visit.

"They're only a handful," she answered. "I'm talking more generally. The change to the free market has polarised society and created two classes: the super-rich and the super-poor. Middle-range services have disappeared because ordinary people cannot afford them, and the rich prefer classier, more luxurious establishments like this restaurant. These super-rich live in a different world. This immense wealth cuts them off from ordinary life."

Ed looked around.

She sensed his question.

"Those who work in foreign or private companies can earn high wages in Russian terms, and can afford foreign holidays, one or two cars, and a decent living standard. But to be rich in Russia means to be incredibly rich, and wealthy people have a lot of power.

A younger generation have pushed aside their elders— financially, psychologically, and even physically. More than in most cities in the West, people in their early twenties are highly visible, spending extravagantly in restaurants, driving expensive cars, and dressing in pricey foreign clothes. Age discrimination by employers is widespread, with many choosing to employ only recent, more malleable graduates."

A popping champagne cork marked the crescendo of laughter from somewhere close by. Within the cocktail of merriment it was unremarkable, except for the lightning reaction of the two muscle men at the nearby table. Their hands were almost instantaneously in and out of their jackets, holding the unmistakeable butts of revolvers.

The others had their backs to the duo and so missed the spectacle. When he had recovered his composure, Ed, who had been oblivious to the topic under discussion during the sideshow, brought the conversation around to what had been worrying him since he was eyeballed by the two toughies on arrival.

"What about law and order? Moscow has an unenviable reputation for gangsters and killing."

"Yes," she answered. "It was bad—in fact it's still very bad, although it has improved considerably from the time I first came to the city. With the transition to capitalism, the whole economy came up for grabs as ex-party bureaucrats acquired vast assets through privatisation, and black marketers became merchant bankers. Legitimate entrepreneurs and foreign investors were forced to pay protection money to one gang or another, while in turn, leading Mafiosi found their own protectors among the political elite, police, and the judiciary. This has lead to a situation resulting in everyone being covered by what the Russians call a Krysha—or in English, a roof."

*Seems a bit like the system Tom Bergin operates back in Dublin.* Ed looked across at Brennan to see if there was any acknowledgment. There was none. Brennan continued to probe his well-done steak.

"I've just recently been to Saudi Arabia, where Westerners consider themselves to be the target of a fanatical hatred that seems to have gripped that part of the world. Are you concerned about your safety, or should I be concerned about mine?" asked Ed, gesturing at the two heavies at the next table.

"Not really," she answered. "Personal security in Moscow is generally in inverse proportion to personal wealth. The main targets of crime, both Mafia-related and petty, are rich Russian businessmen, next to whom tourists are considered small fry. Most have their own bodyguards, which accompany them at all times. There are two at the next table," she said, with a nod identifying the two that had worried Brant. "While local financiers are in danger of assassination, the average citizen or visitor is no more likely to be victim than in any other large European city."

"You mentioned the Mafia. Is it still a threat? Ed asked, anxiously watching their dinner-table neighbours.

"It can be. Sure, like everywhere else, the term 'Mafia' includes the criminal underworld, but in Russia, it mainly refers to  the violent enforcers that businesspeople use to gain and keep control of various sectors being privatised. Strange as it might seem to a Westerner, the Mafia were particularly active in the banking sector of the legal economy. Literally hundreds of bankers have been assassinated."

This discourse on modern-day Moscow was interrupted with the headwaiter informing Scott that they had a telephone call for him from the Irish Embassy. He seemed rather excited when he returned.

"Great news. Our meetings tomorrow with the Deputy Minister for External Affairs and the First Deputy Energy Minister have been changed. We'll now just have one meeting," he said pausing, when his voice took on a higher pitch. "Its location has also been changed. We're meeting them in the Kremlin."

Ed looked at Brennan but got no acknowledgment. The spectre of the wedged phone, and the Secretary General's conversation with the Minister from the floor of the embassy Mercedes, as it sped along the motorway, was a subject that Matthew Brennan obviously wanted to forget. Scott was taken aback at the lack of visible empathy, but couldn't hide his own excitement at the opportunity of seeing, first-hand, the inner sanctum of that infamous citadel. Ed, up to then, didn't know whether or not Sam Travers had been aware of the meetings, but her next comment opened up a whole new spectre in Ed's mind of what was really going on.

"The First Deputy Energy Minister—is that Andreevich Matlashov?" she asked, in a tone that Ed thought was a trifle obsequious. "He's actually my husband's boss. Andreevich is a good friend of ours. In addition to being First Deputy Energy Minister he's also Vice-Chairman of the state-owned oil company, Rosneft. I wonder will my husband, Sergei, be attending? He's the President of that company. I mentioned that I was meeting you this evening. He probably arranged the change of venue."

Ed caught the flashing acknowledgment in Brennan's expression. *What was it that Samantha had said about everyone in Moscow business having a roof? It looks as if the lovely Sam is married to one. But by God it seems to work. Tom Bergin would definitely feel at home here.*

Brennan looked at Ed but said nothing. The glint in his eye was enough.

---

Clip clop, clip clop, clip clop.

"Jesus, it'd be funny if it wasn't so awesome."

Clip clop, clip clop, clip clop.

He wasn't even trying. In fact, Matthew Brennan seemed totally oblivious to the racket he was making with those leather-soled shoes as they walked briskly over marble floors, along corridors decked on either side with huge, oil-painted portraits, through huge gilded doors, to the inner sanctum of the Great Kremlin Palace—the very heart of Russia.

The clip clop, clip clop seemed to reverberate forever throughout those hallowed halls, that had seen Czars and kings and Presidents before them. The bouncing sound seemed to give depth to the feeling that they were alone in the entire building, as they marched behind their escort, and were led into what appeared to be a library as the shelved walls, on two sides, were laden with leather-bound books.

As Ed Brant and his companions stood and looked about them, it seemed that they were in a different age, that the five or ten minutes since they walked across Red Square to the giant gates, and through the metal detector and identification check, had brought them to a different time zone. The library of the great Kremlin Palace, if in fact that was what it was, bore all the hallmarks of a different century.

Through the large bay windows overlooking the gardens, they could see the Moskva River and, to the left, the beautiful but familiar golden onion-shaped domes of the Cathedral of the Annunciation. Ed had on many occasions seen the pictures of the Great Kremlin Palace and the domes of the Cathedral behind its great walls. That familiar view was from the embankment. He now suddenly realised that he was doing the opposite—viewing that embankment from inside the Kremlin Palace. It was an eerie feeling.

They were invited to make themselves comfortable in what was a fairly formally structured meeting area within the huge room, and were served tea. Tom Scott informed them that this is the tradition in Russia: black tea with a slice of lemon, sweetened with jam and drunk from a tall glass.

"Don't worry, it isn't habit-forming," he whispered.

Although there was absolutely no sense of intrusion, Ed noticed that at no stage were they left in the room on their own. A darkly dressed man, whom Scott concluded was an armed security guard, stood watching, motionless from the corner.

The door opened and two men entered officiously.

Ed couldn't catch the older man's name, but the other was indeed Sergei Mikhailovich, the husband of Sam. He gave them a knowing smile. It was the older one who immediately took charge.

He opened the conversation by welcoming Ed to Moscow, and adding in a mischievous way, "I hope that visiting the Kremlin Palace was a fitting end to your sight-seeing walkabout."

He went on to say that he had a deep respect for Ireland and the Irish, and was happy to answer any questions they had for him.

"We'd like to get an understanding of how welcome Western companies and investment is in Russia," Tom Scott stated, a bit more directly than Brant would have expected.

The Russian seemed unfazed by the bluntness.

"We need technological help and investment from anybody or any company that seeks genuine mutual benefit. We will not sell our natural resources, or allow ourselves be exploited, as the West exploited the Third World."

"Well, the word in the oil industry is that you want to keep Westerners out. It is our understanding that the Kremlin annulled a tender from Exxon to develop Artic deposits, and Amoco was dropped from a Siberian joint venture with Yukos Oil despite having, at that stage, spent hundreds of millions."

"We will not comment on individual companies. Russia was becoming the new gold rush destination for the international energy companies. We would prefer not to have any U.S. or Western involvement, unless the financial risks are too high, or the technology is more than we can handle. Then, out of preference, U.S. companies would be at the bottom of the list. We don't support the United States' takeover of Iraqi oil, and we don't make a distinction between the United States government and the United States oil industry. They are too close."

Just then the door opened and a smaller man entered the room, followed by two others. Although he was extremely gracious, he had an authoritative bearing to which the others immediately acquiesced. He introduced the other two as aides but never introduced himself. He had a shy demeanour but a firm handshake.

"Whew!" exclaimed Brennan, afterwards. "Funny the way he got straight into it; didn't even bother to introduce himself."

He needed no introduction. He was instantly recognisable. He was Vladimir Putin, President of the Russian Federation.

Before he had reached the table, Scott's last question still hung in the air:

"Rumour has it that you intend to renationalise the Russian oil industry. Do you have such plans?"

Putin himself answered.

"In July 2000, at a meeting in this very room, I told the Oligarchs that they could retain their acquired businesses but would no longer be allowed meddle in politics. I meant what I said."

Scott was in no way intimidated by the presence of the President.

"What was their response?"

"Some disagreed in an open way. In an interview with the BBC, Mikhail Khodorkovsky of Yukos admitted that he continues to support and finance two opposition parties. He recalled our discussions, and agreed that business should not participate in politics. He then went on to advance some inane argument that, according to our constitution, he had the same civil rights as other citizens, and would not renounce his civil rights to guarantee his private property."

His tone intensified as he continued:

"I cannot accept this claptrap. The Oligarchs abused, and are still abusing, the trust that was placed on them by my predecessor, President Boris Yelstin. The auctions where they purchased the natural resources of the state were rigged, the purchase price was criminally understated, minority shareholder rights and share values were diluted, and the cash advanced in the first instance was, in fact, government money that the banks had retained by delaying payments to state creditors. This was confirmed by a subsequent investigation by the Audit Chamber, our Parliament's financial watchdog."

One of the aides that had entered with him, but left, now re-entered, and whispered in Putin's ear.

"Can you please excuse me? The delegation I was scheduled to meet this morning is about to arrive and I must welcome them. I will not be more than ten minutes. If you can wait, I will be glad to come back and continue this conversation."

With that, he and the others left, leaving Ed, Brennan, and Scott wondering whether this had really happened; had the President of the Russian Federation really been in the room discussing his foreign policy with the head of a small Irish oil company and two relatively minor public officials?

"Shush, they're not all gone, and besides, the room might be bugged," warned Scott in a whisper.

As if to reassure himself on that point, Scott stood up, and unobtrusively, wandered past the silent watcher to the window. He stretched his arms above his head as he looked, as if the movement was for exercise, before casually drifting back to the two others.

"It's a bloody Arab delegation. I couldn't get a good look, but those getting out of the car have the Arab headdress."

"Did you see what type flags are on the mudwings?"

"Couldn't see clearly, but they're green, with some Arabic over a sword."

"Saudi Arabia," confirmed Brant, only too familiar with the colours from his previous trip. It was then that he remembered Papandreou mentioning something about an expected Saudi visit to Moscow. It was during their discussion in his office in New York, when they first talked about Ed's mission to Russia. *What was it he said? Yes, I remember: Papandreo's 'ears' had reported that Crown Prince Abdullah, the head of the Saudi Royal Family, was planning to visit Putin – the first time since 1930 that a Saudi leader had made an official trip to Moscow. Papandreou seemed worried that the visit had implications. I wonder what it's all about.*

"Well, you don't often see a Saudi prince in Moscow," confirmed Scott. "Something's up."

The door reopened and, within seconds, Putin and his entourage were again facing the trio, and were back in deep conversation as if nothing had happened.

"Yes, I was talking about Mikhail Khodorkovsky. Well, he has publicly challenged my government's policy on Iraq, claiming that Russia's paramount loyalty should be with the U.S.A. He talked about forming a strategic partnership, even a merger of Yukos with the U.S. multinational oil giants. His purpose was to ingratiate himself with the Americans, and to drive up the price of crude oil. High energy prices are not in our national interest. Our industry needs support at this stage of its development to grow, indeed to survive."

"What support do you expect from private companies?"

"They must help the national effort, they must get into more patriotic avenues of economic activity. Whatever form privatization took in the 90s, there was an underlying social contract; people were given property in order to improve the economy and raise the population's living standards. Even now, I hear rumours of plans to sell a stake in Yukos to a U.S. oil company, and another has plans to purchase Britain's Chelsea soccer club. It was not part of the deal to sell Russia's national assets to foreigners or to buy English football clubs, and I won't permit it."

Scott was getting direct answers to his direct questions. There was no attempt at evasiveness, and certainly no Western style political waffle. Putin's responses were too spontaneous to be anything but heartily felt. He was eliciting exactly the information that Brant needed to take back to Papandreou. Both Brennan and he felt absolutely no need to intervene.

"I don't know the detail of the privatization programme in the nineties, but surely it was incumbent upon the state to ensure that the sale was properly supervised?"

"I know that we have major problems with corruption in this country, and I am determined to stamp it out. Despite the fact that these Oligarchs got the state's natural resources at a fraction of their worth, some of them are still not prepared to pay their due share of taxes. I have just been informed that one of them is committing major tax evasion. Mordovia was persuaded to approve tax exemptions, and sales are being routed through that country to get the benefit of these corrupt exemptions. Should this be proven, not only will those criminals be severely punished, but any Western company involved with the offender will never again do business in Russia."

Ed felt the blood draining from his face, despite the efforts of his heart to double its pumping rate. The reference to Mordovia was like a cannonball hitting his chest. The only other time he had ever heard of that former Soviet Republic was when Papandreou was boasting of how he had wooed and won Khodorkovsky. He shifted in his chair to relieve his aching chest. The movement caught Putin's eye, who shifted his attention. Ed didn't speak. He couldn't. After what seemed like ages, but was probably only seconds, Putin continued, but now slowly and deliberately, as he continued to scrutinise Ed with those clear, bright, confident, and now suspicious eyes.

"The main signal I want to convey is that you shouldn't steal, and that everyone should obey the law regardless of your position or how many millions you have."

He then seemed to dismiss any internal misgivings, and continued with a resurgence of his initial confidence to what, Ed sensed, was his main interest and reason for being there.

"The Irish Prime Minister will be the President of the European Council during the first six months of next year. I expect the first summit meeting of the European Union, following its enlargement, to be with Russia.

We expect that considerable progress will have been made towards agreement on the terms of Russian accession to the World Trade Organisation before then, and that the Summit will confirm the successful conclusion of those negotiations. This will give a major boost to employment, and to trade and investment levels, between the European Union and Russia. It will be a joint step forward for open markets and trade liberalisation in Europe."

"And, Mister President, are there outstanding difficulties?" Matthew Brennan interjected rather obsequiously.

Putin seemed disappointed that his tête-à-tête with Scott was interrupted, but now, looking at Brennan, continued unabashed.

"The European Union considers that Russia's energy prices on the internal market are providing a competitive advantage to our industry, and is demanding that Russia introduce what it calls a 'competitive market.' Despite the fact that Maxim Medvedkov, Russia's chief negotiator at the talks, insists that energy prices are not part of the World Trade Organisation's brief, Russia will agree to gradually increase domestic gas prices and give private companies access to our state-run pipelines."

"Surely, with the high level of hydrocarbon reserves in Russia, it is in your interest to have prices as high as possible," Ed interjected.

The suspicion returned to Putin's demeanour. He seemed to take an inordinate amount of time in framing his response.

"We believe that high oil prices are being promoted because of the associations and connections between the present incumbents of the White House and the oil industry. This approach is totally at odds with their war on international terrorism. These terrorist organisations, including those coming out of Chechnya, are funded by the oil dollars of Saudi Arabia. The higher the price, the more that corrupt regime can afford to pay for its very survival. It openly funds these fundamentalist training schools that spread their doctrine of hatred all over the world. As a result of the influence that the Saudis have on educating these young Muslims, the ranting of Wahhabism is becoming the dominant form of Islam."

*Those Arabs are in for a roasting.* Ed glanced at the others and knew they were having the same thoughts. *It's probably the only bit of good news, though. I'll be able to reassure Papandreou that he needn't be concerned about any relationship developing between these two boyos.*

Putin continued.

"Having said that, of course, Russia needs the oil revenue to develop its economy. It is our intention to double the size of the national economy within ten years. But, as I have said, too high a price is counterproductive. Our industries cannot afford it without subsidy, which is prohibited under the rules of the World Trade Organisation. I think it appropriate that a reasonable price would be set through negotiation by governments, rather than let oil companies and speculators set the price through market manipulation."

The last sentence was delivered with slow deliberation and emphasis. Ed felt that it was being directed at him.

Matthew Brennan, who had said little since the introductions, seemed at that stage to transform himself into the caricature of a British diplomat. The melody with which he generally revealed his deliberations to the world was replaced with an accent that was decidedly West-British. To Brant and Scott, the words hardly seemed to be coming from him.

"Mister President, I have not had any instructions from the Irish Government on the matters that you have raised, but I do assure you, that I will report your concerns back to my government. My role on this occasion is to accompany Mister Brant, who wished to explore the possibility of negotiating the supply of oil for the Irish market."

Putin seemed unfazed by this transformation. In fact, on reflection, Ed wondered how he would have coped with the West Cork equivalent.

"I understand," Putin responded immediately. "I've had extensive discussions with your Prime Minister. I assured him that we would facilitate Mister Brant, who, I understand, is the proprietor of the biggest oil company in Ireland—eh--Brantoil."

Ed hoped nobody on their side would correct the error. Having listened to Putin's tirade against international oil companies, American in particular, his status as a representative of the world's largest, Global Oil Incorporated—probably the biggest culprit— would have been very unhelpful. He found his open disapproval of a proposed Yukos merger with an as yet unidentified American oil company, and his reference to the tax-planning scheme in Mordovia, as particularly nerve racking. Once again, Papandreou's 'ear' on the ground was not hearing.

Ed suddenly realised that the Putin was still talking.

"I understand there cannot be—how do you say it?—a quid pro quo, but I know that I can rely on Prime Minister Ahern to use his undoubted influence in our World Trade negotiations. If, on the other hand, you can negotiate a fair contract on the supply of oil with our company, Rosneft, it will have my approval. I have appointed my senior aide, Igor Sechin, as Chairman. He'll see you tomorrow at ten in his office."

With that he rose to his feet, and shook hands with each one of them with much aplomb. The meeting was obviously at an end. He disappeared as quickly as he had arrived.

His aide took Ed and the others back through the Palace.

Clip clop, clip clop, clip clop.

"Jesus, when we came to Moscow to find out what was happening, I never thought that we'd get it from the horse's mouth," commented Brennan as they reached the gates of the Kremlin. "Beats wandering around keeping your ear to the ground."

"And your arse in the air," said Ed with a grin that his heart didn't share.

Brennan felt for the comfort of his mobile but said nothing. The pipe again protruded defiantly from the corner of his mouth.

———◆———

Igor Sechin's office was on the top floor of a four-story, yellow stoned, white-window-framed building of impressive design on the Sofiyskaya Embankment on the south side of the Moskva River, directly across from the Kremlin. Ed felt it was an extraordinary coincidence that the first Moscow meeting was in the Kremlin Palace overlooking the Rosneft head office—although he didn't know it at the time—while the second was that situation in reverse.

The office itself was minimalist in the extreme; 'if it doesn't need to be there, then it shouldn't' would appear to have been the policy behind its decor and furnishings. The same degree of austerity seemed to have infiltrated its personnel selection. Contrasting with the bubbling confidence of most of Russian youth, the old stereotypes seemed to have taken refuge here. An atmosphere of gloom and doom pervaded the building. Ed was escorted along polished linoleum-clad corridors into a wire-encaged lift that struggled with the challenge of reaching the fourth executive floor.

Following his meeting with Vladimir Putin, Ed had telephoned Norman Kem in New York to find out what he could about this Ivor Sechin, whom he was to talk to on the following day. As he expected, Kem knew a lot, but his information did not connect Sechin with the Rosneft Oil Company. Igor Sechin was Putin's aide-de-camp and deputy chief of staff. He had no known experience of the oil business.

"The appointment of Putin's closest and most secretive lieutenant as head of Rosneft must be a sign that he is, at the very least, about to tighten his grip on the Russian oil industry."

He went on:

"There have been reports that Rosneft has claimed that it will soon account for twenty percent of Russia's oil production. At the moment it has only four and a half percent. I can't help but believe that Sechin's appointment, and that ambitious claim, are connected. But where will Sechin pick up that additional fifteen percent, unless by grabbing back chunks of the privatised sector?"

Ed was eventually led into a reception area that housed the executive offices. Apart from some dark wall hangings and pictures of tank ships, oil derricks and some very Russian-looking gentlemen, the ambiance was no better than at the lower levels. Out of this dullness stepped a man with his arm extended. It was, after Vladimir Putin, the most powerful man in the Russian Federation.

Igor Sechin's manner was youthful, casual, and confident, and his perfect English gave testament to the accomplished linguistic skills that Kem had spoken of. After the initial handshake, he seemed to revert to character. He became somewhat taciturn and withdrawn, but business-like to the point of abruptness, yet there was no trace of the confrontational demeanor that some Russian officials used to mask inferiority complexes when dealing with Westerners. Like Vladimir Putin, he came across as one of the new breed of Russians who meant business, knew where they were going, and were impatient to get there. He bore little resemblance to the heavily-yoweled and buttoned-up bureaucrats, reminiscent of the Soviet era.

He wasted no time. He sat behind a wooden desk and faced Ed, who had been directed to the only other chair in the room. The sparseness of the earthly comforts inhibited Ed from deliberately looking around. But the only noticeable trace of luxury seemed to be Sechin's black leather swivel chair, a modest photograph of his mentor President Putin, and a colourful and much-flagged map of the Northern Hemisphere, with the Russian Federation at its core.

He looked unflinchingly into Ed's eyes, and when he spoke it was deliberate and precise.

"The President has asked that, in a spirit of mutual cooperation and interdependence, I would look to assisting Ireland to avoid the inevitable shortages and high crude prices that will follow the hostilities in Iraq and perhaps, Saudi Arabia." He paused for emphasis but no response was sought. "What is the consumption level of your country?"

"Oh, eh—about seven and a half million metric tonnes."

Ed was taken unawares by the question but felt reasonably confident of the number. He silently prayed that he was right.

"That'll be no problem. Let's talk about price. While we insist on a fair price that will enable us to develop our industry, we do not want to establish or underpin an unduly high world oil market price where the precedent would enable some regimes to use the excess to fund international terrorism in Chechnya and in other parts of the world."

"I don't understand how you could do that," Ed said. "I know that, after Saudi Arabia, Russia has the largest reserves, but the supply demand balance is so tight, and getting more so with the increase in demand from China and India, that Russia would have to be able to put significantly larger quantities onto the market to force the price down."

"Yes, and that is exactly what we intend to do. Our industry is presently in a shameful condition." As if to emphasise the point, he extended his arms, inviting Brant to look around at the empty office. After a moment he continued:

"It is operating at no more than thirty percent efficiency. We intend to energetically address that problem, and we will do it ourselves. As the President has indicated to you, we will not permit the international oil companies to exploit our natural resources or destroy our economy by manipulating market prices."

Ed didn't know whether it was the now-familiar pain in his chest or the determination, passion, and belief with which Sechin spoke that reminded him a lot of his first encounter with Jim O'Raghallaigh in the Royal Marine Hotel in Dun Laoghaire. Despite their distinctive national features, they were very similar characters. He felt that he was again being backed into a corner, but this time he didn't have that paragon of diplomacy, Patricia Harvey, to bail him out. This powerful figure, who had the ear and confidence of the President of the Russian Federation, was here talking to him in the belief that he was there to negotiate a crude oil supply for Ireland, when, in fact, his only brief from Papandreou was to establish the situation on the ground. The information he had already garnered, on Putin's misgivings about Global Oil's prospective partner, Yukos Oil, Mikhail Khodorkovsky, and the frosty Russian Saudi relations would more than justify the visit, yet he had no option but to play along with the charade.

"Seven and a half million tonnes a year I know does not seem a lot, in the context of total Russian or even Rosneft oil production, but it is a large additional quantity from a region that would be geographically convenient to Ireland. Where in Russia is Rosneft's production?" he asked, hoping to create an obstacle and get some measure of control of the discussion.

Sechin pointed to the wall map.

"Rosneft plans to produce oil and gas in the North of European Russia. Its proximity to the industrially developed, and energy consuming markets of Western Europe, makes the region particularly attractive. In the next two years oil production at the fields will amount to a minimum of seven million tonnes a year, even without further development. The Irish market will fit in quite well. We should not have a problem in stretching production to what you require."

Ed said nothing; his mind was working furiously and his chest was throbbing. *Jesus, what have I got myself into? These guys have made it abundantly clear that American companies are not welcome. They won't be too happy when they discover that I've wasted not just this man's time, but also President Putin's. Christ, why didn't I correct him when he first indicated that he thought I was representing Brantoil, and that that little distributorship in Ireland was a major player in the Irish oil market? Not only will I have some explaining to do to whatever is the modern equivalent of the KGB, but this episode could also create a fuckin' international incident that'll embarrass both the Irish government and Global. Papandreou will probably not believe that Global's failure to do business with Yukos was doomed from the start, and will probably conclude that my fuckin' tinkering with his negotiations was the cause. Jesus, how do I get out of this? Ah, I know—the price will probably be unacceptable anyway. I'll be able to gracefully withdraw on that pretext.*

"Can we talk about price?"

"As I said, we want a fair, sustainable price. I know OPEC was looking at a range of up to twenty-eight dollars a barrel. We think that's too low. We would require thirty-two dollars with thirty days payment."

Ed was dumbstruck. That morning in the hotel he had accessed his e-mails. The price on the New York Mercantile Exchange was $42 and rising. As far as the oil industry was concerned, prices below $50 would, in the short term, be history.

"Thirty-two dollars!" He tried desperately to keep the incredulity out of his voice and the tightness in his chest from showing in his expression. "Fixed for what period?"

"We'd be happy to maintain supply over ten years, and to fix the dollar price for that period, with an annual adjustment to compensate for the higher of U.S. and European inflation. We insist that the purchasing power of our oil revenues be maintained."

"Where's the port of loading?" Ed asked, knowing that, quite often in winter months, the most northerly Russian ports are ice-bound.

"That I can't say right now. But we will guarantee delivery into your nominated storage, west coast United Kingdom, in super-tankers. We know that you do not have a catalytic cracking refinery in Ireland, so you would probably want to use the U.K. refineries."

This was astounding. Ed had assumed that the astonishingly low price that he was offering was for loading at some port in northern Russia. But no, he was incredibly confirming delivery into a refinery close to Dublin, which was easily worth another several dollars per tonne in freight costs.

"That sounds fair," he heard himself saying. "What happens if we can't place all of the crude oil? We don't have one hundred percent of the market—yet."

"You can confirm your option to take up your annual quota each year, with three months notice. If you overestimate and have to place some elsewhere, that'll be okay, but we would have to charge you a freight differential if that was further. It'll be your product, and we will have discharged our commitment to your Prime Minister."

*This gives me the flexibility of assigning the crude to Global Oil. My God, if I'd sat down to write the contract, I couldn't have done better!*

"You've got a deal. It's a pleasure to do business with you."

"Thank you very much. The President will be pleased. Please advise your Prime Minister." With that he outstretched his hand.

"I'll have a contract to you at your hotel later today. I would hope we can sign it tomorrow."

That was clearly the end of the meeting. Both travelled down in the elevator and Sechin saw him to the door.

Windfalls happen in the oil business. They generally relate to discoveries of crude oil in areas where hope had been abandoned, or where reserves are suddenly found to be much larger than expected. They are rare, but do happen. What never happens, is that seven and a half million tonnes of oil a year is sold to somebody at up to fifteen dollars a barrel, or over a hundred dollars a tonne, under the market price. This is what Sechin was doing. It would be worth almost a billion dollars a year to Global.

*Jesus! Almost a thousand million dollars a year for ten fuckin' years.* It was the most bizarre business experience of his life. It was the key to his life-long ambition. With Patricia as his wife, he could have started a new life in the corporate clouds of Houston, as the Vice President of North American Petroleum Operations, en route to succeeding Dino Papandreou as the Senior Vice President when he became Chairman.

*Yes, Dad! I've done what you wanted me to do. I've risen above it. I'm secure. I'm invulnerable. I knew you were wrong about me. I've made it! But you know what, I don't care anymore. It means nothing. You've seen to that.*

———◆:◆:◆———

# CHAPTER 9

The bottle of Charles Heidsieck 1989 stood unopened as Ed Brant sat on the edge of his four-poster bed and pondered on what might have been, as he stared vacantly at the mustard-coloured magnificence of that infamous building across Red Square. It stared back with defiant complicity, and he wondered what drama was now unfolding behind those dark, white-framed panes.

Funny how such a historical symbol of oppression could, in a matter of minutes, catapult me and Global Oil into the super league of capitalism's earners. His achievement was greater than even he had ever imagined possible. Now he could  negotiate the terms of that promotion. Now he could have slowed down and done the things that Patricia wanted. Now he could have everything. Everything that is, except what he really wanted – a future with the only real love he had ever known. He slipped off his shoes and socks and lay back on the bed. The rest would ease his heartburn.  He knew he to had to shake himself out of this state of hopelessness, despondency and dejection. He had to live, he had to go on. Global Oil would not be concerned about his shattered love-life; in fact about any aspect of his life except in his continuing ability to produce; to add to its bottom-line. He had to call Papandreou. He would do that now as he awaited delivery of the contract from Igor Sechin's office.

He considered what he should say. It would be a classical 'good news, bad news' situation. On the one hand, he would be telling Papandreou that his contact man in Russia was not exactly a favourite son of the system and seemed intent on self destruction, but also, that the Morovian scheme that Papandreou had been so proud of, was being unravelled and could be explosive. On the other hand his emissary, the one Ed Brant, the son of Paddy, had sipped tea with the President of the Russian Federation, and had negotiated a deal that, if prices reached the magical fifty dollars—which we both know they will—would be worth the guts of one billion dollars every year, for ten years, onto the bottom line of Global Oil Inc.

The timing was perfect. He was certain that it was Tom Roden's job that he would be offered. Sure, hadn't Roden talked his way out of his job with his crude incitement to mutiny? Hadn't Papandreou said as much in the company plane when they crossed the Atlantic together? But how could he negotiate terms on the phone? No, he decided, he would have only one shot at it and he had to make it count. What was another couple of days anyway? He'd see about his heartburn as soon as he got back to Dublin and then he'd travel to New York. There he'd announce that he had negotiated the contract single-handedly, and accept nothing less than the multi-million dollar compensation package, that Papandreou himself had said was now available on the market.

Yes, the good news could wait. His mission was to report on the current climate, and he could most certainly tell Papandreou what he needed to know. The supply contract was another issue. He would hold that bit of news until he was face-to-face with Papandreou, when he would use the euphoria that would create to negotiate terms and conditions to go with Roden's old job. *Yes,* he thought as he reflected on the strategy, *I'll also be in better shape to drive a hard bargain; this bloody heartburn doesn't help the concentration.*

He sat up and put his feet on the floor. The soft comfort of the hand-woven rug on his bare feet enveloped his whole being as a harbinger of things to come. He would inform Papandreou of the abbreviated essentials of his Moscow visit, as he had planned, and then take advantage of the plush décor and services of the National Hotel. It was time that he learned to enjoy the comforts that wealth and success would bring.

Maybe it was his relaxed state following the champagne, which he had now opened, maybe it was the vision of a future life without the stress and strain of the never-ceasing competitive pressure; he wasn't to know, but before he had time even to think of his reason for calling, he had dialled Patricia's mobile number and was again captivated by the glorious sound of her Americanised Irishness, interspersed with the yapping sound of a frisky dog in the background.

"Hello, Ed, I'm delighted you called. I didn't expect you to call from Moscow. Is everything alright? I've so much to tell you."

"Everything will be fine, Patricia. Don't worry. I know what you've discovered about your mother. We'll work it out somehow. Everything will be different from now on, I promise."

The words had flowed before he knew what he was saying. *Christ, what have I done? What have I said? She'll know that it's impossible! We're brother and sister.*

In his consternation he hardly noticed the pause before she spoke, but he did pick up the emotion in her voice. *Is she crying?*

If she had heard his words she didn't react. *Did I really say that?* He couldn't say.

"Ed, I'm so happy and I've so much to tell you, but I need to see you. When will you be back in Ireland?"

"I'm just waiting to sign a contract and then I'll get the next plane out of here. I feel so happy too. I could make it without the plane." He had said it before he knew what he was saying, but again, Patricia seemed to ignore the passion in his voice.

"Don't try; I'll meet you at the airport. Let me know when you're coming."

"How is bus...?" He almost said it, he almost ruined the moment, he almost asked her about the business. He was learning you can't mix business with pleasure, especially with somebody as sensitive as Patricia. *But it doesn't matter anymore, it's different now; we're brother and sister.*

"How is Bergin?" He hoped she didn't notice the change of subject.

"Ed, he's fine but I haven't been into the office for some time. That's one of the things I need to talk to you about. Ed, I'm leaving Global. I've already told New York."

Ed Brant's mind went into a spin. She continued.

"I have to Ed; you'll understand, with our relationship—"

Ed understood perfectly. Why didn't he think of it? Patricia, coming from the corporate office, would have been very politically aware. She would have seen that it would not have been appropriate for the Chief Executive to have a romantic liaison with his Executive Assistant and the scandal of their relationship would have had catastrophic consequences for his career. Patricia was so clear-headed that she would have seen the difficulties. That was obviously the reason she had been distant since his outburst on the balcony; she didn't want to compromise his position.

"I understand perfectly," he said, although his gut-wrenching sense of loss was in no way alleviated by this reward of corporate salvation.

"But Ed, we need to talk. I can't wait to tell you everything. Hurry home!"

He was left with a feeling of despair. He was devastated. Patricia must know that their relationship was impossible yet this sickening realization did not come across in her voice. Had those feelings that they had for one another been so smothered, by that one outburst on the balcony, that now this revelation of the true identity of her father meant more to her than the unsurmountable obstacle it created for their future life together.

❖•◆•❖

While Ed Brant sat on the side of the four-poster bed, luxuriating in the comfort of the deep pile rug under his bare feet, the rimless glasses of Dino Papandreou glinted in the light of the shaded lamp on the large, leather-capped desk that had been the workstation of David F. Coleman, recently retired. The resonating sound of his heavy breathing contrasted sharply with the silence of the other American sitting motionless to the side. Both combined to intimidate the middle-aged woman, standing expressionless before him, awaiting some acknowledgement of her work. If she resented the intrusion of this overweight bully with the Greek name and clipped American accent, it didn't show through her dignified stance. As Personal Assistant to the Chief Executive of Global Oil (U.K.), she had seen many incumbents come and go. Although it would not be professional to show preference, David Coleman would have been one of her favourites. He had brought their company forward and had shown great humanity and compassion in all of his dealings with the staff. Certainly the personal qualities of this invader, and temporary occupant of the office, didn't measure up to previous standards, and the notice that he had dictated, and was now reviewing, would undoubtedly be seen by all as insulting to the memory of her former boss.

*'David Coleman, Chief Executive of Global Oil (U.K.), has resigned to pursue other interests and to spend more time with his family.'*

He eventually passed the one-page typewritten notice back to her, and with a grunt dismissed her before returning his attention to the Texan who sat behind her during this intermission in their discussions.

"That gal didn't seem at all happy with that notice," the visitor commented sardonically, in a heavy West Texan drawl. It was Tim Savage, former CIA operative and Military Strategist, although more recently and more often, earning his fortune as advisor and confidante to Dino Papandreou.

"She knows that this is the usual baloney that is issued on this side of the Atlantic to cover a dismissal. I'm sure she has seen it all before. How else can you say it? We fired his ass? I doubt it. The staff will also know, but fortunately for us, will just see the change at the top as opening up possibilities for them. They never upset their chances of promotion by displaying too much regret or admiration for the departed. 'The King is dead, long live the King' applies to more than the monarchy over here. I've relied on that response before when terminating clapped-out executives. I've never been disappointed."

"Well, Dino, you asked me to cross the Atlantic. What's on your mind? I reckon it's more than to discuss the ambitions of your foot soldiers."

"You bet your ass. I had half expected Coleman to show up and cause a scene. I've already alerted security to prevent him from entering the building. I hope he has more sense. Not that I give a shit about the son-of-a-bitch, but I've got a corporation to run, and am concerned with that other wimp, Tom Roden, causing problems back in New York. I need to get back there to keep the board cool on our Saudi strategy. Coleman is history and Human Resources can deal with the detail, but I need a security presence here. It should just be for a week or two."

"Sure thing, Dino, I've always fancied a paid vacation in London; haven't been here since the seventies. I hear what you're saying, but if you're wrong, what type of problems would you expect from Coleman?"

"Well, I can clearly remember his expression when I fired him in New York. He was apoplectic with rage, and left threatening all sort of action against me personally and against the company. I believe they were empty threats; I've heard them all on numerous occasions in the past in similar circumstances. It's generally a first reaction, but when the bastards take advice they soon learn that I've got them by the short and curlies. Their pension and deferred stock options are vulnerable. I make sure of that. This usually has a sobering affect. The Global Oil benefit plan has been deliberately constructed to ensure that disenchanted executives cannot afford to damage the company's interest. I've always been careful to ensure that this protection is in place before I allow any executive to participate in discussions of a strategic nature, where disclosure could be embarrassing or commercially disadvantageous. No, that bastard is out of the system and good riddance. I've no time for these do-gooders or wimps."

Coleman's Personal Assistant returned with a number of letters for Papandreou's signature. To Savage, bearing in mind that this woman had worked for Coleman and probably had a sense of loyalty and loss, Papandreou's attitude seemed to be deliberately provocative to the woman. He grabbed the sheaf of papers and, as he scribbled his signature, snapped, "Coleman won't be coming back so pack any personal possessions of his that are lying around and send them to his home address—and, eh, can you fill this coffee pot?"

She nodded with blank acceptance. There were no questions as to where he was or where he had gone. When she was gone, Papandreou used her sad demeanour to demonstrate his point.

"There, you see, a well-trained corporate disciple. They're so predictable. They compartmentalise that section of their lives where they earn their living, but their creative energy or real talents lie undiscovered or only emerge outside of their professional lives. I bet she does just enough to keep her job, day after day, year after year, until she retires having effectively wasted almost a third of her adult life."

Tim Savage got the benefit of the Papandreou stare and tone, and the glistening beads of sweat on the shiny, hairless crown, to indicate that what he was saying was being delivered with conviction and disgust.

"I can never decide which is worse to have around—the wimp like Coleman, who shirks the hard decisions, or the automaton like his secretary, who never really gets emotionally involved in anything of real importance: like the issues affecting this great corporation."

As he talked, he instinctively clicked into his personal e-mail address to update himself on the operating statistics of the Global subsidiaries all over the world that reported in to him, and to monitor the market intelligence provided by his 'ears' in those same operating regions.

The lady, that had been the subject of the disparaging comments, returned with a tray containing a steaming coffee pot, two cups, and biscuits. She placed it on the desk with a faint smile to Savage. If she expected any form of acknowledgment from the great man, she was to be disappointed; there was not even a grunt of recognition as he stared with increasing intensity at the illuminated screen.

Savage was used to Papandreou's regular diversions during their sessions and accepted this, not just because he was being paid handsomely whether or not he said anything, but because over the years, since he had first met Papandreou as fellow operatives in the Secret Service, he had come to accept that this man could deal with the minutiae of several subjects at once.

He sat patiently awaiting Papandreou's attention. Only occasionally was the silence broken, and that was by the slurping sound of swallowed coffee, until the Personal Assistant interrupted to advise him that Ed Brant was on the secure line from Moscow.

"Ed, you've had a session with whom? Well, I'll be darned!"

The manipulation of the computer mouse immediately ceased and Savage could see that the caller was uniquely getting Papandreou's undivided attention. It was apparent that the 'Ed' was the Irish guy who was on some mission for Papandreou in Moscow.

"That goddam crazy son-of-a-bitch."

Savage could see that Papandreou's whole being was in the handset of the telephone. He looked at the receiver as if it were the enemy, and for a moment it seemed to Savage that he was about to hurl it across the room.

"You really believe that Putin has it in for Khodorkovsky? Okay, well done, Ed, let me think about it. I'll get back to you. Stay where you are. Do you think you could discreetly talk to Khodorkovsky? No, don't do that. I'd better talk to Francis Baker. He's the only one that Khodorkovsky listens to."

Tim Savage could see that Brant had obviously asked who Baker was, but Papandreou's attention had shifted back to his computer monitor.

"Jesus Christ."

The profanity was accompanied by an explosive spray of coffee that only avoided Savage by the umbrella affect of the computer monitor.

"Do nothing until I get back to you, Brant. You understand? Do nothing!"

With that he slammed down the phone, and with an ashen expression and coffee-stained shirt turned to Tim Savage.

"That goddam son-of-a-bitch is in Kuwait heading for Saudi Arabia."

"Who's in Kuwait, Dino?" Savage spoke with a timidity that was uncharacteristic.

"That fucking David Coleman has arrived in Kuwait City on his way to meet Aramco officials, and, reportedly, a member of the royal family in Riyadh. If he talks about your strategy to invade Saudi you're finished. Do you hear me?" he shouted at his compatriot. "You and he both!"

"Let's slow down a bit here, partner, I take it you've read something on your monitor. Is it reliable?"

"You bet your ass it is. It's from Jiluwi in al-Khobbar. He's totally reliable. I have him in my pocket. That other snake in the grass, Seb Cooper, is helping Coleman with the contacts. Luckily, he doesn't know that bin Jiluwi is one of our most expensive 'ears' in the Middle East. He's just e-mailed me with the details."

"Where's Coleman now?"

"Jiluwi has taken the initiative and offered him accommodation at the Oasis Resort at al-Khobbar. He'll pour the booze into the bastard pending instructions from me."

"How do you see it playing out?"

"If it's his intention to seek revenge by divulging our strategies to the Saudis, it'll cause a major international embarrassment for the U.S. government, but more importantly, it'll mean the end to Global's privileged position in Saudi Arabia whether or not the military strike ever does take place."

"I don't believe the Saudis will take the word of a clapped-out executive," responded Savage with less confidence than his tone carried.

"The U.S. government will, as a matter course, deny that any such plan existed, and the Saudis will go through the motions of accepting such a denial. But wheels will be set in motion to protect the Kingdom against even the slightest possibility of it being true. The board will need a scapegoat to keep Washington happy. I won't be falling on my goddamn sword." The final few words were said with a menace that made Savage reminisce of their days together in a different era and a different world.

Savage leaned forward and, with the intensity that Papandreou remembered from their time behind the Iron Curtain, he spoke with a deliberateness that left old comrades under no illusions as to what needed to be done.

"Dino, you sort out your Russian problem and I'll stop Coleman."

With no further word he rose and left the office. Papandreou remained deep in thought. He hadn't really heard Savage. He knew everyone had his price. Coleman would be costly, but that couldn't be helped. There was only one man he could trust with getting a job done. Luckily, he had finished in Moscow. He'd tell Brant to meet Coleman in al-Khobbar. He himself would get back onto that Russian problem with that maverick Khodorkovsky, and his company, Yukos.

———————◆•◆•◆———————

The sun glinted on the whirring rotary blades of the Augusta A 109 helicopter as it hovered high above the narrow streets of Palma de Mallorca before edging northwards, where the built-up landscape gave way to open countryside dotted with citrus groves, and dissected with blacktopped motorways. The blue sky, and clear cool air of the spring morning, afforded spectacular views of the approaching Sierra de Tramuntana mountains that cosseted their thirteenth century castle destination, in a peaceful embrace. However, their majestic dominance did little to attract the interest of the lone passenger. The offer by the pilot to circle the area's beauty spots was dismissed ungraciously by the heavyset American oilman, who was clearly focused on getting on with whatever business he had with the pilot's employer, the multi-millionaire solicitor, Francis Baker. *So unlike the Russians,* he thought, who generally were childlike in their enthusiasm for the tour and generous in their appreciation.

Although Francis Baker normally worked out of his plush London Park Lane office, he proposed that, 'for reasons of confidentiality,' Papandreou would be collected by limo at his central London hotel and taken directly to Heathrow. From there, he would be flown by private jet to Palma, and then by helicopter to Baker's private mountain residence, close to the beautiful Soller valley of northern Majorca. Offering hospitality in a castle of thirteenth century vintage, in such an exotic location, was designed to impress stressed-out executives and, generally, enabled the host to extract concessions that otherwise might not have been possible.

Francis Baker had a reputation for knowing Russian corporate law as well as anyone; he had framed and drafted most of it at the request of the Oligarchs, following privatisation. The Oligarchs knew that the fortunes they had amassed, by being quick-witted and fast of foot during those days of winner-take-all, could just as easily be lost. The violent turf wars, that were the order of the day in the mid 90s, were behind them, and the consolidation of their gains needed a more stable legal environment. Prior to Putin coming to Moscow, it was possible for businessmen with money to use their Krysha, or their roof, as their political protégé was called, to have almost any requirement enacted into law. Francis Baker, on behalf of Khodorkovsky and others, had invested millions of dollars in creating a legal framework that enabled them do almost anything with the companies they controlled. Baker was now, on his own account, reaping additional millions by steering Western multinationals through the legal maze that he had created for the Oligarchs, and with their money. Visitors like Papandreou, alighting from the blue and white cabin of the private helicopter in the gardens of the beautiful villa, high in the mountains overlooking the sleepy town of Soller, were now a familiar sight to the welcoming staff of this mountain retreat.

"I can't believe Putin will do anything to upset the applecart," Baker was assuring Papandreou as they sipped white wine and enjoyed canapés on the garden terrace overlooking the valley. "To attract Western investment, and to gain membership of the World Trade Organisation, it is essential that Russia presents a convincingly stable environment."

Although it wasn't prudent, from a fee standpoint, to minimise the difficulty when talking to Papandreou, Baker showed little concern that Putin would upset their plans.       "P r o v i d e d companies act within the law as it stands, the authorities can do very little without damaging their credibility. Arbitrary or retroactive laws would destroy the confidence that Putin is so anxious to develop."

Francis Baker was a close friend and confidante of Mikhail Khodorkovsky. It was through Baker that Papandreou had negotiated the Yukos deal, and it was to finalise those negotiations that Papandreou had really now, personally, come to London.

"I know Mikhail is headstrong, and he does have some strongly-held political views, but I know him well and know that he will always stop short of provoking a reaction that would jeopardise our plan. There's too much at stake."

The plan he was referring to was simple. A new company was to be formed through a merger of Yukos Oil and Sibneft, Russia's first and fifth largest oil companies, with the European assets of Global Oil. This would create the largest publicly traded oil and gas company in the world. To obscure the sale and the gradual transfer of total ownership to Global Oil, Baker had set up a network of offshore companies through which the share ownership would be passed. The entire scheme had been Baker's brainchild, and it was to him that Papandreou now turned to discuss the disturbing news that he had received from Brant in Moscow.

"No, it couldn't happen," he said confidently. "The publicity would make it impossible for Putin to interfere, no matter how much he resents the surrender of control over Russia's natural resources to an American company. Besides, so much has happened in Russia in the last ten years, that if Putin was to turn over rocks looking for something on Khodorlovsky, he wouldn't know where to start."

For emphasis he swept the beautiful valley stretching far below with his outstretched arm. The thousands of boulders and rocks, of all shapes and sizes, illustrated the point but hardly satisfied his client. Prompted by Papandreou's quizzical look, Baker continued.

"To be on the safe side, we'll just delay the news of Global's involvement. The Kremlin will already have publicly approved the merger of the two Russian companies, Yukos and Sibneft, and any subsequent objection would be seen for what it is: blatant anti-Western bias."

"I find it hard to believe that breaking up the deal into two transactions will cause Putin any great difficulty if the son-of-a-bitch has it in mind to scuttle the merger."

"Well, as I said, I don't believe Putin will have the nerve to upset the West, but okay, I'll also talk to my friend, Khodorkovsky, and persuade him to back out of any politics he's been involved in, until we can put the deal to bed."

Papandreou had no option. It was critical that he kept Baker onside. He was vital to the plan. It was due to Baker that he had been able to conclude the deal with Yukos and Sibneft despite the interest of some of the other multinationals, and it was due to Baker that he had been able to put the Morovian tax scam together.

Papandreou, for good reason, hadn't told Baker about Putin's reference to Mordovia. Although Baker had been unwittingly involved in that part of the plan, he had not been told that the payment was an inducement. Papandreou had led him to believe that it was to purchase exploration rights on a property that had been privatised. The legalities, he had been assured, had been dealt with by Global's in-house lawyers, and he had been asked just to transmit the payment under cover of a pre-drafted agreement. The cheque had been drawn in the name of Baker's firm, and had been recorded by the Global Oil accountants as legal fees. Baker had thought it strange, at the time, that he would not have been asked to check out the title, but he had been paid his fee and made the payment. He had thought no more of that transaction.

"Right. And the extended timescale will enable me deal with that other goddamn problem that has arisen," he mused absent-mindedly.

"What problem is that?"

He got no answer, but he couldn't really have expected one. Papandreou had not been as probing or as domineering as he had on other occasions, and for the first time since they had met, he had declined the offer of overnight accommodation. Nor had he demanded coffee. He was very obviously preoccupied.

———————◆·◆·◆———————

Ed Brant knew that Tom Bergin was clearly frustrated as he listened to him from the comfort of his Moscow hotel suite. The merger of Anglo Oil and Global Oil was proceeding, and Bergin claimed Jim O'Raghallaigh was doing an excellent job with the integration of staffs. But despite their best efforts, industry events were causing major staff upsets.

Bergin was acting out of character. He was a good news messenger, but what he was now reporting was anything but good. It appeared that Ed's now regular absences from Ireland, the turmoil in the crude oil markets with reports of shortages, and the rumours of an impending sale by Global of its European subsidiaries, was undermining morale. One of Ireland's illustrious economic commentators had apparently come to the conclusion, that the turmoil in the Middle East would prompt American companies to retrench, and focus investment and marketing in North America. The fact that Brant wasn't around to comment was taken as a 'no comment' or implied confirmation that something big was afoot. The staff were jumpy, and the good ones, according to Bergin, were leaving.

"Patricia Harvey going is a major setback; she's hugely respected, and the staff sees her going as a vote of no confidence in Global's future," he told Brant.

"Well, that's unfortunate, but I'm sure she has her reasons. Maybe you could get her to delay her departure until we offload those offshore stocks. At that stage the crude price will be dropping and the market won't be as restless."

"Not a chance," he said. "I've tried already. Patricia has another job, and was not even prepared to discuss terms."

"Oh, she's got a job already. Who is she working for?"

"Jim O'Raghallaigh," Bergin said after a moment's pause.

Ed talked business, but thoughts of Patricia kept entering his head. He respected and agreed with her reasons for leaving Global, but working for O'Raghallaigh? He'd have to do something about that when he returned to Dublin.

Business results were good. Apart from the staffing difficulties that Bergin had alluded to, the managers were getting on with their business. He reported a quiet market but with significant gains available through the standard industry practice of increasing prices before reported crude price increases really affected the cost of their refined products, like petrol and heating oil.

"Careful, Tom," Ed urged. "There are bigger things at stake. Don't rock the boat with the government. I don't want any price enquiries at this stage."

"Don't worry, Ed, I've got that situation well covered. We won't be bothered. Apart from that, we're letting the other companies lead the market; we're keeping a low profile."

Ed knew better than to pursue the issue on the phone but was concerned at Bergin's confidence. He really would have to find out the basis for his apparent inside track with government officials. But for now he would let it rest.

"How's the crude price?" he asked.

"I don't know how you knew it, Ed, but the crude prices closed on the New York market at the highest ever; it was just below forty-five dollars a barrel."

Ed surprised himself at his ability to show interest and enthusiasm. The more successful was his business life, the more desperate his personal life seemed to be. It was as if they were on the two sides of a scale – anything added to one took from the other, and at this stage, his sense of satisfaction, achievement, and personal worth were almost at zero. However, Bergin was doing a surprisingly good job, and if it wasn't for the damn pain in his chest, Ed would have been more appreciative. That would have to wait.

"Well done, Tom," he said. "When it hits fifty, start offloading."

"I think we should start now," he answered.

"No, don't lose your nerve; wait for fifty. Sorry, Tom, the front desk is calling, I've got to go."

Sechin's messenger had arrived with the contract for signature.

It was in English and of the standard format used in the West. The essential clauses were as agreed and stated in simple but legally-effective terms. The discharge port was described as *'anywhere in North West Europe as nominated by the purchaser'*, which was stated as Brantoil.

Brant added his signature to that of Sechin, and looked forward to a few hours rest before his return flight to Dublin.

His rest was short. A very agitated Papandreou was again on the phone. There were no preliminaries.

"Ed, I need you to get to al-Khobbar as soon as you possibly can. That damned Coleman has lost it. I've had him intercepted and bedded down in the Oasis Club, but you need to get to him, and fast."

That mission didn't suit Ed one bit. He was concerned that his chest pain seemed to get worse under pressure, and although he wouldn't admit it, even to himself, there was this niggling doubt that maybe, just maybe, it was more than just heartburn. But he had spent the last several hours, while he waited for the contract documents from Sechin, visualising life as the President of Global's North American Petroleum Operations. He would be able to immerse himself in that challenge without the daily fear of meeting Patricia and, although it had lost its lustre, he was so close to the goal that had been seared onto his brain, that now was not the time to let his benefactor down. Papandreou, he sensed, was near to panic, and Ed had no doubt that a refusal on his part would have met with an unmeasured reaction, probably leading to the redirection of Papandreou's ire from Coleman to him.

"Sure, Dino," he heard himself say. "What do you want me to do?"

"Get that son-of-a-bitch out of there," Papandreou was shouting. "He's on his way to the Saudis to spill the beans on the committee's Persian Gulf oil zone strategy. If he gets to them we're all gone—you, me, the Chairman; the whole fucking company. We'll be another Enron, only worse."

"I'll do what I can," Ed said, easing his aching body back onto the four-poster bed.

"I knew I could count on you. I'll be away from a secure phone for the weekend, but we'll talk next week."

———————◆∙◆∙◆———————

To David Coleman, relaxing by the pool in an exotic resort was not an entirely unique experience. He was a man with a balanced attitude to life. His rapid promotion within the industry was earned through hard work but not at the expense of leisure pursuits, and his ability to enjoy the offerings of the Oasis Club was well within his capacity. Although he had spent many years with Global Oil, he was probably one of the few of its top executives that had never stayed there previously. He had, however, heard of its lavishness, and looked forward to several days of extravagance at Global's expense. The Club was, he thought, disappointing in its absence of Arabic culture, but the blue skies and the warm sun of the Gulf was sufficient consolation as he lazed and sipped, and sipped and lazed, and awaited the details of the financial bonanza that his principled stand had extracted.

Coleman knew that Global Oil had its own intelligence service, and that Papandreou had his 'ears' in every region in which they operated. He wasn't really surprised, therefore, when he was approached in Kuwait City. What did surprise him was the hospitable offer of accommodation at the Oasis Club.

He despised Papandreou, but he appreciated the gesture. He intended to continue working in the oil industry, and he had no doubt that their paths would cross in the future. The scene at that final dinner, and again the next morning, in that infamous thirty-first floor office overlooking Central Park, had convinced him that Papandreou was merely a pawn of the political establishment whose mission was to transform Global Oil into another Halliburton, which was itself no more than an agent of the administration. He wanted no part of that, and was intent on resigning when Papandreou fired him.

The turbulence in the oil market, essentially the result of the invasion of Iraq and the many strategies that were in place to keep the price up, had created many opportunities for people like himself with long experience and many contacts in the oil business. He had received many offers from investment banks that were now keen to get into oil futures, and were waving multi-million dollar contracts at those who could deliver. That was the purpose of his mission to Saudi Arabia; to renew acquaintances that he had established over the years with Aramco officials, but also with members of the extended royal family, with the view to securing supplies, either on his own account or for his new employers, if he elected to take up the offer.

It was through these contacts that he knew that the picture being painted by Brant, and that ex CIA agent, Tim Savage, at the Strategy Coordination Committee meeting was not complete. He knew that the Saudis were very concerned that the American invasion of Iraq was possibly the start, and not the end of their determination to gain security of their oil supply sources in the Middle East. Even if a change in the political leadership in the U.S. aborted any expansionist plans, the Saudis knew that it was only a question of time before Iraq supplanted them as the main Middle Eastern supplier. This would eliminate their influence on U.S. foreign policy and leave them vulnerable to internal and external threats.

They needed a nuclear protector with a dependency on their oil to ensure their survival. Who better to replace the U.S. than the next emerging superpower, The Peoples Republic of China. The Chinese had been very receptive to their approaches because of their surging oil demand, and the Chinese National Oil Company was about to be favoured with preferential status that, up to now, had been the sole preserve of Global Oil Inc.

Because of the friendly rather than official business relationship with his informants, Coleman was not prepared to raise these issues at the meeting, but had tried, on two occasions, both at dinner and again on the following morning, to advise Papandreou. On each occasion he had been interrupted in a confrontational manner, and it seemed clear that Papandreou had his own agenda and was intent on forcing his resignation. In the circumstances, with two job offers each worth a multiple of his Global Oil compensation package, he was happy to comply, and accept the golden handshake and paid up pension benefits and stock options.

It seemed that Papandreou was anxious to ensure that there were no hard feelings, and Coleman appreciated the trouble he was taking in sending Brant with details of the package and, undoubtedly, instructions to remind Coleman of the confidentiality and non-compete provisions of his contract. This was standard procedure, and Coleman's only surprise was that Papandreou had waited until now and had not referred to them at the final showdown. However, it didn't really matter. Coleman was very conscious of the legal constraints on him, and he had no intention of jeopardising either his pension or his stock options.

The sunshine of the Persian Gulf beat down mercilessly while he cooled in the crystal clear waters. The female company, and the illicit poolside service, provided an added bonus as he passed the time, and waited the arrival of Ed Brant.

———————◆•◆•◆———————

The star shone brightly through the fog. It was magnetic. He couldn't take his eyes off it. He knew that if he did he would sink into the morass that was trying to engulf him. He moved his head; a cold wet softness touched his cheek. *Jesus where am I?* He tried to focus on the star. *A star in daylight? It can't be!* Ed Brant struggled for consciousness. He became very frightened. He knew he was not right. *God, where am I?* Gradually the star came into focus and metamorphosed into a glint, darting from the gold stem of a chandelier. Gradually the familiar shapes of the bed canopy and the chandelier, bathed in sunlight, came into focus.

He awoke with a start. He knew he had been semi-conscious, but for how long he had no idea. It was the chandelier, picking up the sunlight streaming through the large bay window, that had broken through his comatose state. He raised his head from the sweat-drenched pillow and struggled with the nausea that the effort provoked. *Jesus, where am I?* He tried to place his surroundings: the four-poster, the ornate ceiling, that indomitable walled palace across the square. It all came flooding back. *I'm still in the National Hotel in Moscow*. The contract with Sechin; had he been dreaming? *No, thank God; there it is*. He picked it off the bedside locker and flicked over the pages. Yes, clear as anything. *'Igor Sechin'* immediately above the familiar scrawl of his own signature. He tried to stand. The pain in his chest had ameliorated but he felt ill as never before. Sweat streamed down his face. He made his way into the bathroom. The deathly pale figure that he met in the mirror was hardly familiar. That sickly greenish hue. He felt he could vomit, but knew he wouldn't. What he did know was that he was sick and in Moscow. This was not part of his deal with Global Oil. If he was to be hospitalised it would not be in Moscow, Kuwait City, or al-Khobbar. It would be in Dublin. Coleman and al-Khobbar could wait.

He looked at his watch. He had just enough time to get to Moscow's Sheremetevo-2 International Airport. From there he could get a British Airways direct flight to London's Heathrow with a connection to Dublin.

David Coleman was living in luxury in the Oasis Club. He wouldn't mind waiting a few days. In any event, right now Ed Brant had other things to worry about.

———◆•◆•◆———

It took some time for Ed Brant's eyes to adjust to the half-light. The canopy of the four-poster, the ornate cornice, and the glinting chandelier had been replaced with the sterility of a flat white ceiling and sunken spots. He had an oxygen tube in his nostrils, he was wired to what he took to be a blood pressure monitor, and there was liquid being fed into his system through a tube that entered his arm. A middle-aged, white-coated woman was standing over him with a concerned expression.

"Good morning, Mister Brant, how do you feel?"

"Not great. Where am I? What happened?"

"Don't worry," she said. "You're in good care. You're in intensive care at Saint Vincent's Hospital. You've given us all a scare, but you're a very lucky man. You've had a heart attack, but you'll be okay."

"How did I get here?"

"You had your attack on a plane approaching Dublin Airport. Fortunately, they had a defibrillator on board. That kept you alive. You were very lucky. Had you no symptoms?" she asked.

"I've had a bit of heartburn. I've been busy and had no time to have it checked out."

"Mister Brant, can I say one thing to you? Every week I see people dying. Some will express regrets of one form or another, but I've never heard anyone regret that they did not spend more time working."

"Okay, I take the point. What's happening?"

"Well, now that you're back with us, we'll have to give you an angiogram. That'll tell us where the blockage is. After that, I imagine, it'll either be an angioplasty to clear the blockage or a bypass. Doctor Pat Murphy will be in to see you shortly, and he'll explain the options."

"When do you think I'll be able to leave? I need to get to Saudi Arabia very urgently!"

"You won't be travelling anywhere for some time, and, if it's a business trip you have in mind, forget it. You won't be allowed to even think about work for about two months. I'd strongly advise you to put those rebellious thoughts out of your head; the next time you might not be so lucky; they might not have a defibrillator on the next plane you're on. Enough of that for the moment," she said. "Who is your next of kin? Who do you want us to contact?"

"Yeah, phone Tom Bergin in Global in Dublin and Dino Papandreou in New York."

"Mister Brant, have you not been listening? Forget about the office. Give me the names of those who care about you," she insisted.

Ed stared at her blankly.

"Have you a wife?" she asked.

"No, not yet, I never had time."

"Why doesn't that surprise me? What about mother, father, brother, sister?"

"Yes, phone my brother, Ben, and ask him to tell John. But don't forget to tell Papandreou," Brant pleaded.

"I'll talk to Ben. He's your next of kin. He can decide who he needs to tell," she said.

Listening to Staff Nurse O'Brien, Ed Brant knew well why he had never wanted to marry—that is, until he had met Patricia Harvey.

———————◆•◆•◆———————

Ben Brant was in an uncharacteristic foul mood. He had just left a meeting with government officials, where he had been representing a number of public servants who were members of his union. He could never fathom those higher civil servants. They were on a salary scale where increments came regardless of performance, yet when they came to discommoding their staff, they were as ruthless and inconsiderate as the bosses in the private sector. This lust to exercise power seemed to be endemic to a certain personality type, and that type always ended up in management.

He could never understand how managers could make decisions without regard for the human consequences. They seemed capable of wreaking havoc on the lives of subordinates and of disassociating themselves from the misery. And for what? In the case of the civil servants whom he had just left, for an inconsequential saving to the taxpayer, and a public relations opportunity for some bloody politician.

Ed, he thought, was a case in point. He accepted that management had to maintain a certain aloofness, but how a brother of his, coming from their relatively unprivileged background, could be so unconscionable as to ignore the fallout from a redundancy programme he had launched, and now not even be around to address the genuine concerns of the remaining employees.

Rumours relating to the sale of Global and other oil companies were rife. Ben suspected that they were groundless, as were all of the other allegations of stock hoarding and price manipulation that were circulating. But it was sheer arrogance for the Chief Executive to not think it worthwhile to reassure employees and the public.

He had heard that Ed was in Russia, but even Russia had phones and he could have issued a statement. How he acted professionally was his own business, and he had no doubt that Ed would have no hesitation in telling him that if he commented, but how he treated John, well, that was another matter. To ignore their younger brother's plea for help in saving the family firm was not on. The more he thought about it, the angrier he became. He'd ring him now. Ed would answer his telephone call, or his next call would be in person. He stopped the car and angrily dialled Ed's personal mobile number.

"Hello, this is Edward Brant's phone," a female voice said.

"Oh, I'm looking for Ed; this is his brother, Ben."

"Oh, Mister Brant, I'm glad you called. This is Staff Nurse Collette O'Brien of Saint Vincent's Hospital. I'm afraid I've bad news for you. Your brother has had a heart attack."

"Jesus!" Ben exclaimed. "Is he okay?"

"Well, he's stabilised but still on the danger list. The next forty-eight hours will be critical. He was anxious that I phone a Mister Bergin in Global in Dublin, and a Mister Papandreou in New York. He gave me a mobile number for both. Maybe you would do that?"

"I will, of course," Ben answered. "Can I visit him?"

"Yes, but no one else," she said. "Your brother has had a near miss. He needs to rest and be quiet. He'll be heavily sedated, so don't expect him to entertain you, and don't, under any circumstances, talk about business or get him in any way excited. He is very stressed."

"I understand," Ben replied. "I'll be in right away.

--------◆-◆-◆--------

Papandreou anxiously paced the floor in the Presidential Suite of London's Churchill Hotel.

His innate caution had prompted him to tell Ed Brant that he would not be reachable over the weekend. He had no wish to alarm Brant but, at the same time, he did not want any direct telephone calls that would be traceable if things went wrong, and if it became necessary to deny all knowledge of Brant's mission. He didn't expect things to go wrong. He had confidence in Ed Brant and in the idiom that every man has his price. He knew that Coleman could be bought; that's how the world worked, and Brant was the man to handle the delicate negotiations.

Still, he hated situations like this; a loose canon in Saudi Arabia intent on letting his personal rage drive him to what was really a treasonable act, and then that other, brain-dead multi-billionaire in Russia allowing his ego to provoke a confrontation with the President that could jeobardise his entire fortune, and maybe even derail their merger deal, which would be of historical significance.

He felt the beads of sweat on his forehead as he paced up and down. His career, the fortunes of Global Oil Incorporated, and the more he thought about it the vital interest of the United States, were all dependent on the successful outcome of these two issues. For the first time in his career, he felt he was losing control.

The ringing tone of his mobile phone jarred him back to reality. He noted the caller identification.

"Godammit Brant! I told you I didn't want you to contact me over the weekend. These goddamn calls can be monitored."

"So?" came the casual response.

"So, if you have something to tell me, telephone me on the secure line, not from your cell phone."

"Listen Mister Papandreou, this is Ben Brant, not Ed." There was no effort to disguise the frustration and anger. "I don't know what you expect Ed to be telling you on a Saturday evening that you're concerned about being overheard, but I don't have your concerns. I'm phoning at Ed's request to tell you that he's fighting for his life in a Dublin hospital."

"What!" exploded Papandreou. "You mean he's not in al-Khobbar?"

"No, he's not, and thanks for your concern. I'll pass it on to Ed."

With that the phone went dead.

———◆◆◆———

Completely oblivious to the turmoil his travels were causing in the lives of his former boss and of his aide and protégé, David Coleman relaxed as he waited the arrival of Ed Brant. He was enjoying the lifestyle of the expatriates, and felt life was getting better by the minute.

He recalled Brant's view of the sense of siege that he claimed afflicted the residents of the Oasis Club. That had certainly not been his experience so far, but rather than risk any unpleasantness with locals outside of the resort, he decided he would dine in the plush surroundings of its gourmet restaurant, the Oasis Tent. He had often heard of the quality of its Mediterranean cuisine, and of its very unofficial, but very extensive wine list. He looked forward to the evening when he would also have the opportunity of, perhaps, networking with the other affluent expatriates.

He had just finished dressing for dinner. The Arabian sun and cocooned atmosphere of the resort had already began to show, he thought, as he noted his tanned and relaxed reflection in the bathroom mirror. *Yeah, a chap could get to like this lifestyle, provided one could jettison all morality and be a good corporate disciple—like that Irish guy, eh, Brant. Still, it wouldn't be for me; I'd prefer to sleep nights.*

Coleman's reflective serenity was exploded by a commotion outside, preceded by several loud bangs. The sound of Arabic voices, at a hysterical pitch, was close—very close. Before he could get to the handle, the door suddenly crashed open, hitting him on the face, and momemtarily converting his utterances of indignant protest to dazed taciturnity. His backward stagger across the room was accelerated by the uniformed figures waving guns who unceremoniously invaded his bedroom. He froze in alarm with his hand to his grazed nose.

"You Muslim? You Muslim?" screamed the one who seemed in charge.

Coleman said nothing. He stumbled backwards, further into the room in alarm. Without warning of any kind, he received a vicious rifle-butt blow to his head. He dropped to one knee, dazed, with blood streaming down his face.

"Show passport, infidel," shouted the lead Arab, pointing the gun directly at his head.

The passport was on his bedside locker. Despite his blurred vision Coleman managed to stagger to the bed and, with blood-stained hands, he passed it over.

"You Coleman?" the lead man shouted.

"Yes, yes, I'm David Coleman. I'm an executive with Global Oil. I've friends in the House of Saud."

There was a blinding flash and a loud bang.

Coleman didn't hear the shot. He was already dead.

———◆•◆•◆———

As soon as Ben Brant had unceremoniously terminated the call, Papandreou phoned Sebastian Cooper at the Oasis Club. The attack was occuring at that very moment. The security forces had arrived, but the terrorists, dressed as uniformed militia, were indistinguishable from the compound guards. They had already killed a number of the guards and were now holding some of the residents as hostages. Cooper was not yet aware of the fate of David Coleman. It was some hours later that news of the murder was confirmed.

Papandreou had disliked Coleman intensely—the constant challenging and undermining of his authority in front of the others. *But still, to be mowed down by a bunch of terrorists in a godforsaken desert is a death that I wouldn't have wished for anyone, even a double-crossing wimp like Coleman.* This philosophical concern for Cooper was inevitably short-lived, and it wasn't very long before Papandreou began to relate the possible impact of the event on his plans and strategy. *He can't do any further damage...but what has the bastard done already?* Jiluwi couldn't tell him whether Coleman had talked to anyone of importance since his arrival. *Christ, though, if he has disclosed our strategy and the recommendation we have made to the Pentagon planners, there'll be serious repercussions. It's a political and diplomatic bombshell.* Papandreou visibly shivered at the prospect.

It could not have happened at a worse time: the supply contract between Aramco, the Saudi state oil company, had expired, and the military had not been able to secure the production facilities in Iraq where, it was reported, the situation was deteriorating rapidly. On top of everything, Ed Brant had reported hostility from Putin to the Yukos deal, which at best, on Francis Baker's advice, was now to be postponed.

Papandreou's thoughts moved from the impact on Global to concern for his own situation. If the source of Global's crude supply was in any way interrupted, his own position would be in serious jeopardy. Saudi Arabia was his responsibility. Global Oil would dump him with no more regard than he had shown to Coleman. In every corporation there was, he knew, vultures like Tom Roden, who despite the damage to Global would gloat at Papandreou's discomfort and would, in all probability, be taking advantage of his absence from New York to ingratiate himself with the Chairman.

Yet, he thought, perhaps he was being unduly pessimistic. Perhaps the whole attack was a fortunate coincidence. He didn't know for certain that Coleman had talked to any member of the royal family, and if he did, well, that family was so extensive that not every member would have official status or be at a level that would have access to Prince Abdullah. After all, there were almost as many royals in Saudi Arabia as there were commoners. Maybe he was worrying unduly.

It was then he remembered Tim Savage; his peremptory departure from Coleman's London office that day when they first learned of Coleman's arrival in al-Khobbar. He knew Savage's capability. *Christ, I don't think I told him that I would cover the situation by sending Brant to buy off the bugger. Is it possible that Savage used his CIA contacts to preempt the situation? Christ, is it possible that Savage in fact orchestrated the attack?* Was it possible? He had no way of finding out.

All he could do was wait and see what the fallout would be.

He hadn't long to wait. That afternoon he was summoned to attend an emergency meeting of the board to be held on the following day in New York.

————◆————

# CHAPTER 10

Ed Brant was drifting in and out of consciousness.

He was vaguely aware of his surroundings, and of the regular visits by the nurse to check the readings on the equipment he was wired up to, and enquiring as to how he felt. He knew he was alternating between sleep and wakefulness. He was in a twilight zone. His dreams were bizarre, but he couldn't distinguish between the dream and reality.

He could hear voices—some of which he could recognise, others he couldn't. Some were up close, others seemed to be in the distance. He thought, on occasions, that he heard John and Ben and, once or twice, he could feel Patricia's presence in the room. He knew she was crying and holding his hand, but when he opened his eyes he was alone. He drifted off again into confused thoughts about desert sands, and Red Square, and glinting chandeliers.

He could clearly hear the voice of Papandreou. It wasn't his usual self-righteous tone, but it was his voice. "Condolences to the family of our colleague David Coleman, and condemn his dastardly murder."

Brant knew this was no dream. But what was Papandreou talking about? He struggled for consciousness. It was a television broadcast. Papandreou was being interviewed by Sky News.

"It is rumoured that Mister Coleman had recently been fired by Global Oil. Is that true? And if so, what was he doing in the company apartment in the Oasis Club?"

"Mister Coleman had recently resigned to pursue other interests," Papandreou was saying. "He was visiting the company's locations to say his good-byes to former colleagues."

"Rumour has it, Mister Papandreou, that Global Oil has lost its supply arrangement with the Saudis, and that the Chinese National Petroleum Corporation is likely to take up the production that formerly went to Global. Would you like to comment?" asked the reporter.

Papandreou was clearly taken aback by the question.

"No, that's pure speculation. I've no comment to make on that," he said lamely.

"Do you deny that the issues are connected: Mister Coleman's dismissal, his unannounced visit to see a member of the royal family, followed by the refusal of Aramco to renew the Global contract?" pressed the reporter.

"Absolutely," blustered Papandreou. "I came here to express my personal and my company's condolences at the death of a colleague, not to talk about business at this sensitive time."

"Well, can you comment on the reports that Global Oil and Yukos are in merger negotiations, Mister Papandreou?" pressed the interviewer.

"No comment," said Papandreou, in the tone that Brant knew so well.

"Thank you very much," said the Sky reporter.

Ed stared at the screen in shocked disbelief. Was this real or was he still in the twilight zone? Just then the nurse came in, followed by Ben.

He gasped for breath, his mind in turmoil. David Coleman had been killed in the Oasis Club apartment. He had been there only a few weeks ago, and he would have been there now if it was not for his heart problem. He tried to sit up.

"Ben, did you see that? I could have died too," Ed blurted out.

"And you will too if you continue to excite yourself," the nurse said.

"I'm sorry, Mr. Brant," he heard her say to Ben. "You'll have to leave. Your brother's blood pressure is dangerously high. I'll have to sedate him."

---

Dino Papandreou held the most senior executive position in Global Oil Inc., reporting only to Tim O'Reilly, the Non-Executive Chairman of the board. In that capacity, he had effectively run the corporation, securing the support of the Chairman, and, through him, the board whenever required. In the five years occupying the position of Senior Vice-President, Petroleum Operations, he had never been summoned to a meeting. Meetings had always been held at his initiative. The notification of the meeting, although framed as a request, was clearly an instruction. Papandreou immediately responded.

He boarded the company jet, and within a few minutes was airborne. It was only then that he remembered Ed Brant. He had been totally preoccupied and had not followed up on the perfunctory call from Brant's brother, who, he now recalled, had said that Ed was fighting for his life. He would remember to make a call to the Dublin office when he reached New York.

That didn't happen either. A limousine waited at JFK to whisk him to the corporate office on Manhattan's Fifth Avenue, where a full meeting of the board was already in session.

"Welcome back, Dino," the Chairman said.

Papandreou took his place at the polished mahogany table. He sensed the tense atmosphere as he quickly scanned the pre-typed agenda.

### Report by Senior Vice-President, Petroleum Operations:

1. **Atrocity in al-Khobbar**
2. **Saudi Arabian supply position.**
3. **Iraqi supply.**
4. **Yukos merger.**
5. **FERC Report.**

Papandreou reported on each agenda item, 1 through 4, as he saw them. He had no knowledge of the FERC Report, but knew that this referred to the powerful Federal Energy Regulatory Commission, the government agency that monitors the energy business.

The Chairman addressed the meeting while looking directly at Papandreou.

"I want to express my sincere sympathy to the wife and family of our former colleague, David Coleman, and to confirm that I have personally spoken to his wife to express our sorrow. I must say that I was most embarrassed to hear that you had seen fit to dismiss David without consultation with me. I would have thought that, as a matter of courtesy and natural justice, you would have taken a second opinion before taking such drastic action with a senior executive. I was also dismayed to be told that, although David reported in to you directly, you did not see fit to contact his wife or family after the tragedy."

Papandreou had never been reprimanded in this way before and, in shock, stared blankly at the Chairman.

"On the second point, Mr. Papandreou, I am alarmed that you are not aware that our traditional main crude supplier has just committed almost three million barrels per day to the People's Republic of China. This means that they cannot also supply the United States.

The preservation of relations with the Saudis was your priority responsibility until we got the Iraqi infrastructure under military control, and increased the production to displace the Saudi supply. Instead of doing that, we are told by the government, that you sponsored some ridiculous scheme of our military taking over the Persian Gulf oil zone, which, I needn't explain, would involve invading three sovereign states, as well as Iraq. That plan of yours somehow got to the Saudis. Their deal with China is a direct reaction, and we are told that Prince Abdullah went to Moscow, no doubt to secure Putin's support. Which brings me to the next point."

He hesitated, inviting Papandreou to respond. For the first time in his life he couldn't speak. The Chairman continued.

"My understanding, Mister Papandreou, is that you have a special relationship with Mikhail Khodorkovsky, the majority shareholder of Menatep, the company that controls Yukos Oil."

"Yes, I do," Papandreou spluttered. "He and I have negotiated an excellent deal that I will shortly be bringing to the board," he said, desperately trying to gain control.

"Are you aware, Mister Papandreou, that Mikhail Khodorksky was this morning taken off a plane at gunpoint by the Russian authorities and is now imprisoned on a charge of fraud and tax evasion? Unless you've got some other contact in Yukos, I doubt that your deal will ever be presented to this board."

Papandreou had paled and looked totally defeated as he slumped in his chair.

"Finally Mister Papandreou," continued the Chairman. "The report of the Federal Energy Regulatory Commission. I assume you've heard of Enron and the price gouging and market manipulation they practiced in California?"

Papandreou nodded assent.

"Well, I expect you've heard of the infamous 'burn baby, burn' recorded exhortation by those juvenile traders that was discovered by the Commission and produced in evidence. I would expect you have. It helped to convict several of their top executives."

Papandreou said nothing, trying to understand the relevance of the Chairman's comment.

"Well, we've got one of our own, which I hope never gets the same notoriety. How about 'I've never met a bunch like the Russkis; you don't even have to put it in a brown paper bag like you do here?' Or in discussing how high we can push up the price of crude, 'fortunately the industry has a lot of friends in the American administration.' These are your people, Papandreou; they're on tape, and that tape is with the FERC."

"I don't understand," said Papandreou meekly. "Can the voices be identified?"

"You bet your life they can," responded the Chairman angrily. "That Irish lilt of your fair-haired boy comes across loud and clear. Where is he now?"

"He's back in Dublin. He's ill, I think."

"What do you mean, 'he's ill you think?'"

"He could be dead," said Papandreou. "The last I heard, which was three days ago, he was fighting for his life."

"You're really people focused, aren't you?" said the Chairman.

Papandreou bristled but said nothing. How this man, O'Reilly, had ever been appointed Chairman of one of the largest corporations in the world was beyond his understanding. He was clearly another wimp who had risen through political patronage and hadn't got the backbone to stand up to the political pressure that was obviously now being brought to bear.

It was crystal clear to Papandreou too that Roden had been undermining him and the Oil Zone strategy in his absence. He was angry at the public admonishment, but had no doubt that, over time, he would be proven to be the one who was right. That would be the time to persaude the board to get rid of this part-time Chairman, and his puppet Roden, and appoint him as Executive Chairman.

After all, it was Papandreou who had discovered the false picture being painted of the progress by the military in Iraq, and the Saudi action had long been anticipated. Wasn't the insecurity of oil supplies in Saudi Arabia the whole reason for the invasion of Iraq in the first place? So, he would argue, to be surprised at something that was expected to happen anyway, would just support his argument that the Chairman was completely out of touch.

The proposal to take over the Saudi and Kuwaiti oil zone was a recommendation based on real understanding of what could be accomplished by those with backbone and patriotism. It was not for wimps.

The time to make his move would be when he delivered on the Russian supply. He listened to the rest of the board's waffle, but his mind was on Khodorkovsky and on what the Chairman had said.

---

The mist had cleared from his brain and, for the first time in a while, Ed Brant was fully conscious. He knew he was not alone, but lay there with closed eyes until he could identify his visitors. Ben and another, whom he took to be the doctor, were in the room. The doctor was speaking.

"Your brother was very lucky. The damage to his heart could have been a lot worse. But he was extremely agitated and stressed, and our fear was that he would have a second, and more damaging attack."

"How is he now, doctor?" The note of concern evident in Ben's voice stimulated an emotion in Ed that he knew he had smothered many years ago.

"He's stabilised and off the critical list. But he needs to be kept quiet. Staff-Nurse O'Brien tells me that he's preoccupied with that atrocity in al-Khobbar. That doen't help his recovery. Do you know why that would concern him so much?"

"Not really," Ed heard Ben say. "I know he's been out in Saudi Arabia, but I don't know why that attack should excite him. They're happening all the time out there."

At this stage Ed, fully alert, was struggling into a sitting position. Ben immediately reponded and fixed the pillows.

"I'll tell you," he said, reaching to the bedside locker and picking up the copy of the Irish Independent newspaper that had been delivered earlier. "Do you see that picture?" he gasped, pointing to a photograph under the headline of 'ATTACK SPARKS OIL PRICE SURGE,' which dominated the page. "Well, one of those body bags you see lying there probably has the body of a colleague of mine in it. I was about to visit him. And if it wasn't for this heart attack, I'd probably be in the other."

Ben and the doctor just looked in horror and disbelief. Putting his hand on Ed's shoulder, Ben continued in the big brother role.

"You're joking," he said quietly, but in a way that didn't require an answer. "Well, I'll be fucked. You're probably the only man alive who's lucky to have had a heart attack."

"Let's keep it that way," said the doctor. "Whatever happened, happened, and nothing you can do will change it. So just put it and your business problems out of your mind and let your body heal." He stopped for emphasis. "Otherwise, you might not continue to be so lucky."

The doctor left, and as Ben was seeing him to the door of the ward, Ed scanned through the rest of the article, desperately looking for mention of David Coleman and details of what had happened in that desert oasis that he knew so well.

"Isn't this disgusting?" he said to Ben as he returned. "Fifteen people have been murdered, and this article is just about the impact it'll have on the price of oil. It puts their value of human life into perspective."

"Well, to be fair, the weekend press has been full of the atrocity. You were sedated and obviously missed it, but I take your point. It doesn't take long for the real interest of the media to shine through."

"Ah, come on Ben, you're back on your effin hobby-horse. It's all the fault of big business, is it?"

Ben hesitated before accepting the challenge.

"Look, Ed! This is not the time, but the media is owned by big business. Independent editors don't survive in the long term, nor do those truth tellers that forget that their newspaper or television channel, or whatever their organ is, exists primarily to make a profit for its shareholders. I know! I've represented enough of them to know."

"You're a real cynic. The media in Ireland have uncovered all of the scandals we read about, day in and day out. If it wasn't for the media, look at the corruption that would continue to exist unabated." As he spoke, Ed couldn't help but wonder what his deputy, Tom Bergin was up to, and what he was telling Papandreou now that he had free rein.

Ben seemed tempted to leave the debate for another day but couldn't resist the dialogue that was a feature of those dinner table discussions of their youth. For the first time in years he felt that they were really communicating. He unconsciously reverted to the older brother tone of those distant years.

"Ed, you amaze me. For a smart man, you can be incredibly naïve. The media is just like any other business. Investigative journalists are encouraged to dig up material, but not for any altruistic reason as you seem to be suggesting. It's their product, in the same way as yours is oil. They dig it up, dress it up, sell it, and make money."

Seeing the look of interest in his brother's expression, he continued.

"It's always been like that. Remember Dad talking about the U.S. President, Dwight Eisenhower? In his departure speech in 1960 he apparantly warned against the dangers of the Iron Triangle. This was a term he used to describe a United States where power was concentrated in the triumvirate of government, military, and big business. I suppose since those days another side has been added—the media. You could say it's now a squared triangle."

Ed liked the sound of that: *The squared triangle; Government, military, Global Oil, and the media. The formula for controlling the riches of the world, for changing regimes and international boundaries, for lifting a young Irishman branded a failure by his father, to a position of power that Ben couldn't even imagine.* He said nothing and Ben continued.

"You know yourself the power of the media. That's why Putin has retaken control of it in Russia. It wasn't so much that he did not want fair reporting, but he wasn't prepared to allow the Oligarchs to further their own political interests and agenda by biased reporting. Take the U.S. on the other hand. There the media, Fox News in particular, is so slavishly supportive of the administration that you must ask why. Their stage-managed participation in the government-controlled and edited news coverage of the war in Iraq is such, that it is almost an arm of the military effort, like that other symbol of what's wrong with capitalism, Halliburton."

Their eyes met, and for a fleeting moment they seemed to recapture a brotherly tenderness from shared experiences and emotions of bygone days. But Ben continued. The hurt of the global rampage of what he clearly attributed to Ed and his like had taken over.

"Why do independent media companies act that way unless it's rooted in the profit motive, either directly or indirectly?"

He picked up the newspaper, still lying on the bed, and pointed to the headline that Ed had found so offensive.

"Take the subject that's closest to your heart—the price of oil. You know that despite the surge in consumption in China and India, there is no great physical shortage in the world. So why is there such hysteria? You needn't answer that, but I would suspect that there is a big business conspiracy that includes the media and the producing countries. And Ed, I'd say the whole act is orchestrated by your effen company. I'll be watching for your results. I'd bet there'll be record profits set this year and, need I say it, record payoffs for the top executives."

"Ben, that's the system. You're looking at, and talking to me, as if I created it. I didn't. It's called capitalism and, for all its faults, its better than the alternative."

"Ed, don't talk to me about systems. You'll win any theoretical or philosophical argument, but you still won't convince me. Galbraith, that giant of old-fashioned U.S. liberalism, summed it up for me when he said: 'Under capitalism, man exploits man. Under communism, it's just the opposite.' The systems are designed by the elite, for the elite, and are preserved by the elite. My members, those men and women that I meet every day, are fodder for your system. Galbraith also knew where they fitted into your systems: 'If you feed enough oats to the horse, some will pass through to feed the sparrows.'"

Ben would have continued, so Ed feigned exhaustion. Totally devoid of the energy for a reasoned and credible response, his head rang with the sound of Ben's scorn. *Just like our dad, Ben, you wouldn't understand. You never had to prove anything other than scoring a few goals to get his approval. You're so lucky: you've got a philosophy that underpins your life. I've had to do it the hard way, and now you're knocking even that. I couldn't even begin to explain to you what I'm about.* Through half-closed eyelids he looked at his brother in a way that he had not done for years. *He's so true to his ideals, regardless. With me, it's caused a heart attack, and here he is telling me that I've been chasing a rainbow.*

He lay back on the pillows until Ben was gone. He then flicked through the rest of the paper. The business section carried the next headline that got his attention: 'TWO RUSSIAN OIL GIANTS TO MERGE.' The editorial went on to describe that the first and fifth largest of the Russian oil companies, Yukos Oil and Sebneft, had agreed to merge. There was no mention of Global Oil, but there was a sting in the tail—'*the news is accompanied by rumours that American firms are interested in making a deal with the merged company in order to gain access to the Russian market.*'

He knew that this could be a problem. Putin had left him in no doubt that American involvement in Yukos was not on. It was clear that Papandreou had been able to block any reference to Global being the company involved, but still Putin was obviously on the alert. *Pity the media isn't a party to our strategy.* He knew he'd never use this as a rebuttal to Ben's philosophy. The triangle wasn't square in Russia—not yet at any rate.

———◆◆◆———

Francis Baker was seriously perturbed at Khodorkovsky's obstinacy and uncompromising stance at the suggestion that all reference to the involvement of Global Oil be omitted from the initial public announcement. Baker had assured him that the omission was merely a strategic postponement that would aid their ultimate objective of the outright sale, but Khodorkovsky seemed to see this as some submission of will to Putin. His opposition seemed to be more political than commercially motivated.

"Let's get Sibneft into bed with Yukos first," Baker had pleaded. "That merger will create the fifth largest publicly traded oil and gas company in the world. Without Sibneft you won't get top dollar from Global Oil. It'll only be a couple of months. The Kremlin will have to approve the merger of the two Russian companies and then, when the dust settles, we'll integrate it with Global. I'll have the offshore structures in place and no one will be able to monitor the gradual transfer of total ownership to Global Oil."

Khodorkovsky eventually relented but continued to pursue his political agenda. He had headed off on a week's tour of Russia's provinces, holding what looked suspiciously like political rallies with students, employees, and local residents. His trip was cut short. He was arrested at gunpoint, imprisoned on charges relating to fraud and tax evasion, and levied with a fine of three and a half billion dollars. The Oil Ministry also announced that it had imposed a freeze on the sale by Yukos of its assets. The next contact Baker had from Khodorlovsky was a telephone call in which he calmly asked Baker to arrange his release from prison and, in the interim, to temporarily assume his position as Chief Executive of Menatep, the Yukos holding company.

Baker contacted the Ministry of Justice to protest. He was firmly rebuffed. The Ministry threatened to seize the company's biggest subsidiary, Yuganskneftegas, which accounted for most of its crude oil production. This, Baker knew, would leave the company in ruins.

It wasn't long before the media, both Russian and Western, were heralding this move as a reversal by Putin of the liberal environment that had existed since Yelstin opened the sluice gates on privatisation. Analysts saw a state-owned company, or one loyal to the Kremlin, as being the most likely beneficiary. This event, and the recent appointment of Putin's top aide, Igor

Sechin, to the last remaining state-owned oil company, Rosneft, was seen as part of the one action.

Baker wasn't sure. As Khodorkovsky's lawyer, he had insisted on being given details of the charges against his client. He could deal with most, but was concerned with a charge relating to alleged bribery and corruption of officials in the Russian Republic of Mordovia. The charge also involved an allegation of massive tax evasion.

He could clearly remember being involved with Mordovian officials, but that was on behalf of Papandreou of Global Oil. He was just a middleman, making a payment for some exploration license. At least that was what the paperwork had said, and what he had discussed with Papandreou. With a feeling of panic he instructed his secretary to extract the Global Oil file, and to ask their investigative unit to assemble all of the information they could on Dino Papandreou.

———————◆•◆•◆———————

Dino Papandreou left the meeting of the board a very chastened man. Never in his long experience in business, or in the government service previously, had he been spoken to with such disdain. He was determined to regain his former status within the board, and when he did, he would ensure that Tom Roden would pay for the mischief he had created during his absence in London. But that would have to wait.

He assumed that the information on the non-renewal of the supply contract by the Saudis had come through diplomatic channels, so it was obviously a political decision by the House of Saud and would be best dealt with by the politicians. The loss of the Saudi supply, without the planned-for capacity production in Iraq being available, was nothing short of a disaster for the United States. He had no doubt that the President himself would be using his renowned personal influence with Prince Abdullah.

But, if he could land that Yukos deal before the Saudis were brought around, he would be seen as the saviour of Global Oil, and, at that point, he would make his play for the number one job. Then he would deal with Tom Roden.

He needed to make urgent contact with Francis Baker to get the real facts on the Russian situation. Khodorkovsky was a very powerful figure in Russia. Indeed, he was the personification of Russian capitalism. Although Ed Brant had warned about Putin's annoyance, he couldn't really see Khodorkovsky being treated in the way that O'Reilly had described at the board meeting. Obviously, the report was exaggerated and probably came from the CIA. He wondered why the board continued to listen to them after their disastrous advice on Iraq. No, the only man who would know exactly what was happening in Russia was Francis Baker.

———◆•◆•◆———

Dino Papandreou stared vacantly at the walnut-panelled wall of his plush office, overlooking Central Park. He felt as if he was drowning. The more he tried to save himself and recover his composure, the more he seemed to sink. He had never tried to create friends, either in the company or in the industry, but he never realised that he had so many enemies. They seemed to be feeding off of one another. Now Francis Baker, whom he had made rich, was insinuating that the ingenious scheme he had developed to woo Khodorkovsky was the cause of his predicament with Putin. He was threatening to go to Moscow with the evidence. He had to be stopped.

He could trust nobody. That snake in the grass, Roden, had not only influenced O'Reilly, but he now seemed to have the support of the entire board. In fact, O'Reilly was even now chairing a subcommittee of the board from which, for the first time in his career, Papandreou had been excluded. He guessed that he was the subject of that discussion. Obviously they were looking for a scapegoat. The Iraqi fiasco was not his fault. He had made the recommendation, but had not even been involved in the final decision. It was the invasion that had unsettled the Saudis, well before that traitor, Coleman, had got to them. He had just tried to save the situation with the Russian alternative.

He thought of O'Reilly's admonishment at the board meeting. Coleman got what he deserved, and there was no way he would lower himself to sympathise with his family. Still, he thought, killing him complicated the situation. That was the problem with using his CIA connections. They would certainly respond to any request from a former associate. The trouble was that having paid them he couldn't control their enthusiasm. They would handle the situation in their own way, sometimes with extreme enthusiasm and fatal results. He would have to find another way of preventing corporate wimps from massaging their lily-white consciences with acts of sabotage. Still, the CIA was secure and safe, and Baker had to be stopped at all costs. He would use them just this last time.

He had just finished his call to that unlisted number in Washington D.C. when O'Reilly's Personal Assistant told him that the Chairman was ready to see him.

———◆•◉•◆———

Tom Bergin, as General Manager, was officially second in command of Global Oil (Ireland) Limited, but apart from periodic visits by senior executives from New York and occasional functional meetings of his peers, he rarely had direct contact with corporate management. He had heard of Tom Roden—most executives of Global worldwide would have—but he had never actually spoken to him. He had no reason to, as Roden handled the North American operations. He was amazed, therefore, when his secretary informed him that a Mister Roden from Global New York was on the phone.

"Hi Tom, Tom Roden from head office here," he started. "I'm really sorry to hear of Ed's bad turn, but I've heard from the hospital that his angioplasty has been successful and he should be discharged in a couple of days."

"Yes," confirmed Tom. "I was in to visit him this morning and he's in good form. Looking forward to getting out but, unfortunately, it'll be a while yet before the doctors will allow him return to the fray."

'That's why I'm phoning you, Tom. You will have heard of the difficulty we're experiencing in Saudi Arabia. It looks bad. There is concern that the Saudis may place an embargo on crude supplies to the United States, similar to what occurred in 1973."

"That bad?"

"It's even worse than it looks," answered Roden. "The U.S. Department of Energy has been drawing from the Strategic Petroleum Reserve in an effort to ease the pressure on prices, and its level is now precariously low. We are under directive from the Department to divert all uncommitted stocks to the U.S."

"You mean the stocks that we are holding in Europe?"

"Wherever—anything above your normal operating level has got to be effectively sold to the SPR," said Roden.

"At what price?"

"Cost plus six percent. That's the standard mark-up."

"But that's way below market price," said Tom, frantically reading the average cost that would leave Global Ireland selling the crude to the U.S. government at about eighteen dollars short of the NYMEX quotation.

"That'd cost us almost thirty million dollars," he spluttered.

"Yeah, I know—and probably a lot more when the Saudi news hits the media; the price will skyrocket. It could hit eighty dollars which, taking inflation into account, is exactly what it reached during the '73 embargo."

"However," he continued. "That's all academic. We've been directed to do it under emergency powers that the President can assume in time of national crisis. As an American company, we've no option but to comply."

"I understand," said Tom. "Don't think that I'm querying your authority, but our senior director is Dino Papandreou. In Ed's absence, I'll need to discuss it with him."

"I understand too," responded Roden humorously. "But I'm afraid you won't be able to get Mister Papandreou. He's been reassigned to handle other matters. There will be an organisational bulletin from the Chairman e-mailed this p.m."

"Oh," said Tom, in genuine surprise. "And can I ask who will replace him?"

"You sure can, Tom, it's me. I hope to get over there in the next couple of days to meet you and the rest of the team. In the meantime, send me the paperwork transferring ownership of the stocks, together with your invoice addressed to your parent company, so that we're in legal compliance."

"I'll be glad to," said Tom weakly, wondering how he would explain all of this to Ed Brant.

---

The fact that he could avoid major bypass surgery was the best news that Ed Brant received in what seemed a lifetime. Although nobody mentioned it, and he thought it better to keep quiet, he guessed that this would allow him get back into the office a lot sooner than the two months that Doctor Murphy had mentioned. It was a critical time for Global, both in Ireland and internationally, and he needed to be there to bring the Russian deal to a conclusion by assigning Brantoil's contract rights to Global. He also needed to deal with the staff unrest that both Bergin and the others had let get out of control.

Ben had—purposely, Ed suspected—taken his mobile phone. It was his way of protecting his younger brother from himself, and although it made Ed more isolated than he wanted to be, he secretly appreciated Ben's concern. It meant, however, that he had to rely on the television news and the papers to find out what was happening in the industry that he had being playing such a huge role in shaping, only a few days previously. Despite Ben's misgivings about the bias of the media, with which he totally agreed, it was the only source of business information available to him. He avidly scoured the business sections of the papers and tuned into all of the news and business broadcasts.

He had missed the announcement by Yukos of its merger plan with Sibneft, but the headline 'KREMLIN POWER TURNS YUKOS LIGHT OUT' brought him completely up-to-date, both with the merger announcement, and Putin's reaction with the imprisonment of Khodorkovsky. He noted, with relief, that no mention had been made of Global Oil, although the article did speculate that a Western company had been engaged in discussions with the newly-merged entity. He had almost convinced himself that the whole Russian experience was part of his hallucinations but he now knew it wasn't. It was real. He reread the article. There was no mistake. There it was in black and white.

He wondered how Papandreou would react to the news on top of the tragic events in al-Khobbar. If Coleman had talked to the Saudi royals before he was killed, as Papandreou thought was his plan, then it was likely that his entire strategy was in a shambles: Iraq close to civil war, Saudi Arabia reacting to U.S. hostility, and now his Yukos contact in prison. The consequences for Global Oil's source of supply would be nothing short of catastrophic.

Brant knew that these events were not really helping his recovery but it was a Channel 4 news broadcast some days later that caused renewed concern with Staff Nurse O'Brien.

Standing in a field against the backdrop of a smouldering pile of twisted metal, the Channel 4 reporter was describing the scene of a helicopter crash:

"Francis Baker's Augusta A 109 helicopter slammed into this field about two kilometres south of Soller in Majorca, where it was taking him to his luxury thirteenth-century castle home in the mountains of Sierra de Tramuntana. He had boarded the private helicopter at Palma Airport. Both he and the pilot were killed."

Responding to the News Desk's questions, the reporter continued.

"The pilot reported an unspecified problem to air traffic control at Palma airport and lost control of the helicopter on the final approach. It crashed into the mountain peak that is about a mile from his home. Witnesses have said that the helicopter's rotor cut out. It then struck the ground, nose first and at high speed, exploding on impact."

The News Desk took up the story.

"Mister Baker's death has triggered widespread speculation as to whether he was a victim of a terrible accident or indeed something more sinister.

He had been appointed Managing Director of Group Menatep, the parent company of Yukos, Russia's most valuable oil company, shortly after its major shareholder, Mikhail Khodorkovsky, was arrested on charges of tax evasion and fraud.

Lawyers representing Khodorkovsky said, 'The timing of the crash could not have been worse for the company. If someone planned to do something, this would have been the time that would have been chosen.'"

The News Desk continued with Ed Brant clinging to every word.

"Whatever might have happened between the Oligarch's arrest and the death of Mr. Baker may never be known, but it has been reported that just days before the crash, Mr. Baker approached

Britain's National Criminal Intelligence Service with an offer to provide them with information. Friends of Baker are reported to be saying that he was receiving death threats daily by telephone."

Ed Brant lay back in stunned disbelief. Papandreou had mentioned Francis Baker when he talked about Yukos, although, as hard as he tried, Brant couldn't remember the context. What was alarmingly clear, however, was that being a close business associate of Papandreou was a risky business. Here was the second fatality within a week or two and, as Nurse O'Brien kept reminding Ed, there could very well be a third.

# Chapter 11

"Ya sure you're okay, Boss? Ya don't look the May West. Dat nurse certainly didn't look too happy with ya dischargin' yourself."

Ed Brant grimaced at the uniformed figure that held the door of his mercedes as he gingerly edged his way into the back seat.

"Yes, I'm okay. John, just get me out of here. I've had all I can take of that Staff Nurse O'Brien."

"Yeah, she didn't seem at all pleased with you dischargin' yourself the way ya did. Anyway Boss, you're out now and I'll have you home in no time at all."

"How have things been at the office, John? I've heard the morale has not been great since I've been away."

"Well there was all sort of stupid rumours being circulated... about Global selling out and all that sort of nonsense...caused the staff to be a bit upset and all that. But that's okay now; Mister Bergin has done a great job since you were out...I mean eh, well you know yourself, the people know him and trust him, especially since Mister Roden arrived everythings been good."

"You mean Tom Roden from the corporate office?"

"Yea. He's been over for about a week now. He's usin' the boardroom as an office. Very nice man is Mister Roden, I've been driving 'im around since he arrived."

"You're telling me that Roden has been here for a week. For fuck's sake, turn around and bring me to the office… quick."

"Ah Jesus Boss, I thought ya knew. I hope ya know what you're doin'. You've had a heart attack. It's not like ya had an effen cold or somethin'. Ya need to take it easy. Why don't ya let me bring ya home. I can bring Mister Bergin down to the apartment in a few days and he can update ya with what ya need ta know."

If Ed Brant's driver continued with his commentary on his boss's state of health and his preferred destination, it was lost in the charged atmosphere that suddenly pervaded the car. Within minutes, the back of his boss disappeared within the portals of Global House.

"Oh…" a startled receptionist's embarrassment at her delayed recognition merged into obvious amazement as she gaped at the sight of the informal and somewhat dishevelled appearance of the Chief Executive bounding through the reception area.

"Oh Mister Brant. We didn't expect you back…so soon that is. I'm really sorry to hear about your illness. Are you feeling better?"

The exchange of pleasantries were far from the mind of Ed Brant until the familiarity of the voice jolted him back to reality.

"Helen…I thought you had left!"

"Oh, yes I did, Mister Brant, but Mister Bergin asked me to come back and I must say that I am very happy to have done so."

*I bet you are. I bet that ol' codger has bought you back with an excessive pay packet, in the same way that he gets everything else done. But, well maybe he was right this time. That young fella that he had replacing you was a real disaster.*

"Glad you're back, Helen. Tell me,… eh, is he in?"

"You mean Mister Bergin?"

"No, no...Roden. Where's Roden?"

"Oh Mister Roden is using the boardroom. He is there at the moment. He has just come off the telephone," she said looking at the desk switchboard.

"Tell him I'm coming up."

———————•:◆:•———————

Ed Brant stared at Tom Roden across the boardroom table. The table was strewn with papers bearing the corporate logo of Global Oil. It was obvious to Ed that he had been there for some time. He wondered for just how long; he was obviously feeling at home. On entering the room he had had the audacity to direct Ed to a chair at the side of the long table. *He wants to play his power games. Well I've had enough of this macho stuff.* Ed ignored Roden's gesture and instead took his usual Chairman's position at the head of the table. *You've come to Dublin so obviously your visit is official. You might be President of Global's North American Petroleum Operations but you can wait and play Chairman in your own patch in Houston... for as long, that is, as Papandreou leaves you in your job... which probably won't be for too long.*

"I'm sorry to give you this news on your first day back, Ed," Roden had started. "But your doctors wouldn't let us communicate with you and your cell phone was switched off. I left numerous messages for you, but obviously you didn't get them. Hey, are you okay? Can I get you a water or something?"

Tom Roden looked with genuine concern at the deathly pale complexion and dazed expression of the young Ed Brant. He seemed to be ageing visibly and transfixed as he stared at the wall over Roden's left shoulder.

"No, I'm okay. Thanks. What was it you said?"

Roden repeated what he had said while stealing a glance to establish the cause of Brant's obvious discomfort. The only possible object was the portrait of the original founder of the Irish company, Tom Stone. Brant's Personal Assistant, Patricia Harvey, had insisted on hanging it in place of the framed copy of the company's Mission Statement. "It's far more appropriate" she had said at the time. He hadn't commented, but had privately agreed.

"You're telling me that Dino is gone. I can't believe it," Ed asked in a whisper. "You're telling me that he has been suspended?"

"You know how these things go, Ed. He and the Chairman, Tim O'Reilly, never really saw eye to eye. In fact, they were at opposite ends of the spectrum. Trying to use his old CIA contacts to get his Saudi scheme accepted by the Pentagon was stupid. The President phoned O'Reilly. I don't know what was said but it was serious. Then it transpired that Dino was in the middle of some scheme to help Khodorkovski avoid taxes. Putin talked to the President and that was the end. O'Reilly gave him his walking papers."

"And you've taken over his responsibilities?"

"Temporarily, and that's really why I'm here."

Ed hoped his ailing heart would keep beating. This was it. He'd expected to get Roden's job as President of the North American Petroleum Operations, but it looked as if he was now about to be offered the jackpot. Papandreou was gone and Roden had just told him that he was only temporarily assigned to the role. Obviously that's what Roden had been sent to Dublin to do—to offer him the job of Senior Vice President of Petroleum Operations.

He waited with bated breath. He quickly decided that he wouldn't appear too keen; he would agree to consider the offer but travel to New York to discuss terms. Ed then realised that Roden was still talking.

"I'm sorry to be the one who has to tell you this Ed but, as you know yourself, it always falls to someone."

*What is he talking about?*

"We've lost our source of supply. The Saudis have cut us off completely, and they say they will not deal with Global Oil ever again. The Iraqi oil industry is in chaos and Papandreou has well and truly sabotaged any possibility of a deal with the Russians. The board has been left with no alternative but to sell our European operations. I have been instructed to ask you to act on our behalf with regard to Ireland."

Ed looked at him blankly; his mind in turmoil.

"What will my position be?" he asked, struggling to appear in control.

"You'll be well looked after. You'll be expected to act professionally, get the best price for the assets, and do a reasonable deal with the employees. If you meet the board's expectations on those matters, your pension will be fully funded and there will be a payment of two years salary and benefits."

Ed's mind was a blank. He knew that he was being fired. He tried to grasp the financial details. What he was offering was worse than Ed had offered to the redundant employees of Anglo Oil. He told Roden so.

"Ed, I was hoping we could avoid this part, and so was the Chairman. I didn't outline the full extent of our difficulties. I don't know whether you're aware or not, but the Federal Energy Regulatory Commission has a taped conversation between you and one of your people in Ireland. They intend to use that tape to prosecute the company for market manipulation and price fixing. The board argued strongly for your dismissal with no compensation. It was O'Reilly himself who insisted on recognising your past loyalty to the company. As you know, he's a strong character, but coming on top of the Enron fiasco, the board was concerned that a hefty compensation package would be seen by the authorities as in some way admitting the charge and condoning your action.

What I have offered is the best the board was prepared to sanction in the circumstances." He hesitated. "And it's contingent upon you doing a good deal on the disposal of the Irish operation."

Ed knew there was no point in arguing the point further. He was being told, in no uncertain terms, that he had let down the corporation by his lapse in talking irresponsibly to Tom Bergin, and as far as the board was concerned that cancelled out any other achievement. Despite the fact that he was not the initiator of the strategy that was causing the difficulty with the FERC, it was clear that he was being jettisoned as a scapegoat or, as Tom Roden had told him in their first encounter, as driftwood.

"What is the board's expectation on price?" he asked, not so much to get the answer but not to appear as dumbfounded as he felt.

"The board fully understands the regrettable situation that Papandreou has got us into but, unfortunately, so does the rest of the industry. We've no crude oil source to supply our European operations, but neither will our competitors. In practical terms, Global Oil in Europe is no longer an oil company; it's more of a real estate company and, realistically, our value will be based on our assets rather than an operating business."

"But that will only yield a fraction of what it's worth as a going concern."

"You're right, but that's the reality. The board is concerned that even the asset value will be diluted if it's unsold when we run out of supply. That gives us seventeen days with operational stocks. The thirty million made on the diverted stocks will help the optics but, as you say, it'll still be only a fraction of its worth as a going concern. That's the damage that the megalomaniac Papandreou has caused. It'll cost Global Oil billions of dollars."

"Does the board have a value in mind?"

"If we got fifty million euro, the board would take it."

"You've got it," Ed said.

Roden looked at him quizzingly. "You'll buy it?"

"My offer is open for twenty-four hours. After that you had better move over here and sell the bits and pieces yourself—and tell the two hundred people that they've no jobs. And by the way, that'll cost you ten to twelve million in redundancy payments."

"I'll put it to the Chairman straight away," Roden said.

"Twenty-four hours; you have my number."

With that the meeting ended, as did Ed Brant's remaining life's ambitions and dreams. Ol' Stonyface seemed pleased to have overseen the procedings and to have regained his privilaged position. But somehow or other, those eyes, that still watched relentlessly, now seemed to be sympathetic.

---

Ed Brant had never been to a golf club, although the company had paid his membership fee at the prestigious Powerscourt Club in County Wicklow. In fact, being driven out along the N11 southwards through County Wicklow, without a business purpose, was a huge novelty. It was a beautiful morning; a bright sun was shining in a blue sky that was speckled with snow-white billowy clouds. The serenity of a scene that now, to Ed, seemed eternal was sharply interupted by the memory of a previous occasion— the time he had talked to Papandreou from the floor of the car. *So long ago. So much has happened!*

He had decided that he should tell his brothers about his dismissal before they read the inevitable reports in the press. He also needed to know if they knew about their father and Patricia's mother and - Patricia. *Thank God they never knew about our relationship. I don't know if either of us could cope with that complication.* He had phoned John with great apprehension, not just because of Patricia, but he was conscious that John had been chasing him since before his last trip to New York almost two months ago. He had not returned those calls. However, he need not have worried.

349

John had moved on. From his immediate enthusiastic response it was obvious that whatever problem John had then had since been sorted. There was no mention of it at all, nor did he mention Patricia. Ed was glad. He was tired of these family confrontations. *Patricia has obviously decided to tell the family who her dad was in her own good time.*

"Morning, Ed," John had responded cheerfully. "Great to hear you back in action. We didn't expect you to be out of hospital for ages yet, and here you are ready to socialise. Do the doctors know you're up and about?"

"More or less, John." Ed lied, "you know how they are. They'd run your life forever if you let them. I believe you're now back playing golf."

"Well, I'm trying. It'll take a while to get the fuckin' handicap down to where it was. I really regret not continuing it years ago. I'm trying to make up for lost time now. What about yourself?"

"About the same. Never had time. Always meant to but never got around to it. Like a lot of other things," he said with meaning. "Always too busy."

"Would you like to see what you're missing? Ben and I are meeting up today for a round. We'll be starting with lunch at 12:30. I know you can't play, but would you like to join us? I can hire a buggy for you."

"I'd love to," Ed heard himself saying. "I won't play golf but I'll join you for lunch. I've something I need to tell you both."

"It'll be a day for confessions," John said. "There's something I need to tell you too."

Ed arrived before both. There were few patrons present. The clubhouse opened up onto a wooden decking overhanging a lily-strewn lake. Beyond the water was the most beautiful vista imaginable. The sun continued to shine from what was now a clear blue sky illuminating the lush grass green and heather brown of the surrounding hills. The Sugarloaf Mountain stood majestic to the north, while eastwards the blue of the Irish Sea blended into the horizon so that it was impossible to distinguish what was sea and what was sky. Ed stood alone, momentarily lost in the magical splendour of it all until, as was now happening so often, the dark clouds of depression obliterated all before him and left him reeling with a feeling of hopelessness bordering on despair. Everything he had ever wanted – a feeling of selfworth through achivement and, the love of Patricia – simple enough goals, but goals that were now and forever beyond his reach. *Yes Dad! You were right. I'm useless; wasted space.*

Ben and John arrived. Lunch was ordered. Before long the conversation got around to Ed and what he had been doing. It became obvious that, however illustrious it may have sounded to have dined with an Arab Sheik in a desert tent, to have travelled the Atlantic in a private Boeing, or even to have met President Putin, it was not what they had come to talk about or touched their interest.

Ben, as usual, cut through the chat. "What's really on your mind, Ed?"

"I need your advice, Ben."

Ed ignored the quizzical expression on the faces of both of his brothers. He proceeded to outline the supply difficulties that Global Oil now had and the final assignment that he had been asked to take on.

"Can't say I'm surprised, Ed. I come across similar stories twice a month. What advice can I give you?"

"Well, you recall the last redundancy programme that I announced. I know you think that I could have handled that better. I wouldn't want to cause the same trauma all over again with Global."

"Ed, there is no easy way to tell nearly two hundred people that their jobs are gone, because, in most cases, it isn't just a job they see as being lost, it's their sense of self-worth. I've seen more tough men reduced to tears at the news that their life's work has counted for nothing. You remember our discussion while you were in your hospital bed - before you were able to argue - capitalism values cash investment and devalues human effort."

Ben took on that reflective look that the brothers knew so well from their youth. After a moment or two he continued.

"I firmly believe that a company is not the creation of the shareholders. Yes, they are the legal owners of the assets, but the real worth of a company is in its heart and soul, in its shared experiences, mission, vision, and values. The people look to the executive management to set the direction for the company, and then to nourish these elements and blend them into a culture of achievement that all can take pride in." He had a hint of sadness in his voice.

"You're jumping the gun, Ben, they asked me to liquidate the company and sell the assets, but I didn't accept."

Ed went on to tell them of his offer to buy.

"For fuck's sake, Ed!" Ben exclaimed. "Where would you get fifty million? Fifty - plus redundancy costs?"

"That's not a problem. The company is worth five times that amount."

"But you said yourself, without supply it's only worth the sale value of its assets."

"Yes," Ed responded with emphasis, "But I do have supply. In fact, I could supply the whole of Ireland."

He told his brothers of his trip to Moscow, of his meeting with Putin and the contract with Rosneft.

"But why is Global saying that it has no supply if it has this fuckin' contract?" interjected John, who up to this point had said very little.

"For two reasons. Firstly, with my heart attack and all that, and"— he spoke with a wry grin—"Ben protecting me from myself by taking my mobile, I honestly put it to the back of my mind and never told them. Something to deal with when I got better. The other reason is that it's not their contract, it's ours. It's with Brantoil."

Ed stopped for a moment to let the words sink in.

"And last night the Global Chairman himself phoned me to confirm that the board has accepted my offer. The contract is on its way to my solicitors. The Brants are in the money, fellas. We've made it and I want you both in."

John spluttered and looked at Ben. They both had paled.

"Ed, I don't know how to tell you this. I tried so hard to contact you and couldn't. I don't know whether or not you got my calls, but anyway you never phoned back. Neither Ben nor I own Brantoil any more. It was losing money and we had to sell our shares. We couldn't afford to be hit with fuckin' losses. We don't have that sort of money."

Ed looked at both, speechless.

"But the three of us owned Brantoil; you couldn't sell out without the three of us agreeing. It's not legal," Ed said in desperation.

"I'm afraid it is," said Ben. "I had it checked out thoroughly, I didn't want any screw-ups."

"Who the hell did you sell it to?"

Both looked embarrassed. It was John who spoke.

"Well, as I said, the company was losing money. I couldn't handle it. I'm not a businessman. About that time Jim O'Ragallaigh got all of that fuckin' cash from you for handling the Anglo Oil merger. He wanted to invest, I wanted to sell. So I sold my third to Jim."

"And you, Ben, did you sell your third to him as well?"

"No Ed, I'm afraid I did worse than that. I'm a trade union official. I don't have a huge salary, but I do have a huge mortgage. I couldn't afford to accept the possibility of having to cover Brantoil losses, so I really gave my shares away."

"You what?" Ed shouted in disbelief.

"You're the business brain in the family, but we couldn't get hold of you so we made our own decisions. I gave my one third to the employees. It's now a workers' cooperative."

"Do you realise what you've done?" Ed shouted. "That contract is worth billions, and you two have given it away."

"No point in you having another heart attack." said Ben. "All is not lost. Jim O'Ragallaigh is a good, decent man. He has turned the company around, and it's now making money. He has a third, you have a third, and the workers have a third. What's wrong with that?"

"Everything," Ed said, totally defeated.

"Why don't you discuss it with him? He'll be here shortly."

"Ed, before we get into that, there is something far more important that you need to know."

"Ed, the doctors advised against telling you before, but we can't wait any longer. Ed … we think Patricia Harvey is… our sister."

Ed said nothing. Ben continued.

"You know that Patricia's mother worked for Dad in Brantoil all those years ago. Well, it appears that they were closer than that. Patricia was born, and you know how Ireland was in the seventies. She left and took her daughter, our half-sister, with her. It looks as if she was raised not knowing that her father, our dad, was still alive in Ireland."

"How do you know this?" Ed said quitely.

"Well, Jim talked to some of the old-timers in the company. Among them it was a well-kept secret. Now that all of the principals are dead, our dad and mam, and Patricia's mother, there was no point in continuing the secrecy. As you know, Jim has a way with people. They told him, and he told John and me. Because of your condition, the doctors thought it better to hold it from you until you had recovered."

"It's probably just based on rumour at the time. How would they know? I'm sure it's not true," Ed said, hoping the desperation was not evident in his voice.

"I think it is," Ben said quietly. "But we'll know for certain when Patricia gets the result of the DNA test. It'll confirm the blood-line. I'm sure it'll prove that Patricia is our half-sister. Isn't it great news – for us and for her?"

"When did you find this out?" Ed asked weakly.

"Well, Jim was told about the relationship when you were in Saudi Arabia, but Patricia wanted to keep it private until she got the DNA confirmation. You were still on the critical list. Patricia, John, and I went in to tell you. You were delirious at the time, and the doctors told us to go away and await your recovery. I'm really sorry Ed that you're only finding out now but I hope you'll understand, we thought it was in your best interest."

"That's okay, Ben. You know, I had already guessed it. How did Patricia take it when she found out?"

"Not good, Ed" Ben replied quietly, "to tell you the truth she seems to be in a state of denial. Despite what she was told she is insistent on the DNA test. I suppose I can understand if she had other romantic notions about her father and mother. We hoped she would have been pleased but no – she got very upset, in fact hysterical, when I told her."

"And the DNA test was positive?"

"I'm sure it will be. I think it's only a formality but last time we talked to her she was still awaiting the result."

Ed wanted to find out more. To find out how Patricia was now? How she looked? Had she talked about him? He had a million questions for his brothers, all to do with her. But they would have to wait. Jim O'Raghallaigh came out onto the decking and that conversation came to an abruft halt.

They went through the ritual of pleasantries. Ed found it difficult, but O'Raghallaigh seemed genuinely interested in his recovery. Eventually Ed could restrain himself no longer.

"Jim, from what Ben and John have told me, it looks like you and I are partners in Brantoil. Ben and John have just been filling me in on what happened. Well I'm in the process of buying Global's network in Ireland. Would you have any interest in merging the two companies?"

O'Raghallaigh didn't seem at all fazed by the bluntness of the question. Why would you want to do that? Global is the market leader, while Brantoil is a small distributor that is just on the right side of break-even."

"Sentimental reasons," Ed lied. "It's the old family firm and I want to keep in touch."

"By gobbling it up in a merger?"

Ed could sense Ben and John shifting uneasily.

"Ed, let's start again," O'Ragallaigh said. "And this time let's have no bull-shit. Maybe we'll start with me telling you what I know."

"Okay," Ed said, taken aback.

"I know all about the supply contract with Rosneft. The Russians wanted it sealed, so they sent it to the Brantoil office. I knew nothing about it, so I had it checked out. It's legal, and it's very valuable. I also know about Global. They are pulling out because of supply difficulties. I tried to buy their assets, but know that you got in before me and they're selling to you."

He stopped to weigh the impact of his words.

Ed Brant said nothing; he couldn't.

"Without the supply contract the assets are not worth what you're paying because, before you can sell them, you know and I know, that your brother Ben here will make sure that the workers get fair redundancy terms."

Ed glanced at Ben. He was nodding assent.

"So the real value is in the supply contract. Why don't you let Brantoil buy the assets of Global Oil, and we'll operate the merged entity as we operate Brantoil now? It would mean giving a third of the acquired assets to the employees. You and I would own the other two thirds equally."

Ed could see how O'Ragallaigh was so successful in what he did.

"Can we scale down the share of the employees?"

"Not a chance," he responded. "It's a condition of our Memorandum and Articles. Your brother put that in. I take it that it's non-negotiable, Ben?"

"Damn right it's not."

"Okay," Ed said. "You've got a deal. Tell me, how did you know about Global and their supply difficulties?"

"From my brother, Tim; he's the Chairman of Global Oil Inc. You probably know him as Tim O'Reilly. He uses the English version of O'Ragallaigh over there in the U.S. He got fed up having to continually spell his name. O'Reilly's easier. I talk to him regularly, in fact, I talked to him this morning. He had been trying to contact you. He told me that the guy that you and I had had dinner with in London—you remember, the Greek; what was his name? Oh yes, Papandreou. Well, apparently they found him in his office. It looks as if he committed suicide. The door had been locked. It seems he shot himself."

Ed Brant felt remarkably calm. Despite the fact that this definitely signalled the end – the end of his rainbow – somehow or other he felt remote from it; it just didn't matter any more. The image of Papandreou slumped over the polished mahogany, blood spattered desk, high in the sky, overlooking Central Park, seemed part of another existence; of a dream that was hardly real.

He instinctively changed the subject and desperately tried to collect his thoughts and his composure. "At least I'll retain my position as Chief Executive," he blurted.

"Okay with me," Jim said. "But all appointments are subject to the Employee Selection Committee. Another irrevocable rule written into our constitution at the insistence of your brother."

"So my position is subject to the majority vote of the workers?"

"Afraid so, Ed," he responded. "As you said yourself once, what goes around comes around."

"Who's the competition?" Ed asked cynically, looking O'Raghallaigh directly in the eyes.

"No, it's not me," he answered. "I've had my fill of corporate life. It's Patricia Harvey."

The silence was deafening.

"Jim, we've told Ed. He knows that Patricia is our sister." It was Ben. He had been quitely listening to the exchange.

"I told her I was meeting you here and asked her to join us. She should be here by now. I'd guess that if you are interested in the position  she would be willing to step down and give you a clear run." O'Raghallaigh seemed to know more about Patricia than Ed was comfortable with.

He was taken aback. He had intended contacting her when he had got to the apartment. He hadn't told her that he was about to discharge himself from the hospital and, with his diversion to the office and subsequent meeting with Roden, it slipped his mind.  He wanted more than anything to be with her. The fact that their first meeting had to be with others present was bitterly disappointing. He really wanted to tell her how he felt - that although they couldn't have the future they wanted, they would still have something special, even if it was as brother and sister. Their past would be their secret.

It was no more than five minutes but, to the duelling protagonists and spectators, it seemed interminable. Eventually she arrived. She wasn't alone but she was radiant. Ed and she embraced. He could feel her emotion as he kissed her cheek. He sensed a nervousness and uncertainty. Tears started slowly as their eyes met but soon streamed down her beautiful face. He silently cursed the others for being there. He again felt helpless. He wanted to hold her. He wanted to tell her that they would be okay. He sensed the awkwardness of her companion and he turned to face him for the first time.

"Ed, I want you to meet my father." Her words were barely audible.

Ed took the extended hand. "Mister Stone – wha… I don't understand?"

Ol' Stoneyface looked at Ed and the others but turned back to Patricia.

"Yeah, after all of these years I've found my daughter or, should I say, she found me, with the help, that is, of an old friend of mine"

Then facing the brothers he continued:

"I believe you lads were claiming her as your sister. Well, sorry about that but you're out of luck. Your dad, Paddy Brant, was another good friend of mine - my best friend all those years ago. But we fell out. He wouldn't tell me where Maureen had gone with her little girl - my daughter – he had given his word. I was married to someone else - so what could I do? Mo left and I never heard from her again. It destroyed me. It destroyed my life. But now …" He left it at that - further words were superflous.

Ed could have hugged him. Those last words were lost on all except him. He knew exactly what was meant - Stone's millions meant nothing – he had lost his lover and their daughter – the only things of real value to him - and Ed had regained a reason for living.

Ed embraced them both. The three became submerged in a sea of emotion. Tears turned to laughter and reverted to tears. The others were lost in their confusion but the sun continued to beam from a cloudless sky and nature itself seemed to be rejoicing.

"Jesus, Ed, will you leave her alone? Did you not hear what the man said, she's not your sister."

Ben looked embarrassed at the display of affection which seemed at odds with what he had just heard, but Ed was oblivious to his brothers and the staring diners. Global Oil, Dino Papandreou, murders and suicides, trans-Atlantic flights in a private Boeing, the Iraqi war, Saudi Arabia and its desert cuisine, Red Square, the tete-a-tete with President Putin and gained and lost positions and fortunes were irrelevant in the context of what they had secretly lost but now publicly found.

Tom Stone seemed to understand.

"Heard you took my picture down, Son. Can we negotiate on that one? Believe we're all now going to be family? How about all three of us in the one picture– me, my daughter and you. I believe we'll be one hell of a team?"

John looked impatient.

"For fuck's sake, Ben, can we go and play golf now, and maybe you or Jim can explain to me what the fuck is goin' on?"

———————◆•◆•◆———————

The familiar sound of his mobile brought Ed back to reality. He was glad at the distraction. He had to somehow recover his composure. He moved aside to take the call.

"Jesus, Ed, are you coming into the office today?" It was Tom Bergin.

"No, I'm not, Tom" he answered quietly. "What's up?"

"Ed, I need to talk to you. Urgently. We've just had a summons, you and I, to appear before the Planning Tribunal. They're not happy that some of the professional fees we've being paying are legitimate. They're claiming they were bribes. They say that the US Federal Energy Regulatory Commission are cooperating in their investigations. The media has got hold of it. It'll be all over the papers. Ed, it's serious. We're talking big money. I don't know what to tell them."

An explosion seemed to have been set off in Ed'd head.

"Deal with it yourself, Bergin. You paid the fucking money. See if your buddy, that slimy bastard, Papandreou, can help you now. I suppose this is your second call; as usual you probably already tried his mobile number. Well, he won't be answering your calls ever again."

There was silence. Ed was almost enjoying the anguish that he knew he had created at the other end. He could picture those fluttering eyelids, that ashen face and misshapen beard.

"Ed, I don't know what you are talking about. The payments were made by Patricia but under your authority. And why should I phone Papandreou? I don't know him, I've never talked to him in my life. He's been on on several occasions looking for Patricia, but recently she refuses to talk to him. I don't know what's going on."

Ed couldn't take any more. He switched off the mobile.

Ben had waited before following John to the first tee-box. He put his hand on Ed's shoulder and, in a big-brotherly tone, said "Ed, I must say I've got to hand it to you. In that cut-throat world of big business you've really made it. In a few short years you've really become something. You must be very proud. I know Dad would. I remember him telling me that you were the only one of us who would get anywhere. Yes, he'd be so proud of you."

Ed said nothing. If this was success, you could have it. He was empty inside. He looked at Patricia; even her. Despite what they had shared she had betrayed him. *How could she act as Papandreou's snout? How could she criticise my actions and betray our love, for the sake of her own corporate advancement?*

He made his excuses. As he slid into the leather-upholstered seat of his S600 Mercedes he watched her. Against a backdrop that had clouded over she radiated happiness in the company of her newly found father.

"Hold it for a minute, John" he instructed the driver.

The memories of their brief life together came flooding back. *What am I thinking about? What am I doing?* He asked himself. He thought of Papandreou. Although on occasions he had been surprised by Papandreou's prior knowledge of events in Ireland, never had it been negative. *It never hurt me - in fact it always helped.* His rise within the global sphere had been nothing short of meteoric. *I wonder would it have happened at all without a gloss being put on the facts.* The more he thought about it the clearer Patricia's role in his success became. *She used her New York connections to help me along. How could I have doubted her, even for an instant?* He thought back on the occasions he had asked her to watch Bergin. He remembered her look of disappoinment bordering on disgust. *Yes! How could I have doubted her? Bergin had said that she, and not he, had authorised the payments. Well, in that case I know they were honest. Obviously the FERC have communicated the contents of the tape of that stupid conversation I had with Bergin to the Tribunal. Well! now that I know there's no basis to it that won't be a problem. Jesus, poor Tom Bergin. I'd better get him back and apologise – the poor man. What have I done to him?*

Ed made the call and then strolled back to where Patricia and her father, Tom Stone, were seated.

"Patricia, Jim O'Raghallaigh tells me that your name is down for consideration by the Employee Selection Committee for the position as Chief Executive of Brantoil."

"Yes, I do believe so," she replied. "Jim himself was not interested and submitted my name. Now that the two companies will be merged no doubt you will want to take that position."

"No I won't," he responded, "I'll have other things I want to do but I do have a recommendation – Tom Bergin - one of nature's gentlemen."

Her eyes glistened again.

"And what will you do?" she asked, anxiously.

"Oh - I'll sit on our balcony and watch the stars - I'll walk the hills and smell the roses - I'll play with Blondie and - who knows - I might even write a book."

"Write a book? You're serious! What about?"

"A hard lesson I've learned – 'You reap what you sow'. I think I'd call it - Crude Justice"

Lightning Source UK Ltd.
Milton Keynes UK
19 August 2010

158676UK00001B/30/A